THE WOMAN
WHO FELL IN LOVE
FOR A WEEK

THE WOMAN WHO FELL IN LOVE FOR A WEEK

Fiona Walker

sphere

SPHERE

First published in Great Britain in 2015 by Sphere

1 3 5 7 9 10 8 6 4 2

Copyright © Fiona Walker 2015

The moral right of the author has been asserted.

A CIP catalogue record for this book
is available from the British Library.

ISBN 978-0-7515-5610-0

Typeset in Plantin Light by M Rules
Printed and bound in Great Britain by
Clays Ltd, St Ives plc

Papers used by Sphere are from well-managed forests
and other responsible sources.

MIX
Paper from
responsible sources
FSC® C104740

Sphere
An imprint of
Little, Brown Book Group
100 Victoria Embankment
London EC4Y 0DY

An Hachette UK Company
www.hachette.co.uk

www.littlebrown.co.uk

This book is dedicated, with grateful thanks, to the amazing ed from the Land Down Under, who never stops aiming for the stars. And to women everywhere who are afraid of failing. Dive in.

THE WOMAN
WHO FELL IN LOVE
FOR A WEEK

I

Thursday

1

TO DO LIST

Copy-edit Carla's book
Eat lots of super-foods
Read a novel a day
No alcohol
Quit electronic smoking
Do something about depilation
Swim 40 lengths a day
Have sex with Roger

It wasn't hard for Jenny to close her front door and walk away from home, these days. When her marriage had ended three years earlier, so had her long love affair with the only house she'd ever wanted to take root in. She felt no great affection for the modern mews in which she lived now, bricks and mortar bought with her share of the sale of the North Oxford home in which she and Robin had raised a family and razed a marriage. She was potted out, waiting to be replanted.

She glanced back at it in the rear-view mirror as she pulled into the communal drive, her little terracotta safe haven sitting neatly among its architect-designed clones, all overlooking the Oxford canal. After the ambush of divorce, she'd eschewed any ambitions of home-making, merry-making and love-making in favour of practical necessities. At the time, the children had needed to stay close to school, and the cycle into work along the canal towpath suited Jenny perfectly too. The mews development's gated community kept her safe, locked in her own self-protective shell. The twins complained that there was no room to move amid the relics of the old family home, its antique furniture crammed into the small modern house – Robin had taken almost nothing with him to the States – but Jenny had needed the comfort they brought. Now she found it increasingly impractical to live in a museum of her marriage. Abandoning it for brief bursts of reinvention had become a great treat, and house-sitting was her favourite means of escape.

Waiting for the electric gates to slide back, she fed the postcode of the Old Rectory, Hadden End, into her sat-nav with the excited exhilaration of a space traveller inputting the co-ordinates to a new galaxy.

Most of Jenny's house-sitting work came through a free online agency, whose members' area she scanned with more enthusiasm than the online dating sites to which she also subscribed. However, her best-paid and usually most inter-esting work came via the books of the exclusive Home Guardians run by a flirtatious ex-estate agent called Henry, whose glossy ads promised *Tatler* and *Telegraph* readers that his sitters were bastions of home and pet care. Henry had called Jenny late the previous night, entreating, 'I know I can rely upon my absolute *stellar* sitter to help out in an emer-gency. These clients are well known, so they require discretion, good security and, above all, an experienced dog lover.' The Lewis family's usual house-sitter – one of Henry's ex-army stalwarts – had broken his leg the day before their fortnight's holiday, Henry explained. 'They leave tomorrow. I've told them you're my secret weapon, darling Jenny. Please tell me you're free.'

While she knew that she was probably the only person on his books with a life so organized and dull that she could drop everything at a moment's notice – and, judging from the late hour of the call, he'd already tried others – Jenny was rather boosted by the notion of being a secret weapon with a mission. She was also in Henry's debt because he'd agreed to find her an idyllic house-sit during her autumn term sabbatical, preferably overseas, in which she could finally write the novel she'd always wanted to have a stab at.

And when she learned who the Lewises were, Jenny was only too happy to step into the breach. What better place to start seeking inspiration for her sabbatical than a fortnight spent looking after the home of two successful writers? Richard Lewis was a critically acclaimed, media-savvy biographer whose pithy, meticulously researched insight into the lives of literary heavyweights had won him a legion of fans, Jenny among them. His fame, though, was far overshadowed by that of his wife, Geraldine Scott, the author of passionate page-turning sagas that were opened *en masse* on sunloungers the world over by devoted followers like hymn books along church pews. Most legendary among them was *The Dust Storm*, sections of which a whole generation of women could quote verbatim.

Accepting the last-minute job with a rush of impulsive, almost reckless enthusiasm that was quite out of character for her now, Jenny was incredibly grateful that she hadn't already committed the first two weeks of the summer holidays. The independent school at which she taught always broke up a fortnight earlier than state ones, and many of her pupils' families and her colleagues took advantage of this by escaping as soon as the bell rang after the term's last lesson. For Jenny, these two weeks had once been among her most precious, filled with indulgent domesticity and time devoted to her own children. This year, with the twins overseas, they had become fourteen hollow days. Jenny had lined up plenty of distractions to keep her occupied, but until now nothing had seemed a perfect fit. She'd been dabbling with the idea of a cheap Med break, urged on by her English department head, who took pot luck on last-minute deals to devour the Booker short-list at this time every year. Her regular date, Roger, was equally keen to lure her into a week's hill-walking in the Peak District. Instead, to her delight, she was stepping into her favourite role: custodian of a beautiful home, with a generous bonus and the opportunity to see inside the life of one of the literary world's most successful marriages.

Driving the short hop from Oxford into Buckinghamshire, the squeak of the whiteboard marker and thunder of feet along corridors faded from Jenny's ears as the Heart FM presenter shared the happy news that the current heat-wave was heading into a second week, cueing Donna Summer's 'Hot Stuff'. She cranked up the volume and let her new house-sitting persona wash over her. She was no longer Mrs Rees, deputy head of English at a solid home-counties school, mildly OCD, neatness fanatic and devotee of Angela Carter, Oscar Wilde and the eighteenth-century novel, who guiltily smoked her electronic cigarettes outside in the back garden under cover of darkness and read all books with a pencil tucked behind her ear to correct typos. She was Jane Eyre, about to enter Thornfield Hall, Tess heading to the d'Urberville mansion or Dorothea idealistically setting out for Lowick Manor. She was about to step into the world of Geraldine Scott, doyenne of the sweeping modern romantic epic, a passionate charity campaigner and rock-and-roll bohemian, married to art-loving academic Richard Lewis, whose soft voice had lulled Jenny to sleep on many occasions while she was listening to the late-night culture show he hosted on radio.

To be true to the spirit of this adventure, she was tempted to glide sedately along the left-hand carriageway at stage-coach speed, listening to Beethoven to savour the moment, but she couldn't resist putting her foot down in the fast lane as she sang along with the disco diva, thrilled at the liberation.

Even though the Old Rectory was in the heart of the very small village of Hadden End – Jenny had cruised past it several times on Google Street View late the previous evening – its discreetly hidden driveway took her a long time to find, and she was already running late.

Street View had captured the scene in winter, a full-frontal of High Gothic splendour through spindly hazels, but now in midsummer the lane that looped around the little Saxon church and its historic consort looked different: thick-topped trees and fat hedges created an enclosed tunnel that narrowed claustrophobically as verges bursting with desiccated cow parsley almost met in the middle, then twisted on through chicanes of ancient brick walls tumbling with ivy. Higgledy thatched cottages leaned out into the thoroughfare as though eager to share gossip.

Jenny, who hated being late (crueller pupils called her the Daft Punk because she was always banging on about punctuality, punctuation and punctures in her bicycle tyres), grew hotter and more tense as she drove repeatedly around the narrow circle past the church lichgate, blinded by bright sunlight each time she turned back onto the main road. After a few false starts up grand driveways, she assailed an elderly dog-walker to ask for directions.

'Just follow the sound of flying Crown Derby and insults, my dear.' The pensioner pointed to a narrow gravel track curling away between two crumbling, urn-topped stone gate piers that were half buried in foliage and overhanging branches. One small very bright blue eye winked mischievously between canvas hat brim and dark glasses rim before she tugged her overweight Cairn terrier onwards.

There was no house sign, but Jenny remembered reading that the grander the incumbents, the less likely they were to help you to locate their homes.

As she cautiously nosed the car into a tree-lined driveway, canopied by acid-green lime leaves, she caught a glimpse of cusped mullion windows and Gothic gables peeking around the shoulder of an ancient yew.

'Home sweet home,' she breathed, the full scale of the house coming into view now. It was on a par with the school she taught in, which housed fifty boarders, two live-in staff and a hundred day pupils. This, however, was a family home for just two writers, three children and one dog.

A luxury off-roader was parked directly in front of the ecclesiastically arched porch, its tailgate and doors open, a trio of small heads, in wireless headphones, lined up on the back seat in front of the Disney Channel on headrest screens. There were suitcases spread out on the gravel alongside the car, several open and spilling colourful contents.

Having parked beneath the shade of the yew, Jenny picked her way carefully around them towards the house.

A male voice bellowed from the hallway, 'Get BACK and lie down NOW.'

She hesitated.

'GO *BACK*!'

Jenny realized the voice – unmistakably Richard Lewis's – was addressing a dog. 'In your BED, Gunter!'

'We have to leave in *five minutes!*' came a woman's voice from further inside the house, husky and urgent, accompanied by feet running on flagstones.

'I wish you'd bloody told me you'd arranged to have lunch with your mother, Gee. I said midday to the agency – LIE DOWN, Gunter! I think the house-sitter's coming from the other side of Oxford, so he's probably en route by now. We'll have to leave him a note.'

'Gunter will eat it. And him! And what about setting the alarm?' A tall, curvy figure burst out of the house carrying a pile of sarongs, several summer hats perched on her head, brims flopping over her face. Not seeing Jenny, she hurried to the nearest suitcase.

In her wake bounded a dog that was part rusted steel scourer, part werewolf. Spotting Jenny, he went into a frenzy of barking and jinked towards her, eyes like conkers glaring beneath huge grizzly eyebrows.

Jenny adored dogs. She'd grown up with them, and had looked after many during her recent summers of house-sitting. She always enjoyed their company, anthropomorphizing them in her mind to have human voices and personalities. But in Gunter she immediately sensed trouble. From the moment she set eyes on the Lewises' big, overexcited dog, she knew which human he resembled – and in canine terms, he was a doppelgänger for the one person she never wanted to share house space with again. In the split second she had to assess him as he bounded up to her, Jenny registered the same prospector's beard, unkempt salt-and-pepper hair and passive-aggressive expression as that of her ex-husband in the worst throes of his mid-life crisis.

9

'Argh!' Glasses flying, she was flattened against a creeper-clad wall by twenty-five kilos of uncontrollable wiry neurosis.

'Who the hell are you?' Geraldine Lewis swung round in surprise, hat brims revolving like spinning plates. She was plumper and older than she appeared in her author photographs, but no less glamorous or intimidating, her phosphorus yellow eyes as bright as flames as she regarded the stranger on her doorstep being body-slammed and bear-hugged by her dog.

'I'm the house-sitter.' Jenny crossed her arms and looked up, as she'd learned to do when dealing with unruly dogs. Gunter dropped his paws obligingly to the ground, thrust a cold nose between her legs and inhaled deeply.

'Welcome!' Geraldine shook off the hats. 'How marvellous – you're early! Don't worry, Gunter's quite harmless. Oh, God, he's ripped your sleeve, you poor thing. He pulled the shirt front clean off a Jehovah's Witness last week. He loathes artificial fibres.' She caught her lower lip with a perfect pelmet of white veneers as the dog continued goosing the new arrival with appreciative snorts. 'Richard! We need the zapper. The house-sitter's a woman.'

'GET OFF, Gunter!' yelled Richard Lewis's deep, authoritative voice. 'Get off her NOW!'

A little box attached to Gunter's collar let out a loud-pitched beep and he sat down promptly, let out a contrite whine and glanced ruefully towards the figure emerging from the house.

Richard Lewis might be a literary heavyweight, but in physical terms he was far less substantial than his wife. He was much shorter and built like a jump jockey, with kind, pale-lashed eyes and a narrow mouth that seemed perpetually curled in mild amusement. Jenny knew from her Wikipedia research the previous night that he was over sixty, but he looked much younger. If it hadn't been for the silver wings fanning over his ears, she would have taken him to be the same age as Geraldine. He was also immaculately turned out, from cuff-linked wrists to shiny brogue toes.

'Welcome!' He thrust out a lean, long-fingered hand. 'We were told to expect a chap called Reece.'

'It's Mrs Rees.' Jenny shook it briskly, aware that she sounded as starchy as if she were covering a rowdy class of year-eights. It was disconcerting meeting two people whose public profiles were well known and whose life-changing words she had absorbed in her intimate world of reading and late-night listening. 'Is that a problem?'

'Not at all.' He gave her a diffident smile. 'Gunter and I both far prefer the company of women.'

'Whether women prefer their company is debatable.' Laughing throatily, Geraldine rushed forward to grasp Jenny's hand, her smile as warm as the Mauritian sun that awaited her. 'We thought you were one of Henry's army blokes. Welcome! You've caught us trying to make a quick getaway. Geraldine Lewis.' The Australian accent was still pronounced. Close to, she smelt heavenly and very expensive.

Resisting the urge to blurt, 'My friends and I loved *The Dust Storm*', Jenny studied her, the wild fringe tangling with blonde lashes. Although Geraldine was very different from the photograph in Jenny's battered copy of her seminal debut novel, she was still a natural beauty, whose eyes remained as wide and fiercely clever as those of the girl who had seemed to write about Jenny's eighteen-year-old heart more than two decades earlier. Amazonian in height, with golden, freckle-dusted skin, acres of flame-blonde hair and Rubenesque curves swathed in a brightly patterned maxi dress, she made the debonair, greying Richard look even smaller.

11

'Forgive us, Mrs R' – the abbreviation made Jenny feel like a hoary old housekeeper – 'but we're in a tearing hurry. Richard will take you on a whistle-stop tour of the place while I throw in a few more essentials.' She waved at her suit-cases, gasped, 'Flip-flops!' and dashed off, calling over her shoulder, 'Show Mrs R how to use Gunter's remote control, Richard.'

'Please do call me Jenny.' She eyed the ominous battery-like block against the dog's neck. She'd read about training collars and was pretty certain most were illegal.

'The collar is a perfectly harmless training device that emits a sound he associates with a reprimand,' Richard assured her. 'German wire-haired pointers can be very excitable – can't you, Gunter?'

Gunter cast a resentful glance at the remote, but looked the picture of gundog obedience, beard bristling. He reminded Jenny of Robin on his best behaviour in the divorce court.

Ushering her in through the front door, Richard enquired politely after her journey. 'Did you find us easily?'

'Of course.' She didn't bother him with her bad naviga-tion, which would hardly instil confidence that she was the Mary Poppins of house-sitting. Equally, she forced herself not to gape at the sensational interiors, maintaining a polite, professional focus as she followed him through an echoing tapestry-hung hall and into a cavernous scrubbed-wood kitchen.

'Forgive the squalor.' Richard waved vaguely at surfaces crowded with paperwork and washing up. 'Just leave it until the cleaners come tomorrow.'

Jenny's fingers itched to tackle it. Everything would have been cleared away before the family had reached the M40.

'We inherited a live-in domestic couple when we moved

here,' Richard explained, as he hunted for something amid the debris, 'but they retired last year and Geraldine took over the staff cottage as a studio.' He pointed through the window to the end of the garden where a sagging tiled roof was just visible above a tall hedge. 'Now we have contract teams that come in each week. I've written all the details in the notes, if I can find them among the wreckage – aha!' He extracted a sheet of printed A4 from beneath a packet of Sugar Puffs and wiped it with his cuff. 'It's all listed here. Cleaners every Friday. Laundry service collects Thursdays, returns Mondays. The gardening lot are a bit eccentric and turn up when they want, but the main chap is a genius who wins gold at Chelsea every year and you'll get terrific tips if you bribe him with a cup of tea. The pool man comes every Wednesday – I've said our neighbours can use it while we're away, so don't be alarmed if you hear splashing. Whatever you do, don't let Gunter out when they're here or he'll dive in too – he wrecked the liner twice last year. Don't let him go upstairs either because he raids the laundry baskets. Here, I'll show you how to use the training collar.'

He held up the remote. Gunter, who had been furtively goosing Jenny from behind, sat down obediently with a gruff huff.

'This green button activates the warning beep – that should be all you need, but if he gets loose when the post-man's around, you might need the yellow one, which releases a puff of citronella spray. Whatever you do, don't press the red button, unless he's chasing old Myrtle's cat again, in which case it's the only thing that'll stop the carnage.'

'What does the red button do?' she asked, imagining the collar self-destructing and vaporizing the dog in a puff of smoke.

'Best not to ask. You'll need to charge the collar overnight every two days. Take it off when he goes to bed. He sleeps in there.' He pointed through a door to a metal mesh kennel construction in the utility room. 'Put him in it if you go out, but never leave him for more than two hours – and make sure he has the radio on, anything but pop music, which makes him even more neurotic.'

Jenny thought it no wonder Gunter was neurotic if he was caged by night, Tasered by day and forced to listen to Radio 3, but her job was to look after pets as their owners instructed. And this dog's alarming resemblance to the man who had turned his family's lives upside-down and left her rudderless made her distinctly suspicious of him.

In the hallway, Geraldine was shouting that everything was packed and they must bloody well leave. 'Mrs R will be fine, darling! Leave her to have a good old snoop once we've cleared off.'

'I never snoop.' Jenny bristled in shock.

Richard gave her a sympathetic smile. 'Apologies. Gee assumes everybody's as inquisitive as she is. Writer's mind.' He handed the page of notes to her. 'All you need to know is here. We were going to put male Reece in the Zen bedroom above the garage, but that's a bit bleak, so I suggest you use the guest suite – it's furthest to the left on the first landing. I'll let you find that for yourself. The fridge is fully stocked – please help yourself. The wine in the kitchen racks is all drinking plonk, so do have a glass or two. Ocado will deliver again the day before we return – it's all ordered.'

Jenny suspected that Richard did the online grocery ordering, just as he orchestrated the domestic teams on a spreadsheet, arranged his children in height order before plugging them into car entertainment and controlled the dog by remote. In her experience, immaculately dressed men were often perfectionist over-achievers. By contrast, Robin had never taken the slightest interest in what he wore or how the house ran until he had decided to take his share in court.

'Richard!' The voice in the hallway was cranking up to a Nellie Melba aria of high drama.

He looked at his watch and grimaced. 'I'll quickly take you through the security system.'

In the utility room with the dog's cage, he opened a cupboard discreetly camouflaged in the tiled wall. It was full of keys, above which was a high-tech touchpad. 'It's self-explanatory to anyone with a basic understanding of alarms. The code is 1887, but if you forget it just look above the front door – it's the date carved there, the only way to get Gee to remember it. The main keys are all on this fob, so keep it with you at all times. The garden cottage isn't alarmed, and those keys are here if you need them – they're the ones marked Gee Studio. And this is the keyless ignition to the dog car.'

'Gunter has his own car?'

He glanced at the gundog, which had skulked miserably into the wire kennel, eyebrows shifting left and right as he looked from master to stranger, well aware he was about to be abandoned. 'You'll need to drive him somewhere quiet for exercise. He can't be walked in or around the village. Take him to Beacon Common first thing in the morning and walk him there, ideally before seven – the end with the gravel pits. Nobody goes there so he's safe to be off the lead, but always take the remote control. For his late walk, take him along the river on the lead, never off. And *never* leave him unaccompanied in the car. You'll see why when you first drive it.' He swung the cage door shut and slid the bolt. 'Easier to keep him here while we set off. He chased me halfway to the station yesterday.'

'He must be very loyal to you.'

15

'Good to know someone is.' He sighed as he stooped to press his forehead to the mesh where the brindle whiskers were poking through. 'You behave, big fella, d'you hear?'

Gunter turned his back and slumped down in a leggy sulk, grizzly back hunched and chin heavy on big paws, letting out a self-pitying groan.

2

When the Lewises had finally set off in a flurry of spitting gravel, Jenny turned back to the house, eager to explore her new surroundings in peace. This was always her favourite house-sitting moment, the knowledge that she could claim custodianship.

Looking up at the Old Rectory's handsome sunlit face, she imagined the centuries of previous incumbents, who had gazed from the leaded casement windows at either side of the grand porch as carriages swept in and out, church services were called, sermons composed and domestic dramas enacted below stairs.

She could hear Gunter barking dementedly, the metalwork confining him rattling and crashing so much it sounded like a canine cage fight. Hastening inside, Jenny let him out. As soon as he was released, he ran from window to window, paws scrabbling on the stone ledges, panic-stricken and mournful at being left with a stranger.

Picking up the remote and hooking the long neck-strap that was attached to it over her head, Jenny hurried after him, catching a lightning tour of the house in the process, although she took in little beyond bright colours and mess.

Eventually he settled for baying forlornly at a mullioned window halfway up the back staircase. She perched between him and the landing, remote in hand, hoping this didn't constitute a green-button misdemeanour. Richard Lewis had specifically said the dog mustn't be allowed upstairs, but surely halfway was neither up nor down, like the Grand Old Duke of York's hill?

'It's okay, Gunter, you poor thing.' She approached him gently, laying a hand on his back. 'I know it's horrid when they go, but you have me and I'll look after you.'

Another great yowl shook his body for a full twenty seconds, making her ears hum.

However firmly she jollied, patted and encouraged him back downstairs, he just cried and howled more desperately. After he'd deafened and ignored her for a full ten minutes – so like Robin on a whisky-soaked rant – she decided to leave him mourning in peace while she got her bearings.

The reception rooms in the main Victorian body of the house were individually as big as the entire ground floor of her little mews house. The formal drawing room had hand-painted wallpaper and antique eau-de-Nil sofas facing one another like Regency dance partners, overlooked by a grand stonework fireplace. Across the hallway, an equally impressive carved wooden fireplace dominated the red-walled snug, over which hung a huge portrait of the yellow-eyed Lewis family – the children all looked like Geraldine, she noticed, like Midwich Cuckoos. Beside the snug, a dark-panelled dining room spoke of riotous feasts, with huge, deep-silled sash windows revealing tantalizing tableaux of the walled garden through their old glass. The long oak table was covered with ring marks and wax from dripping candelabra. Each room she looked at was beautifully styled with a great eye for colour, furniture and art, but they were also incredibly untidy, with books and papers piled everywhere. By contrast, the cool French grey library she found through a door at the furthest end of the vaulted hall was meticulously ordered, the shelves all alphabetically stocked, every pen lined up in parallel on the vast George III desk, the floor to ceiling windows perfectly aligned with topiary arches in its own private wing of the garden. Above its marble fireplace hung a beautiful stylized painting of the house. Jenny liked this room most, her eyes running along the book spines as she passed, making her tingle with anticipation. She could be imprisoned in a room like this for a year and not care.

Steps led down through a stone archway from the hall to an older part of the house, with deep mullioned windows and flagstones, in which she found a playroom. It was impossible to make out the floor for massacred Barbies, scattered board games and drifting Lego, triggering a maternal nostalgia that made her fingers twitch afresh. She remembered the long-suffering devotion with which she had once reunited decapitated Kens with their smiling heads, and picked up a thousand tiny Meccano bolts. A television room opposite was dominated by a plasma screen as big as a ping-pong table, still playing a muted kids' satellite channel, the table in front of the squashy leather sofa cul-de-sac littered with dirty plates and drinks cans. Further along the passage, past a small cluttered ante-kitchen and a door that seemed to lead to the cellars, she found a still-steamy wet room, with sodden towels thrown on the floor. Unable to stop herself hanging them on the high-tech rail to dry, Jenny noticed that somebody had failed to flush the loo or aim very well. She pressed the button on the cistern and experienced a misplaced rush of affection for family life.

Reversing out before she was tempted to get on her knees with the Domestos or sort the pile of boys' clothes left in one corner into lights and darks, she headed back through the house to check on Gunter, now with his paws on the front door, howling through the letterbox. This time when she made soothing sounds, he bounded towards her, goosed her against the newel post, then threw himself back to cry through the letterbox again.

19

It was progress, Jenny acknowledged, wishing it didn't make her think of Robin clutching her as compensation when a love affair ended.

Shaking the thought from her head, she went to admire the kitchen, trying to see past the debris of breakfast, half-opened post, soaking pans, abandoned mugs and food spills.

Here, Jenny – who had a secret addiction to all house-buying programmes on television and could spend happy hours searching million-pound-plus properties on the inter-net – had to admit it was among the best kitchens she'd ever seen, regardless of mess. If the Old Rectory's library was a ten, then its kitchen was a Spinal Tap eleven, including boiling water tap, sparkling water tap and retractable high-pressure tap.

It must once have been several rooms but had been opened out to create a vast, light, open-plan run of space from cooking through dining to sofa-sprawling and on through a Gothic arch to another wing of the house. Standing at the cooking end – itself twice the size of her beloved old Oxford open-plan kitchen – she let her eyes roam from flagged floor to hand-made surface to vaulted ceiling in pure, unadulterated pleasure, thrilled that this was her domain for a fortnight.

Embarrassed into action by her own indulgent delight, she started clearing up the clutter.

Now that she had time to study it in action, she could see that the kitchen was immensely practical, as well as beautiful. It had been exquisitely crafted to seem old and distressed. At its heart was a top-of-the-range Aga in the same defiant red as the one she'd had in the Oxford house. Surrounding it, the cupboard doors had been designed to echo the shape of the Gothic arches of the windows and doorways, and concealed a mountain of white tableware and polished glasses, a plethora of modern gadgets, from steam oven to Italian coffee machine, and a fridge as big as an industrial cold store. It was obvious that the Lewises were regular party-throwers who loved their food and wine. There was a walk-in larder you could park a car in, plus a two-storey drinks fridge and a wine rack as high as a climbing wall. One cupboard was filled floor-to-ceiling with sauce-flecked recipe books; another was crammed with Emma Bridgewater pottery, an indulgence that Jenny had collected for years and received for birthdays and Christmases without fail. If she lived to a hundred she wouldn't own this much.

To Jenny, the Old Rectory was a dream house. She even loved the mess, because it gave her something to do – she had never been good at doing nothing. Pausing by the hall door to check that Gunter was still snorting and yowling through the letterbox – less frantic now – she danced to the larder to put away a pot of Marmite and a packet of crisp-bread, lingering there to turn all the tins and jars face front and breathe in the smell of farmers' market, food-hall and foreign-holiday foraging.

Singing now, she loaded the dishwasher, wiped the surfaces, neatly folded the dishcloths, aired the tea towels and looked around at near-perfection. The only things she couldn't bring herself to tidy away in the kitchen were the books. Books were her comforters, her escape rooms beyond even this beautiful house. The Old Rectory had books absolutely everywhere, Jenny's idea of Heaven on earth. As well as the meticulously ordered first editions in the library, there were bookshelves short, tall, wide and narrow in every room, books on every table and surface, piled on their sides against walls, lined up on every step she passed, waiting on mantelpieces and fading on window-sills, clustered spines forming colourful barcodes wherever she looked – fat reference books, broken-backed novels, biographies, notebooks and children's reading lay everywhere.

Jenny found it impossible to inhabit the Old Rectory for more than an hour or two without loving the Lewises and their lifestyle. But it wasn't just the books that made the house unique, or the sumptuous furnishings or even the cataclysmic family clutter. It was the art in the house that struck her most, the walls crammed with works that showed an extraordinary eye for originality and talent. Portraits, animal studies, still-lifes and landscapes lined every wall, and the most noticeable motif was a delicious sense of humour.

There was a veritable gallery on the long wall that ran opposite the row of french windows in the part of the kitchen where the family ate at a big scrubbed table, then more in the sitting area and under the arch into the formal morning room. Jenny counted no less than fifty paintings, almost a quarter of which were by one artist, an extraordinary palette of vivid colours depicting scenes filled with joyful personality and life, from Moroccan markets to English country fayres, French circus acts to American dog shows, all by the hand that had painted the vibrantly characterful picture of the house in the library. The style was familiar, although the signature, a strange hieroglyph that looked like a table lamp on its side, meant nothing.

Beyond the bright morning room there were two studies, which, she guessed, had to be the creative Lewis engine rooms. Richard's workspace was easily identified, as meticulously ordered as the library, a simple Mac yachting alone on a slate-topped desk, a Herman Miller desk chair, and an iconic Absolut Crystal pinstriped bottle with an ironic lamp plugged into its neck on a black marble pedestal table nearby. Yet the pared-down furnishings were at odds with the walls, barely visible for tightly packed canvases. This was clearly the hub of the art collection. There were more paintings signed with the table-lamp scribble, plus cheery Mackenzie Thorpes, several Nicholas Hely Hutchinsons, a small Hockney of a dog, and some fantastically corpulent Beryl Cook ladies. Jenny found it surprising that an urbane academic like Richard Lewis had taste so defiantly popular and upbeat. Geraldine was the obvious candidate for collecting such carefree splendour, but when Jenny looked into the adjacent study, it was the only room in the house that was devoid of art, its walls crammed with framed book jackets, posters and photographs, mostly of the children. Here, the personality of the room came from real life, not artefacts. The only pretence was the fictional world created within it.

This is where Geraldine Scott's books are conceived, Jenny thought in awe. She could almost feel the dry heat of Western Australia fill her lungs as she breathed in deeply, the faint tang of Geraldine's distinctive perfume that lingered here becoming the scented flowering gums beneath which Jack had first kissed Victoria in *The Dust Storm*.

Although Richard had said that Geraldine now used the cottage in the grounds as a writing studio, the room was far from abandoned. It seemed that she worked wherever the mood took her and, as Jenny had seen elsewhere in the house, there were piles of notes, cuttings and reference books. Geraldine Scott was well known for writing her books in longhand, and her extravagant, looping handwriting was like a repeating pattern, featuring on every surface, papering the furniture and lined up among the ornaments on the sills and shelves, the scatter cushions on the sofas, teetering foolscap towers of inky prose. This room was the most chaotically cluttered in the house by far, yet Jenny found it profoundly beautiful and exciting. She kept her little mews house as immaculate as if she was expecting prospective buyers, a subconscious longing to flee. Her own mess disturbed her, but other people's was fascinating, especially that of a couple like the Lewises, whose clutter represented creative thought. And while Richard confined inspirational chaos within frames on the walls overlooking his minimalist desk, Geraldine's was an explosion of word and thought.

A mournful howl from the opposite end of the house made her turn guiltily, realizing that she was guilty of snooping just as Geraldine had cheerfully predicted, and that she'd abandoned her canine charge.

'I'm here, Gunter! It's okay!'

As she hurried from the room, Jenny caught her toe on a chair leg and it tipped over, upending a pile of paper resting on top. Turning, she watched in horror as three hundred pages of tightly written loose-leaf A4 spilled across the floor.

Stooping to gather it up, she heard a clattering of claws on flagstones as Gunter skittered energetically into the kitchen, bounded on through the morning room, bearded mouth smiling with relief as he spotted her.

'Gunter, no! Argh!' She fell back on the sea of paper as he leaped at her, his body gyrating with joy. She was the only human soul in the house so he had to stick close and make friends. He tried to wash her face enthusiastically, paws wrapped around her, before upending himself on the paper pile alongside her. There was a loud scrunching and ripping as he offered her a hairy chest to rub and a lot of hot, panting breath.

'Calm down.' Jenny tried to drag the ever more creased pages out from beneath him, but he took that as an invitation to hug her some more. He was Robin to a T, persistently crowding her and insisting his planet had the only gravity.

'No, Gunter! Get back. Sit!'

He ignored her, long claws scrabbling through the manuscript.

In desperation, she reached for the remote hanging around her neck and pressed the green button, the collar letting out its warning beep.

Gunter sat up suddenly, his face full of remorse and betrayal.

'I'm sorry, but I said no,' Jenny told him firmly, straightening up and looking down at the mess.

While she gathered up the rest of the paper – the pages now impossibly creased and out of order – Gunter slunk out to the morning room and sat underneath an occasional table, bushy eyebrows twitching in the shadows as he peered mournfully at her.

'Friends?' She tried to coax him out, but he stayed stubbornly wedged beneath the antique marquetry.

Murmuring gentle nonsense at him to try to gain his trust, Jenny sat at the kitchen table and started to put the pages of the manuscript back into order. To her relief, Geraldine had numbered each page in her looping hand, but her zeros, sixes and nines all looked the same and she had added extra pages later, with a numbering system that Jenny couldn't fathom, involving asterisks and roman numerals.

After a few minutes a warm pressure on her legs and a weight on her toes told her Gunter had crept out of the morning room and was sitting on her foot, leaning against her shins. She could hear his anxious breathing beneath the table, and when she glanced down, she saw that he was resting his chin on the chair next to hers, eyebrows moving from side to side as he alternated between watching the birds through the french windows, the hands above his head sorting papers, and the kitchen door through which he longed for his master to return.

The pages of extravagant handwriting moved left and right into piles of ten and Jenny tried not to sneak peeks at the content, but two words kept catching her eye. Jack. Victoria. Surely it was too much to hope for a return of the characters from *The Dust Storm*, who had shaped her romantic dreams more than twenty years earlier.

When Jenny found the title page of the manuscript, her squeak of excitement sent Gunter into a frenzy of barking as he body-slammed his way from windows to door, then dived back under the table to cower at her feet. Jenny barely noticed, still staring rapturously at the page in her hands.

THE STORM RETURNS – A Sequel
Second Draft for Transcription
Geraldine Scott-Lewis

Laying it on top of the sorted pages, she pressed her hands together and touched her nose with them in delight. Geraldine Scott, gifted story-teller, emotional rollercoaster driver and sexual guide to a host of teenage girls in the nineties, had finally answered the prayers of millions, Jenny and her friends included. She had brought back Victoria and Jack.

. She longed to text her old friend Rachel straight away to break the news – they could still quote Victoria and Jack's lines in the closing scene verbatim – but she knew that would be the height of unprofessional house-sitting behaviour. As would reading the book without permission. She would have to get the pages into order then put the whole thing back where she had found it without snooping. And somehow flatten and mend it too.

Fingers tingling with excitement, Jenny sorted the first three chapters, trying desperately to smooth out the creases.

At the other end of the kitchen, her phone rang in her hand-bag. She had yet to tell anybody that she was here, apart from her neighbour, who was watering the plants and bring-ing in the post.

She got up to answer it, but was hampered by Gunter upending two chairs as he scuttled out from beneath the table, raced once around the kitchen island, then jumped up to lavish her with more unwanted kisses.

She fingered the remote. 'Down!'

He lapped the kitchen island in the opposite direction, sending two bottles flying from the wine rack, then threw himself onto the big patchwork sofa beyond the table and lay upside-down, offering his stomach with an inverted smile and a lot of white eye.

That's Robin engaging in a new flirtation, Jenny thought darkly.

By the time she reached her phone, the call had gone to voicemail.

She settled beside Gunter on the patchwork sofa to listen to the message, looking out through tall, foliage-fringed win-dows to the walled garden she had yet to explore, a covered swimming-pool stamped perfectly in the foreground. The garden was a work of art in itself, the borders a Monet of blurred blues, purples and reds, the shrubbery a green Henry Moore sculpture park of clipped curves, and the beds a Jackson Pollock riot of joyful primary colour. Richard was right about the genius of the gardener: the beauty of the formal landscaping probably beat the perfect-ten library and Spinal Tap-eleven kitchen to a round dozen.

The missed call had been from her mother, the familiar warm voice enunciating slowly because she mistrusted tech-nology and always talked to answer-phones as though relaying a message via a particularly dim doctor's receptionist. She was eager for the regular lunchtime offload about the trials of living in a feud-ridden Hampshire retirement community, Haven Hall.

'Do call, darling. It's been a tricky few days. Lots to say.'

Jenny felt a fleeting urge, quite common when she was house-sitting, to let the fantasy of disappearing into somebody else's life wash over her, a feeling akin to diving into water and letting it take her weight, suspending her in a moment of total absorption before she kicked to the surface. She was sitting alone in a magnificent house that spoke of feasts, play, laughter, success, the confidence of a united book-, art- and fun-loving family. It was a house that felt happy and full of movement, not like a museum of marriage past. Her current surroundings possessed the essence of family life she had wanted to keep. It was the one thing she would never get back. She wanted to hold it in for as long as she could.

Still upside-down beside her, Gunter let out a squeaky yawn, short tail thumping, and she realized he had forgotten his absent family and transferred his affection to her as his most likely source of food and tender loving care. Robin's *modus operandi* was similar.

Jenny let out her breath, knowing the moment of suspension had already passed. She returned the call, already guessing her mother's reaction when she found out whose house she was sitting. Mum was the one who had discovered *The Dust Storm* in the first place, staying outside on a Mallorcan sun-lounger until she had read its last chapters by moonlight, sunburned and mosquito-bitten.

'You'll never guess where I am,' she started, as soon as her mother picked up the call, then hesitated. The news of her stay at the Old Rectory would be around the bridge and book-club circle within hours, doing the dinner-party circuit of the Rotary and am-dram shortly afterwards, filtering to

28

the WI before she knew it. Within twenty-four hours it would be viral.

But her mother was too eager to offload the latest home gossip to play twenty questions. 'Someone's been putting kipper skins in the wheelie-bins again. We all voted against it at the last committee meeting because they smell terrible now it's a fortnightly collection. Bob Kermode set up a CCTV camera to catch the culprit, but the hanging basket kept swinging in front of the lens . . . '

Jenny settled back to listen, content in the knowledge that it would be at least ten minutes before her input was needed. About eighteen months earlier, not long after her father's third heart attack, her parents had moved from their village house to the show flat in the Haven, a nearby country pile that had been converted into luxury apartments for the over-fifty-fives complete with spa, gym and café. It was obvious they both loved it because they hadn't stopped complaining about the neighbours since.

After a long description of Wheelie-Bin-gate, followed by indignant chuntering about the state of the communal parterre, the price of other apartments up for sale, and some salacious rumours about the Carmichaels' marriage, Jenny's mother suddenly asked, 'Where did you say you are?'

'Buckinghamshire,' she fudged, wondering whether it would be unprofessional to tell all. She hadn't signed anything about confidentiality, and the Lewises were hardly in a league with Posh and Becks.

'Is it something to do with your new chap?' The excitement was almost palpable. 'Are you on the walking holiday you told me about?'

'It's work,' Jenny said, in her no-nonsense, teacher voice, getting up to return to the table and adopt a more businesslike stance. 'I'm being paid to look after a house.'

'Has he lost interest?'

'No! I just preferred the idea of coming here. You'll never guess who—'

'You must learn to let your hair down, Jennifer,' her mother interrupted. 'I know you can do what you like with your holidays now that the twins are based in the States with their father, but—'

'They don't *live* with him, Mum,' she said tetchily. 'Amalie lives on campus, and Jake's stopping off to see Robin for a bit on his travels. He's only met his half-sister once.' She still couldn't say her name out loud, even though she was almost two.

'You could go on one of those singles holidays,' her mother said pointedly.

'I'm not really single any more, and this is work. I've got Carla's manuscript to correct while I'm here. Remember I told you about it?' She delved into her capacious bag to pull out her laptop.

'Vaguely.' Her mother dismissed it. There followed a moment's breathless excitement. 'So if you're not really single, is it still on with the new chap?'

'Still on.' Jenny shifted her feet, which were going to sleep because Gunter was once again Velcroed to her legs beneath the table, chin resting on her knee as she fired up the computer, letting it find 3G broadband.

'Good. He sounds lovely and old-fashioned.'

'He is lovely and old-fashioned.' She sighed, thinking of Roger's mannerly reliability. Polite, oh-so Britishly shy, clever and respectful, but unreconstructed and sporty enough to be sexy, he was a rare find amid the World Wide Web of internet dating lies. Even the eternally cautious Jenny had allowed herself to hope for more from the tall, witty conveyancing solicitor, who had described himself as 'forty-something, unmarried, solvent, straight and young-at-heart' (whose acronym was FUSSY, as her friends loved pointing out, although as two divorcees, Jenny felt she and Roger were both technically FDSSY, and her own D had left her extremely self-protective). 'I'm just not ready for a holiday together yet.'

'Someone else will snap him up if you don't,' her mother warned, catching Jenny with an inadvertent blow. Trusting anyone again was proving a lot harder than she'd imagined. After all, someone had snapped Robin up from right under her nose, wedding ring and all.

Jenny stared out through the french windows, watching dead petals drift down from the rambling roses tangled above them, embarrassed at the selfish little-girl urge to say that *she* wanted to be the one who was snapped up. 'I found out last week that Roger was still advertising for girlfriends.'

It had come as a shock to learn, several months after they had first met and started dating, that Jenny might have secured the regular Thursday theatre and dinner slot with Reliable Roger, but his time wasn't yet exclusively hers; his profile was still active and the website through which they had met reported that he was online most days. She'd let her own membership lapse weeks ago, although if she was brutally honest that was as much about hating internet matchmaking as liking Roger.

Her mother was gratifyingly indignant. 'I hope you gave him what-for!'

'I tackled it, yes.' She could still feel the sharp pinpricks of humiliation when she'd finally raised the subject, her jokey approach edged with irritation in an awkward candlelit conversation over a bowl of post-Playhouse linguine. She'd felt like a jealous wife again.

'What did he say?'

31

'He took his profile page down that night.' She clicked on the dating site on her laptop now and found no trace of Roger. 'He said he'd been waiting for me to ask.' To her surprise, Roger had seemed rather chuffed by her indignation. Doubtless his invitation to share a week's Peak District yomping together – issued swiftly after her confrontation – was an indication that he felt the relationship was ready to move up a notch. It was time for the initiation ceremony to reach the next level: His and Hers toothbrushes in the bathroom, weekends together and fidelity.

But as soon as this twist was offered, Jenny had started to panic that it might be better to stick where they were. Roger was a charming midweek date. Her libido, so long in the deep freeze, was all over the place right now. She didn't yet trust her self-control enough to take it further. Neither could she call her attraction to the man who was only three years her senior yet seemed to belong to a different era. Given her secret plan to escape overseas for at least part of her sabbatical – news she had yet to break to Roger or anyone else – she wasn't convinced that toothbrushes, cosy weekends and fidelity were wise. While she might not crave sex, drugs and rock and roll, it all felt suffocatingly tame.

'What a gentleman!' her mother enthused, about Roger's declaration of loyalty. 'I'd love to meet him.'

Jenny suspected that if Roger went to Haven Hall, the swooning of elderly ladies would swing the hanging baskets in full circles. By contrast, if he strode into the Old Rectory right now, she feared the reaction would be as wilted as the lilies in the troughs by the swimming-pool. He had fitted perfectly into her Oxford life thus far, but she wasn't sure how suited they were to more than a weekly play and after-theatre supper.

It was true that she had often wondered what Roger

would be like in bed, but nowadays she thought about sex an alarming amount – and no longer with the puritanical, resentful recoil that she'd felt in the later stages of her marriage. She found herself regularly wondering what strangers she met would be like as lovers, from the Polish plumber who'd fixed her shower and winked as he left, to the financier fathers who came to parents' evening and joked that their sons adored her. (It was through one father's inadvertent comment that she'd learned that MILF was not an abbreviation for mille-feuilles pastry, but slang for 'mums I'd like to fuck', with dedicated Tumblr feeds featuring seductive cougars bent on physical pleasure). In the past six months, Jenny's brain had acquired a hitherto undiscovered MILF porn channel. To her shame, she'd fantasized most about Nice Married Matt, the rugby-mad, wide-shouldered, twenty-something trainee teacher, who flirted with everyone over the biscuits in the staff room. Most weeks poor Roger barely featured in her top ten, although his regular availability on Thursdays had bumped him up the charts recently. She was starting to suspect that he was the best option if she was going to have a sex life again. Her friend Carla had even given it a name, 'Roger Roger Night'. Jenny wished she could shake the worry that, as soon as it happened, they would be over and out.

But she could hardly talk to her mother about this, a woman who occupied the strange orbit between middle and old age, and was of a generation for whom making love had once been an Age of Aquarius pleasure. They had once smoked without fear of demonization, driven drunk without seatbelt or stigma, and had enjoyed unsafe, Pill-protected sex until the Aids epidemic had reclassified it. They saw it now as something to be discussed in romantic euphemisms: they believed love still grew in a rose garden with bullshit as bedding manure.

'You need to have a man's love again, Jenny,' she said earnestly, kettle boiling in the background.

'So do you, Mum,' Jenny replied, with feeling. Carefully removing Gunter's dribbling bearded chin from her lap, she realized that had sounded wrong. She'd meant that her mother deserved more devotion, her husband's attention lost in curmudgeonly neighbour-baiting, but it had come out far too glibly. While mother and daughter occasionally flirted with romantic notions over a bottle of wine in front of a box set – they'd recently agreed that one wouldn't say no to Jeremy Irons while the other felt the same about his son Max – it was never serious, sober or repeated in phone conversations.

A proud sniff. 'I love your father.'

'Of course you do.' An apologetic laugh.

There was a brief lull in which Jenny chewed her bottom lip, wondering if she'd crossed an invisible line.

Then her mother's warm voice resumed its familiar hot-chocolate gush. 'Dad might be a tricky bugger, but at least he's not like Frank Jamieson. He can no longer get into the car since his stroke. Poor Anne and the carers have to feed him, like a corpse in a carpet. Apparently they had a terrible time in Morrison's car park last Wednesday when he got wedged between the Prius and a people-carrier ... '

They were back on track, and Jenny could slip into her rhythmic descant of oh-no-mm-mm-ah-ah-poor-you, sympathy and laughter. When they finally rang off, she pressed her eyes with the balls of her hands, ashamed at her inability to say what she was really thinking.

Selecting another speed dial and slotting her mobile phone under her ear, she opened the email program on her laptop. She started to type, certain the call would go straight to voicemail: *Hi, Roger* (he had started to sign himself 'Rog', these days, but she couldn't bring herself to use it. 'Roger' was tricky enough – she suspected he'd be far higher up her Sex Fantasy Top Ten if he was called 'Zac' or 'Ryan'). *Quick note to let you know I'll be away for the coming fortnight, so have to say a regretful no to the Peaks, also cancel tonight and the following two Thursdays until I'm back, when I will drop you a shgkjt*

Her call was answered with breathless enthusiasm. 'Don't tell me you're working on it already?' demanded Carla, voice infused with Marlboro. 'What do you think?'

'Are you off sick?' Jenny tapped the delete button. 'You never answer my calls when you're at work. I was going to leave a voicemail.'

'I'm out on the fire escape with the suicide smokers winding up the trolls on my Twitter timeline. Is that typing I hear? You are *amazing*, Jen – I only emailed the final draft yesterday, my multi-tasking chum.'

Jenny had first met Carla when they'd worked together on a local newspaper, her own youthful pedantry as sub-editor smoothing the rough edges of the journalist whose appalling spelling let down her addictive style. While Carla had gone on to embrace better computer spell-checks en route to her staff job with a national tabloid, the demands of motherhood had long since diverted Jenny's editorial career hopes, her work life pared down to part-time piecemeal when raising young children, then to teaching, which fitted in better with family life. Her friendship with Carla had endured, however, and the journalist still rated her as the most eagle-eyed copy-reader she'd ever met, a skill Carla abused with a regular torrent of libellous prose, charm and dreams of e-book best-sellers.

'I'm not editing your manuscript yet,' Jenny said briskly, continuing her email to Roger *drop you a line and* ... 'I'm away for a couple of weeks.' She typed on ... *we can meet up* ... 'But I'm going to work on it while I'm here' ... *and maybe go to bed.*

'Anywhere interesting?'

She tapped backspace twenty times in a rhythmic tattoo, added a full stop after 'meet up' and signed the email with three kisses, then removed two. They still largely communicated by email, maintaining the polite formality of business colleagues, and she didn't want to encourage him. She knew Carla would recommend adding something ground-breaking, like *PS If you want to find my High Peaks, let's fuck in Bucks.*

'I'm house-sitting for a family called Lewis,' she explained as she tapped the keyboard, adding an alternative PS: *Give me a call if you're in the High Wycombe area,* 'or Richard Lewis and Geraldine Scott, to use their professional names.'

Carla combined a grudging snort and a respectful whoop to acknowledge the literary luminaries. 'Don't they live in Gothic splendour with dozens of marauding children and animals? I read a profile in the *Sunday Times* mag recently.'

'The children are staying with Granny while they take off to bask in the Indian Ocean. I'm looking after the art collection and marauding animals. And the house isn't strictly Gothic – it's sixteenth century in origin, although a Victorian make-over admittedly camped it up a bit with turreted gables and towers.'

'Spare me the Pevsner, Rees. I bet you were up all night Googling the place, along with the sales history and online planning consents.' She laughed affectionately. 'You are a totally addicted perv of property porn, Jen.'

Jenny spell-checked her email to Roger, wondering if she'd

fancy him more if he advertised himself on Zoopla. 'I always like to know the history behind the houses I take on.'

'Jenny Rees, the SAS of house-sitting, so discreet they'll never know you were there, yet somehow always leaving it in much better shape than before. This time, I insist that you leave a book behind too. Mine. The Lewises must read *Tour Divorce*. This could make all the difference – their endorsement will guarantee we're a best-seller. They're like Richard and Judy with doctorates. In fact, can we email a copy to them to read on holiday?'

'They're on a romantic break in Mauritius, C – I hardly think they'll want two hundred pages of typos about surviving a marital break-up.'

'There aren't that many errors!'

'I've spotted three in the first paragraph.'

'Good. That means you're reading it.' Carla was defiantly upbeat. 'And I want you to promise to read it very, very carefully, Jen.'

'It's my job, C.'

'That's not what I mean. Look especially closely at the chapter called "An Empty Nest Is Not a Glass Half Empty".'

Jenny glanced around the unfamiliar kitchen, its polished-granite and oiled-wood surfaces no longer cobbled with half-full glasses and breakfast debris. 'I'll read every word assiduously,' she promised, and Carla moved on, predictably, to Roger.

'Are you luring him for nights of sordid passion on the Lewises' four-poster?'

'That would be highly unprofessional.'

'So you still haven't rogered Roger?'

Jenny removed the one remaining kiss from her email. 'No.'

'Jen, you're going to have to face the very real possibility that you may be about to have sex again.'

'I know that,' she scoffed, throat dry.

'And Roger is as f-u-s-s-y as you are. He's made it abundantly clear he's attracted to you. So what's stopping you?'

Jenny thought about the formal clinches they had smoothly manoeuvred into at the end of dates, some quite sexy in a staged way, like pre-rehearsed seductions in old-fashioned movies, which cut away to her travelling home in a cab, face flushed with anticipation. Roger was among the most polite men she had ever met, yet he couldn't hide the increasingly predatory look in his eye, the way his gaze felt at liberty now to roam her body, although he always asked, 'Would you mind if I kiss you?' in much the same way one might seek permission to open a car window. She still wasn't sure if that meant she was in the driving seat or not. Their journeys between theatre seat, restaurant seat and home felt like outings in a dual-control driving instructor's car, with one of them pressing the brake as fast as the other was opening the throttle. And, like map-reading en route, they were far better sitting down studying a theatre programme or restaurant menu than looking at the road ahead.

In early middle age, Jenny found, different sexual rules applied to dating, especially with an old-fashioned consort like Roger. Her own inability to let go frustrated her, the need to stay in control still largely eclipsing desire. It was so different from the fun, fumbling kisses on doorsteps, dance-floors and sofas she remembered first time around, the first-second-third-base experimentation of her teenage years. There was now an obstacle course of venues, entertainment, food and formal small-talk to navigate. The slow-burn flirtation could quickly go off the boil in the face of bad stalls seats or poor restaurant service. She envied her undergraduate self the easy way in which she'd slipped into that brief, hedonistic phase of drunken, daring student promiscuity before she'd met Robin and gratefully settled down to couple culture and Sunday-morning love-making. She missed those mornings enormously.

She had a sudden mental image of Robin's sunlit, tousled head between her legs, heard 'Perfect Day' on the radio and saw the framed *Withnail and I* poster on the opposite wall. The Jericho flat in the nineties: a cheap Ikea duvet cover, pillows flat as pitta bread and mattress as soft as quicksand.

'I'm not ready,' she told Carla.

'Like fuck you're not.' She cackled.

The memory of Robin going down on her wouldn't go away, so visceral it made muscles clench deep inside her. It was like fantasizing about a stranger, the quirky Rhodes Scholar she had met at twenty, with his boundless sexual confidence, his full head of hair and insatiable desire for her. Robin Rees. The last man she had fallen in love with. The only man she had ever fallen in love with.

Two decades later, as adult professionals whose romantic profiles had been matched before their eyes met, she and Roger had kept their clothes on through twenty dates: their bodies and social circles had yet to touch. She knew more about his opinions on Jacobean drama than she did about his own life tragedies. But when she thought about it, the same had been true of Robin, the only difference being that they'd slept together on the second date, straight after sitting in the cheap seats for *Othello*, lighting the touch-paper that had ignited her love.

'Roger is a gentleman,' she told Carla starchily now, all too acutely aware that sex on top of the *Observer* – accompanied by St Giles's peal of eight bells while the coffee in the cafetière went cold – was unlikely to be an option with a man whose love of canoeing meant he got up at seven each Sunday to hit the water. 'We're both waiting for the right moment.' She replaced the kiss on her email and pressed send.

'Don't wait for a fantasy figure, Jen,' Carla lectured her. 'Having sex increases your libido. It's a known fact. Read the chapter in my book entitled "Sex Is Not a Battle But Making Love Is War". And, FFS, roger Roger.' She blew a kiss down the line and rang off.

In Jenny's mind's eye, Robin's thick pelt of chestnut hair instantly switched to Roger's neat grey short-back-and-sides. She crossed her legs tightly to banish the thought.

Determined to stop thinking about sex, she wrote hasty email messages to daughter Amalie, who was staying on in the States during her summer vacation from NYU to help out at a kids' camp, and to Amalie's twin Jake, who was on the last leg of his gap year with his girlfriend, now en route from a voluntary aid programme in India to New York via an alarming number of countries ending 'stan', his hotmail account woefully neglected of late. As always, she found herself peppering her prose with far too many exclamation marks and platitudes, tropes she would never accept from a student but which she had started to coin in private in an attempt to connect with her children, emoticons concealing the roaring mother love that she feared embarrassed as much as it protected them, these days. Finally, switching off her laptop, she texted her old friend Rachel to suggest they rearrange their lunch in a week's time so that it was closer to Buckinghamshire. *So excited by this one: remember us fighting over* The Dust Storm *at uni?*

Rachel had three children under six and a frantic home-life, which made their monthly get-togethers increasingly difficult to orchestrate. Yet unlike Carla, who was very hit and miss to communicate with, often going weeks without replying to a message, Rachel was always straight back in touch.

I WORSHIPPED that book, Jenny read, as she headed upstairs to check out her bedroom. *Isn't GS our age? Bet she doesn't have a broken dishwasher and kids with nits, the lucky thing. And you lucky thing too! Enjoy the luxury . . .*

Jenny's first copy of *The Dust Storm*, 'borrowed' from her mother's bedside shelf twenty years ago, had eventually disintegrated, passed around the school common room so much that it fell open obediently at the points of most interest, which had raised teenage girls' pulses and expectations to melting point. Jack and Victoria had been up there with Jason and Kylie as the Greatest Love Story Ever to her generation, the difference being that the former had gone way beyond closing the wobbly television set bedroom door, with Bouncer tail-wagging on the other side. *The Dust Storm* was a common language, the book every teenage girl of Jenny's acquaintance had read, no matter how pretentiously they spoke about Marina Warner or Kazuo Ishiguro in their university entrance interviews. It marked, for many, a sexual awakening. They *were* Victoria, rebellious daughter of a wealthy mine owner; Jack, a miner's son with an explosive temper, was their first love; Geraldine Scott – barely older than they were when she wrote the novel at university in Sydney – was a role model and guide, the genius who had made millions of women shriek with joy when Jack had taken over the mine and claimed Victoria from her well-born fiancé, their passion as deep as the shafts beneath their feet.

Jenny thought about their story carrying on in *The Storm Returns* and felt a shiver of anticipation. She must not read it, she reminded herself. But she *was* going to have to iron it . . .

3

The guest suite that Richard had told Jenny to use was a haven of blue and white Provençal shabby chic, dominated by an ornately carved white bed piled with vintage-fabric cushions. Above it hung a blue and white *ciel de lit*. It would be like sleeping in a Victorian bathing tent, Jenny thought.

It was an intensely feminine room, and she guessed it had to be Geraldine's taste. By contrast to the rest of the house, there were no flamboyant paintings on the Toile de Jouy walls. Instead clusters of artfully framed antique French silhouettes were grouped over the painted *bombe* furniture, featuring delicate dogs, birdcages, musical instruments and slim-necked girls in plumed hats. Beyond the swagged silk curtains, the view was of vibrant pea-green leaf and lawn, across the walled garden to the shrubbery and the woods beyond. The casements were open, letting in a faint breeze that carried traces of freshly cut grass infused with swimming-pool chlorine. She could hear bumble bees drifting lazily through the climbing quince below and the church clock ringing two.

Jenny closed her eyes and breathed deeply, longing to freeze-frame the moment and bottle her own draught of private paradise. But she needed a pee and she wasn't sure where the dog had got to.

Throwing her bag onto the navy silk slipper chair at the foot of the bed and padding across tracts of glossy dark floorboard and thick hand-woven rug, she found an en-suite located beyond découpage screens featuring flirtatious corseted ladies in compromising positions.

The little bathroom's walls made her gulp in alarm. They were entirely covered with antique French mirrors tiled together, from floor to ceiling across every surface, including the alcove housing a marble bath with taps shaped like lions' heads and a shower rose as big as a serving plate above it. The only way to take a wee without seeing oneself from every angle was to close one's eyes.

As Jenny sat on the high antique loo, her reflection bounced off cushion mirrors, speckled giltwood mirrors, Venetian mirrors and mirrors with candleholders. It was like sitting in a lavatorial fairground attraction. A hundred dark-haired women of average age, average build and average height looked back at her, middle-aged, middle class and with thickening middles. It reminded her of walking through Marks & Spencer one day when the twins were young and seeing a harassed, overweight mother of two who looked like she'd dressed in the dark. She had cast her a sympathetic glance, then realized it was her own reflection.

Looking up, she groaned to find herself reflected from the ceiling as well, the angle emphasizing her hollow cheeks and startled eyes. She tried to pull a comedy face, but it looked grotesque. She smiled instead, which was just as bad. Her dentist had recently told her that she was grinding her teeth so much that her smile would soon be gone. He'd fitted her with a gum shield that she had to wear in bed, so now she squeaked her way to sleep and always smiled with her lips closed.

Finishing as quickly as she could, she washed her hands, surrounded by a crowd of her mirrored likeness.

'Learn to love yourself first' was one of Carla's mantras – no doubt *Tour Divorce* would be peppered with it – and Jenny had tried hard, but she barely recognized herself, these days.

43

When Jenny had first lost a lot of weight, triggered by the stress of her marriage falling apart, she'd developed a habit of staring at her reflection for far longer than normal, which those who didn't know her well might have ascribed to vanity. More accurately, she'd been getting to know the unfamiliar face and body she saw, the slimmed-down, scruffy divorcee who looked a bit like her but whom she had never imagined was the woman she would become, a newly single forty-something with a twenty-something waist. Jenny had always played down her hang-ups, but years of sexual rejection by Robin had left her acutely body-conscious, a perfectionist whose flaws had become silent enemies. For years it had been her size, the pregnancy pounds that had become a long-term investment gaining annual interest. Now, with her skin loosened by weight loss, it was ageing.

The last time she'd met Rachel for their monthly get-together, they'd indulged in an afternoon's pampering at a child-friendly country spa. Rachel, who was the same age as Jenny but had become a mother in her late thirties, had incredible skin – porcelain pale, taut and regularly fed with Lush's finest. By contrast, Jenny's swarthy hide sagged and creased more each day, long starved of nutrition, any pampering time stolen by years of early-morning school runs and late-night marking, its surface bearing blotches from sun exposure on Cornish family holidays, weekend walks and playground duty. Appalled by the beautician's declaration that her 'skin age' was closer to fifty than forty, she'd come away armed with a small fortune's worth of products, which she applied with assiduous care morning and night in place of the usual supermarket brand. Apart from smelling rather nice, she had yet to see a difference.

But today, with the sun streaming through gauze window blinds behind her and the speckled, yellowing glass casting her olive skin to gold and her high cheekbones into soft chiaroscuro curves, she allowed herself to believe that for the next fortnight, in this amazing house, she might just see a different angle of herself. Nevertheless, she decided she would use the en-suite loo only after dark with the lights out.

In the bedroom, she lay back on the super-king-size mattress and smiled up at the striped canopy. 'What a place! This is the— Oof!' A great weight of wiry hair and sinew landed on top of her, licking her face eagerly, whimpering with excitement to have tracked her down.

'Gunter! You are definitely not allowed up here!'

Spooning winningly, he upended himself to offer his belly, cramming her against the pillows and bolsters and grinning across at her, all white teeth and square beard. The parallels with Robin struck her afresh. Even at his most unpleasant and secretive, days away from leaving her, he'd been a bedhog and restless sleeper. While she'd hung off one side of the mattress, cocooned in breathless grief, he'd sprawled in the middle, chest up, snoring defiantly, tossing this way and that, occasionally turning to enfold her in an unconscious bearded hug that she'd clung to, believing right up until the last possible moment that he would change his mind and stay.

Gunter's dog-hug was just as selfish, domineering and primitive, she thought, as she glanced across at the witless, bristly smile. There was nothing malicious in his instinct to cleave to her for comfort. Sandwiched against such warm neediness, exhausted from end-of-term mania, late-night Googling and Roger-dodging, Jenny closed her eyes.

Six hours later, when Gunter rested his hairy beard on her forehead to suggest he might like a walk, Jenny woke up with a guilty start. Dusk was falling.

4

The 'dog car' was a snazzy high-spec silver Evoque, just like the yummy-mummy models Jenny had admired in the school car park all year, and far superior to her own modest Japanese runaround – or, at least, it had been before a German wire-haired pointer had eaten his way through the leather upholstery. She distinctly remembered Richard warning her never to leave him alone in the car. Both driver's and passenger's seats had been chewed, as had some of the dashboard, and it was obvious Gunter had broken down the dog grille more than once, although he seemed happy to bound into the boot now and steam up the windows with impatient barks.

An on-board computer greeted Jenny warmly before showing a multi-angle rear camera shot of the garage door opening and asking where she wanted to go. To Jenny's relief, it offered 'Gunter River Walk' among the first pre-programmed options. She reversed out amid much sensor-beeping and barking, then set off along the drive. Turning left onto the lane as directed, she found Heart on the digital radio with just a couple of screen taps. The car also suggested she might like to connect her phone via Bluetooth. She agreed, charmed by the gadgetry.

But before she could play with more controls or call a friend or two to boast that she was talking hands-free in the most high-tech car she had ever driven, the sat-nav voice announced that she'd arrived at her destination.

She caught Gunter's eyes in the rear-view mirror. 'We've come half a mile. You must be seriously tricky to walk.'

Gunter *was* seriously tricky to walk. As soon as he was out of the car, all bonding was forgotten. He was on a mission to upend fishermen, capsize canoes, flatten bicycles and jump on and off boats.

As she was dragged, mortified, past furious riverbank users, Jenny grabbed the remote control that was swinging around her neck and pressed the green button. Collar beeping all the way, the overexcited dog took no notice, hauling her along behind him at high speed towards a terrifying-looking weir. When she thought she was going to be pulled into its gushing depths, she pressed the yellow button. Snorting from a puff of citronella up his nose, Gunter swerved left just before they both fell in, but then homed in on a row of houseboats moored further along the bank and charged towards them.

'No, Gunter!' Green button. No response.

Two Rottweilers appeared on the deck of the first boat, letting out baritone barks warning them to keep away.

'Gunter, stop!' Yellow button. No response.

The Rottweilers' hackles rose, barks turning to savage snarls.

By now Gunter was baying furiously, bounding towards them, dragging Jenny with him. As he drew close to the boat, the Rottweilers hung over the side, teeth bared, snouts wrinkled, ready to fight. Gunter put on a surge of speed. Closing her eyes, Jenny pressed red.

Gunter let out an indignant whimper, leaping away so violently that he pulled the lead from her hands and fled, jinking left into thick woods, with several trees that bore big signs, saying 'KEEP OUT' and warning that 'Trespassers Will Be Prosecuted'.

'Shit!' Jenny ran after him, then shrieked as the Rottweilers threw themselves off the houseboat, almost landing on top of her.

'Down!' ordered a voice.

The dogs fell to the ground.

Swinging round, Jenny saw a man standing on the boat, dark hair dripping wet. From wide shoulders to well-hung bulge, he was wearing nothing but water drops and a small cotton towel round his hips.

'Get back here!'

The dogs obediently trotted up the gangplank.

'I'm sorry,' he called to Jenny, the accent gruff and Scottish, his face set with bad temper. 'They don't usually do that.' He was squinting along the towpath, now veiled in dusky shadows. There was a distinctive pale streak in his dark hair, which looked pink in the lowering sun. 'Was that a dog with you just now?'

'He's run off.' Jenny found herself still staring at his body, as though her eyes were being controlled by a third party. The towel was really very small and his torso fabulously ripped. A blush stole up her face as he turned sideways and she saw the bulge in profile, its magnificent projection telling her it was fresh from active service.

'What's going on, baby?' purred a seductive voice, as a girl appeared on deck wearing an even smaller towel, white against her ebony skin. She was also dripping wet.

Jenny looked quickly away, cheeks burning.

'Your dogs tried to chase this woman's and now it's run off. I'll get some clothes on.'

'They're not my dogs, baby,' the girl pointed out petulantly, watching him bound down into the boat. 'They're Perry's.' She sighed, her beautiful face even grumpier than Pink Streak Man's, furious to be interrupted *in flagrante* by a dog fight. 'Perry owns this boat,' she told Jenny. 'He'll be back tomorrow.'

'That's good to know,' Jenny muttered, backing towards the woods and raising her hand, eager not to have to form a search party with the girl's priapic, bad-tempered lover. 'Tell your man there's no need to help, thanks! I'm sure I'll find him.' She hurried along the path and clambered over a gate marked 'Strictly Private'.

Gunter was cowering behind a large beech tree in near-darkness, big eyebrows constantly on the move as he blinked uneasily, certain he was about to be zapped.

'I am so, so sorry.' Jenny crouched and wrapped her arms around him. 'I will never, ever do it again, I promise.' Gunter licked her face and put a woolly paw on her knee.

Clicking open the remote-control case, she pulled out the rechargeable battery and held it up to show him before pocketing it. 'We'll do this our way.'

In the crepuscular light, Gunter looked more like Robin than ever, his bright-eyed, hirsute devotion hiding uncontrollable baser instincts. As Jenny fumbled for the broken lead, the dog cocked his head to listen to a rustling in the nearby undergrowth. With a squawk of alarm, a pheasant flapped from cover. Gunter bounded off in hot pursuit. Within seconds, the bird was dead. Another bird squawked and he killed it just as quickly.

'Stop it!' she cried, spinning round. There were pheasants everywhere. And Gunter was killing them all.

It took Jenny almost twenty minutes to catch him, convinced at every turn that a gamekeeper was going to appear with a shotgun and despatch him with a cartridge blast between the eyes. She even tried to slot the battery back into the remote, but the plastic guard had wedged at an impossible angle. Eyes rolling, Gunter dodged her and dashed past. By the time she finally caught him and hauled him out of the woods, he'd killed at least a dozen birds.

'Oh, Christ alive, what do I do?' she muttered, under her breath. Did one leave a note with a phone number, like when you pranged a car? Try to bury the evidence, like a mass murderer? Take a few for the pot like a poacher? Right now, running away from the scene as quickly as possible seemed the best option.

Creeping out of the woods with the wiry murderer at her heels, she looked up and down the riverbank, now in near darkness, apart from the houseboats' lights. Low reggae music, fabulous cooking smells and the unmistakable tang of weed floated to her from Perry's boat. The Rottweilers were, thankfully, nowhere in sight.

Tip-toeing past, Jenny made a hurried getaway to the dog car, which welcomed her with strings of illuminated coloured lights around its dashboard, a computer update on its performance and a selection of available television channels for her enjoyment. She half suspected it would make her a much-needed cup of tea if she found the right command. As she drove home, she almost veered off the road when the car speakers let out a shrill ring. Then she saw Roger's name on the dashboard computer screen and two touch boxes marked 'Accept' and 'Decline'. A call was coming through on her phone via Bluetooth.

She remembered the PS she'd added to her email: *Give me a call if you're in Bucks.* Surely he wasn't in the area right now. She was covered with pheasant blood and riverbank dust, hadn't even unpacked her bag, had stubbly legs and hadn't tackled her bikini line in weeks.

Indicating to turn into the hidden driveway, she pressed 'Decline'.

5

Despite being put to bed with a late-night radio phone-in and a selection of well-chewed dog toys, Gunter howled and thrashed in his cage from the moment Jenny left him to head up to the guest suite. The attention-seeking hullabaloo reminded her of nights lying awake while Robin crashed around downstairs, argued with the television or listened to loud music, peeved that she'd taken herself off to bed to read. But tonight Jenny found it impossible to concentrate on any of the books she had so joyfully carried up from the Lewises' library. Unable to sleep because she had napped for so long, or to shut out the dog's cries, she couldn't bear to leave him so alone and unhappy, no matter how furious she was about the dead pheasants. Eventually she decided to keep him company. She had something very practical in mind to pass the time, something that needed doing and which was one of the household chores she always enjoyed with the radio for company. On this occasion, she had a large dog in a cage too.

She set up the ironing-board, then went in search of the battered pages of *The Storm Returns* and started to flatten each one on the lowest setting.

After the title page came a dedication: *To my darling RL. Out flew the web and floated wide . . .*

How romantic to dedicate a book to one's husband with a line from Tennyson, Jenny thought wistfully. She recognized the quote from 'The Lady of Shalott', which she'd taught as a set text so many times, the tragic epic poem that told of the beautiful, mysterious victim of an evil curse, bound to stick to her enchanted weaving task day and night without ever looking out of the window, but whose self-discipline snaps when, reflected in the mirror, she sees Sir Lancelot riding by on his return to Camelot.

Unable to stop her eyes running down the first lines of *The Storm Returns* as she ironed, Jenny started to look for errors. Then she stopped and started reading as she found Victoria and Jack waiting for her, the two lovers who had been united against all odds at the end of *The Dust Storm*. The story picked up over a decade later, with the couple at breaking point.

By two in the morning, she had ironed the first two chapters and was totally hooked.

II

Friday

6

TO DO LIST

Copy-edit Carla's book
Eat lots of super-foods
Read a novel a day
~~No alcohol~~ ✓
~~Quit electronic smoking~~ ✓
Get on top of depilation
Swim 40 lengths a day
Have sex with Roger

Jenny was having the strangest dream. She was in a house –
a very beautiful, vaguely familiar house – sitting on a button-
backed patchwork sofa. A dog was lying on top of her and
pages of manuscript surrounded her, while she looked out at
a pool in which her younger self was swimming naked, her
dark ribbon of hair reaching almost to her small, round buttocks.

She'd had a beautiful body. Why had she never thought so
at the time? She hadn't known then the ravages that child-
birth, weight loss and middle-age gravity would bring.

The young Jenny walked out of the curved steps at the far
end of the pool, reaching for a robe that was draped over the

rails and pulling it on with a flick of her wet hair that sent out an arc of water droplets. Then she turned back towards the house to pick up the strap for the pool cover. She saw the older Jenny looking at her and smiled, lifting a hand in recognition.

In her dream, Jenny lifted her hand too.

Gunter woke with a start as he felt the movement overhead. They both heard the screeching rattle of the winding mechanism as the pool cover went on. Barking furiously, he leaped from Jenny's lap with such force that the sofa tipped back with Jenny still on it. By the time she had scrabbled up, the pool was covered and the girl had gone.

7

As Richard had predicted, the drought-parched, featureless expanses of Beacon Common were deserted at dawn and Jenny yawned her way across the sandy scrub with Gunter, admiring the sun rising over the pine woods on the horizon. To her relief, Gunter steamed in a relatively straight line, with far less force than he had on the riverbank, from the car park to the gravel pits where she could let him off the lead. It was like being swept along in a mistral's slipstream rather than caught up in a typhoon. She found it quite helpful to be towed: her legs ached from the sleepless hours she had spent standing at the ironing-board.

Last night, she had sorted, pressed and read the first five chapters of *The Storm Returns*, in which Jack and Victoria's marriage had continued to disintegrate and ultimately collapse amid a lot of highly charged sex, with one another and with their lovers – Jack with the young British teacher who was educating their children in their remote outpost of Western Australia, Victoria with her ex-fiancé, the neighbouring landowner, whose own unhappy marriage was also racketing towards a dramatic end. The book was positively heaving with erotic tension, making for addictive and unsettling reading. Just as *The Dust Storm* had made her feel gauche and naïve as a teenager, so this novel made her feel middle-aged and priggish.

She stooped to let Gunter off the lead, sending up a small prayer that she would catch him again as he bounded off along the water's edge.

Picking up speed to keep him in sight, Jenny thought about Roger and the message he'd left on her phone the previous evening. His voice had been as crisp and practical as ever, saying he quite understood about the Peaks, and that he had a lot of work on so had been thinking much the same himself, but that by coincidence he had clients in Buckinghamshire he would be seeing next Thursday and would take her out to dinner afterwards, if that was convenient. Jenny had smiled – he'd slotted it neatly into their usual date night, his routine uninterrupted, a creature of habit. Perhaps Carla was right and she really should sleep with him. A week away together would have been too much – and she doubted she would feel up to bed action after yomping in the Peaks – but perhaps a night together at the Old Rectory could take them through the bedroom door at last. She had a very sexy bedroom, after all, and she was sure Gunter would have calmed down by then.

Would it be so unprofessional to share a night with him here? The Old Rectory was a far more seductive house than her own gated museum, and Roger's neat terrace in Summertown was even less appealing, his student lodgers leaving bicycles in the hall and an all-pervading smell of Super Noodles.

How much easier to have the confidence of Geraldine's fictional characters, who leaped into bed at the suggestive lift of an eyebrow, then had the energy to do passionate slithering, bubbling, pumping things until dawn.

She was thinking about sex again – her mental MILF porn channel was flashing a disturbing image of yesterday's towel bulge on the houseboat now. Jenny decided it was time to turn for the car park.

To her surprise, Gunter came bounding back to her when she called, sitting for his lead with something close to

58

obedience and towing her along at a relatively low speed until the sight of another car arriving beside the Evoque sent him into a frenzy of pulling and barking, matched by the furious snarls of several Westies inside the new arrival. Without the remote control, she was forced to pick Gunter up and heave him bodily through the tailgate. As she closed it with relief, the driver's side window of the other car buzzed down and a voice said, 'It's okay – I always wait until Gunter's in before I let mine out. We all do.'

Back at the house, Jenny put on some toast and continued sorting the pages of *The Storm Returns,* most of which were still muddled. Despite Geraldine's eccentric numbering system, she was determined to put them all in order. Her conscience told her that she must resist the temptation to read any more, however desperately she wanted to. With luck, Geraldine would never know it had been moved. Jenny was guardian of her house and keeper of the secrets.

Taking a break to make more coffee and stem her hunger, she was confused to find the toaster empty – had she eaten it already? – but then she was distracted by Gunter barking and hurling himself at the french windows. Laughter and splashing came from the pool – the neighbours were swimming. Jenny took hold of Gunter's collar and raised a hand to give them a cheery wave, then froze. A middle-aged couple were frolicking in the shallow end. He was small, round and bald. She was very overweight with dark roots growing into her wet blonde hair. Their tiny bright triangles of swimwear, lashed together with flesh-digging straps, left nothing to the imagination.

Gunter was now body-slamming the glass with such force it seemed destined to break. Jenny dragged him away and put him into his cage with several rope toys and a dental-health chew that she'd found with the dog food, but he howled miserably.

Settling on the floor beside him, she recited Thomas Hardy's 'The Ruined Maid', which he seemed to like, slumping against the mesh wall beside her and barking between verses. Encouraged, she shared Coleridge's 'Kubla Khan' and the Prologue to Chaucer's *Canterbury Tales*.

Twenty minutes on, creeping back to the kitchen for coffee and praying they'd gone, Jenny saw that they were now riding two Lilos astride and having a play fight with two tubular foam-rubber pool noodles. The woman's blue-veined breasts rested pendulously on her belly, and her thighs were dimpled with cellulite. The man had a hairy, sunburned back and thick creases in his bald neck.

Aware that it was terribly rude and anti-social to keep ignoring them – especially now that Gunter was napping quietly in his cage after the poetry recital – Jenny summoned a bright smile and slipped outside: 'Hello there!'

As they turned to face her, a pool noodle caught a small lycra triangle and hooked it off a large brown nipple. Jenny's flustered explanation that she was the house-sitter was greeted with gales of laughter and warm introductions that she didn't take in because the woman had now pulled her bikini top off altogether.

'Bothersome thing.' She lobbed it towards the paved side and it fell short, plopping into the water and floating like dis-carded bunting. 'It's far too hot for modesty. This pool is such bliss, isn't it?'

'I've not had time to swim yet,' Jenny went into reverse. 'I must just check on the dog. Lovely to meet you both.'

Embarrassed, because she felt she was invading their private joy and ashamed because she was repelled by it, she made a cup of strong instant coffee and shut herself back in the utility room to play the latest gaming craze on her phone. She'd become secretly addicted to Cranky Bird, although she reprimanded children she caught playing it at school, and was witheringly outspoken against it in the staff room. She'd only tried playing it in an attempt to understand why teenage children were so obsessed with it, and now it was her guilty mind-dump. As it loaded, she let Gunter out of the cage and turned on the radio to soothe them both, tuning it to her favourite station and letting out a whoop as a Queen track came on. But Freddie Mercury – and her singing along – seemed to terrify Gunter: he tried to climb into her lap, whimpering loudly, hot breath on her face.

Now remembering Richard's warning about pop music – although she would have classified Queen as classic rock – Jenny tried to wrestle free, irritably recalling that Robin had behaved in much the same way whenever she'd retuned from Radio 3. But Gunter refused to budge. Her phone, trapped in her hand beneath him, let out several beeps of protest.

When she finally broke free and switched off the music, she discovered that she had accidentally 'shared' several screen shots of her pink budgie avatar's Cranky Bird progress with all her Facebook friends. Someone had already liked them.

Gunter leaned against her and panted in her ear while she deleted the posts and scrolled down her newsfeed. Jenny had never been comfortable with Facebook – she was very private, a little proud and prudish, and very pernickety about grammar – and found it hard to publicize elements of her life *en masse*, especially after her marriage had ended. She hadn't been on it for weeks, and looking now, the high volume of comedy-cat memes, home-baking shots, drunken selfies and inspirational quotes with misplaced apostrophes reminded her why.

Yet the insight into the lives and thoughts of people she knew made her feel nostalgic for life's random transient friendships and for the person she had been: Jennifer Asadi, the self-conscious, vintage-cardigan-wearing student who had shared a litre of cheap wine and a long snog on a punt with Tom Grogan (561 friends, now living in Australia with long-term boyfriend and posting a Buzzfeed link to '15 Worst Beards', no doubt to make him feel better about his own); Jen Rees, the sociable, coffee-shop-haunting young mum who had pushed a double buggy around the College Gardens talking baby poo, diets and parenting politics with Nancy from NCT classes (237 friends, posting a long rant about residents' parking permits in Summertown); Mrs Rees, the inspirational teacher, who suffered no fools but had encouraged class joker Alice Tattersall (983 friends, a blurry mobile-phone photo of her toddler on a swing – how had that happened? She'd been a child herself moments ago) to understand and love Margaret Atwood; Jenny Rees, the sociable divorcee, who despised badly written fiction and literary snobs, and had briefly belonged to a book club where she'd often got the giggles with Gupta Choudhury (179 friends, just reached Level 20 of Sweet Squash Saga). There they all were, so many familiar names with unfamiliar lives, reminders that she had once been schoolgirl, colleague, single, married, self-effacing, self-improving and a lot more likeable. On here she had just 43 friends and Cranky Bird was the most likeable thing about her. She didn't belong.

Feeling uncomfortably like a spy, she checked her children's walls, first Jake to see whether he'd posted an update (nothing since a body-surfing shot of his feet on a Bali beach in April), and then Amalie, whose profile picture was a close-up of one of Jenny's Sunday roasts. Her daughter's most recent activity dated back even further, to before she had left for the States. Both she and Jake now had other ways of connecting with friends, mysterious app worlds of instant photo shares, mood boards and trending that they encouraged Jenny to embrace but she could never hope to master before they fell out of vogue and another set of rules had to be understood. Her only consolation was that their father was even less technically adroit. With the same furtive guilt she felt playing Cranky Bird, she clicked on his name among Amalie's friends and found herself on a page as sparse in detail as their marriage had been in affection. There wasn't even a photograph of him, just a white on grey silhouette with a regulation Tintin quiff.

Robin Rees's 'About' list stated that he worked at NYU and lived in New York. He had only five Facebook friends, two of whom were his children, and another his new wife.

Jenny's cursor hovered over that young smiling face, but she couldn't go there, couldn't face the belly-flop sting it inevitably brought, the deep, jealous mourning and protective-mother urge when she saw the photographs of the baby, saw the boasts about her first tooth, first step, first birthday, the bursting happy-to-share confidence of a proud mother. That had been Jenny once, when Facebook hadn't existed. If it had, maybe she wouldn't find it such an alien world, so capable of inflicting pain.

If she found the perfect overseas house-sitting job to fill her autumn sabbatical, she would embrace it, Jenny decided, imagining posting photographs of her computer on a Tuscan balcony, wine glass refracting the sunset, or selfies of her tanned legs and brightly painted toenails stretching out on a poolside sun-lounger shaded by cypresses as she re-read every Dickens, Eliot and Henry James for fun.

She returned to the comedy cats and inspirational quotes on her timeline, 'liking' as many posts as possible because social-networking aficionado Rachel (1269 friends, added eight new photos to her album 'My Dysfunctional Kids' ten minutes ago) had hauled her up on her poor social networking effort several times, insisting that it was an important part of life's fabric that showed you cared. Jenny called friends regularly, never forgot birthdays, still sent Christmas cards with individual messages in them, threw parties and was a staunch ally, which showed a degree of loyalty that didn't require the added click of a thumbs-up under a photo of somebody's cupcakes. Rachel had told her, though, that in cyberspace small gestures sent big ripples, so she had a go now, increasingly sociable and affectionate as she liked, commented and shared, grateful for the distraction from the near-skinny dipping outside.

After another half an hour had passed, she crept out. The couple had gone, leaving the cover off and a brace of Lilos dripping on the diving board.

8

The contract cleaners arrived mid-morning in a small pink car emblazoned with *Va Va Vacuum* on one side, *Ladies Who Launder* on the other, and what looked like a chewed pipe-cleaner on the top.

'It's supposed to be a feather duster,' one of the cleaners told Jenny, as she bustled through the door in a pink tabard, carrying a Henry Hoover. 'Shelley's husband fixed it up there – he does custom cars as a hobby – but it went a bit funny in the car wash. You the house-sitter? You ready to hold the dog down? You'll need that zapper thing.'

Jenny was already hanging onto Gunter's collar as he strained to goose the new arrivals. 'Why should I do that?'

'Terrified of the vacuum-cleaner. Tries to attack it. Vernon, the usual sitter, used to kettle him.'

'We'll go out in the garden,' Jenny said, clipping a lead on Gunter and grabbing her laptop so she could work on Carla's book. She also took the manuscript of *The Storm Returns* because she didn't want the cleaning ladies report-ing back to Geraldine that they had seen it spread out on the kitchen table. She'd tuck it under the laptop while she worked.

Tied to a heavy cast-iron table leg beside the swimming-pool and far from the sound of vacuuming, Gunter settled in the shade with a resigned grunt to catch up on last night's missed sleep.

Carla's book – based largely on her own traumatic and

acrimonious marriage breakdown – was funny, irreverent, incredibly frank and politically incorrect, a disturbing cross between Germaine Greer and Nigel Farage. It was also littered with errors. Fingers tapping on the keys, she corrected two chapters before the computer battery warning heralded a coffee break.

Weighing down the pages of Geraldine's manuscript with a heavy terracotta pot containing a citronella candle, Jenny gathered up the laptop and carried it inside to connect it to the charger.

The walled-garden side of the house was less formal and imposing than the front, showing the soft, shy face of the Old Rectory. It had been artfully designed by the Chelsea-gold-winning gardener to look lost and unkempt, although Jenny felt it had been allowed to run riot – you almost needed a machete to get along the paths – but it was very romantically Frances Hodgson Burnett. Three of the six doors in the row of french windows into the kitchen were so overgrown they wouldn't open, woven tightly shut by the ropes of clematis, honeysuckle and rambling roses that tumbled, like Rapunzel's hair, in a scented mass from the balcony that Jenny assumed must lead out from the master bedroom.

On it, out of sight above her head, she could hear the cleaning ladies talking and, from the bittersweet tang, realized they had stepped outside for a cigarette. Jenny paused and drew a deep breath, her old addiction still biting although she'd quit again almost a year ago. They were talking about the Lewises.

'Definitely a make-or-break holiday,' one said.

'She'll never give up this place.'

'It's those poor kids I feel sorry for.'

Not wanting to hear more, Jenny hurried inside and

plugged in her computer before putting on the kettle. She then searched her bag for her electronic cigarette and took a few puffs. It seemed impossible that this wonderful house, filled with so much creative life and positive energy, could contain anything other than the perfect happy family.

She looked outside to check on Gunter – still flat out under the table snoring happily. A movement at the back of the garden caught her eye and she thought she saw a shadow cross behind the soft-fruit cages. She stepped closer to the window. There it was again, moving behind the potting sheds and on towards the garden cottage. Lifting his head, Gunter saw it too now, letting out a bass bark and scrabbling to his feet. A moment later, the heavy cast-iron table he was tied to lurched left and toppled towards the pool.

'Gunter, no!' As Jenny ran towards the door, she heard a loud splash, followed by panicked shrieking from the balcony.

'Help! The dog's drowning!'

The table was now upside down in the pool. Somewhere beneath the flotsam of handwritten manuscript pages floating on the surface, Gunter was tethered to the bottom of the deep end.

Jenny kicked off her shoes, ripped off her dress and dived in. Paper shadows moved overhead as she swam down towards the maelstrom of foam, bubbles, wet fur and scrabbling claws. Using the table to anchor herself, she grabbed the lead, which was still knotted tightly to its leg, and hauled Gunter towards her. In his terror and confusion, he bit her arm. Fighting the instinct to let go, she groped around the snapping alligator jaws until her fingers found the lead's clip to release it. Grabbing Gunter's collar, she hauled him up to the surface.

One of the cleaning ladies was at the side of the pool and

helped drag Gunter out. He tried to bite her too, wild-eyed and shaking. Then, realizing he was safe, sun-baked tiles beneath his paws, he let out a victorious bark, shook himself and charged off around the garden, disappearing behind the potting shed.

'You okay, love?' The cleaner, who had leaped back to avoid the drips, was standing in a flowerbed. 'Shelley's calling for help.'

'I'm fine, thanks.' Jenny removed a page of wet manuscript from her head and almost cried with relief when she saw that the ink wasn't running. Wonderful, talented Geraldine Scott wrote with a down-to-earth ballpoint.

'I hope you've got a copy of that.' The cleaning lady chuckled. 'Not like Mrs L. Supposed to keep hers locked in the safe, she is, but she's always leaving it lying round the place. I'll fetch you a towel.' She turned towards the house and shrieked as Gunter charged out of the shrubbery ahead of her and raced in through the french windows. Squawking about her freshly mopped floors, she ran after him.

Still treading water with the only copy of one of the most anticipated books of the decade floating around her, Jenny started gathering up the pages as fast as she could, separating them and lining them up on the side before they turned to pulp, praying the cleaning ladies wouldn't notice exactly what had fallen into the water with the dog and the table.

The clunk of a gate closing made her look round nervously, but there was nobody in sight. She swam to the lip of the pool and crouched there, eyes scanning the garden for the shadow that she'd seen crossing it, but apart from two fat wood pigeons perching flappily on a spruce which struggled to take their weight, it was deserted.

She collected the last few pages, clambered quickly out of the pool and wondered about the best place to dry the manuscript. Tucked away behind the shrubbery, the garden cottage's black-tiled roof and dormers were just visible, drenched in sunlight. Working as fast as she could, Jenny arranged all the wet leaves of foolscap in a long, neat rows on the cottage's little suntrap terrace. As she did so, she saw Gunter's wet paw prints leading to the front door. There was a key in the lock, a heavy bunch of others hanging from it, including the distinctive black rectangle of a car key.

Geraldine's reputation for scattiness was clearly well founded. Making sure the door was locked, she took the keys to put them back on a hook in the security cupboard in the utility room, surprised that a romantic novelist would have a key ring with a heavy leather tongue stamped *Ironman Cozumel 2009*. She liked Geraldine's quirkiness more each day, from her obvious adoration of her children and love of writing to unexpected hints at practicality and now endurance. It saddened Jenny that Geraldine's marriage was in trouble, and made her all the more determined to ensure that the Lewises would find their beautiful house picture perfect upon their return.

9

That afternoon, the Ladies who Laundered insisted that Jenny drank copious mugs of sweet tea, made on the hoof as they folded loo-roll ends into triangles, re-rolled the bathroom towels, sprayed a lot of lemon disinfectant and gossiped endlessly about their clients – never the Lewises, whose marriage they dissected in private during cigarette breaks. Shelley's husband, who had been summoned to help haul the table from the pool, arrived with a young workmate in an electrician's van that had an oversized three-pin plug fixed to its roof. Assessing the damage, the pair tutted a lot about the likelihood of the pool liner being damaged while they drank two mugs of regulation sweet tea. On close inspection it proved miraculously intact, as was Gunter.

Apparently unbothered by his near miss, he raced around the pool, barking and trying to jump on both men as they attempted to fish out the table until eventually he had to be confined, howling, in his cage.

'What are you doing?' Jenny asked, in shock, when she came back out to find Shelley's husband had stripped off to reveal a lot of faded blue tattoos and a pair of *Simpsons* underpants.

'Someone needs to get in there. Or are you offering, darling?' His eyes twinkled as they gave her the standard male three-point check – tits, crotch, legs. 'I'm happy to stand aside if you are, eh, Andy?'

Andy didn't look up from checking a message on his mobile phone. 'Whatever.'

Jenny shook her head, the thought of them seeing her in her costume too appalling to contemplate. Even on women-only evenings at her local pool, she slipped in and out of the water with self-conscious stealth, hoping nobody was looking. 'I've only just got dry – you go ahead!'

The wind had picked up, threatening to scatter *The Storm Returns* over the roof of the garden cottage and into the churchyard; Jenny gathered up the manuscript and returned to the house to lay out the few remaining damp pages to dry on the Aga in batches, handwriting side down. It was looking truly dreadful now, the paper crumpled into water-damaged ripples and even more creased and bent. Jenny's face burned with shame, and she wondered if she could make amends by spending the next ten days transposing the entire book onto her laptop, then printing it out using the laser machine in Richard's study. Knowing her reputation as a house-sitter was already in peril, she decided doing that would make her look even more interfering and unprofessional. She'd just have to go over it with the iron and hope that by some miracle she would be forgiven. It was all still perfectly readable, at least.

Gunter's training collar was drying out beside the last few pages of manuscript, looking horribly like an S & M fetish accessory. He was whimpering softly in his cage now, curled up in a tight sulk in the far corner with his toys under his chin, his whole body shaking because he knew he was in trouble.

'It was my fault for tying you up,' Jenny assured him, making a mental note to buy dog treats so that she could try bribery and positive reinforcement before she had to resort to putting the battery back in the remote control.

To her relief, Shelley's husband was fully clothed again when she brought more tea outside, the dripping table back in position. 'You're both stars. I owe you a very big thank-you.'

'Nice gaff this.' He looked around admiringly. 'Think they'd mind if we bring the kids for a dip later?'

The day was impossibly hot, and the pool beckoned, cool and inviting, the little machine trundling round its base already sucking away any signs of dog hair, rust and papier-mâché.

'We can't go to the local lido since they banned Maddison,' he went on. 'Something about health and safety, what with the broken glass and blood and everything, but he's calmed down a lot since going on the ADHD drugs, and Shel can wear a verruca sock. No need to tell the Lewises, eh?'

Still thinking about her tarnished reputation as custodian, Jenny gave him her starchy Mrs-Rees-to-year-ten look, said perhaps not, then felt mean. To make up for it, she hurried to fetch them two bottles from the kitchen wine rack as thanks, noting down the labels so that she could replace them.

She knew she would be honour-bound to tell the Lewises about the accident in the pool, but only after their return, by which time she would have minimized the damage and they would hopefully be too loved up to care. It might be best to keep quiet about the pheasant massacre too, she reflected. If the cleaning ladies were right and this was a make-or-break holiday for the couple, she wanted nothing to blight their homecoming to the Old Rectory.

As soon as the cleaning team had left, Jenny gratefully reclaimed the house. It certainly smelt clean and there were vacuum stripes on the carpets, but a quick appraisal told her that the two tabarded ladies came nowhere close to her own standards. They hadn't cleaned behind doors, de-cobwebbed the recessed lights or dusted the tops of the picture frames. The kitchen bin hadn't been wiped out after it was emptied, and all the dirty plates and mugs gathered from around the house had been dumped in the machine without rinsing. In the playroom, the mess had been stacked precariously to one side so that it resembled a mountainous toy landfill. It would never have passed muster in Jenny's house-proud heyday when the twins were toy-distributing missiles and her knees had worn constant Lego indentations from picking up and sorting. Looking at it, she was hit by another wave of home-sickness for the house to which she would never return, so strong that she had to go in search of her electronic cigarette.

To make amends for the manuscript disaster, she would not only iron it back to easily transcribed neatness, but restore order and perfection to the house. Every book or paper would be neatly stacked, every picture polished, every ring mark removed. The Old Rectory would soon be at its most beautifully welcoming.

Electronic cigarette clutched between her teeth and Gunter once more liberated from his cage to bound around supportively and wrestle with cushions, Jenny spent several hours tidying the Lewis children's toys, matching up sets, colour-co-ordinating Lego, piecing together jigsaws to make sure no bits were missing, re-dressing dolls and repatriating dice and counters with boards, breaking off only to pad back through the house and sort a few crisply dried A4 pages into order at the kitchen table. Her ironing pile was growing, with the five chapters she had read now back in chronological order and ready to re-flatten, along with another thirty pages on which she caught tantalizing glimpses of action and dialogue.

When the playroom was a haven worthy of an interior-design brochure shoot, she switched on the iron. Sorting another pile into numerical order while she waited for it to heat up, she realized that at least one page was missing. She went to search for it in Geraldine's study. A photograph on the wall caught her eye as she entered, a studio shot of Geraldine and her three doppelgänger children, sharing a hug of tremendous affection, four identical, irrepressible, white-teeth-and-pink-tongue laughs in a line. They were beautiful children and Geraldine clearly doted on them. More framed shots of them stared, smiling, from the walls around her, the three cuddled to their mother's chest as bald babies and white-blond toddlers, or with her arms around them on ski slopes and beaches, in forests and by lakes.

Studying them, Jenny felt the familiar pang for her own children at that age. She loved them now no less fiercely, but in their prolonged absence that love sometimes felt like lightning refracting around her with nothing to earth it. Their father's domineering love was Zeus's thunder, pulling the children towards him now that the storm of the marriage breakdown had passed, the count between one's strike and another's boom five hours' time difference apart. At first they had been reluctant to go to him, but that had changed, and she could see why. Life with Robin offered the constant roar of the City That Never Sleeps; their mother slept alone amid the dreaming spires, the family photographs neatly lined up on the shelves and sills in her museum of married life.

Like the photographs in Geraldine's study in which Richard rarely featured, so Jenny was absent from most of hers. She'd never minded that because she'd been the one clicking the shutter, and so self-consciously overweight – especially when her comfort eating and drinking were at their peak – that she'd found pictures of herself depressing. She still hated being photographed, even though the weight had dropped off between decrees Nisi and Absolute and stayed off, her appetite now held in check by her rechargeable electronic cigarette.

She puffed furtively on it now as she resumed her search for the missing manuscript pages. Using it inside the house was another blot in her copybook. At home, she took it into the garden, still guiltily replicating her behaviour when she'd smoked real tobacco. But here at the Old Rectory, holiday rules applied. It was a big house and there was nobody to tell her off, as her children once had, not even her own conscience. The fumes were odourless and invisible, she reassured herself. If only she could make the water damage to almost a ream of crumpled, chlorine-scented, handwritten manuscript similarly undetectable

She spotted one of the lost pages poking out from beneath a big oil canvas that was turned towards the wall – Geraldine had a work of art in her room after all. Unable to resist, Jenny tipped it back. Several pairs of amused yellow eyes peered at her.

It was the same family portrait that was hanging in the snug. She turned it around and studied it, wondering why they had two identical paintings. Perhaps it was a gift for grandparents, or another family member. The artist had captured them perfectly, their characters alive on the canvas. She recognized the sideways lamp signature alongside this year's date.

Not entirely trusting her eyes, she carried it carefully through to the snug to check that the Va Va Vacuum Ladies hadn't moved the painting from there without her knowing, but the duplicate was still on the wall: Geraldine's yellow eyes were clever and teasing, Richard's big brown ones full of wisdom and compassion, the children ravishingly mischievous and animated, Gunter sprawled on the floor, savaging one of his toys just as he was doing now in the kitchen. Jenny stared at them both. There had to be a difference.

Deciding to compare the two side by side, she reached up to hook it off the wall. The canvas caught on something behind it with an ominous rip.

Jenny gripped the frame, trying not to panic. Slowly inching the picture from the wall, she saw what she had just done. Behind the portrait was a large safe from which protruded a dial that had just sliced through Geraldine Lewis's smiling face.

'Hell, hell, buggery hell.' She looked at it helplessly.

Carefully, she set the picture down and propped it beside its duplicate.

'Keep calm,' she told herself, her heart racing.

Thinking fast, she picked up the second painting and hung it in front of the safe. She'd leave it there for now and take the ripped one to be repaired first thing. All would be fine.

In the hallway, Gunter was body-slamming the door, breathing deeply through the letterbox, eager for his evening walk. Yet again she was reminded of Robin, desperate to get away from being trapped in domestic confinement with her and the twins.

'We both need fresh air,' she agreed.

She took him for a sunset walk along the riverbank in the opposite direction from the houseboats, and was dragged at speed through reed tuffets, nettle beds and hedges for an hour, leaving them both coated with burrs. Back at the Old Rectory, Jenny picked them off and doused her nettle rash in TCP before setting up the ironing-board to perfect her manuscript-flattening technique and keep Gunter company until he settled. She was keen to avoid another late-night howling session. Armed with a damp tea towel, greaseproof paper and the heaviest recipe book she could find, she discovered a way to smooth the pages to the point at which the damage was barely noticeable, but it was dull and time-consuming – it took her almost two hours to reach the point at which she had stopped reading it the previous day. After that, her eyes kept disobeying her, taking in sentences, then whole paragraphs, greedy to know when Victoria and Jake would get back together and spark that extraordinary chemistry once more. But it wasn't going where she wanted it to go: the lovers were now arch rivals, passion replaced by bitter enmity. Forcing herself to stop looking, she switched on the radio and listened to a debate about Middle Eastern politics.

At this, Gunter headed inside his cage of his own volition, flopping down with a deep sigh and starting to snore. Closing his door as quietly as she could, Jenny stole upstairs to bed to dream that she was ironing the ripped painting, the Lewises' smiling faces melting as she did so, screaming at her to stop.

With the dawn chorus edging into her consciousness, she dreamed she was watching herself swimming naked again. This time she was looking out of the bedroom window, seeing her body sliding effortlessly through the water, a smooth ivory dolphin. Her eighteen-year-old self swam twenty lengths then got out. She stepped into her clogs and flipped her hair in a tiara of raindrops before lifting it to pull on her robe. She had a tattoo of a butterfly on the back of her neck. This time she didn't pull the cover back across the pool, wandering instead through the long shadows of the shrubbery and disappearing through the gate to the church track.

I never had a tattoo, Jenny thought, shaking her head hard to wake herself up and finding she was standing by the window with the curtains closed. She must have been sleep-walking, she decided, and went back to bed.

III

Saturday

10

TO DO LIST

~~Read and proof Carla's book~~ ✓
Eat lots of super-foods
Read a novel a day
~~No alcohol~~ ✓
Quit electronic smoking
Get on top of depilation
Swim 40 lengths a day
Have sex with Roger

Returning from her early-morning walk with Gunter on Beacon Common, Jenny heard splashing and laughter. The neighbours were using the pool again. As the dog raced through the house to launch his customary snarling frenzy at the french windows, she edged across the kitchen to extract him, head averted as though approaching Medusa. Inadvertently catching sight of a drooping pierced nipple and a lot of untamed pubic hair, half shielded by inadequate bikini bottoms, Jenny retreated to the other side of the house with her computer and Gunter, shutting herself and the dog in the library to sit at the antique desk and Google picture restorers.

The closest she could find was in High Wycombe. She checked out the customer reviews on two sites, researched the going rate for repairs on several others, plotted the route via online maps, dropped down to Street View to check out the parking, then called to book an appointment later that day.

Sitting back with a creak of Victorian desk chair, she sighed with satisfaction, convinced order would soon be restored and her role as Old Rectory custodian justified so that she could enjoy her stay and briefly fantasize that the house was hers. This was the room she coveted most, her admiration for Richard Lewis and his oasis of calm growing whenever she spent time in it. The sight and smell of so many books, so beautifully ordered, filled her with an over-whelming sense of happiness and belonging. Even Gunter, sitting heavily on her feet beneath the desk, his chin on the rim of a wicker wastepaper basket, seemed at his most relaxed.

Jenny returned to her computer, opened *Tour Divorce* and devoted the next hour to tightening and neatening Carla's assertive prose in the chapter titled 'Men Might Have XY Chromosomes but We're the Exes Who Need to Know the "Why"'.

Reading it, she winced at Carla's bitterness against her ex, poured out in the guise of self-help, but too close to the surface to hide. Her heart stung for her friend, with whom she'd sat up through many late-night calls as her hopes were smashed on the rocks of his hidden debts and drunken denials. Soon the shipwreck of her marriage was spread across the shores of her Facebook, Twitter and blog pages for all to see. Jenny's own sense of betrayal was deeply buried. Her reaction had been more controlled and private. Robin had been a flagrant adulterer, his years of infidelity building thick ice walls behind which she still existed, the smoke and mirrors of everyday happiness never generating enough heat to melt them. Carla's prose burned with anger, and Jenny envied her that heat as she remained beneath her glacier, correcting errors and adding a bubble comment beside the chapter heading: 'Is this book intended just for women? Suggest men may benefit too.'

Contemplating the state of the Lewises' marriage, she looked around the library again, each book spine like a military stripe in a long battle of the sexes. Without warning, her allegiance changed. I like Richard, she thought resolutely. He loves difficult women and dogs, collects joyful art, and has an alphabetically indexed library of classics. He wouldn't turn lovers into rivals for profit: he has too much integrity.

Richard's notes had repeated that Gunter was fine to be left in his cage for up to two hours as long as he had fresh drinking water and the radio on. It didn't specify which station, but having established his fear of nineties indie pop and classic rock, and his disinterest in late-night debates, Jenny thought he looked like a Radio 4 Extra kind of a dog, so left him with a vintage episode of *Round the Horne*. He looked distraught at the prospect of abandonment.

'I won't be long,' she promised, as she set the burglar alarm. 'And I'll buy you treats.'

Navigating her way back through the narrow lanes two hours later, Jenny drove into Hadden End with a heavy heart and a lighter purse. It had been an expensive morning. The picture restorer wanted to charge double for turning the job around in ten days; the wine from the Lewises' rack that she had given Shelley's husband and his workmate turned out to cost twenty-five pounds a bottle and was only available by the case.

Feeling stressed, she'd brazenly bought a packet of cigarettes at Tesco Express only to throw them away in a car-park litter bin minutes later to stop herself giving in to temptation.

At the till of the pet shop in the next town she discovered that she'd also accidentally thrown away her debit card and eighty pounds cash-back with the fags. When Jenny had driven back, they'd all gone from the bin. She now desperately wished the opportunist thief had at least been a non-smoker because she hadn't felt like sparking up so much in months, and the battery in her electronic cigarette was flat. The dog treats, at least, had been on a two-for-one offer, which she had paid for by scrabbling around for parking change in the glove box.

As she turned into the Old Rectory's drive, the house alarm was shrieking.

Visions of armed raiders sprang to mind, and she imagined them already sprinting off across the walled garden with the Lewises' valuables while Gunter crashed his cage onto its side in fury.

'Please, no!' Jenny raced along the drive and parked in a *Sweeney* flurry of gravel, dropping her keys twice in her hurry to get inside, then doubling back to check the date above the door before running through the house and jabbing the numbers into the touchpad.

Ears still ringing, she turned to the dog cage. It was empty.

Trying not to panic, she examined the door, still bolted but now gaping open, its hinges forced by persistent claws and teeth. The surrounding mesh was twisted and ragged. There was, at least, no sign of blood. The cushion inside the cage was still warm. Her first thought was that Gunter must have been terrified by the alarm going off. Then her heartbeat revved: had he broken out to attack an intruder?

'Of course not,' she told herself. The alarm in the Oxford

84

house had gone off every time a petal dropped from one of the flower arrangements or a spider trotted over the sensor; old buildings had too much life for modern technology. The reinforced Alcatraz dog cage must have taken Gunter the best part of two hours' hard work to break out from, and as soon as he'd achieved freedom, he'd tripped the security system.

'Gunter!' She hurried around the house, the tinnitus ring of the sirens still in her ears despite the silence. There were no windows or doors open to the outside. He had to be in there somewhere. She pulled her T-shirt out of her waistband and raked her hair off her sweaty forehead. It was stiflingly hot.

The house phone rang. It would be the police – Richard's notes had explained that the alarm was programmed to notify them when it went off. Jenny grabbed the nearest handset as she checked through the dining room then went on to the snug, relieved to see that the safe seemed untouched, the duplicate portrait hanging exactly as she'd left it.

'Mrs Lewis?' a flat voice demanded in her ear.

'No, I'm Jenny Rees, the house-sitter.'

It was then that she finally realised what the difference was between the two portraits. She'd stared closely at the beautiful face with the rip in it for a long time this morning as the picture restorer had talked about resins and varnishes, too relieved at his assurance that it would look exactly as it had before the damage – and that only another trained expert would ever spot the repair – to notice that it wasn't at all identical to its twin now hanging in front of the safe. 'It will be like the portrait of Dorian Gray,' he'd boasted. 'The lady will age, but this picture never will.'

Irritated by his flagrant abuse of literature, Jenny had

pedantically pointed out that the portrait aged while the subject did not.

Now she looked at the picture on the wall and saw the distinction. Geraldine's face was not the same as it was in the one she had taken to be repaired. This face was older and more expressive, its cheeks wider, chin softer and eyelids lower. It was no less beautiful, but it was entirely different. It had aged. And, despite the familiar smile, it also looked incredibly sad.

'Are you all right, Ms Rees? . . . Is there an intruder in the house? . . . Ms Rees, are you still there?' The police receptionist was clearly hopeful that an armed burglary might be in progress to brighten up a dull day at the station.

'I'm fine! It was just a false alarm, I think. The dog probably set it off. I'm checking round now, but there's no sign of forced entry.'

'Before we go any further, could you confirm the security password, Ms Rees?'

'The what? Oh, yes. Hang on.'

She ran back to find Richard's notes in the kitchen and read it out with a sardonic laugh. 'Gunter. The password is Gunter.'

On cue there was a bark from upstairs.

11

Gunter had made his way into the master bedroom first – there was evidence of much bed-bouncing and pillow-chewing – and somehow, from there, he'd got locked into an en-suite. He was now trying to break out, using much the same technique he had successfully employed on the cage.

'No, Gunter!' Jenny entreated, rattling the door handle in vain. He must have turned the lock while scrabbling to get out. He was howling and body-slamming the door now, reminding her of when Robin had accidentally locked himself into the spidery cellar during a power cut.

Making soothing noises, she went in search of a screwdriver and tripe sticks then set about dismantling the handle, feeding treats through the gap beneath the door to keep him quiet. The handle was fashioned to look like old black ironwork, and took a long time to prise apart. She was soon running short on patience and tripe sticks, wondering whether locksmiths accepted PayPal or internet banking transfers, given she had no cash or debit card.

There was always Henry at the house-sitting agency, who loved to boast, 'I'm here in an emergency, night or day', but that hardly looked good for Jenny's professional reputation, and Henry could be embarrassingly flirtatious. The one previous time she'd called in his help – when a client's very valuable pedigree cat had vanished for three days – he'd arrived with a bottle of wine and a Nicole Kidman DVD and offered to wait with her until it came back. She would deal with this alone: she was good in a crisis.

Sitting back on her heels to regroup, she looked around for inspiration. There had to be a Kirby-grip somewhere. Detectives were always cracking locks with hairpins, and Geraldine had acres of hair to control. A quick scout round the surfaces yielded no more than a few *raku* sculptures and a hand-thrown bowl full of foreign coins.

You could tell a lot about a marriage from the master bedroom, Jenny always found. Her own, in later years, had been a beautiful no man's land that gave away its secrets if you looked closely enough: the six-foot mattress with parallel ruts two feet apart, like two shallow graves; the his and hers antique wardrobes, beautifully restored chests of drawers and Heal's laundry baskets entirely separated to stop her clothes picking up the stale smell she associated with his skin and their marriage; the clock radios set to different wake-up times and stations; the bedside reading piled high on her side because she went to bed early and devoured escapism, one slim volume on his table that stayed there for months on end because he came to bed after she'd gone to sleep and snapped the light straight off.

At first glance, the Lewises' bedroom was nothing like her dormant, loveless, Arts-and-Crafts battlefield. It was clad in the high-grade, coffee-coloured froth of interior design. The bed was a huge antique *lit bateau* large enough for a frolicking foursome; chaises-longues lay beneath the windows inviting sideways seduction with a view; the deep golden rugs were thick as barley fields and made for finger-raking, toe-ploughing fun. The art on the walls was a clever mix of sepia-toned erotic sketches and sleepy line drawings. The bedding, dishevelled from Gunter's gambolling, was the coolest, crispest, thickest Egyptian cotton beneath a buttermilk counterpane, all of which she carefully remade now. It was all tastefully, lusciously, full-fat creamy. But that was the point. It was all so beige. It was like stripping off a sequined, feather-plumed stage costume from a burlesque dancer and finding flesh-tint undies beneath. These colourful long-married peacocks, whose vibrant house spoke of laughter and fights, creativity and chaos, had a bedroom that looked like a *Dangerous Liaisons*-themed suite in a boutique hotel, where couples who no longer had anything to say to one another came for vanilla sex once a year.

Hearing an ominous shredding sound from beyond the en-suite door, Jenny resumed her screwdriver assault on the lock, levering and hooking blindly into its depths. On the point of giving up, she felt the mechanism loosen and spring. The door swung open and an ecstatic, tripe-smelling ball of panting relief burst through it to flatten her, then bounded onto the big sleigh bed to ruck up the Egyptian cotton again, then onto each chaise-longue in turn, jettisoning cream cushions, rolling noisily on the rug and returning to slap her face with a grateful tongue.

Laughing and pushing him off, Jenny hurried through the door to assess the damage. The room was much bigger than she'd anticipated, a wide dressing area leading through to an en-suite with the biggest claw-footed bath she'd ever seen. This was clearly Richard's personal space, the dressing room recesses shelved up to the rafters with cubist boxes of neatly folded striped shirts. In contrast to its creamily neutral bedroom neighbour, all the walls were painted in deepest claret and predictably crammed with art. It was neat, ordered and smelt of expensive aftershave and hand-made suits. There wasn't a dropped towel or a pile of loose change in sight. Except now the wall around the door was covered with scrapes, the lining paper hanging off.

Running her hand over the clawed plaster, certain it was beyond her Polyfilla skills, Jenny wondered if any local painters and decorators accepted PayPal.

As she contemplated the best solution, her eyes were drawn to the paintings around her, neat rows of ornate frames hung well away from the threat of bath steam. This collection bore all the marks of Richard's distinctive, colourful, comic taste in original art. Here, the essential difference was that the paintings were naughty or saucy. There were lots of frolicking plus-size ladies, adorable semi-dressed older couples canoodling on picnic blankets and enough fat-bottomed girls on bicycles to inspire Betjeman and Queen for a lifetime. Others were more traditional nudes, but with no less appealing good humour. She stood up and examined the familiar sideways-lamp signature on one. It was incredibly sensual, almost overtly erotic, the model reclining on a bed with a come-hither wantonness that left no doubt as to what the artist had wanted to do with her and wanted all those who saw it to share. She looked young – no older than eighteen or nineteen, Amalie's age, a hand resting idly between her open thighs like a beckoning invitation.

For a moment, puritanical scorn rose in Jenny, defensive and righteous, despising such a carnal cliché. Yet the cat's cradle of her own desire drew tight without warning before she turned away from its colourful sensuality, a pleasure pain that reminded her she had been that girl once, uninhibited and unquestioning, her body something she'd explored as a new-found land.

She turned to study the damage by the door, thinking hard about sandpaper and paint. She could hear Gunter bounding around in a room to her right. Realizing he might lock himself in there too, she dashed back out into the bedroom and swung a U-turn through the door immediately to the left of the damaged one, where she found him rolling joyfully on a sheepskin rug, smile upside-down and paws in the air.

Geraldine's dressing room and en-suite were laid out in a mirror image of her husband's, but that was where the resemblance stopped. Like the couple's studies, their private sanctums were like two contrasting continents leading off the neutral territory of their shared bedroom.

Her rooms surprised Jenny: the colours were all earth – terracotta, ochre, peat and bleached-bone white. Unlike the rest of the house, the furniture was ethnic, artisan and humble. There were more photographs of her children everywhere, and no mirrors in the dressing area, apart from a speckled hand-held one buried among the familiar clutter of paper and pens on the dressing table. The chaos was predictable and high-grade, from the pages of notes in the all-too-familiar handwriting to the splashes of colour provided by swimsuits and knickers, hats and flip-flops pulled from the wall of dark-wood wardrobes raided on departure day, rejected holiday packing that the Ladies Who Launder had whisked off the floor and arranged in a high tide along a deep window-seat.

The bathroom had big marble tiles that were Bondi golden, a suite white as surf and walls blue as the sky. Yet it was also a scuffed, messy haven that spoke of long baths, rampaging children and a love of indulgent toiletries, of overflowing scented bubbles and hours of pampering.

This is where she escapes, Jenny registered, remembering her own marathon baths, the radio and a book for company, the tears and the steam indistinguishable sometimes, the fantasy of escape only permissible when one slid totally under water and submerged active thought.

'The cleaners missed that.' She tutted, noticing the smears

on the driftwood-rimmed mirror set in a vaulted recess above the walk-in shower.

Then she saw it was a message, written with a finger when it had been steamed up.

RUN AWAY WITH ME.

Please let this be a pre-hols husband-and-wife flirtation, she willed, trying very hard to visualize dapper little Richard Lewis scaling a stepladder and breathing hard on the glass before issuing the challenge. She could still remember the cold, clammy terror with which she had read the text message on Robin's phone, in which he had arranged a night away with the woman who had gone on to become her replacement. She'd sensed even then that this one was different. His midlife crisis had mutated, the hair and beard trimmed from misunderstood academic to slick silver fox, the motorbike leathers replacing ageing denim and velvet jackets, creaking in and out of the house at odd hours, the roar of the Japanese engine sounding a death knell to family life.

Jenny jumped as Gunter started drinking noisily out of the loo beside her.

'In fairness to Robin, he never did that.' She sighed, deciding she needed a large glass of wine. Hadn't she just bought a case of very expensive Burgundy? It was the weekend, after all.

Halfway down one of her bottles of Montrachet – which was indeed delicious – Jenny started to see the funny side of her disastrous start at the Old Rectory. Sitting at the kitchen table, the bulk of *The Storm Returns* still spread out in front of her in piles for each hundred-page group, plus side piles for unexplained asterisk numbering and ambiguous nines, sixes and zeros, she tipped back in her chair, a small chuckle escaping. Maybe this job played to her strengths, after all – a love of animals, beautiful homes and order.

Sprawled on her feet, exhausted after hours of battling solitary confinement, both prescribed and accidental, Gunter's speckled dew flaps billowed between dreams and snores. When the house phone rang, those cheeks sucked in temporarily and one conker eye opened, but he didn't raise his head. As Jenny's warmest tones reassured the caller that all was well, he closed his eyes and resumed snoring.

'*Nothing* to worry about here,' Jenny told Richard Lewis in Mauritius on a breaking-up line.

'Gunter behaving himself? Not been chasing Myrtle's cat?'

Had she not been slightly tight, Jenny would have been inclined to admit more of the truth about his dog's misdemeanours and her manuscript-soaking mishaps, but his voice was so kind, clever and amusing, and she so desperately wanted his marriage to work again, that she adopted the same reassuring tone she did with parents whose evil-genius children were a nightmare in class but very likely to ace English A level.

'No cats have been chased, I'm happy to report.' She tried to remember exactly who Myrtle was, vaguely recalling a note about a neighbour with a grudge against Gunter. In fact, it was more of a *fatwa* now she thought about it.

'Marvellous!' Richard seemed delighted. 'I know Geraldine was worried that you might not be strong enough to hold him, but you obviously know your gundogs.'

At her feet, Gunter let out a long tripe-smelling burp. He still had dark red paint in his claws, she noticed.

'Has the rude gardener been yet?' Richard was saying. 'He can be a bit of an oddball, but I don't want to lose him. Expert plantsman.'

'Not yet, but you said about bribing him with tea. It's all in hand.'

'You're magnificent, Mrs Rees.'

'Please call me Jenny.'

'I hope you're helping yourself to food and drink, Jenny. There's a Montrachet in the rack I'd recommend. Do try that. We've cases more of it in the cellar – drink it like water. *Ipso facto* dipso fattos.' He laughed uproariously – he sounded really rather drunk too.

She looked at the label on the wine she was drinking, registering that the cases in the cellar now had a plus one.

'Treat the place as your own,' Richard went on, as Jenny pictured him swinging in a double hammock with Geraldine, sharing Coco Locos on a sun-drenched balcony with the Indian Ocean stretched out before them. 'If you want to have a friend or two around for supper, that's not a problem. Invite the neighbours if you're lonely. Great chums of ours – have you met them? Terrific free spirits.'

'Only briefly,' she said, trying not to think about the pierced nipples and stray pubes she'd witnessed in the pool.

'Daughter's as bright as a button – babysits for us and idolizes Geraldine. Reading English at Somerville next year. Wants to be the next Dorothy L Sayers.'

Jenny winced, remembering her own identical boast when she'd started at Oxford, her ambitions a seemingly boundless panorama ahead of her, until the day she'd sat down opposite an American PhD student in the Bodleian and developed an instant, fierce crush that had narrowed her focus to just one point on the horizon, never imagining that the journey would end in the divorce courts more than twenty years later, her ongoing passage transferred to the superhighway of virtual matchmaking.

'I do have somebody I might invite, actually,' she told Richard, feeling a wine-fuelled rush of affection towards Roger, his reliability and old-fashioned courtesy. She imagined Richard Lewis to be much the same. And she hadn't given up hope that Roger had a wild, sensual side, just as Richard's private art collection had revealed the scholarly biographer's vibrant inner world. He was probably deliciously imaginative in bed, she reflected dreamily.

'By all means!' His jollity snapped her out of her MILF-channel moment. 'Just watch out for Gunter. He can be a bit overbearing with strangers. Neurotic canine.'

After the call ended, Jenny rolled Richard's summaries around her head: *expert plantsman, terrific free spirits, dipso fattos, neurotic canine.*

'Academics love labels,' she told Gunter, thinking about Robin and frowning. 'It's a limit they impose because they're frightened of what lies beyond.' She reached for the wine bottle. 'Speaking as a plain old teacher, my furry friend, I'm more concerned with the three Rs – Roger, Robin and Richard.' She snorted with amusement, then stopped herself, hoping she hadn't just flirted on the phone. That would be beyond reproach: the man was on a romantic holiday with his wife. Just because Jenny coveted his house, loved his library and found his saucy dressing-room pictures sexy, it didn't give her the right to harbour even the tiniest crush. He was married to the woman who had first caught Jenny's romantic imagination and spun a story of such intense love that it remained the pinnacle to which she aspired. Roger's wild sensual side had a lot to live up to.

Looking at the piles of *The Storm Returns* criss-crossed in front of her, she set down the bottle carefully. 'Gunter, I apologize. I might be a bit squiffy. Let's walk this off.'

Too tight to drive, she decided to ignore Richard's warning and risk Gunter on a local leg stretch. The dog deserved a chance, she reasoned. He'd been unfairly tarnished. They were starting to understand one another, and he'd been very well behaved on the morning run. As long as she avoided the village centre, she was certain she could control him, although she'd put the training collar back on as a precaution.

But when she tracked it down to the back of the Aga where she'd left it drying yesterday, she found it had melted against the rim of the hotplate lid, the plastic strap reduced to a gluey black tar.

12

Having studied the Ordnance Survey map and identified a path that led through the churchyard, then out into the woods and the farmland beyond, Jenny worked out that she and Gunter could walk for an hour or more without needing to cross a road. She'd have to keep him on the lead and a close eye out for other dog-walkers, but she was sure she could manage, even without the training collar.

As soon as they were through into the churchyard, Gunter did his out-of-control speedboat impersonation, throttle on max, as Jenny water-skied behind.

The heat-wave was now in its second week, the grass yellowing above scorched, cracked earth. Jenny held on tight and slalomed through the headstones, towed by the jet-powered gundog, overshooting her turns each time he slammed on the brakes to cock his leg on a grave.

On the outskirts of the woods, they met a man with a bull mastiff. Jenny only managed to stop the overexcited Gunter launching at it by wrapping his lead around a nearby tree-trunk and hanging on tight until her fellow walker had passed, casting her a wary look over his shoulder.

'Lovely day!' she said, before seeing he was wearing earpieces. At least that meant he didn't hear her swearing a moment later when Gunter towed her into a bramble-choked ditch in pursuit of a bumble bee, then threw himself down and rolled indulgently in fox poo. When he stood up, he lifted his head and drew in a deep sniff that reminded

Jenny alarmingly of Hannibal Lecter. Slowly, he turned to look back towards the churchyard.

Before Jenny had time to adjust her grip, he was charging back in the direction they'd just come. Ligaments straining, she clung to the lead loop as he pulled her with him, dragging her through a clump of stinging nettles before tearing straight across a kerbstone plinth, scattering green grave chippings.

The Old Rectory's chimneys poked over the yews alongside them once more as he raced back through the churchyard. Then, just as suddenly, he cut the engine and stood stock still, leaving Jenny cannoning into a shiny granite headstone commemorating Reg Sparrow, 1926–2001.

Gunter was frozen in animation, head cocked.

A few feet ahead, a curled ginger tail twitched behind a stone urn filled with dead chrysanthemums.

Before she knew what was happening, Jenny found herself hanging on to the headstone for dear life, silently apologizing to Reg. She battled valiantly to hang on, but Gunter seemed to have turned into Cerberus with three heads all wrestling and straining at the leash, and it was a losing battle as, inch by friction-burning inch, the lead was dragged from her hands. In a streak of hissing ginger tom and another of barking bristly grey dog, the cat and Gunter were over the churchyard wall, through a laurel hedge and gone.

The scream that went up behind the laurel hedge chilled Jenny's blood. She hurried to the wall, but there was no way of following the animals through the dense laurel so she was forced to run out into the lane and around to the row of quaint thatched cottages whose gardens backed onto the churchyard. There she saw a familiar-looking old lady along the side return of the first cottage threatening Gunter with a grass rake, a fat Cairn terrier growling furiously alongside her.

'This time, you are going to the RSPCA, you mark my words!' she shouted.

Cornered by the compost heap, Gunter cowered in terror. The ginger cat, now sitting on top of the garden shed, licked its paws and stared at him disdainfully.

Jenny hurried up the narrow drive to reclaim him. 'I am so, so sorry!'

'I told Dicky I'd report the dog if I caught him again. He's already on a parish-council warning after he tried to eat Mrs Green's little girl's guinea pig – it keeled over with a heart attack that very night. He'll be given a rehoming order this time. I've threatened him with the Dangerous Dogs Act and an Antisocial Behaviour Order.'

'I'm truly so sorry,' Jenny repeated, as she hurried to extract Gunter. 'This is entirely my fault, not Mr Lewis's. I'm Jenny Rees. I'm looking after the house while they're away. He told me to use the control collar at all times, but I didn't put it on, *and* he told me not to walk the dog locally. I must take full responsibility, Mrs—?'

'Call me Myrtle.' The old woman eyed her suspiciously. 'So you're the teacher from Oxford who threw the table in the swimming-pool?'

'That's right.' Jenny knew she shouldn't be surprised that details of her identity were in circulation: she'd grown up in a village. The Ladies Who Launder had clearly spread the news. She hauled Gunter out of the compost heap, letting out an exasperated cry when he launched into another show of bravado at Myrtle, the Cairn and the cat. 'Sorry!'

Myrtle shook her head and tutted. 'I've told Dicky to send him away to be trained, but he won't listen. I'm glad you took off the collar. Horrible thing.' She turned her beady gaze to Jenny. Barely five feet tall with her hair in a neat white cloche, pink-rimmed glasses and a bosom like a life-saving ring tightly buttoned beneath a floral shirt-waister, she looked like a ready-made ACME granny. 'I shall have to report this attack to the council, nevertheless, and to the churchwardens. That dog has been banned from the St Peter's graveyard since the digging incidents. Dicky has to understand the seriousness of this. The brute shouldn't be left in the hands of a little slip like you.'

'If there's anything I can do by way of apology, please just say,' Jenny entreated, clutching Gunter's collar more tightly as the Cairn came out from behind Myrtle's thick, mottled ankles and growled its way closer. 'Perhaps you'd accept a bottle of wine as a small gesture.'

'I don't care for wine.' She gave Jenny a penetrating stare. 'But I can tell you do.'

Jenny was appalled. She knew she could hardly deny it today, but the accusation made her feel as though she had a red drinker's nose, gout and a cirrhotic liver.

'I can smell it,' Myrtle explained, which didn't make Jenny feel any better, convinced now that she reeked like a pub, and amazed that Myrtle could smell anything above the pong of fox poo coming from Gunter's coat. Her house-sitting reputation would truly be in splinters now. 'It's impossible to spend more than an hour in the Old Rectory and not come out plastered,' Myrtle went on, loosening up with a despairing chuckle. 'My friend Joan used to be con-vinced that one of those flashy taps they installed in the kitchen dispensed claret and another Chardonnay. Lovely woman, Joan. She lived in the garden cottage there when she kept house for Dicky and Geraldine.' She said the latter's name with a disapproving sniff. 'When Joan and Norman retired, the family got in two women with a pink loo brush on their car, and a very rude gardener who has the mulching machine going at all hours. Place has gone to pot if you ask me.'

Jenny silently concurred that the Va Va Vacuum team were distinctly average, and she certainly wasn't looking forward to meeting the gardener.

Myrtle was peering at her intently over her pink spectacle rims. 'Actually, there is something you could do by way of reparation.' She glanced darkly at Gunter.

'Just name it,' Jenny was being dragged backwards towards the gate now.

Myrtle and her Cairn marked her, both growling ominously. 'Could you lend me the garden cottage keys?'

'Whatever for?' Jenny stopped, backed up against the side gate, harbouring sudden images of nefarious, clandestine over-sixties gatherings in the little cottage at the end of the Lewises' garden.

Myrtle mustered a benign pensioner smile. 'Joan and her husband Norman live in a retirement flat in Aylesbury now. It's her birthday coming up and I want to do something special. There's a hand-painted tile surround in the garden cottage at the Old Rectory that she was always terribly fond of. I'd like to photograph it so I can get the tiles copied. I can be in and out without you knowing. I'd ask Geraldine, but you know what she's like – so ditzy, working in there all hours of the night and day, lost in her world.'

Having pulled Geraldine's keys from the door of the cottage the day before, Jenny suspected she was far from strict on security, but she didn't feel it was her place to let in neighbours, however well-meaning. 'Perhaps I could take the photograph for you.'

Myrtle crossed her arms in front of her, clearly irritated again. 'I'm sure Geraldine won't mind me popping in there –

we're good chums. Have you read her books? I've enjoyed them, especially that one about the young couple, although I'm more of a true-crime fan. Did you know she's been busy writing another one about them?'

'*The Storm Returns*, yes.' She could feel her cheeks redden, her own crime uncomfortably close to hand, the piles of crumpled manuscript waiting for her. If Myrtle knew about the garden table going into the pool, did she also know that the document sitting on it had been that long-awaited sequel?

But she was looking surprised. 'Is that the title? *The* Storm *Returns*?' she repeated, grey eyebrows lifting above the pink specs.

Jenny nodded. She'd checked online where it was listed as coming out the following March, so it was no betrayal of trust to say so. 'It's being published next year.'

'No wonder she's been working in that cottage round the clock these past few weeks.' Myrtle sighed. 'I haven't liked to ask her about the tiles. Shall I come round in the morning, after church?'

Something about her fixed smile made Jenny hesitate. She gathered what were left of her house-sitting wiles. She had the distinct sense that she was being led up the garden path, and that possessing the keys to the cottage door at the end of it was an advantage she should keep hold of.

'I really can't let anyone in there without notifying the Lewises first,' she said firmly. 'Perhaps it would be better to wait until after they're back from holiday.'

Myrtle dropped the smile, very put out. 'In that case, I'll take the bottle of wine you offered by way of apology. I have a friend who drinks the stuff visiting this evening.' She looked at the narrow gold watch on her wrist. 'You can put it in the milk-bottle holder on the doorstep. And if I catch that grey brute chasing my cat again, Dicky will be coming home to find his pointer under close arrest in my coal cellar.'

Hiding behind Jenny's legs now, Gunter let out a low whine.

13

Historically, Jenny had often struck upon what seemed like a simple and brilliant idea after a few glasses of wine, which had turned out to be a very bad idea indeed. Investigating the little cottage that stood at the end of the garden at the Old Rectory was one such mistake.

She'd worked out that she could take a picture of the fireplace tiles on her phone, then print it on the snazzy Wi-Fi photo printer in the main house. That way, when she took the bottle of wine to Myrtle, she would be able to add a handwritten apology on the back of the photograph. It was exactly the sort of gesture she loved making, and made her feel less of a battleaxe for refusing the old dear's request.

But when she let herself into the cottage, the scene of chaos that greeted her made her step back outside, cannoning into Gunter. It had been ransacked, resembling scenes in spy movies when hotel rooms are turned inside out in search of missile-launching microchips or phials of continent-destroying poison. It must have been burgled.

She pulled her phone out of her pocket to call the police, then hesitated as it dawned on her that this might just be Geraldine's mess after all. With a deep breath of trepidation, she edged inside again.

The Ladies Who Launder clearly didn't Va Va Vacuum in here. There was dust and detritus everywhere, the windows silted with dirt. Several reams of scribbled A4 leaves and crumpled paper balls littered the floor, along with abandoned clothes and shoes, mugs, glasses, ashtrays, CDs, a scree of pen lids and ballpoints, like twigs after a storm. It smelt of stale cigarettes, spilled wine and late nights. The mirror above the fireplace was cracked, as though something very heavy had been hurled at it.

While Gunter charged around rearranging the debris with bounds and body rolls, Jenny picked her way hurriedly across the mess to take a photograph of the tiles surrounding the little cast-iron hearth, trying to frame the shot tightly to miss out anything that would offend Myrtle. Then she lowered the phone from her face as something caught her eye. On the dusty, cracked face of the mirror above the fireplace – distorted now by the smashed glass – was written the same message that she'd seen in Geraldine's bathroom: RUN AWAY WITH ME.

Jenny hurried back outside. She definitely needed another glass of wine.

Unable to leave Gunter in the broken cage, Jenny was forced to haul him back with her to deliver the bottle of Montrachet and the printed photograph, on which she'd written a profuse apology. She tied him to a lamppost, then headed up the path to Myrtle's cottage, lavender scent pluming up as it brushed against her ankles, bumble bees reverberating in the last of the lupins. I had a garden like this once, she remembered, thinking wistfully back to the high herbaceous borders at either side of her front path in North Oxford, bursting with delphiniums and hollyhocks as tall as soldiers, alliums and sweet peas grown over an arch, cottage perennials that Robin had thought a terrible cliché and out of keeping with a townhouse, but that she'd tended and adored with a passion that seemed to belong to another lifetime, sometimes taking an hour to get from gate to door as she stopped to weed, dead-head and gather seeds. On the small decking square at the mews, she had minimalist phormium in containers, as tough and spiky as she was.

A garden sprinkler was spluttering out of sight, deeply buried in one of the borders, its spray just catching her leg as she passed. Richard had made no mention of the need to water the Old Rectory's garden in his notes, but with no sign of his horticultural team in evidence, she doubted the plants could hold out much longer.

Gunter was starting to whimper on his tether, the lamp-post rattling as he ran around it like a big hairy swing ball.

He would strangle himself in a minute – or take off, Jenny thought, as she hurried to the black-painted door. She could hear voices inside the cottage: the old lady's rattling laughter and the deeper, sexier bark of a man. Leaving the wine on the doorstep as instructed, she rang the bell once and hurried back to spirit Gunter out of sight before he could do any more damage.

Dodging midge clouds and storm flies in the muggy evening heat, Jenny polished off the rest of her wine as she wandered around the Old Rectory's garden with a hosepipe that she'd discovered wasn't long enough to stretch to the thirsty borders, meaning she could only water the tubs and troughs closest to the house. Thinking this a terrific game, Gunter chased the water 'tail', tangling himself in hosepipe and tripping her. As she moved between the containers, watering herself almost as much as the plants, Jenny pondered the message on the mirrors, *Run away with me*.

Her logical, no-nonsense brain had worked out the practical if unlikely scenario that Geraldine Lewis had written them herself as some sort of inspirational *aide-mémoire*. Her fantasist's heart dwelled upon the possibility that she was having a wild affair, like Victoria in *The Storm Returns*.

She was being eaten alive by midges now. Heading inside, she opened another bottle of wine to enjoy while she ironed a few more chapters of *The Storm Returns*, now sorted back into page order, apart from a few unfathomably numbered ones that she knew she'd only fit back into place if she actually read it. Thus justified, with alcohol blurring her moral principles all the more, she devoured each page as she ironed, unable to resist following the story.

The star-crossed couple were now apart, Victoria – a double marriage-wrecker – marrying her former fiancé, and Jack descending into alcoholism, buying love wherever he could find it. The characters were far crueller than Jenny remembered them but no less brilliantly written. She barely recognized them as the young lovers she'd adored. She'd once even considered emigrating to live and work in a Western Australian mine and find her own Jack, whose talent for carpentry and love-making meant he handled lathe and inner thigh with equal skill. This older Jack was an embittered drunk, his ex-wife a harlot. They had children together, but that didn't seem to count for anything in their mutual quest for revenge and sexual fulfilment. When Victoria discovered her new husband could not satisfy her in bed as Jack had, she took a Sapphic detour over several pages, seducing the young British teacher Jack had already deflowered earlier in the book, then lost through his violent drinking. The seduction scene – heavily influenced, Jenny suspected, by *The Rainbow* and *Tipping the Velvet* – was among the most graphically written in the book.

She carried a freshly pressed page with her to the loo, took another into the kitchen to read as she put on some toast and waited for it. She wasn't really hungry, but she knew she had to soak up the wine and stop feeling horny. This was bad old out-of-control unhappy-wife behaviour. When she'd reluctantly read *Fifty Shades* at Carla's insistence, she'd cannoned around the mews house like an unexploded bomb all week, despite covering the book in pencil corrections and putting it straight into the recycling afterwards. She felt the same reading this, without the need for pencil marks.

Geraldine's young teacher was positively shuddering to a climax guaranteed to make the reader's nether regions twitch when Jenny realized the next page was missing.

'Blast!'

She was tempted to go for a naked swim to cool off, but she knew she'd had too much to drink to risk a late-night dip. The last thing she needed to cap her appalling luck on this house-sitting job was for her naked body to be discovered floating in the Lewises' swimming-pool.

Instead, she reached for the toaster only to find it empty. She must be drunker than she thought if she'd eaten without remembering. She put the cork back into the bottle and headed upstairs for a bath, grateful to discover that the walls of mirrors in the guest en-suite steamed up too much to see one's reflection, which meant she could leave the light on and shave her legs: she'd been showering with her eyes shut so far. Now, as she rather haphazardly mowed tracks up and down her shins and thighs, inadvertently leaving small stubbly islands on her knees and ankles, she sang Norah Jones's 'Turn Me On' in a throaty alto and looked up at her reflection in the mirrors on the ceiling, a satisfyingly blurred pink blob with an unsatisfyingly large brown triangle halfway down it.

Given her possible seduction plans – and the lack of much shaping beyond basic edging of the bikini-line department lately – she decided to give it a trim. Robin had always far preferred the wild-meadow look, but Roger was probably a formal-border fan, like most men, she told herself, as she worked her way along each side, blinking woozily as she struggled to match them. Chin propped on the bath rim, bubbles on the end of his nose, Gunter watched in fascination as she tipped her head this way and that, Venus razor twirling, wishing she had a protractor. It finished up a bit wonky – more scalene than isosceles – but it at least wouldn't stray from her swimsuit if she decided to try out the pool again, she concluded happily.

Now that his cage was broken, Gunter clearly had no intention of staying downstairs. When she went to bed, Jenny banished him to the landing where he lay outside her door, snorting under it and letting out baleful moans. Plugging in her earphones as she climbed into bed, she lined up some favourite radio comedy shows on her phone's iPlayer and tried to ignore him. Within minutes, she was fast asleep and Gunter had stolen in to clamber happily alongside her.

Jenny dreamed she saw herself swimming naked in the pool again that night. This time it started with a nightmare in which she was lurching to the loo, dry-mouthed and bladder bursting with wine, keeping the light off to pee among the mirrors, although dawn's steely fingers were creeping in through the gauze blinds, casting her many reflections as mottled-grey stone statues with an alarming lack of pubic hair. It was like weeing among a Terracotta Army of clones. She tried not to scream. She could hear the rhythmic strokes of someone swimming outside and knew it was herself. Pulling back the blind, she saw the ivory dolphin powering back and forth.

Then she almost fainted as a cold, wet nose was thrust against her bare thigh.

'Gunter!' She swung round.

In the half-dark, his whole body wagged and she could see the gleam of his front teeth in his bearded smile. Then he bounded back towards the bedroom.

In her half-conscious, semi-sleepwalking confusion, and still slightly tipsy, Jenny walked into the shower twice and into the wall once before tripping after him and collapsing back into bed.

IV

Sunday

14

TO DO LIST

Eat super-food (NOT toast)

Read a novel a day

<u>Quit alcohol</u>

~~Do something about Depilation~~ ✓

Swim 40 lengths

Have sex with Roger

Jenny had one earphone unaccountably up her nose when she woke on Sunday morning. She'd been having a disturbingly erotic dream about Matt the rugby teacher and an Ibiza foam party. It had been gloriously guilt-free, leaving a tic between her legs, a long-dormant urge revisited.

She knew it must still be early because the stripe of sun through the curtain crack was still above her bed and had yet to move right over the painted *bombe* wardrobe, which signalled Gunter's early walk. The sun-stripe was a lot wider than she'd expected and appeared to be wobbling, a dog-shaped shadow at its centre. Head pounding with a tell-tale hangover, she turned to see Gunter's tail wagging like mad as he stood with his front paws up on the window-sill looking out. He let out a few eager barks.

She glanced at her watch and groaned. It wasn't yet six.

Clutching her head, mouth dry and acidic, she wandered to the window to look out, bracing herself for the lumpy neighbours swimming after an all-night 'free spirits' pot-smoking marathon. But the pool cover was on. Beyond it, just visible through the shrubbery, a figure was crouching by the french windows of the garden cottage.

Gunter barked again, his whole body waggling in welcome. It was clearly no stranger.

She turned back and groped for her glasses on the bedside table. Under them was an untouched copy of *Bonjour Tristesse* she'd brought up to bed to read, although she'd ended up listening to the radio instead to drown Gunter's whingeing from the landing. She must have been three sheets to the wind because she'd brought up the French-language original. She closed her eyes guiltily as she remembered drunkenly binge-reading *The Storm Returns*, then getting to a very steamy sex scene only to find another page missing. No wonder she'd been having erotic dreams. She only hoped she hadn't left the iron on.

She held her glasses up to her eyes and turned back to peer out at the garden. The figure seemed to have a pair of secateurs, pulling a rampantly overgrown Russian vine from around the cottage windows.

It must be the rude, eccentric gardener, she remembered with a groan. She hadn't anticipated he would be so rude and eccentric that he started work at first light on a Sunday.

Heading through to the bathroom to clean her teeth, the sight that greeted her made her reel back. Her hung-over face reflected in a hundred mirrored panes was bad enough, but the sides of the bath appeared to be coated with animal hair. Had she washed Gunter in there? Then she remembered her drunken depilation. Lowering her sleep shorts in trepidation, she found that where yesterday there had been perfectly shaped – if old-fashioned – pubes, there was now a lop-sided triangle shaped like the Isle of Skye.

By the time Jenny made it across the garden with a cup of tea, still dressed in her sleep T-shirt and shorts, the gardener was already wrapped in a bear-hug of gundog welcome, his arms mouthed with eager play-bites.

'Get off, Gunter!' he hissed, not sounding at all pleased to be the object of such devotion.

'Milk and one!' Jenny announced brightly.

He sprang back against the cottage wall.

Jenny started, scalding tea slopping over her fingers. She was normally very good with faces, but she was woolly-headed this morning and it took her a moment to work out where she'd seen him before. Unshaven and covered with Russian vine blossom, he was far removed from the neat, overall-wearing plantsman she'd once employed to help her keep the narrow walled garden behind the Oxford house in perfect order. He looked like he'd been for a run. His faded blue T-shirt already bore dark tracks of sweat from navel to breastbone and his unruly mop of black hair was damp at the roots. He pushed it back with a paint-speckled hand and looked at her angrily, eyes the same pale green as blackbirds' eggs. Running through that unruly black mop, close to his forehead, there was a white bolt of hair, which her mother called a 'witch's streak'. Closing one eye, she tried to imagine it in sunset pink. He was the man on the boat.

His Rottweilers had tried to take on Gunter. Or, rather, they were Perry's Rottweilers on Perry's boat, and the pretty girl was quite possibly Perry's girlfriend, but Jenny was far too fuzzy-headed to work all that out.

'You certainly start work bright and early.' She handed the tea to him, noticing that his secateurs were odd-shaped and very rusty. 'I don't blame you in this heat. It must have been close to forty yesterday.'

'Close enough.' He nodded, eyeing her warily over the mug rim as he sat on the step.

She remembered the Scottish accent now, the rough, heathery voice that had ordered the dogs back. 'Close in every sense of the word!' She forced a laugh, fanning the hem of her T-shirt, acutely aware that her hangover was making her feel as though she was sweating fifteen per cent proof Burgundy from every pore. 'It's so muggy already.'

His eyebrows shot up and she realized that, from his low angle, he could see right up the T-shirt she was flapping. She still had no bra on, her unsupported breasts drooping horribly low. She stepped back hurriedly. 'I'm Jenny, the house-sitter. Richard said to make you lots of cups of tea.'

He looked astonished. 'He did?'

'He says you'll give me brilliant gardening tips if I keep them coming. I'm sorry, I don't know your name?'

'Euan.'

'Jenny.'

'So you said.'

Jenny nodded again, aware that she wasn't simply flustered because she was sweatily hung-over. It was because she'd last seen him standing on a boat in a hand towel and a state of arousal. He was undeniably physically attractive, if one went for the brawny rugged Scot thing. She was more of a Cumberbitch, a fan of intellect and wit, but it was hard to shake the memory of that bulge from her head.

'I'll just get dressed so I can take the dog out. When you've finished trimming that vine, perhaps you could have a go at the climbers around the kitchen at the main house too.

116

They're so overgrown the doors won't open, and it's far too dark in there.'

'That's how Geraldine likes them,' he muttered, blowing on his tea. 'They hide the pool from view when the neighbours use it.' He glanced up, the green eyes unexpectedly direct.

He probably knows a lot more about life here than I do, Jenny thought. Some of the more bohemian elements of the Old Rectory made her very uncomfortable. Meeting the 'rude' gardener was doing nothing to change her opinion. If he was happy to stand on a houseboat deck without a stitch on, skinny dipping was probably his idea of fun.

'More tea in half an hour.' She hurried back inside to take a head-clearing shower amid the steamed-up antique mirrors. There, she tried to even up the triangle of hair beneath the soft ledge of her belly, but the razor was blunt now and the triangle just grew even smaller, scratchier and no less wonky until it was a tiny Hebridean island, possibly Uist or Jura. She forced herself to stop before it shrank to Eriskay. Wiping a small letterbox of steam from the nearest mirror, she tipped back and tried to imagine what her breasts would look like viewed from a low step. The sight reminded her of the drawings her son Jake had made when he had first become fascinated by breasts, big rounded Ws with two full stops at their lowest points.

Strapping on her most supportive and uplifting bra, she dressed in a prim, high-necked sundress that allowed no inadvertent flapping, and went outside to fetch the gardener's tea. He was still sitting on the step, looking bad-tempered and smoking a cigarette. 'Ready for a top-up?'

'No.'

The acrid smoke made her recoil, the reflex craving non-existent at that time of day. Even at her most addicted, she'd never smoked first thing in the morning, apart from as a student, usually after having sex all night, still drunk or stoned or both. But that had been the girl who'd swim naked in the pool as dawn broke, someone she no longer recognized as herself, the middle-aged mother with drooping breasts who showered with her eyes closed.

Unusually benign, Gunter was passive-smoking companionably as he leaned against Euan, having eagerly transferred affection again, bearded chin on one shoulder.

'Where's his training collar?' Euan asked, scratching the dog's neck.

'I took it off.' She didn't mention that it had got knocked too close to the hotplate while it was drying out on the Aga and the strap had melted.

The cigarette end dangled from a half-smile, green eyes squinting up at her, amused and admiring. 'You'll never control him without it.'

'You'd be surprised.' She mustered much-needed bravado and fixed Gunter with her most authoritative teacher's look. 'Walk!'

She was cannoned against the cottage wall as fast as a goal net taking a penalty. Showing his readiness, Gunter body-slammed her again, kissed her face with a drippy beard, then raced off towards the garages to throw himself at the door in case she'd forgotten where the dog car lived.

Dusting herself down, she gave Euan a victorious smile. 'I won't be more than an hour. Are you sure you'll last without another cup?'

His brows lowered. 'Just leave the back door open and I can help myself.'

Jenny hesitated, glancing over her shoulder at the house. Richard Lewis might revere the man's horticultural prowess, but that didn't mean he trusted him not to tread topsoil all over his cream floors in search of Darjeeling. She'd barred a pensioner from taking snapshots in the cottage with less justification. 'I must lock and alarm it every time I leave.'

'I'm here to keep an eye on it.' The direct gaze landed on her again, challenging her to refuse.

'The cleaners have only just been.'

'I promise I'll take my boots off.' His single-mindedness played to her double standards. 'I can wash myself off in the pool too, if you like.'

She had a sudden image of his wet footprints on the boat's deck and felt her cheeks colouring, trying hard not to think about the towel. Finding her eyes doing their involuntary crotch-check thing, she backed quickly up the path with a terse nod. Richard had told her to keep him sweet. 'That would be appreciated.'

As she drove away, Jenny cursed her hazy head, wondering again if it was wise to let him have the run of the house. She'd been too hung-over and eager to escape to think it through. Based on Euan's houseboat bonking, there was every reason to doubt his moral fibre. She'd probably return to find him wearing her knickers and lounging in front of Sky Sports with a can of lager.

'I don't know why you were so pleased to see him,' she berated Gunter, as they headed to Beacon Common. 'I bet Diarmuid Gavin doesn't turn up in clients' gardens first thing on a Sunday morning looking that miserable, do you?'

Bounding around behind his grille, panting, whining and taking bites at the interior trims, Gunter barked in agreement.

The walk around the gravel pits cleared Jenny's head and woke her up. She was grateful that the only thing Gunter

chased was his shadow. Her bikini line was already be-
ginning to feel uncomfortably itchy and she longed for
Sudocrem.

Back at the Old Rectory, she hurried to inspect the garden
through the french windows and noticed the vine around the
garden cottage door looked exactly the same. The Lewises
should seriously reconsider their domestic contractors, she
thought irritably. The rude gardener seemed even less effi-
cient than the Va Va Vacuum duo. Neither did he appear to
have any sort of vehicle. Wasn't it compulsory for landscape
gardeners to drive around in ancient flat-bed trucks dropping hedge trimmings everywhere?

'Want one?'

She swung around in shock to find that Euan was in the
kitchen, still wearing his boots, looking oversized and undomesticated as he clumped to the island with the kettle. Was
it her imagination or was he slightly out of breath as he threw
a teabag into a mug and poured in the water. 'Just making
that cup of tea.'

'I'd prefer it if you boil the kettle first,' she pointed at the
cold Dualit in his hands, suspicion rising.

'Sure, if you like it prepared the old-fashioned way.' He
thrust his mug into the microwave and selected two minutes
at max power, glancing at her over his shoulder. She couldn't
tell if his expression was mocking or wary. 'Good walk?'

'Excellent.'

He turned to her, arms wing-spanning the island behind
him as he lounged back against it. 'You go along the river?'

'Not this time.' She smiled stiffly. He must have recognized her too. She tried hard not to think about that towel
bulge in profile. Now he was in the house, he seemed to fill
it with his presence. The sunlight streaming through the
thick foliage cast dappled green shadows on his tall, broad-

shouldered frame, making him look as though he was covered with dragon scales.

Being confined in a room, even a cavernous one like the Lewises' kitchen, with a man she had so recently seen in a state of semi-erect arousal, and who was now staring at her without making a comment, that made Jenny beyond uncomfortable. She retreated to the other side of the long table, perching on the arm of the patchwork sofa and glancing through to the morning room where the two doors to the Lewises' studies were closed. Had they been like that when she left?

She was just being paranoid, she told herself firmly.

Euan had turned away to pull open the door housing the vast fridge and draw out the milk. He seemed very familiar with the Old Rectory's built-in appliances.

'Where's your van?' Jenny asked, trying to sound casual, but sounding instead like Jane Tennison interviewing a murder suspect. Her bikini line was itching again.

His brows furled. 'It's not driveable at the moment.'

'What about all your equipment?'

'It's here already.' He held up his hands. They were big, tanned and calloused, but finely hewn beneath the outdoor armour, with strong square nails and knuckles tight as gauntlet joints. The colourful flecks on them struck her as odd.

'Is that paint?'

'Nail varnish.' He smiled up at her briefly to let her in on the joke, turning back to claim his mug from the microwave. 'Jack-of-all-trades, me.'

Blood boiling alongside the kettle, she stood up to move closer to the window and pretended to look out, hoping he'd bugger off back to his Jack-of-rough-trade bad pruning. She hated being teased, and he was like a tiger with one claw out. She found his presence incredibly unsettling.

121

Perhaps it was the word-association. Jack, the character from *The Dust Storm*, whom she'd fancied like mad at eighteen, but who was now letting her down in its grown-up sequel by going off the rails and embezzling the family fortune while nefariously bedding women left, right and centre. And this ripped, scruffy gardener – who apparently did no gardening – was a prime candidate for life far from the rails.

The Lewises had lousy domestic staff, she decided. Bring back Joan and Norman.

She knew she was probably just projecting her own guilt. She was the one who'd been ripping paintings, nosing around the cottage and drowning dogs. She glanced nervously in the direction of the utility room where *The Storm Returns* was spread out on the ironing-board. Please don't let Euan have seen it, Jenny prayed, edging back towards the kitchen. Having finished his breakfast, Gunter was drinking noisily from his water bowl just out of sight.

Feeling dehydrated too, she diverted to the fridge and drank half a carton of freshly squeezed orange juice straight from its spout. It was just starting to turn, an acid fizz corroding her tongue. But it kicked in much-needed sugars.

When she turned back, Euan was watching her again. Gunter was wiping his wet beard on his huge dusty desert boots and weaving around him, wagging his tail, sucking up again.

'He likes you,' she said brightly, edging towards the utility room.

'He likes everyone.' His green gaze tracked her. 'Are you a friend of Geraldine's?'

She stood in front of the door and crossed her arms like a bouncer. 'I'm from an agency.'

'A professional house-sitter.' That Scottish accent lent a sardonic tone. The corners of his mouth turned down and his eyes slid away. She had the distinct impression that he disapproved, probably well aware that she had fallen short of the mark so far.

'Actually I'm a teacher,' she said conversationally as he turned to make her tea the conventional way. When he didn't answer, she forged on, 'But I've always thought horticulture would be a fabulous thing to do. Isn't there a saying that gardening's all about sex and death, and beauty is just the by-product?' Where had that come from? she wondered in horror, as he glanced at her curiously. Her MILF channel was in danger of tuning in, and he really was far too grubby and nefarious to dwell on.

'Do you want me to give you one?' he asked gruffly.

It was a moment before she saw that he was holding up a bowl of sugar lumps.

'No, thank you.' She took the tea briskly. 'Tell me, what are you planning to work on now? That Russian vine might need a bit more trimming.' Her bikini line itched in sympathy as she remembered her drunken bathroom pruning.

He dropped two lumps into his microwaved mug, then looked up at the plant-laced windows for a long time, eventually saying, 'I think you're a bit in the dark here, Jenny.'

'Absolutely!' She marched to the windows under the guise of clematis scrutiny, but in reality to shake off an almost overwhelming urge to scratch. 'The climbers here are just as bad as the cottage, although please don't cut back anything you think Geraldine would disapprove of. She gives the orders around here, not me.'

'I do what I like.' He stalked out.

Jenny had no doubt she would have fired him by now if she was the Lewises. Checking he was out of sight, she

123

nipped through to the laundry room and tackled the itching before hastily hiding *The Storm Returns* among mesh laundry bags in a drawer. Then she collected her laptop and took it through to the library to work on Carla's book.

15

Jenny was correcting the chapter entitled 'Sex Is Not a Battle but Making Love Can Be War' when she realized she was being watched again.

Looking round, she saw Euan leaning against the library door frame. The sweat had dried on his T-shirt and his hair was now a matted confusion of black spikes and curls, the white streak poking up like a single horn. He was covered in more blossom petals than ever, as though he'd just walked through a wedding. Gunter was still glued devotedly to his side. Pale green eyes above intense conker ones, man and dog were regarding her thoughtfully.

'It's been an hour and you've not offered me any more tea.'

She was tempted to tell him to sod off and make his own tea. But Richard's lecture about his oddball manners and keeping him sweet stayed with her. 'Tea. Perfect timing. I'll just save this.'

'What are you writing?' He stepped closer. The words on the screen were Carla's cougar-on-the-pull mantra, written in bold.

Let's celebrate! It's the twenty-first century, ladies. Women are allowed to enjoy sex and not feel guilty about it!

She hastily minimized the page. 'I'm correcting something for a friend as a favour. I trained in copyediting a long time ago.'

'Is it Geraldine's?'

'No, it's a self-help book.'

'Who will it help?'

'My friend's finances mostly, if it sells. And divorcees.'

'Is the advice any good?'

'It's very good,' she said brightly, although she had serious issues with Carla's take on sex.

'In that case, I'll buy it in case I ever get divorced.'

Jenny wondered what his wife was like. Long-suffering, undoubtedly. His glibness shocked her, and the thought of the bulge on the boat made her prickle uncomfortably.

Yet he seemed a lot friendlier and less intimidating now, his mood brighter. Perhaps he'd been a bit sleepy and hung-over too this morning. It was Sunday, after all. She checked the clock, astonished that it wasn't yet nine. At home, she'd be stretching out in bed listening to Clare Balding, review-ing her Saturday and contemplating a long shower and pamper. She was glad she was up, had already walked off her hangover and done an hour's work. It felt good.

When she went into the kitchen, she saw the sunlight streaming over the table, the drapes of climbers cut and tied back, all but one set of doors thrown open. 'What a difference!'

'The light's better.'

'Just look at the way it reflects off the pool and dances round.' She laughed. 'Thank you. I'm sure they'll love it.' She ignored a niggling worry that she'd overstepped the mark. What had Carla called her? The SAS of house-sitting? She stood to get court-martialled on this one. But she loved it, convinced it was much better. Gunter certainly approved, dashing in and out of each window in turn in a new slalom game.

'The keys were already in the locks, apart from one,' he pointed out.

'It'll probably be in the key safe.'

'Tell me where it is and I'll look.'

Even though she'd hidden *The Storm Returns*, she didn't want him asking awkward questions about the greaseproof paper and recipe books still laid out on the ironing-board. 'It's fine. I'll get it later.'

As she waited for the kettle to boil, she found herself under scrutiny again. Those pale green eyes were appraising, working their way around her face and nose as though studying a rare plant species and working out where to take a cutting.

'You have unusual bone structure.'

'My father's Persian. I get my cheeks from him.'

'And those lips.' He fiddled with a teaspoon, still staring. 'They remind me of Rossetti's *Proserpine*.'

She glowered at the mention of a painting she knew well, a Pre-Raphaelite postcard classic, its sulkily pouting subject doomed for eating a single pomegranate seed. 'I always think she looks like Rupert Everett in drag.'

'The model was William Morris's wife.' He gave her lips a final once-over before turning away to admire the liberated windows, eyes creasing against the sunlight streaming in. 'Rossetti was screwing her.'

Jenny shifted uncomfortably, glad he couldn't see the blush already stealing up her cheeks. It didn't take a lot to shock her these days, her innuendo alarm highly sensitive. She was pretty sure he wasn't flirting with her – he seemed very matter-of-fact – but the shift in conversation confused her. He was a lot more cultured than she had given him credit for, even if he looked like he'd slept on a park bench. On balance, it was easier to cope with his surliness, like a standard-issue disruptive pupil, as opposed to an over-bright screwed-up one.

She made the tea, noticing as she lobbed the squeezed bags into the recycling that he was holding the teaspoon's glass handle up to the sunlight and casting spectrums on the kitchen wall, which Gunter was watching, entranced, head tilting this way and that.

'The best light in this house is in the library,' Euan told her. 'That's north-east-facing with skylights in every apex of the octagonal roof. Apparently it was designed for a reverend who was an astronomy-nut and liked to compose his sermons beneath the constellations, although how he squared the Big Bang Theory with God hasn't been made public. I've spent hours in there and never tired of it. It's basically a light box by day, an observatory by night.'

Jenny wondered if he knew the Lewis family socially, which would explain why he was so familiar with the house and why they retained such an unconventional gardener. He was probably a cousin or old university friend who was down on his luck, she guessed, as she tried to work out his age, settling on anywhere between thirty-five and fifty. His hard-muscled body seemed younger than his face, which had deep laughter lines, and she noted the first threads of grey in the thick black hair, along with the distinctive white streak. It really did need a wash. Allowing herself a small surge of pity, she regarded him more kindly.

'The library *is* fabulous.' She sipped her tea. 'The collection of first editions is out of this world, isn't it?'

'I'm pretty dyslexic. Books don't interest me.' His voice had hardened.

The English teacher in Jenny wanted to launch into a long diatribe about strategies that could get any adult or child reading for pleasure, but she stopped herself as she guessed he was embarrassed by it. 'You seem to know the room terribly well.'

'I painted in there,' he explained, threading the spoon through his fingers, studying her cheekbones again, his head cocked.

'You paint as well as garden?' she asked, an idea forming.

'I paint.' He nodded.

So the Lewises employed their old acquaintance to do decorating work around the house as well as gardening. Jenny thought of the ravaged en-suite that she had to put right. 'Are you available to paint this week?'

'Are you serious?' He frowned.

'It's a huge, huge favour, I know,' she rushed on, 'but this would be much less time-consuming than the library project.'

He tilted his head thoughtfully. 'So you like my work?'

'I've admired it every day.' She already planned to replicate the cool French grey library walls in her sitting room at home. 'The biggest problem is payment.' She pulled an embarrassed face, seeing his expression darken further. 'I promise I will pay, but I threw my cash and debit card away by mistake yesterday, so I have nothing to offer at the moment, apart from nine bottles of Burgundy and an IOU. How much do you charge for this sort of thing?'

'Nine bottles of Burgundy is a good start.' To her relief, he smiled. 'Van Gogh worked for less.'

'That's wonderful news.' Jenny hoped the Lewises hadn't taken their friend under their wing to help him recover from alcoholism. But she had no desire to drink any more of the stuff right now, and it was a fair trade for a day's filling and painting. 'When can you start?'

'Tomorrow's good for me.' He looked at the clock, yawning widely before his mouth turned into a big and surprisingly winning smile. 'I just need to fetch my kit from Perry's boat. I'm through with painting her now.'

So that was the story. He'd been repainting Perry's house-boat and abusing his trust by sleeping with his girlfriend while he was away. Empathizing with his poor wife, she was no longer feeling quite so sympathetic to his plight, and wondered if she should really trust an immoral freeloader with a paint scraper in Richard Lewis's en-suite. The Lewises were probably paying him good money to look after their garden. She wouldn't give him an easy ride.

'That's excellent news,' she said, in a business-like voice. 'Now, I need you to set up the sprinklers at the back of the lawn.'

A black eyebrow shot up. 'Why?'

'I'm sure it hasn't escaped your attention that there's a heat-wave. I need the hose to stretch as far as the flowerbeds along the far wall. And please make sure all the sprinklers are working.'

'Are you always so bossy?' Not waiting for an answer, he headed back outside with his tea and wandered across the lawn in search of sprinklers and hosepipes.

Soon he'd gathered together a yellow plastic mini Stonehenge of devices to try out. He wasn't particularly good at it, Jenny decided when she heard cursing. A few minutes later she looked out, to see him alternately standing in a mist then being doused by a whipping snake of water as the hose end blew out, Gunter leaping joyously through the rainbows all around him. Euan was soaked, the pale blue T-shirt clinging to his torso, reminding her of his bare-chested, caught-in-the-act anger on the deck of the houseboat. Then she remembered the perfection of Perry's girlfriend's smooth skin and long, slim limbs, as she paused briefly from being wrapped around him to deal with a harassed, middle-aged dog-walker.

The church bells started ringing puritanically for morning

service, and Jenny retreated hastily to the library to resume work.

Catching sight of her reflection in the hall mirror, she noticed how unflattering the dress she'd put on was, emphasizing the round curve of her belly. She hadn't exercised all week, apart from a few dog walks. She made a mental note to do some sit-ups and swim later. While the Lewises holidayed, the parishioners worshipped and freeloader Euan made a romantic getaway, she was going to feel the burn.

She started by selecting one of the heaviest books in the library, a huge coffee-table tome about the Pre-Raphaelite Brotherhood – she felt as if she was pumping iron just lifting it across to the desk. Flicking through, she found Rossetti's famous *Proserpine* and studied it closely. The figure still made her think of a man in drag, with rugby-player shoulders and hands like an undertaker's. Scowling, she flipped through the book, remembering her passion-hungry eighteen-year-old self lining her college room with John William Waterhouse posters of Ophelia, *The Tempest*'s Miranda and the Lady of Shalott. The movement was no longer one of Jenny's favourites, however beautiful the paintings; similarly, the romantic poetry with which it was synonymous contained great works she admired for their skill but found too fanciful for her taste now.

She slammed the book shut, then lifted it over her head and from side to side a few times to feel the benefit before slotting it back in the shelf with a relieved 'oof'. She'd work with something lighter from the poetry shelves next time.

She reopened *Tour Divorce*, battling her way irritably through the highly opinionated sex-is-not-a-war chapter before she was forced to go in search of paracetamol in her handbag for the headache that wouldn't shift. In the kitchen she clicked on the kettle and stewed over Carla's glib assumption that everybody had her own self-confidence. In her book, she urged readers to lose their inhibitions and sample life's sexual tasting menu before it was too late. Not so hard for an urban predator who ate out a lot, like Carla, but a self-deprecating internet dater like Jenny undertook twenty weeks of slow-cooking followed by indigestion before dessert.

She still hadn't called Roger back to confirm Thursday. Roger Roger Night, she thought with a shiver of anticipation and fear. Richard Lewis had said she could invite guests so there was nothing stopping her, she reminded herself, moving to another window to see if Euan was on the side lawn. Admittedly Richard had been drunk at the time and unaware that she had already tried to smash up his pool, kill his dog and trash his dressing room, but the sentiment had been genuine, and she wasn't planning rampant bonking all over his house, just a much-needed seduction beneath the *ciel de lit* in her room.

You're a grown-up, Jenny Rees, she heard Richard's clever, jolly voice in her head. You surely have a lover. Invite him over to my beautiful house. We're all grown-ups. We make love. I'm pleasuring my wife in the Maldives as often as I can. My neighbours swim joyously together and share regular orgasms despite middle-age spread and excessive pubic hair. My gardener is a grown-up who's been rocking the houseboat with Perry's beautiful girlfriend in a steamy shower as well as sharing his wife's bed. This is what grown-ups do. You are one of us, aren't you?

She picked up her phone, then put it down again, deciding she'd do her sit-ups before calling him. For that, she needed total privacy.

Unable to spot Euan from the house, she carried two mugs of tea outside, dodging the deluge from several different designs of lawn sprinkler that spluttered and snaked drips over the Old Rectory garden. Gunter was scrabbling miserably at the big arched door set in the wall that divided the garden from the churchyard. Euan had clearly just left.

Jenny stomped inside, wishing she hadn't asked him to do the painting. He was very rude and unreliable.

Heading upstairs with a screwdriver, trailed by a panting Gunter, she refitted the dressing room door handle, overlooked by frolicking, flirtatious paintings from which she averted her eyes. She then marched down to the garages where she'd spotted a wall of shelves filled with hand-mixed Farrow & Ball colours labelled with the rooms they had been used for. There, between the Classic Cream of 'master bed' and Dayroom Yellow of 'G dress/bath' was the familiar deep claret, fittingly named Rectory Red. She gathered it to her chest, with a tin of off white marked 'woodwork master suite' and carried them upstairs, returning with dust sheets, brushes, fillers and acres of newspaper. She'd give Euan no excuse not to get straight on with the job.

She studied the damage again, wondering whether she could do it herself – practical, perfectionist Jenny, who could turn her hand to most things. She'd painted a few walls when she was first married, before there was money to pay professionals. She'd been far more impatient and slapdash then, covering quite a lot of herself with paint, which Robin had helped her scrub off in the bath afterwards, amid much squealing and splashing. She hadn't been much good at decorating at all, she reflected. Or at frolicking in the bath, judging by Robin's eagerness to get his back scrubbed elsewhere as soon as the twins had come on the scene.

She glared at a nude of a lusciously curvy woman dancing through a surrealist topiary of box trees clipped to look like faceless supermodels, an affectionate and comedic work, which did nothing to cheer her up. Sweat was dripping off her, reminding her how unfit she was, exhausted by just two trips upstairs. It didn't matter that the day was so hot even Gunter had no energy left. Jenny felt monumentally out of condition.

She went to her room and dragged out her swimming costume – the dullest navy blue Speedo, bobbly-bottomed from hauling herself in and out of the school pool for the past three years. Pulling it on, followed by her rubber hat and nose clip, she hurried back downstairs again and rolled back the pool cover with the vigour of a pirate hoisting the mainbrace for an ambush. Then she dived in.

The thing that Jenny loved about swimming was water's ability to silence thought. Today, she needed her thoughts slowed by the heavy, submerged drag.

She opened her eyes, watching the light refracting on the blue pool liner, her shadow gliding over it. Something white on the bottom of the pool caught her eye. She dived down and found a missing page of manuscript, sucked to the filter grille, still intact but now as soggy and fragile as tissue. Picking it up by the corners, she carefully carried it to the surface and placed it on the hot paving stones beside the shallow end. The chlorine had bleached the page almost pure white, Geraldine's writing barely visible, although she could just make out a *hungry tongue* and *ripe papaya* – it was the missing page from the Sapphic love scene. She weighed it down with a pebble and dropped back into the blissful cool. After ten more lengths, she wondered where Gunter was, the only sounds in the garden being her strokes whooshing, the water slapping the filters and birdsong.

She climbed out, then up onto the pergola, tipping her

head from side to side to unblock her ears, the sun-bleached wood burning her feet. She heard loud snoring. Looking down, she saw that he was asleep in the cool beneath the cast-iron table, his grizzled back cross-hatched with shadows.

Jenny crouched to give him a stroke. 'Does this mean you're starting to trust me enough to relax and hang out with me?'

Waking with a start, he opened his mad conker eyes, looked around anxiously, then shot off into the house, reappearing with a massacred pillow from her bed, feathers pluming, which he dropped reverently at her feet. Jenny knew from experience that this was a seminal moment. It was his first gift. Gundogs liked fetching things for the humans they considered leaders of the pack, a replication of the job for which they'd been bred, carrying back the spoils of the shoot. Admittedly he'd just destroyed a very expensive item of home furnishing, but it was an act of affection she badly needed.

'Thank you.' She kissed his domed head as he slumped companionably beside her.

Jenny decided that, despite the greying beard and hyperactive neurosis, Gunter no longer reminded her quite so vividly of Robin, who had stopped giving her things very early in marriage, preferring to slip a cheque into a card if he remembered a birthday or anniversary, which wasn't often.

Leaving him to sunbathe, she took her pillow gift back to the house before the feathers could spread around the garden, stooping to gather up the wet page from beneath its pebble and take it to dry on the Aga. She picked out a few more faded words, including a *shuddering sweet spot* and *wet fingers delving to their hilts*.

16

The swim had invigorated her. No longer sweaty with the self-pity of *ennui*, she spent the rest of the afternoon working on *Tour Divorce* between more swims, at her most focused and eagle-eyed, wishing every hour of her life could be as four-cylinders-firing, super-efficient as these few. She was even starting to embrace Carla's go-get-'em mantra. Sitting outside in her Speedo swimsuit, back tanning in a strange cut-out circle, she conjoined infinitives, closed parentheses and cross-checked references.

Every so often her phone beeped. She checked messages and replied immediately, editing hand still hovering over the keyboard. Roger – retreating behind texts to repeat his offer of dinner – was soothed with platitudes but still given no answer; Carla bounced queries back, delighted Jenny was three-quarters of the way through the first read; Rachel shared silliness from her sofa as she fought sleep through a Sunday-afternoon movie with the kids; Jenny's department head shared links to a cheap package to Kos and promised to raise a glass of ouzo in her absence; other friends caught up and wound down; son Jake sent a picture of Brooklyn Bridge and a Gordon Gekko quote. Jenny replied with a selfie of herself and Gunter and a quote from Carla's book: 'Use every one of your senses to remember each new experience, most of all your sense of self.'

'It's codswallop, of course,' she told Gunter wisely. 'Seventy-five per cent of perception is visual. Most of us wouldn't want to know what Hudson River water tastes like. You are an honourable exception. Besides which, seventy-five per cent of you is smell. And, boy, do you smell.'

Gunter looked up from a long, indulgent session of personal ablutions, panting and grinning at her.

He'd brought her more gifts. The carnage was great: several cuddly toys from the children's playroom had been sacrificed, plus a pair of shoes and two scatter cushions. But Jenny knew 'gifting' was a huge sign of trust. Instead of telling him off, she was now trying to encourage him to stick to one offering, a battered rope dog toy she'd unearthed in the utility room, rewarding him when he handed it over as a soft-mouthed gundog should. He spent the following hour sitting on her feet savaging it, but at least it kept him quiet. It was obvious he'd never had much training beyond the cage and remote-control. Jenny guessed the Lewises had seen an expert, but she thought they'd been given bad advice, and was determined to do her best to look after him without gadgets.

She called her mother at their usual yardarm hour, their Sunday calls inevitably briefer than the midweek marathons because Jenny's sister hosted lunch and took the brunt of complaints about wheelie-bin politics at Haven Hall. She felt a great wave of homesick nostalgia for Persian cooking and family love, but it was a wave that propelled her further out to sea, not inland today.

'You sound very up.' There were sounds of a gin and tonic being made in the background. 'Is that to do with your new man?' her mother probed hopefully.

'I like looking after other people's homes.' She tilted her face up to the sun. 'It was a shaky start, but I think I'm getting there now.' Opening her eyes, she looked at the handsome house, cast from pure gold in the evening sunlight.

Myrtle's ginger cat was sunbathing on one of the dormers, she noticed. Thankfully, Gunter hadn't spotted it.

'You've always put other people's needs first, Jennifer.' Her mother sighed. 'Make sure you look after yourself too.'

'I'm swimming and walking, Mum.'

'That's not what I mean. Pamper yourself. Have a massage and a few salon treatments. Your man will appreciate it too.' Her mother had always believed that happiness came out of a bottle and was expensively scented, preferably applied by a beauty therapist.

'I'd rather relax with a good book.' Jenny thought uncomfortably about her bikini line, which was now starting to itch again. If she couldn't face showing it to a trained waxing expert, she knew she was going to struggle to cope with anyone else getting a close look. Roger Roger Night would have to kick off after dark.

Her mother had moved on to bitch about Veronica Carmichael not returning a borrowed recipe book. 'I don't mind how long Josceline Dimbleby stays out, these days, but I still need Mary Berry in my kitchen where I can see her.'

Before she worked on the final section of *Tour Divorce*, Jenny closed her laptop lid and used her smartphone to Skype Amalie as they'd arranged, fighting an urge to hug it tightly as soon as she saw the smiling face, the chestnut hair drawn up in a bandanna, like a dancer's. The twins had their father's hair. But the lips are all mine. Jenny smiled as she studied the Cupid's bow blowing her lots of welcome kisses, remembering Rossetti's *Lady Lilith* and *Venus Verdicordia* in the book she'd flicked through earlier – they'd shared her daughter's colouring, if none of her *joie de vivre*. She suddenly grasped why the Pre-Raphaelites increasingly left her cold. Not one of the paintings bestowed any joy whatsoever. Instead, it was a procession of ravishing, pouting female miseries from history and myth, mostly damned or suicidal. Richard Lewis's collection of colourful landscapes and plump ladies offered far more reasons to be cheerful than all those rooms of beautiful, vibrant sadness. Staying here was like living in a jolly private art gallery.

'Let me show you round,' she told Amalie eagerly.

'Mum, are you in a swimsuit?'

'There's a pool – look.' She turned the phone to scan round the garden. 'I thought I'd try to get a bit fitter while I'm here.'

'Are you remembering to eat?'

'You sound like Granny.' Jenny laughed. 'There's an amazing kitchen.' She carried the phone inside, trying to remember when she had last eaten. She kept making slices of toast, but she had no recollection of actually swallowing them.

'Cool!' Amalie whistled as Jenny held up the phone and wandered round, showing off the Old Rectory. 'You really have it all to yourself?'

'All to myself. Let me quickly show you Geraldine's study. I'm sure she won't mind.'

'Who's Geraldine?'

'I told you, she's the writer who lives here. I gave you her book, remember? *The Dust Storm.*'

'Oh, that. I couldn't finish it. Too long.'

She'd managed to read all four books in a series about vampires in under a week in Malta last summer, Jenny remembered, but let it pass. She had been the same at that age, spurning adult recommendations, wanting to discover books for herself. Even though she had first found *The Dust Storm* on her mother's shelf, she hadn't wanted to acknowledge it at the time, just as she hadn't wanted to acknowledge that Geraldine had nicked half the plot from Émile Zola.

139

Amalie was entranced by Gunter, cooing at him and making him bark into the phone, and she found him all the more adorable when Jenny told her about the swimming-pool rescue and the damage to the dressing room. 'Poor thing must have been so stressed out.'

'I've found somebody to fix it in exchange for a few bottles of plonk.' She thought about Euan irritably, hoping his decorating prowess was greater than his dedication to gardening.

'Doesn't the agency deal with that on its insurance? Surely it's not your liability.'

'You might have a point—' The phone was knocked from her hand as Gunter jumped up with a new gift, this time her own granny pants, which she'd discarded in the bedroom earlier.

Amalie's face was looking up from the floor where the phone had landed, affording her a close-up of Gunter's smiling face, pants in mouth, and gyrating tail.

'Oh, Mum, we must get a dog like that. He's fantastic.'

For a moment Jenny envisaged the children at home with her again, playing with a new puppy, walking it along the canal, sharing the joy. Then the cold bolt of a reality check reminded her that Amalie was on a degree course in the States for two more years, Jake was about to start university in Scotland, she was hoping to spend part of her autumn sabbatical overseas, and even after that leaving a dog like Gunter at home when she had returned to teaching was not an option.

'He looks far too like your father,' she joked, as she picked up the phone, then felt terrible for falling into the Dad-sniping trap.

But Amalie's face was still smiling widely. 'He's shaved off his beard. Lindsay said it made him look too old. They're on vacation in the Hamptons this week – some high-powered friend of her family's. Honey looks so cute in her first wet-suit.'

Hearing this, Jenny experienced the same self-harming pain as always when the subject of Robin and his new family was discussed. When she next spoke, her voice was as artificially bright as a blade: 'He's really shaven off his beard?'

'He looks loads younger. He's joined a gym.' She giggled. 'Don't say I told you, but he put his back out on the bench press last week. He's had to have emergency osteopathy and acupuncture.'

Jenny had no idea why Amalie imagined that her parents still shared the sort of conversations where one another's gym goofs were currency, but she found it rather sweet that she did. She tried to picture Robin without the beard. He'd grown it as an experiment not long after the twins were born and kept it because everyone told him he looked like Kenneth Branagh, strangers occasionally even asking for his autograph. Through the rest of their marriage he'd lost most of his hair, but never his academic's beard. Without it, he seemed more of a stranger than ever.

Amalie had moved on to talk about camp, chattering about people she had met and the kids she liked. She'd already picked up an American inflection in her speech. Listening to her excited voice and watching the full lips moving as she carried the phone back outside, Jenny brimmed with love, longing to be with her.

'Are you really not able to get home this summer?'

'It's crazy busy, Mum.' Was it her imagination, or had Amalie said 'Mom'?

'Never mind, there's Christmas to look forward to.' It seemed a long way off, but Jenny was a Christmas aficionado and had already vowed she would make it the best ever after last year's damp squib, during which Amalie had been laid up with flu and Jake had been travelling in Australia.

'That's another thing.' Amalie's big eyes blinked on the little screen. 'Dad kinda wants me in New York this year, given the new baby's due, and I missed Honey's first Christmas. You get Jake with a term's worth of washing from St Andrew's, and I get Dad reciting all Jimmy Cagney's lines as we watch *It's A Wonderful Life* for the hundredth time.'

Jenny tried to keep her face composed, although she was too hurt to speak. Was this the new deal, she wondered, a twin each on alternate years? Robin had barely engaged with Christmas when they'd been a family together, but now he wanted to share it second time around with Lindsay and Honey and lots of all-American family love.

'I'll try to get back this fall,' Amalie promised, 'or, hey, you can come here. It's your sabbatical term after all, and you'll *love* New York.'

'I've been to New York,' she said tightly.

'Okay, we'll sort something out, Mom.' Amalie moved forwards, scrunching her face up as she peered into the camera. For a moment Jenny thought she was studying her worriedly, aware that she was close to tears and fury, and she hurriedly composed her face into an approximation of a smile, but Amalie just muttered, 'My battery's about to run out, Mom. Let's Skype again this time next week. We can talk about it then. Love you!'

'Wait! I need to talk to you about fall – I mean autumn.'

Amalie didn't seem to hear. The big lips were in close-up now as the kisses flew out, and then the image disappeared with a synthesized sucking noise.

'I'm thinking of going away for my sabbatical.'

But Amalie had gone and only a bright blue screen remained.

Hollow with frustration and disappointment, Jenny wandered inside to put on some toast, heading listlessly to the fridge for butter and jam but forgetting what she was there for as soon as the cool air rushed against her hot face.

Anger flaring, she marched to the library and pulled two of the stoutest books she could see from a shelf, gripping them carefully and holding them like barbells to raise above her head several times. But she was forced to stop as Plato's complete works threatened to drop to the floor. She lay down beneath the eight skylights, slotted her bare feet under the sill of a bookcase and did twenty energetic sit-ups.

This was how she had behaved when first separated, she realized, as she flopped back and stared up at an octet of sky-blue rectangles. Three years later, she'd patched up her ego as best she could, but the anger still leaked out sometimes. She had to calm down and eat.

There was no toast in the shiny Dualit when she checked it. Gunter was lying on a sunny patch of decking just through the french windows with crumbs on his whiskers. That must be why she couldn't remember eating much of the toast she kept making.

To test her theory, she slotted in two more bread slices and crept behind the kitchen island to hide and observe. Sure enough, as soon as the warm, nutty smell of it toasting drifted out to Gunter's sensitive nose, he awoke and crept inside to wait furtively beneath the slate surface. When the toaster clicked, he stood on his hind legs and removed the hot toast with his teeth, tossing it down with a deft flick of his head so that it cooled on the floor before he wolfed it up and sauntered back towards the French doors.

'Gotcha!'

When Jenny sprang out, he bolted guiltily into the shrubbery.

She knew she should cook something but she no longer felt hungry. She swam a few more lengths, then tackled the final chapter of Carla's book, Gunter panting back out of his hiding place to lie companionably on her feet, both of them pausing to scratch occasionally.

In summary, Carla's rallying cry was convincing, calling upon women to see divorce as liberation, not condemnation, to reclaim their confidence and spirit, to eschew society's demands for perfect youth and instead to celebrate the beauty of experience and wisdom with all its baggage and imperfections, to learn to love themselves again. Reading it, Jenny felt a hot rush of concord.

'You've been living in the museum too long,' she muttered, as she re-formatted quotes and tidied commas. 'You're going to use your time here to take control of your life. You will read worthwhile books and swim, exercising body and mind. You are afraid of nobody. You must love yourself, although not necessarily in a self-pleasuring way. You will have sex again.' She picked up her phone.

'Roger!' she hailed, after his smooth greeting had invited her to leave a message. Even to her ears she sounded a bit overeager and artificial, like a news reporter trying to collar a politician in a crisis. 'You and me, luxury meal and a bottle of wine here, Thursday.' She hung up and rubbed her forehead, then turned to Gunter. 'Who was that woman?'

Gunter jumped up, letting out a bass bark. Voices were approaching the gate in the garden wall, and Jenny recognized the laughter as the swimming neighbours.

Grabbing his collar, her phone and laptop, she hurried inside, well aware that there were still a few aspects of maturity's baggage and imperfections she was struggling to embrace.

17

That evening, in the lengthening shadows of another muggy sunset, Jenny pulled on her trainers, took Gunter to the river and jogged for the first time in a decade, taking the bank past the houseboats, chin thrust up as she powered her way to Perry's mooring. She'd decided that if Euan was there she'd cancel the painting job. Amalie was right: it probably wasn't her liability. She must call Henry at the agency first thing tomorrow for advice, however reluctant she was to admit to being a less than perfect house-sitter. Even if it transpired that she was honour-bound to fix the dog damage, she now suspected that most decorators would do it for far less than two hundred pounds' worth of fine wine. Her new bank card was on its way: better to cancel Euan and wait until she had cash to pay a professional. She blamed the heat for making her impulsive.

But the boat was in darkness and shuttered, not a Rottweiler in sight.

Jenny ran on past it, putting on a rush of speed to shake off her frustration, sprinting along the bank, like Mo Farah eyeing the tape. Twenty yards further on, she stopped and bent down, clutching her knees, her lungs bursting.

'Note to self,' she gasped to a worried Gunter. 'Never hold your breath when running.' As she said it, a pheasant shrieked twenty yards away and he was gone, the lead pulled straight out of her grip.

'Oh, please, no.' Jenny took after him, her legs full of lead, lungs like flat balloons.

It took several painful rugby tackles to catch him before another massacre took place. Jenny made skin-stripping dives through brambles followed by long wades through a drought-shrunken pond and ditch, eventually emerging looking like a bog-snorkeller with an equally filthy dog under her control. The only parts of Gunter not covered with black mud were his white-rimmed conker eyes.

As they made their way back along the river path, Jenny saw two figures standing on top of Perry's houseboat. She ducked out of sight, pulling Gunter closer, listening for dogs.

One of the figures was Perry's girlfriend and at first she thought the other was Euan, her gaze instinctively flicking bulgewards – only to find flat-fronted shorts and very thick thighs. This man was shorter and bulkier, she saw, built like a professional boxer, with Popeye muscles and copious tattoos. The couple were arguing.

'Why the fuck d'you invite him to stay here?'

'He had nowhere to go, Perry baby. He could hardly stay on in the cottage.'

'That's his problem. Where is he now?'

'He says he's got something lined up. Some old bird who's sweet on him has offered him some work apparently.'

Jenny's eyes narrowed murderously.

Gunter tensed muddily beside her and let out a low warning growl. Shushing him, she could distinctly hear the clatter of heavy choke collars against dog bowls from below decks, indicating that the Rottweilers had just been given supper after an evening walk. She had no choice but to brazen her way past before they re-emerged. Holding Gunter's lead tightly, she towed him past the boat.

'Lovely evening!' she called, as she did so.

Not waiting for an answer, she put on a spurt of speed, despite her aching legs, as Perry dived for the hatch to block his dogs' path, their snarls audible all the way to the car.

'This is getting a bit too like a dysfunctional love affair,' Jenny told Gunter, as they took a shower together that night, sharing the downstairs wet room, which was the only place she could hope to scrape off the thick layers of black mud. 'Let's call this a dress rehearsal for Roger. I'll probably keep my underwear on with him too.'

When she deemed him clean enough, Jenny dried him as best she could, leaving him smiling upside-down by the Aga, and went upstairs for a proper bath. She'd no sooner stretched her legs beneath the warm, popping bubbles than she heard Gunter bouncing around on her bed, finishing his drying off with a final polish of the antique French silk counterpane. When she got out, she found him under the silk cover, a grizzly nose poking out at one end and a docked tail thumping at the other, faintly obscene as it moved beneath the fabric.

'You cannot stay on this bed,' she insisted, pulling off the counterpane. The blue and white ticking on its reverse was covered with damp dog hair. She carried it downstairs to hand-sponge in the utility room and hang to dry over the Aga rail.

She picked up the last rescued page of *The Storm Returns*, now poppadum crisp and faded bone white, and carried it to the drawer in the utility room to reunite it with the rest. She resisted the almost overwhelming temptation to take it out and read more. Instead she fetched the English translation of *Bonjour Tristesse* from the library, then tracked down an old blanket to throw over her bed for Gunter, conceding defeat in the light of his stubborn determination to share it. She needed printed words and sleep.

Before settling down to read, she put on twice her usual helping of age-defying moisturizer, applied a liberal amount of Savlon to her bikini line and took an ibuprofen.

Then she started the seductive tale of a philandering father whose daughter feels threatened when his long procession of young, flighty girlfriends is succeeded by a woman of his own age. Soon she'd fallen asleep with the light on and her mouth open, dreaming that she was running around a cemetery in Brooklyn being chased by Robin's current wife, who was a vampire, her school's headmaster in a *Scream* mask, and Gunter, who was dressed as Frank N. Furter from *The Rocky Horror Show*.

V

Monday

18

TO DO LIST

Finish ironing GS's manuscript
Do something else about depilation
Eat super-food (NOT toast)
~~Swim 40 lengths~~ ✓
Do not drink
Have sex with Roger

Jenny thought she heard somebody diving into the pool in her dream, but she was buried underground in a coffin, unable to move. It took a long time to force herself to wake up. When she did, she discovered that she was almost paralysed. Her back had seized up; her leg joints were fused; her stomach muscles had knotted together in constant spasm. Her eyes were red raw from too much chlorine after swimming yesterday. Despite taking both shower and bath before going to bed, she smelt of stagnant ditch water. Her arms were laced with bramble scratches. She couldn't feel her feet.

Doubting she could even get out of bed, she knew that she'd totally overdone it the day before. She tried to roll over and felt a large canine weight lying across her ankles. At least that explained the dead feet.

Sensing that she was awake, Gunter wriggled up to the headboard to offer her a face wash, smiling as whitely as a breakfast-television presenter. Turning her face away, Jenny felt her neck crick. At least the view was good, sun streaming in through the curtains and hitting the corner of the bed, which made it close to six thirty.

Outside, the dawn chorus was enthusiastically predicting another hot day.

It took Jenny a long time to crawl to the bath and run it, then heave herself in with a groan and a bow-wave splash.

A twenty-minute soak loosened her trapped nerves enough that she could get out with more conventional ease and step into some clothes, albeit loose ones. She creaked downstairs and perched stiffly on a kitchen stool, knocking back more ibuprofen as she waited for the kettle to boil.

Gunter was eagerly pacing between the kitchen and the door leading to the garages with a percussive click of claws, eyebrows as animated as those of a Muppet in a musical number. Jenny pretended not to notice, shuffling her stool closer to the kitchen surface to prop herself up.

'What possessed me?' she asked him, as he came to sit underfoot, whining miserably.

She knew, of course. With sexually competitive, age-defying bluster, she'd decided to test her limits. She blamed *Tour Divorce*. Carla's book insisted that a failed marriage was a gauntlet thrown down, an iron fist in a velvet glove that had to reach higher than ever in a sisterly power salute. Jenny had set out to high-five life and let off steam, but now she could barely walk and her precious self-esteem had escaped again. In her dark heart, she also knew she'd gone overboard because she'd heard Robin had got rid of his beard and joined a gym. How ironic that they were both shaving and getting fit. She reached down and scratched, making a mental note to buy depilatory cream and some high-grade body lotion by Thursday. Roger Roger Night minus three.

She felt a spasm of nervous anticipation followed by a rush of hope. Roger had replied to her voicemail with the short text *Much looking forward.* He was where she needed to be, she reminded herself. He was healthy without over-doing it: he played squash once a week and enjoyed his canoeing, drank in moderation and liked to be in bed for *Newsnight*; he preferred women his own age. He admired her mind as much as her body. She only hoped that her body would have recovered enough to move normally by Thursday.

Gunter was up again and starting to sing mournfully as he paced back and forth to the door. Jenny pondered his morn-ing walk, wondering whether she could lift her legs high enough to get into the dog car and, if so, whether she'd ever climb back out. Holding on to his lead would be totally beyond her if he took off.

'You are a professional,' she reminded herself.

When she went to set the house alarm, she found her arms wouldn't stretch high enough to reach the keypad in the hidden cupboard. Neither, she suspected, would her legs move fast enough to exit the house in the thirty seconds allowed before it went off. Abandoning the idea, now moving like an aged crone walking through clay, she made it into the garage block. Immensely grateful for an electronic tailgate, she let Gunter into the car and eased herself into the driver's seat with difficulty.

Opening the garage doors with the fob button, she pressed the automatic ignition and selected reverse. The car's reversing cameras were blinded by the low morning sun shining straight into its lens, but it also had sensors that beeped as she edged past the big pillars in the oak frame.

153

Jenny, who had first learned to drive in her mother's vintage Mini twenty-six years ago, still had a deeply ingrained need to look over her shoulder when reversing. After two decades of driving every shape and size of car, she knew no other way. Her cricked neck could only make it part of the way for her to see a clear path, but she knew that she was reversing into a wide, yew-shaded gravel skidpan. As soon as the car was past the pillars, she pressed the accelerator firmly, swinging the wheel to turn.

The warning beeps shrilled and Gunter yelped a fraction of a second before Jenny heard the crunch and felt the jolt. Her first reaction was disbelief. Then fear. Then anger. The three emotions kaleidoscoped as her eyes ran around the mirrors and she saw a silhouetted figure staggering out from behind the car. Gunter let out a bass bark of welcome.

The silhouette approached the car door. Now she recognized the wide shoulders and the white streak in the black hair.

'You could have killed me!' Euan raged, when she eventually buzzed down the window.

'I didn't see you! Are you hurt?'

'You only glanced off me – I jumped clear in time. My kit is trashed, though.' He squatted down to peer beneath the car. 'It's all under your back wheels. Pull forward.'

Jenny started the engine and stalled it again, fighting tears. She was normally calm in a crisis, but anger at her aching paralysis and idiocy was making her overreact. It could have been his leg or worse under those wheels.

The wild black hair resurfaced at the driver's window. It smelt of the shampoo Jake used, she noticed.

'Hop out,' he snapped. 'I'll move it.'

Jenny winced as she tried to ease her foot off the brake, her muscles locking. 'I'm not sure I *can*.'

154

His expression changed to one of concern, green eyes on her, and he pulled open the door. 'Is it whiplash? Let me help you.'

Jenny batted away the outstretched arm, loath to admit that her injuries were entirely self-inflicted. 'Really, I'm fine.'

'Christ, what happened to your arms?' He had noticed the vicious bruises and scratches.

'BMDS,' she joked, then realized she'd got the acronym wrong, not bondage, dominance and sado-masochism but births, marriages and deaths. She restarted the car, pulling steadily forward with a series of unpleasant crunches. Thinking they were finally on their way, a thoroughly overexcited Gunter started throwing himself around in the back.

Euan dropped out of sight once more to inspect the damage and she heard him groan.

'Is it very bad?' Jenny called out of the window.

'Hard to tell – everything's soaked in turps.' He reappeared looking even grumpier.

Her apologetic offer to replace anything that was damaged was barely audible because Gunter was barking his head off now and making the whole car shake.

'You'd better walk him,' Euan shouted, over the din. 'I'll sort out this mess. Give me the house keys.' He leaned closer to be heard, the smell of shampoo now eclipsed by turps. 'I'll set up while you're gone. Let's hope enough of my kit's salvageable to get started once I've cleaned it off.'

'Shall we rain-check for today?' Jenny leaped gratefully upon the idea.

He was looking up at the house, bathed in pale morning sunlight. 'I'd rather crack on.'

Howling dementedly, Gunter was chewing and clawing at the dog grille, making it clear he was going to eat his way out and drive the car himself if they didn't get going.

155

Paint-flecked fingers rested on her window-sill.

Jenny fished in her bag on the passenger seat for the keys. At least it would get the job done. Determined to wrest back some control, she summoned her speaking-over-the-bell-in-class voice: 'You'll be working in Richard's dressing room. It's upstairs on the—'

'I know where it is.'

'Good. Everything you'll need is already laid out for you there.'

The scowl at the driver's window was lifted by a half-smile. 'Except you.'

Jenny blinked, wondering if she'd heard him right. Was that some sort of threat? Wanting to lay her out cold for running over his stuff was a bit much, she thought, as was his lament over a few snapped Harris brushes and a ripped dust sheet. She chose to ignore it. 'I promise to make copious quantities of tea as soon as I'm back.' She touched the accelerator. 'Won't be long.'

As she drove away, inadvertently mounting the drive's verge and mowing down several box hedges to watch him stoop over the debris of his stuff in the rear-view mirror, she replayed the comment in her head: 'Except you.'

Racketing along the drive and wincing with each bumpy jolt, she remembered the comment from the previous evening: *He's got something lined up. Some old bird who's sweet on him has offered him some work apparently.*

'Oh, God.' She felt her face prickle with colour as she wondered if his comment had insinuated something entirely different. Everything he needed was laid out except her. Was this one of those MILF porn scenarios she'd been allowing herself to fantasize about in her recent build-up to Roger Roger Night? If it was, she was absolutely not about to lift the towel on the rude gardener's bulge. She might be a returning-to-sex divorcee, but she was no way in need of a hired Don Juan.

'I'll give him some old bloody bird,' she snarled, careering out onto the village lane and almost colliding with a rubbish truck. 'We're probably the same bloody age.'

As she drove on, the scenario switched yet again in her head as she reflected that 'bird' might be exactly what Euan deserved if his shaky moral fabric led him to make merry with the Lewises' valuables.

'I gave him the keys.' She groaned, inadvertently accelerating over the road humps. She was already convinced he'd snooped around with his boots on yesterday. Had he been casing the joint?

'C'mon, Jen.' She pulled herself together. 'He's an old friend of the family. Freeloaders don't steal. They have too much to lose.' Nevertheless, she was determined to get back as quickly as she could.

Obstreperous as usual, Gunter chose that morning to go well and truly AWOL. Taking off after a wild duck through the marshes, he was out of sight faster than a cavalry messenger, leaving Jenny fingering the friction burns on her fingers where the loop on his lead had just been.

Hobbling after him, she remembered that she'd left her phone in its charger.

An hour spent chasing distant barks and tracking the local wildlife's squawking panic at least gave her plenty of time to think. She didn't even know Euan's second name. The Lewises had trusted her with their most prized possession and she'd thrown the keys at a virtual stranger. She deserved to be fired. She was in way over her head on this job. She should call Henry and resign.

It took almost another hour to retrieve Gunter from his game-bird hunt, by which time the ibuprofen was wearing off and reed cuts had joined the bramble scratches on her arms and legs. When she finally caught up with him, his lead was long gone, ripped to a six-inch grab handle, so Jenny unthreaded her belt and wrapped it round his collar to tow him back to the car.

There, she found it had a flat tyre, probably punctured reversing over Euan's paint scrapers.

As she battled to change it, assisted by a helpful angler, whom Gunter snarled at from the boot, Jenny imagined Euan loading the Lewises' art into a waiting van, stacking the Hockney and the Beryl Cooks and the Mackenzie Thorpes alongside the high-tech gadgetry and the contents of the safe that was hidden behind the family portrait. No thief would take that portrait, of course. It was too personal, too traceable, those yellow eyes staring happily out from a family tumble in front of the library bookshelves.

Jenny stopped short as a thought struck her. It had been painted in the library. Euan had told her that he knew the house because he had spent a long time painting in the library.

Then she dropped the wheel-nut wrench in horror as it occurred to her what sort of painter he might be.

19

It was almost lunchtime when Jenny got back to the Old Rectory, unfolding herself from the car like a long-distance rally driver after a protracted stony off-road section involving several total rolls and at least one long confinement in neck blocks on a track-side stretcher. Even Gunter, exhausted from his duck hunt, flopped out of the boot, like jelly from a mould. The day was punishingly hot again, no breeze to lift the muggy wall of heat that greeted them. The garage block was like a giant pizza oven.

She found the house keys hanging on the door handle leading to the side path.

Inside, everything seemed exactly as she'd left it. While Gunter drank from his water bowl, like a neap tide lapping at a harbour wall, Jenny hobbled stiffly around checking for missing valuables – nothing obvious – then crab-walked her way upstairs.

Richard Lewis's dressing-room wall was flawless claret once more. Looking at the paintwork around the door, she would never have known Gunter had ever been trapped in there, stripping lining paper like a frenzied DIYer. The repair was only marred by one thing. By the skirting board, so small she had to crouch down to see it, was a small ink doodle resembling a lamp tipped over on its side. It was dated this year.

Euan had signed his work.

Jenny closed her eyes and pressed her forehead to the wall,

ignoring the aches ripping through her as she prised apart her snap judgements and widened her narrow-minded assumptions. The surly Scot that she'd press-ganged into repainting a dog-scuffed wall was the artist whose work Richard Lewis had been collecting for many years. That he hadn't said anything made it doubly humiliating. She'd wasted no time in revealing her hand and showing off that Jenny Rees, house-sitter, was also teacher and copy-editor, a multi-tasking superwoman whose full house had been replaced by three of a kind, her career her most defining success, these days. He'd humoured her, poker-faced, the only card he'd revealed a jack-of-all-trades bluff, hiding a royal flush.

She clambered up and took a tour of Euan's work, starting with the young nude beside her now, legs akimbo, coy hand beckoning, and face suggesting that pleasure awaited all. It was dated that year. This time Jenny felt no cat's cradle of desire tightening, just red-hot embarrassment that she had made such an error. There were two more of his nudes in the dressing room, both dated this year. The landscapes and character studies she counted as she headed downstairs were older, dating back three years or more. There were almost thirty of his paintings in the house.

Humiliation curled at her toes. She was boiling hot, her body prickling in a horse-hair shirt of shame. She knew it shouldn't matter – he'd painted the wall, after all, indicating no hard feelings and that the joke was on her – but it did matter very much. She felt stupidly hurt that he hadn't said anything.

Throwing open the french windows, she breathed deep gulps of air, scented with sweet-pea and swimming-pool. The cover was rucked up at one end, Lilos drip-drying on the diving board. The neighbours had clearly been round for a swim while she'd been out. Gunter bounded outside to do his customary full-pelt patrol of the boundaries, barking excitedly when he disappeared behind the garden cottage yew hedge.

Jenny tried to rationalize the situation. Her assumptions were rarely too far wide of the mark. He could well still be that family friend she'd taken him for, a struggling artist who did odd jobs to help ends meet. He'd definitely been gardening yesterday.

She looked towards the garden cottage where Gunter was still barking, her suspicions rising, wondering what exactly he had been up to there at such an early hour.

Fetching the keys to the cottage, she moved stiffly across the lawn. Gunter had his front paws up on the wall beneath the kitchen window, baying furiously. Above him, Myrtle's ginger cat was perching on the roof of the lean-to hissing back at him, body forming a Greek letter lambda, every hair on end. As soon as it saw Jenny, it shot off.

She slotted the key into the door, then stopped herself. There was really no reason to go inside, just as there was no reason to suspect Euan. She'd already done him a dreadful disservice on that front. And, given her current run of luck, she'd probably flick a light switch, cause an electrical short and burn the whole place down.

As she pulled out the key, she thought she heard a clunking sound coming from inside, but it might have been Gunter, still thundering around the decking on high cat alert.

Determined not to be paranoid, she pocketed the keys and headed back to the house to Google artists named Euan. None of the images she scrolled through came close to matching the extraordinary work in the Lewises' house with a signature like a lamp on its side. Defeated, she flipped down her laptop lid. She had no way of contacting him to apologize for her mistake. It was just one more thing to add to the list of serious cock-ups that she would have to break to the Lewises upon their return.

She went to extract the manuscript she'd hidden in the laundry drawer, wondering how exactly she was going to explain this one: she'd knocked it off the chair when getting Gunter out of Geraldine's study (no need to mention that she was snooping in there) and taken it outside to sort the pages (no need to mention that she'd been reading it avidly); it had blown into the pool (no need to mention Gunter being attached to a table that fell in too). It all sounded plausible.

She called Henry at the agency and tried out this plausible, upbeat version of events.

There was a long silence before he eventually said, 'This is the only copy, you say?'

'I believe so.'

'And it's the book everyone's wanted her to write for twenty years.'

'I think it was supposed to be put in the safe while they're away. But it got left out and—'

'She must not know.'

Lugubrious, laid-back Henry sounded deadly serious. 'The thing is,' he went on, in a hushed voice, 'Geraldine Lewis is not an easy woman to deal with, Jenny. Not an easy woman at all. This could be very bad for us. House-sitting isn't the soft sell it was fifteen years ago. People do it for free. They see it as a second holiday. They're not all professionals like you.'

'What do you want me to do?'

'This script thing is still perfectly readable, you say?'

'The ink hasn't run, but the paper's changed texture. You

162

can't tell the difference so much with the pages I've ironed, but there's at least one that's too water-damaged to disguise.'

'Can you copy it exactly? Trace it or something?'

She swallowed uncomfortably. 'I suppose I could try.'

'Don't let me down. You're among the Home Guardian elite, Jenny.' He made her sound like a fighter pilot being sent back out after a friendly-fire disaster. 'I have possible autumn openings for you in Ibiza and the Riviera, although we'd need to get you top-level security clearance for that one. I've told them you're my top woman.'

Hearing the background rattle of Henry reaching for his blood-pressure pills, Jenny decided it was perhaps best not to mention the ripped family portrait or the mistaken identity of the artist behind it.

Jenny's first few trial runs at forgery were atrocious, not helped by her aching shoulders and the material she was transcribing, which involved a lot of quivering skin and licking from loving cups. Nor could she find the paper and pen that matched the ones Geraldine had used. Her head was soon throbbing and she was relieved when she saw it was already time to walk Gunter again. She decided to shelve the forgery to another day. Shoving everything back in the laundry drawer, she took him to the riverbank, walking in the opposite direction to the houseboats, dragged at predictable speed through tuffets and reed clumps after a scent.

Had she been feeling braver, she might have hauled him round and called in on Perry's houseboat to ask for a contact number for Euan so that she could apologize, but the thought of the Rottweilers, the unfaithful doe-eyed girlfriend and 'old bird who's sweet on him' put her off.

Accelerating her pace to a youthful power walk, Jenny felt a muscle pinch between her shoulder-blades and stay trapped there. Pain ripped through her, and hanging onto Gunter's lead along the riverbank quickly became excruciating. Turning for home, she had to stop at every tree she found, bracing his lead around it so that she could flatten her back against the trunk to try to unlock the spasm.

As she pressed her spine against a fat field maple, she suddenly found herself wondering what Euan had expected to paint if it hadn't been a wall.

20

As soon as she got back to the Old Rectory, Jenny hobbled upstairs to find more painkillers, cursing the empty foil in her handbag. The trapped nerve was like a knife in her back as she checked the Lewises' bathroom cabinets. While the family bathroom housed little more than medicated shampoo and Calpol, Richard's en-suite was gratifyingly stocked with neatly ordered sports wraps and cool packs. The chunky wooden cupboard above Geraldine's basin bore even more treasure, crammed with a boggling array of analgesics, tranquillizers and sleeping pills. Despite the pharmaceutical medley, Jenny couldn't find any paracetamol or ibuprofen, but she spotted the familiar packaging of OxyContin with relief. Jake had been prescribed some when he'd strained a ligament playing rugby. She took two.

She went to her room afterwards to attempt to apply sports strapping around her back while Gunter bounced on the bed, upturning pillows. The thick cohesive wrap was almost impossible to apply alone and, after wrestling for ten minutes, she was left with one breast bound and flattened like an Amazon warrior's, the other dangling, but at least it offered a degree of support.

The sun was low over the garden. Downstairs, it spilled like a golden tide into the kitchen, where Gunter was flourishing a bra he'd extracted from her laundry basket as a gift. He dropped it and barked at two magpies hopping around on the lawn, sending them chattering away.

Grateful for any sign of joy, Jenny let him out and put on some toast.

Realizing that Gunter had distributed the contents of her laundry basket through the house, she started to collect it up, stooping stiffly for shorts and T-shirts in a trail that led through the hallway and into the snug where the Lewis family watched in amusement from the wall as she lowered herself at a strange angle to collect a pair of knickers from the fire irons. Levering herself upright, she stood in front of the portrait, marvelling at its likeness to the couple whom she had met all too briefly, but whose personalities were stamped on her mind. Euan had captured them totally, Richard's cool intellect and pedantry hiding a vibrant warmth, Geraldine's fire and fierce humour concealing old-fashioned earthiness. This man was seriously talented. The humour was just below the surface in those direct gazes, but their expressions were undercut with the sort of truth that could only come from an understanding of human suffering. He'd seen the marriage in crisis, but he'd also seen the shared laughter that kept it alive. Sod the Pre-Raphaelites and their earnest, pouting tragedies, she thought, as she stared at the family tableau. This picture portrays a family who love, laugh and hate on life's domestic merry-go-round like the rest of us. Even Gunter, whom she knew far better than the other subjects, was so perfectly depicted she wanted to reach in to grab his collar and tow him into a tummy-scratching wrestle on the rug alongside her.

'He wouldn't stay still,' a voice said behind her. 'I had to paint him from a photograph in the end.'

Jenny would have jumped sky high, but she was too stiff and only managed a painful lurch. Unable to look at him over her shoulder, she shuffled round, like a jewellery-box ballerina.

Euan was framed in the arched door that led through from the kitchen, the low evening light behind him casting his face in shadow, only the white bolt of hair standing out. 'The back door was open.' He was carrying a battered canvas bag with a large piece of hardboard tucked under one arm. 'You owe me some wine.'

'And an apology,' she said, acutely aware that she was bright red in the face from wrestling with her sports strapping, had one breast flattened and was holding a clutch of dirty lingerie behind her back.

'Accepted.' He stepped back as she lurched towards him, like Quasimodo.

'Why didn't you explain what sort of painter you are?' Not waiting for an answer, she shambled past, heading for the kitchen, cramming the undies into her pocket. 'Your work is brilliant. You deserve every bottle of this.' She reached down for the case sitting by the wine rack, trying not to groan as a spasm of pain shot through her back. 'Take it all with my profound gratitude and embarrassment.'

Still bent over like an aerobics fanatic touching her toes, she saw his legs move behind her and on past the island to the long table, the low sun casting their shadows across the room as he put down the bag and the hardboard. 'Pay me as I paint.'

'You *have* painted,' she blustered, finding she really couldn't lift the wine case. The physical effort at least covered her blushes: he'd obviously been expecting to paint her, not a wall.

'The least you can do is sit for me.' He was rooting through the canvas bag. 'I promise I won't make you look like Rupert Everett in drag, although I may have to use a restricted palette given you've turned most of my gouache into roadkill and thinned everything else with spilled turps. I'm supposed to be starting a commission of an old lady's

167

garden now too – she's putting me up – but most of my greens are history until I can get more paint. Looks like there's plenty left here for skin-tones, though.' Despite the friendly patter, his voice was brusque and workmanlike.

Maybe the woman commissioning the garden picture was the old bird who was sweet on him. Jenny felt slightly mollified, although his reference to 'skin-tones' made her vaguely uncomfortable, and she was now seriously tempted to rush off and put on an all-green outfit. 'You really don't have to paint me.'

'I want to.' He pulled out a sketchbook, wiping its damp leather cover against his T-shirt. 'I like unusual features.' He moved out of the shadows as he stepped closer, his expression serious, the pale eyes already assessing the planes of her face as though it was a piece of architectural salvage he was eager to use. 'Are you okay down there?'

'Fine!' Jenny tried not to be insulted by 'unusual', which sounded one step away from 'interestingly deformed'. She had no desire to become the subject of one of his characterful, raunchy, comedy portraits, filled with cigar-smoking crones and dancing girls. Still stooped over the box of wine, she looked up, trying not to wince as her neck cricked into a tighter knot. 'It's very kind of you to offer to paint me, but I'm afraid I really don't have time. It's entirely my fault for misleading you. You can have all the wine with my blessing.' Now she was stuck at forty-five degrees as her back seized up.

'Are you okay?' He watched her shuffle painfully to the kitchen island to grope for painkillers in her bag.

She tsked as she remembered she'd run out of ibruprofen, and that the pilfered OxyContin should be kicking in soon. 'Bit stiff.' There was no point in lying, given she was stooping like a child who'd just dropped a pound coin. 'I overdid the keep-fit yesterday.'

'Then you need to under-do it for a while.' He was flicking through his sketches, not looking at her. 'Sit for me.'

'I'm like Gunter. I don't do sit.'

On cue, Gunter bounded in from the garden and body-slammed Euan lovingly before picking up the bra he'd discarded earlier and going for a victory lap round the island with it.

'Sit!' Euan commanded.

Gunter sat, dropping the bra.

'You too,' he told Jenny. 'I'll just do a few quick sketches. It won't take long. If they're rubbish we can forget it.' He was still flipping through the sketchbook for a blank page. 'I have an exhibition at the end of summer and need more work to put on show.'

Jenny wasn't sure she liked the idea of her unusual features being put on show, but there was a tetchiness to his tone, a hint of impatient exasperation that made her reluctant to argue any more. It was rude not to co-operate. He had put right the dog damage. Let him draw her hand-me-down Persian cheekbones. He'd soon find she twitched too much to be an artist's model.

'Okay. Perhaps I'll put my feet up on here for a bit.' She shuffled towards the patchwork sofa, kicking the bra out of sight as she passed. 'Don't I keep the picture if I'm paying with wine?'

'Depends how good it is.'

'The wine or the painting?'

He didn't answer, looking at her face intently now. Her mouth seemed to purse and lip-lick of its own accord, her eyes to blink non-stop.

'Do you want me to hold up a pomegranate?' It came out more sarcastically than she'd intended.

He didn't seem to notice, his eyes studying her nose. 'If

169

you like. There's an overgrown old orchard behind the garden cottage.'

'*Woman With Unripe Cooking Apple*,' she mused, now finding her nostrils doing a strange flaring thing they'd never done before. 'Do I take it you're not a trained gardener?'

'I've done a lot of jobs to get by.' He twisted a brief smile, catching her eye before tilting his head to gaze absorbedly at her chin. 'I don't think we need fruit. Don't talk for a minute.'

Increasingly self-conscious, Jenny felt as though she had lockjaw.

She eyed his profile as he turned away to sharpen a pencil with a small knife. His own chin was strongly defined, his nose and forehead set square, straight and masculine, the hair untamed. It made her think of Greek busts, ships' figureheads and the Trafalgar Square lions.

'Have you ever sat for an artist before?' His gaze crisscrossed her face once more and she twitched obligingly.

'Am I allowed to talk now?'

'In moderation.' That half-smile again, which faded as his pencil started flicking this way and that on the page.

'I had my caricature done in Paris once,' she admitted. 'The woman made me look like Gru from *Despicable Me*. My twins thought it was hilarious.'

'How old are your kids?'

The throwaway question she always dreaded, asked with the casual disinterest of a dentist or hairdresser filling the quiet moments between drill and dryer, yet it always made her feel impossibly old. Almost twenty. Twenty! Rachel is my age and can say four, three and eighteen months. Mine are in another continent, drinking more than me, having more sex than me *and* they have more Facebook friends than me.

'I forget.' She tested his concentration.

He didn't react as if she'd said anything out of the ordinary. Instead, he put down his sketchbook and wandered into the main body of the kitchen to pluck up a bottle of Montrachet from the case. 'Let's open one of these.'

'I'd rather have a cup of tea.'

'I didn't offer you tea.' He fetched two wine glasses down from the cupboard, then went in search of a corkscrew, heading straight for the right drawer, she noticed.

'It's a screw top,' she said, with some satisfaction, as he pierced the metal cap.

Jenny didn't want to drink wine or sit as an artist's model, yet somehow she ended up doing both. Lifting her chin, she twitched as best she could.

She hadn't read the warnings on the OxyContin packaging; it took less than a glass of wine for the alcohol to react with the prescription-only pills. The first thing she noticed was that she was pain-free. Then she felt strangely happy. She was talking quite a lot of crap, but she found she couldn't stop blithering on about her wonderful, clever children. All the time Euan looked at her steadily and sketched rapidly. As well as studying her face, he was checking out her body, she noticed, in the familiar, unconscious way men had of dropping their eyes to one's chest. His wasn't the leery three-point check, though: it was more considered and abstract, an artist about to create something magical. She smiled at him enigmatically, imagining herself as Mona Lisa meets Sargent's Madam X. Her voice started to slur and she felt dizzy. Drowsiness swiftly followed. Then sleep mugged her.

VI

Tuesday

21

TO DO LIST

DO something URGENT about depilation
Eat super-food (NOT toast)
Swim 40 lengths
Do not drink
Get rid of Euan
Have sex with Roger

For the second time in a week Jenny awoke still fully clothed on the patchwork sofa with Gunter crammed up against her side, his chin propped on her hip. For a few moments she struggled to piece together what had happened. The dawn chorus was belting out, light stealing across the room. Beneath her T-shirt, she had sticky strapping all over her and one breast hanging out, the other flattened. The counterpane from her bed had been thrown over her. What sort of perverted attack had taken place here?

Then she covered her face with her hands as she remembered sitting for Euan, could still feel his speckled green gaze running over her and her warm, woozy belief that he was unable to resist the instinctive male urge to look at her body. She sat up too fast and her head spun. Her back twinged,

175

and she now recalled wrapping herself in sports strapping when trying to ease her trapped nerve. No wonder Euan had kept looking at her chest. What had she talked to him about? Had she passed out? She had no recollection of what she'd said, or of Euan leaving, but he'd clearly covered her with the bedspread that had been hanging over the Aga rail to dry.

She groaned and slumped back among its soft folds, still woolly-headed and craving more sleep. She hadn't felt so wrecked waking up since she was a dope-smoking student. Two hangovers in as many days, one drug-induced, was not the behaviour of sensible, self-controlled Mrs Rees. This house is a bad influence, she thought groggily.

Hearing a light clunk of a gate closing, she turned her head to look through the french windows. Herself at nine-teen was walking across the dew-dusted lawn, untying her long robe. She blinked hard. Was she awake or asleep?

'Please let me wake up and be her again,' she whispered, closing her eyes and covering them with her arm, listening to the quiet whoosh of a body entering the water at the same time as her own sank beneath the surface of total black-out fatigue.

When she slid the arm away and looked again, the girl had gone. The dew had burned away in the sunlight that was spilling across the lawn, the long shadows of the formal spruces dipping their fingers in the pool's blue surface. Then she spotted Euan's big canvas bag still on the table. He must be planning to come back.

Thirst raging, she made it stiffly to the fridge and threw back the dregs of mineral water from several bottles, press-ing her hot forehead against the cool of the door rim. Then, in a sudden panic, she wondered whether he was still in the house.

Tailed by Gunter, who was gearing up for his walk, she

stumbled around all of the rooms until she was reassured that Euan wasn't there. Her tour took in bedrooms she'd not yet explored, filled with the familiar sights and smells of young children, others arranged as guest suites or unfurnished and filled with boxes of books and files. Showing her around, Gunter bounced from room to room, picking up random gifts to offer her. Carefully putting everything back in place, she made her way to her own room to cut away the sports strapping with nail scissors before standing in the shower with her eyes closed, letting the water pound some of the headache away.

Finding a forgotten twenty-pound note in the back pocket of her jeans cheered her, and she was feeling close to human again by the time she returned to the car after walking on Beacon Common. She drove to the big out-of-town supermarket, which was already open, parking in the shadow of a high wall. Scraping all of her remaining cash together, including the twenty-pound note, she bribed Gunter with the last of the tripe sticks to give herself enough time to dash around the pharmacy section. There, she stocked up on ibuprofen gel, depilation cream, body balm that was on special offer and, to her embarrassment at the till, condoms. She was almost certain Roger would have that one covered – he was a super-safe-all-bases sort of a man – but she wanted to take responsibility too. Buried inside her was a coil, fitted not long before Robin had left. At the time, it had seemed as redundant as a new stereo in a scrapped car, but she hoped it might now justify its existence, even though she would be taking the sensible approach.

'Looks set to be sunny again today,' the check-out girl said chattily.

She watched the Fetherlite packet ping through the barcode reader, wishing she'd thought to go to the self-service check-out. *Look!* the condoms screamed. *I'm going to have sex. It's been three years and I'm finally ready to roll in the hay again.* Hair remover, body balm and pain relief too! This is going to be one mother of a session!

'Yes, lovely,' she said, glancing behind her. A woman was loading twenty loaves of economy sliced bread onto the conveyor-belt, totally uninterested in Jenny's life-changing purchases.

'Do you want a bag for these?'

'Yes, please.'

'Are you sure? It's five pence.'

'Fine!'

As she thrust them hurriedly in, she saw a manager sweating past the tills in a too-tight suit, muttering into a walkie-talkie. 'Mo, some dog's going bananas in the car park trying to eat its way out of a Land Rover Evoque. Put out a call on the loudspeakers. If nobody comes, we'll get the RSPCA.'

Belting back to the car park, Jenny found a small early-morning crowd gathered around the shaking dog car, in which Gunter had already broken through the grille and was alternately crashing from window to window trying to force his way out of the gaps, then tearing the passenger seat to shreds.

'All under control!' She pulled the door open in such a hurry that she dropped the bag and her purchases spilled everywhere.

Puce in the face, she drove back with Gunter quivering on her lap and panting into her face.

To her great relief, there was no sign of Euan at the house. Already boiling hot in her jeans, she went to change, rejecting several outfits before settling on blue cotton Capris and a cool flowered shirt that looked feminine yet professional, with her best balcony bra underneath to emphasize that she had two breasts of fairly equal size. She also put her hair up and added some makeup. If he was going to paint her, she wasn't going to give him an excuse for making her look as wrecked as yesterday.

Jenny then found herself pacing around unable to settle, wondering when and if he would come, and getting increasingly irritated when there was no sign of him. She tried to read *Bonjour Tristesse* in the garden, but couldn't concentrate. She had plenty to do – mostly trying to arrange repairs to the damage wrought by Gunter – but she couldn't settle, too agitated to sit down for more than a few minutes at a time.

When Euan finally loped through the garden gate at close to eleven, she was in a state of high irritation, not gracing him with a hello. 'You should have given me a time.'

'You weren't in a fit state to make appointments.' He stooped to greet an ecstatic Gunter, looking up at her through his mop of hair. 'Are you feeling okay? You seemed pretty out of it.'

'I'm fine. I've just been overtired. Summer term's always a killer.' She stalked towards the house. 'Let's get on with this and make it snappy, shall we? I haven't got all day. Where do you want me?'

'Same place is fine.' He followed her in.

Jenny perched on the edge of the sofa with her hands on her knees, ankles crossed, like a royal in a group shot. Picking up his sketchbook and sitting on the edge of the table, he stared at her for a disconcertingly long time. 'That's just perfect.'

22

After a morning spent trying to sit still and not let the parts of herself that Euan was looking at move involuntarily, Jenny knew for certain that she absolutely hated being drawn. It was a hundred times worse than being photographed: the shutter never clicked its deathly gunshot to put her out of her misery; she remained in the assassin's sights. The pencil merely flicked, the green eyes rose and were lowered but never engaged with hers. He didn't seem to notice her twitching. He was entirely engrossed. Jenny tried to hide her awkwardness behind a barrage of questions, but Euan was even more businesslike and taciturn today.

'Why does your signature look like a lamp on its side?'

'It's an E and an H together.'

'What does the H stand for?'

'Henderson.'

'What part of Scotland are you from?'

'Aberdeen.'

'Is your wife Scottish too?'

'I've no idea. Turn your head to the left. You're very self-conscious, aren't you?'

'I am not!' Mrs Rees could face pupils, governors, head-master and ASBO neighbours with equal verve.

'It's sweet.'

Jenny was so horrified at being called sweet she was momentarily silenced, forgetting to take issue with his glib-ness about his wife.

He was wearing the same threadbare jeans, she noticed, matched with another faded T-shirt that showed off the big, lean triangle of his upper body and his lack of decent stain-removing laundry products. This one was splattered with blue and purple paint.

When she recommended Stain Devils, he looked down at the paint in surprise. '*Nude Reclining in Bluebell Wood*,' he remembered, with a smile, before topping up his glass. 'I can't have worn this since May.'

He'd started on the wine left over from last night as soon as he'd arrived, alternating between Burgundy and coffee in a way Jenny assumed was very *artiste débauché*, but struck her as deeply unhealthy. He had poured her a glass too, but she hadn't touched it, although the coffee was kicking in with high-grade caffeine restlessness as she crossed her legs one way then the other, leaned forward then back, folding and refolding her arms.

'You can read a book, if you like,' he suggested, after a while.

'I'm fine, thanks.'

He was staring at her very intently now, pencil still. 'Take your hair down.'

The way he said it – as curtly as a workman asking one to hold a ladder – made it seem silly to argue, but it didn't stop a tide of self-consciousness stealing through her as she reached up to pull out the clip.

'That's better.' He stared some more, then cast aside his sketchbook and jumped down towards her.

Certain he was going to ruffle her hair, she flinched away, but he merely stooped for her wine glass and handed it to her.

'I really don't want a drink.'

'It's to keep your hands still.'

181

'They'll shake even more if I drink this.'

'You don't have to drink it, just hold it. Your hands are great – so long and angular. We'll work out the pose for the full composition soon,' he explained, settling back in position and picking up his book again, 'but these sketches are a vital reference. Your face has to be at the centre. Its definition is amazing, the skull beneath the skin.'

Depressed that he was clearly entranced by her face for its ageing boniness rather than for its resemblance to Helen of Troy's, Jenny lifted her chin higher, puffed out her cheeks and pressed her tongue to the roof of her mouth: Amalie had once told her that old Hollywood divas did that to knock off five years.

He shot her an odd look but said nothing, drawing on in silence.

Jenny listened to the scratching of his pencil, the pool lapping at its filters and Gunter having a yelping dream out on the decking. A tractor was working in a field beyond the church, whatever contraption it was towing clanking as it came to the headland and needed to turn. The church clock chimed midday.

Fidgeting her way through almost twenty minutes with her chin up, she drank some of the wine, then felt light-headed. She longed to relax.

'Do you mind me moving so much?'

'If I wanted to paint subjects that stayed still, I'd choose fruit and crockery. You're a lot more interesting than a vase.'

'Am I like your usual models?'

'You talk more, but I'll put up with it. Like I said, I need more work to exhibit, and quickly.' He put down the sketchbook and his pencil, then headed outside for a cigarette, leaving her even twitchier. She knew the wine was making her fish for compliments, but he didn't have to be quite so

182

brutally honest. The great-cheekbones line was all she needed.

She watched him stand on the decking sparking up, and felt the cheek-sucking, lung-thumping kick of nicotine desire again. Now she'd had an alcoholic drink, the reflex was at its peak.

Ignoring it, she heaved herself off the sofa with effort, muscles still aching, and crept forwards to look at his sketch-book. There was a drawing of her looking sour, ageing and very cross. Yet it was unmistakably, brilliantly her.

She scuttled to her bag to puff on her electronic cigarette.

23

The interesting thing about posing for an artist, Jenny realized an hour later, is that while they're looking at the angles of your face, the gap between your eyes, trying to capture the dark shadows beneath your cheekbones, you are studying them just as closely.

Since the talk-too-much comment, she had made a conscious effort to be quiet, but it was killing her. She had another go at guessing his age, narrowing it down to mid-forties. He had a strawberry birthmark just visible above his T-shirt neckline that she didn't remember from the boat deck – although she'd probably been gaping too much at the bulge to notice much else – and a habit of raking his hair back with his fingers, then pausing midway as though freeze-framing to think, the long muscles of his forearm taut and grooved. Staring at him made her less self-conscious. She tried to imagine that she was introducing herself – nothing too intimate, just the summary facts he hadn't even asked. Or perhaps he had. She still couldn't remember what she'd talked about the night before.

'Most models don't look directly at me like that,' he admitted after a while, tilting his head back and peering at his sketch. 'If you keep doing it, this will be one of those paintings where the eyes follow you around the room.'

She was embarrassed to have been caught staring. 'When do you start painting?'

'Soon. I'll do it on board.'

'On a boat?' There was no way she was posing on deck between Perry's Rottweilers.

'Wooden board.' He indicated the piece of ply on the table. 'I use it for most of my work. Cheaper than canvas, easier to transport, less liable to rip.'

She looked away guiltily, spilling wine on her lap. Did he know about the ripped portrait?

But he gave no indication that he did, his face frowning in concentration as he flipped through his sketches. 'I'll probably start that tomorrow. We need to establish a pose first.' He glanced up. 'I like the way you're reclining now. That could work.'

Having slipped into a groggy afternoon wine slump between two velvet cushions, Jenny sat up again, spilling more wine, her back aching. She wasn't sure she could take being stared at for much longer. 'Tomorrow's not good for me. Can't we wrap this up today?'

'Nope.'

'So . . . how long do these things usually take?'

'A week.'

'That's too long.'

'Busy?'

She nodded emphatically. 'Wednesday's not great.' The pool men are coming. I can't be seen posing around on a sofa, like Dora Maar sitting for Picasso. 'And I can't do Thursday.' I'll be spending all day in preparation for, then later enjoying, sex with a man named Roger. 'Or Friday.' I will be recovering from aforementioned sex with Roger and ensuring all evidence is removed before the cleaning ladies come. 'Or Saturday.' I have no plans for Saturday, but it pays to look busy. Besides, I anticipate that I will have unleashed the beast in Roger and we'll be back at it. 'And next week's hectic.' Meeting my oldest friend Rachel for lunch, more Roger-ing.

'We'll work round it all.' He headed outside for another cigarette without apology.

Jenny tottered stiffly and rather tightly to her feet and went for another puff on her electronic replica, then limped to the loo, wincing with every step, now seizing up again. Reaching behind her for the loo roll felt like going for the ultimate burn in a fitness class. She needed another painkiller. Scratching her bikini stubble distractedly, she thought about her pharmacy booty bought in honour of Roger Roger Night and longed for privacy to start preparing, a ritual to which she needed to devote twenty-four hours, not sit on a sofa having her boniness captured for immortality.

'You have to get rid of him,' she told herself firmly. 'You were flattered by the idea of a portrait and wanted to help him out by way of apology, but not if he's going to make you look like Dot Cotton. Don't let him bully you into it. Imagine he's a fifteen-year-old boy doodling his way through a detention you're covering for a colleague.'

Returning, she heard the tell-tale splashing and giggling of the neighbours using the pool. Gunter was barking at them through the french windows.

'Aren't those two terrific?' Euan's voice said behind her. 'Did you know they're called Bill and Hilary Clifton?' He chuckled. 'I just love that.'

Jenny shuffled round, surprised to find him there. She'd thought him still outside, but he'd emerged from the utility room carrying a clutch of brushes, bringing a strong smell of turps and soap as he strode back to the table, glancing outside and smiling at what he saw. From the long shadows criss-crossing the table end, Jenny guessed the duo had the pool noodles out again. 'They're far too old to behave like that.' She hugged herself and stayed behind the island unit.

'It's impossible to draw you without a disapproving

expression.' He picked up his board and a chalk pencil as he perched back on the table. 'Come and sit down. I'll go as fast as I can, given your busy week ahead.' His lips twitched, although whether this was irritation or amusement was hard to tell. 'Strike a pose, Mrs Rees.'

Jenny stayed behind the kitchen island, reluctant to take up a position with a front-seat view of the pool. 'Actually, I think I prefer to stand. You can paint me here. How about this?' She splayed her hands on the island, leaning against it with a smile, resembling a celebrity cook on a book jacket.

'That doesn't work for me.' He shook his head, chalk end pressed to his chin. 'And you can't hold that shape hour after hour with a bad back.'

She pulled up a stool and perched on it, replicating the pose. 'There!'

'Far too awkward. You'll look like July in a naked WI calendar.'

She felt her sinews tauten. 'I don't do naked.'

The half-amused, half-irritated expression settled on his face again. 'This exhibition is of nudes, Mrs Rees.'

Jenny forced a laugh. His sense of humour was dry to the point of parched, but she was in control now. He could paint her fully clothed and in Delia Smith pose or not at all.

Gunter was still barking and bouncing. Euan called him back, but he took no notice, steaming up the window-panes as he bayed at the frolicking duo.

'If he barks enough, maybe they'll go away.' Jenny watched a pool noodle fly onto the decking, then averted her eyes as a hairy pair of male legs chased it, crowned in tight red Lycra that was part Speedo, part slingshot. 'Please don't tell me that's a mankini?' she breathed.

Euan was looking at her impatiently, his chalk tapping on the board. 'Are we starting this thing or not?'

'Not until they go away.'

The tap halted. 'If you want more privacy, we could use the cottage. I've painted in there before.'

She was astonished he would even suggest it. 'We couldn't possibly take that liberty.'

He was looking at her very intently now. 'It's supposed to be haunted by a Victorian wraith, but she never bothered me. Have you been inside it yet?'

Perhaps a ghost was behind the messages on the mirrors, Jenny thought, with a shudder, and had trashed the place. She wasn't about to admit to letting herself into the cottage without permission and taking snapshots of the period features, and was immensely grateful that no small, cold, undead hand had gripped her arm. 'Let's stay here.'

'Fine.' His dark brows lowered crossly. Casting the board aside, he loped towards the french windows and reached for a lever that lowered built-in blinds; Jenny hadn't known they existed. Soon the room was striped with fine shadows, the cavorting couple and the pool reduced to a striated reef. Finding himself faced with nothing but cane slats, Gunter let out a surprised harrumph and stopped barking.

Euan turned back to Jenny, who was still holding her celebrity-chef pose, struggling to adjust to the instant change from sunny designer kitchen to Caribbean beach hut. Transformed into a tiger-stripe silhouette, he made his way to a small touch-screen on the wall that she'd assumed had something to do with the central heating. 'Richard Lewis might seem like a nineteenth-century relic, but he's very fond of modern wizardry.' He pressed the screen and Chopin's Nocturnes flooded the space around them, making Gunter dive for cover beneath a chair. 'This house is full of gadgets. Geraldine can't work any of them.'

The sun-streaked shadows and the music had changed

the atmosphere in the room, making Jenny uncomfortably aware of his proximity and maleness.

She cleared her throat, trying to sound cheerily conversational amid the seductive arpeggios. 'Yes, Richard said the only way to get her to remember the alarm was to have it written over the door. Have you known them both long?'

He nodded at the sofa, which was criss-crossed with light. 'Make yourself comfortable, and then you can ask me questions.' His tone was casual, offhand, even, and he was preoccupied, rubbing the surface of his painting board with a sanding block, yet the sudden intimacy of the setting triggered a nervous hot pulse in her wrists.

Increasingly ill at ease, Jenny perched pertly on the sofa, back in her royal-christening position.

Tutting, he strode over, grabbed all the cushions from one end and threw them behind her, along with the antique blue bedcover that was still folded over one arm. 'Snuggle into that lot.'

Now, propped like a small child with tonsillitis having a duvet day, Jenny found she was a lot more comfortable than she had been in hours, but she wasn't about to say so. Euan poured more wine. Sidling out from under the chair, Gunter lumbered up onto the sofa beside her and stretched his chin on her legs, big eyebrows shifting as he looked around anxiously, still worried by the music.

'If he stays there, this will be worth twice as much.' Euan reached into his pocket for a phone and took a photo of them both. 'Nudes and dogs always fetch a high price. Just look at Pierre Bonnard.'

'I don't do naked,' she reminded him quickly. 'Who's Pierre Bonnard?'

'French post-Impressionist, founder of a group known as Les Nabis: "*En ta paume, mon verbe et ma pensée*".'

189

'In the palm of your hand, my word and my thoughts,' she translated, trying to remember where she'd heard it before.

'Intimism was his thing.' He narrowed his eyes, looked around and flicked on a few lights. 'He was an Intimist.' He picked up his board, leaving the word hanging in the air. It sounded distinctly depraved.

Jenny pulled a cushion in front of her and hugged it, grateful that the lights had banished the beach hut in favour of something more Malibu, albeit worryingly closed-porn-set. 'What movement do you belong to?'

He was sitting on the table again, sliding left and then right to get the sightline he wanted, his feet propped on a chair, the board angled on his knee, speckled green gaze eyeing her over it. 'Right now, it's nudes and dogs. Can we lose the cushion?'

'I'm *not* taking my clothes off,' she said, shoving it aside.

'Sure.' He was tilting his head and focusing on her left arm. Jenny had a feeling he wasn't listening. She let the music roll over her for a bit, the piano notes dancing around the room from many hidden speakers. The wine had made her sleepy again and she was fighting not to yawn. Gunter's warm, solid bulk grew heavy against her as he decided that Chopin was okay.

She looked up at Euan's pictures on the walls around her, so many bearing his colourful style and sideways signature. 'Is Richard Lewis the Saatchi to your Hirst?'

'Hardly.' His laugh had a bitter edge and he reached for his glass.

'How did you meet?'

Euan spoke in the same way that he drew, in short intense bursts interspersed with long pauses to stare at her. Five years earlier, he explained, Richard Lewis had been in

190

Dundee on a promotional tour for his much-lauded biography of William Makepeace Thackeray.

'A wonderful book,' Jenny enthused.

'I'll take your word for it.' Euan gazed at her chin for ten seconds before carrying on. With a rare afternoon to himself, Richard had taken a walk around the city, visiting the McManus collection and wandering the side-streets near Murraygate in search of a gift for his wife, at which point a heavy downpour had sent him through the nearest shop door and he'd found himself in a tiny gallery looking at two of Euan Henderson's paintings.

'It was more of a down-at-heel picture framer's, to be truthful – lots of Monet prints and tasteful watercolours of the Tay. I'd persuaded the owner to hang a couple of mine as a punt, but he'd been badgering me to come and pick them up, said there was no demand for them. But that day, Richard Lewis bought both and asked for my number. When he rang to see if I had anything else to sell, I thought it was a wind-up.

'I was renting a cottage up in the Angus glens at the time. I remember the taxi arriving close to midnight – the fare must have cost him twice what he'd already paid for the paintings. I thought he was a tosser.' He grinned. The Montrachet had sharpened his tongue as well as loosening it. 'He'd come straight from addressing a theatre full of book lovers and was tanked on cheap wine, and he bought practically everything I had, which was more than usual because I'd stayed put a while.'

'That was some gift for his wife.'

He shook his head. 'She's not the art lover. He is.' He narrowed his eyes again, and Jenny waited for more, then realized he was just studying her face, changing the pencil marks on the board. He sketched on for a long time in silence, the story apparently concluded or forgotten.

191

'So how did you end up coming down here?' she asked, helping herself to a long draught of wine, fascinated by Richard Lewis's patronage.

'He stayed in touch – pretty dedicated of him, given I move around a lot,' he said, then stopped suddenly, looking at her eyebrow: his mind had abstracted itself as he switched focus to another part of her anatomy. The story resumed as he sketched on. 'He kept badgering me to produce more paintings. For all that academic cool, he's like a terrier when he gets hold of an idea . . . ' He fell silent as he spent a long time studying her ear, brows furled, as though wondering how it had got there.

'He bought a few more pieces,' his focus moved back to the board, chalk moving fast, 'not much, because he was encouraging me to show my work and that meant me keeping the best stuff. And he introduced me to some gallery owners he knew. They all love him. He collects it pretty obsessively, as you can see.' He nodded around the walls. 'Especially when drunk.' He stopped abruptly, attention on her right shoulder for ten seconds or more.

'Since then, I've had work shown in group exhibitions in Edinburgh and York, and some contemporary galleries round here keep my originals on sale.' He drew in sweeping movements now as he outlined the body. 'Then the chance of the solo exhibition down here came up. The only proviso was that they want nudes. It meant preparing a lot of work, but Richard offered me studio space, eager to pluck me from obscurity into the cushiest commercial gallery in the M40 corridor, offering me a base for six months so I could afford to keep enough back for the exhibition. He offered me extra work on top in lieu of rent, including commissioning a big family portrait for his fifteenth wedding anniversary. Frankly I wasn't keen, but he can be a persuasive bugger.'

Jenny found his attitude abrasive. 'If you ask me, Richard Lewis is an amazing patron. Don't take this the wrong way, but I wouldn't give you extra work as a gardener.'

'Neither would I.' He laughed.

'I thought he said you had Chelsea golds?'

His face was hidden behind a flop of hair as his pencil scratched. 'I have Chelsea boots and gold ochre. Painting the Lewises' combined skiing tans took a lot of gold ochre.'

'A portrait is a lovely gift for a wedding anniversary.' She glanced wistfully across the big living space to the kitchen, where the red Aga seemed to pulse like a heart. 'You should be honoured to be asked.'

He looked up, chalk still moving as his eyes ran along her legs, like a horse dealer at an auction. 'I was so grateful, I ended up painting two.'

Jenny felt her nerve ends tighten, wondering if he had noticed that one was missing. 'Why did you paint two?'

There was a long silence. He didn't look up from outlining her feet, his jaw tight. 'It was a buy-one-get-one-free offer.'

'Are you offering me the same deal?' She swigged more wine.

Still he didn't look up. 'If you take your clothes off maybe.'

Her face flooded red. 'That's not going to happen.'

'Shame. I could use some *Nude with Dog* money.' He looked up, green eyes amused. 'And taking your clothes off for an artist is very liberating, they say.' His Scottish voice deepened with instinctive lazy flirtation. 'I think you'd be surprised how good it feels.'

Jenny's cheeks prickled with colour spots – he had made it sound positively orgasmic. 'I'm not an exhibitionist.'

'I paint in private, let the gallery put on the exhibition.'

'It's voyeurism.'

'It's liberation.'

'The day Gunter walks to heel past a cat, I'll strip off.' The joke didn't quite work and she felt immediately foolish, hearing something unfamiliar in her voice. Attention-seeking, unpractised flirtation in return, as clumsily executed as market-stall bargaining.

'I'll hold you to that.'

'Nobody can hold Gunter.' She set the wine glass aside and resumed her pose, as tense as a six-year-old trying to hold the fourth position in a ballet exam.

'Richard's too soft on him.' He was looking her straight in the eyes now, an unblinking direct challenge.

'Fifteen years is crystal anniversary,' she said, flustered. It was the first thing that had come into her head. She'd given Robin two champagne flutes hand-engraved with their initials. He'd given her a cheque a day later and told her to treat herself.

Euan stared at her for an unblinking minute, straight into her eyes, his gaze so intense that she was certain he could see right into her head to that strained, loveless night drinking vintage cava out of heavy-based crystal before heading to a new local restaurant that she'd booked, trying to think of something to say beyond commenting on their food and the décor, and ordering more wine, eventually coming home for drunken, perfunctory sex.

But Euan's gaze simply returned to the board, one eye half closed in concentration as he added detail to her face.

Jenny snatched up her glass and drained it, thinking about Carla's order to take to the dance-floor. You're going to have sex this week, she reminded herself. It will not be perfunctory. Roger Roger Night will be good. You are a woman reclaiming her life. You could strip off right now and pose naked if you wanted to – if your bikini line wasn't such a mess or your body quite so unloved – and nobody could tell you not to. Apart from Mum, who would be horrified, and the kids, of course, and most of the school staff, although the head of geography would probably be thrilled, given his lunges on the last year-ten field trip. And Roger. What would Roger make of it?

She tried to imagine him studying a picture of her naked as she was sitting now, the pose that was everyday and relaxed in blue Capris transformed into something new and strange. Roger's face had two default settings, happy and happy-ish, the blue eyes shy, ever-alert and quick to blink. On reflection, she decided the sight of her on the Old Rectory sofa in the buff was unlikely to be one that triggered happy Roger. His taste in art was very conservative. The one time they'd visited the Ashmolean together, he'd swept her past an exquisite Matisse nude as fast as a motorist accelerating past rubberneckers at a road accident, swerved around a sensual Lucian Freud and positively dodged a homo-erotic Raphael. A depiction of her muffin belly and saggy thighs sprawled on a sofa, captured with comic warmth in oil over gouache would never hang and be admired over his mantelpiece. Not that it would be admired anywhere because she was staying as fully clothed as an outgoing principal posing to join her predecessors hanging along a college staircase.

'Relax,' Euan told her.

She concentrated hard on relaxing, every nerve and muscle of her body straining with the effort. She was so relaxed she was getting cramp.

'Let's take a break.' He reached for his cigarette packet and slid down from the table. Catching sight of figures still moving behind the slatted blinds, he headed through the house to step outside the front door.

Increasingly aware of his complete dispassion, Jenny felt

silly for being so wound up. An artist didn't judge her body as she judged it, on a scale she'd created and on which it scored so low. He wanted to interpret her shape and skin-tones in brush-strokes and pigments; he had no personal interest in it whatsoever. This was all about professional gain. Euan Henderson wanted to paint nudes for a forthcoming exhibition. If the Va Va Vacuum ladies offered to strip, he'd probably be just as willing to prop the board on his knee and sketch.

Jenny still wasn't going to take her clothes off for him, but she could slump back into the cushions and let the wine and music wash over her without the tension prickling.

Realizing that she was in danger of drinking too much to drive Gunter to the river later – and that they hadn't had any lunch – she forced herself to get up and investigate the fridge, pulling out cheese, olives and cold meat, along with a half-baked ciabatta, which she lobbed into the Aga, and a bag of elderly salad that still looked edible.

On food alert, Gunter bounded in from sharing Euan's cigarette break, nose lifting eagerly. By the time Euan followed, Jenny had unpacked everything onto plates and slates, the salad rejuvenated with red pepper and pumpkin seeds, the ciabatta sliced, hot dough-scented steam clouding above it.

'You're full of surprises, Mrs Rees.' He shared a slice of Black Forest ham with Gunter.

'I can arrange deli food. It's a skill passed down through generations of women in my family.' She held up her hands modestly, sounding like Maureen Lipman cast as a Jewish mother. 'Eat. And don't feed titbits to the dog.'

Having piled his plate, he opened another bottle of wine.

She covered her glass. 'I must drive the dog car later.'

'I'll walk him,' he offered, pouring it through her fingers.

She laughed in shock, pulling her hand away. 'You *certainly* can't drive.'

'I'll walk him round the village.'

'He's banned. He chases a neighbour's cat.'

'I'm retraining him to walk to heel in front of cats, remember?' His eyes creased at the corners and he turned away to open one set of french windows. The neighbours had departed and the day was hotter than ever.

24

They ate at the table under the pergola, crammed rather too tightly together under the awning, the butter on their plates already melted, the cheese sweating and the salad wilting.

Jenny tried for more small-talk, but Euan was increasingly focused on the big picture.

'I hate art snobs,' he said, when she asked him about his route to becoming an artist. 'I won a place at Glasgow School of Art at eighteen – had I gone, I'd probably create fuck-off weird installations that only critics and intellectuals like.' He ranted about Brit Art for several minutes with sharp-tongued irreverence, his insight and wit easy on the ear, his face expressive and compelling, mouth always on the move, eating, talking, laughing, revealing very white teeth with a single gold filling.

'Why didn't you go to Glasgow?'

He ate a hunk of bread and washed it down with wine. 'My dad wanted me to man up first, travel the world, get my heart broken. I did as I was told – we all did.' A shadow of pain crossed his face. 'Dad said Henderson men's hands were built for doing not drawing. My brother was overseas working on oil rigs. He swung me a free flight and a few months' work before I took up my place at Glasgow. They both wanted to toughen me up, get this art shit out of my system.'

'But it didn't work?'

He shrugged. 'I never set foot in an art school. I've had no formal training beyond Highers. I painted my passage basically. It was years before I saw Scotland again.'

'How long did you travel for?'

'I still am travelling,' he grinned, ripping off more bread, 'but if you're asking how long I was away from Britain, over twenty years.'

She dropped her fork back on her plate. 'Where did you go?'

'Around and about.' He made it sound like a ramble along a few footpaths. 'I liked South and Central America best – I was there seven years in total. South East Asia was exploited, Africa depressing. Europe cost too much and half the Pacific Rim is Lego towns perched on fault lines. I painted wherever I went and sold enough to get by. When I ran out of money, I took whatever jobs I could – mostly teaching English. It sounds romantic, but it seldom was.'

'What brought you back?'

'My dad was dying.'

'I'm sorry.'

'He had a good life. He liked having a wandering minstrel for a son – he was fifteen years in the Merchant Navy before he started working on North Sea rigs, so his compass had turned full circle a few times before he settled.'

'And your mum?'

He held up one finger. 'The fixed point around whom we all revolve.'

'She must have missed you?'

'She's a tough character, Mum. When you have five boys, you have to be.'

'Tell me about your compass turning full circle.'

'I'm the fourth Henderson son. Dad was away on the rigs a lot when I grew up. We ran riot in a big house outside Aberdeen. Mum's a strict Presbyterian who did local

199

book-keeping to make extra money. At eight, I followed my three older brothers to a boarding school where days alternated between prayer, rugby, Latin and having the living daylights beaten out of you. The art master was a sweet old pouf who encouraged me to apply to art school. My dyslexia meant I was kept down so I finished last, a year after my baby brother, Cal. By then he and two more brothers were all at Aberdeen University. They're the tribal trio. Our eldest brother, Mack, had just qualified as a civil engineer. It was him I followed to the Western Australia to rig up oil pumps before going to Glasgow. He said it would be fun.

'It wasn't fun. It was bloody hot and hard work. We ended up in a sheep station miles from anywhere. The guy who owned it was a shit, intent on screwing the oil company for every penny. His two daughters were the only reason we hung around. They were something else. Mack and I shared a bet that we'd get one over on the old man by getting them into bed. He got a black eye for his efforts. I got my heart pounded into the dust.' Pain crossed his face again, fleeting and visceral. 'When the job ended, Mack moved on to Saudi Arabia and I was supposed to come back to Glasgow to become an art snob. But I went to Sydney instead.'

'To paint?'

He shook his head, smiling ruefully as he mopped up vinaigrette with his bread. 'I worked in a bar in Kings Cross, but I kept getting caught up in fights. Then I met a girl from Sweden who was about to travel up the Gold Coast and invited me along. It's easy to fall into travelling at that age. No agenda, no dependants, no ambitions beyond a bed for the night, a meal and an adventure.'

'What about your family? Your Glasgow scholarship?' She thought uncomfortably of Jake, travelling so long with his girlfriend. The idea of him just carrying on and not coming home was unbearable.

'The tribal trio were enough for Mum to contend with, and I knew Dad didn't want me to be an artist. I sent home a card from every country I visited. I had a broken heart and a British passport. It can get you a long way at eighteen.'

She listened in amazement as he talked about his long time on the road, his restless desire to keep moving. 'I went through bouts of settling down, but it never worked out.'

Jenny sensed that a lot more hearts had been broken, if not his, but she was wary of asking. There was something very guarded about the way he was speaking, as though a tragedy sat at the centre of it. She wondered where his wife came in.

'You said you settled seven years in the Americas?'

He nodded, green eyes impassive as pond water. 'Mexico.'

'Did you find your Frida Kahlo there?'

A smile hooked up the side of his mouth. 'I'm no Diego Rivera.' A forkful of salad hovered by his mouth as he looked her in the eye. 'You remind me of her.'

'Great,' she muttered, distinctly recalling that the Mexican artist was a bisexual Communist in need of tweezers and upper-lip bleach.

'She was beautiful and fierce,' he said, eating the salad, 'friends with Trotsky and slept with Josephine Baker.'

'Two great life ambitions for which I was born too late.'

Both corners of his mouth matched in a gratifying smile of laughter. He reached for his wine. 'I like you, Jenny Rees.'

Embarrassed, she demanded, 'Did you ever have kids?'

He closed one eye, smile transforming to the irritated amusement she'd started to recognize, wine glass hovering. 'Not to my knowledge, but it's quite possible.'

She stiffened, offended by his irresponsibility. If she could buy condoms with the last of her cash, he certainly should have been able to. He was an abomination from another era – a hard-drinking, cigarette-smoking sexual nomad, with no morals. His poor Presbyterian mother must be appalled to have this self-styled Hemingway as a son, now free-loading off the Lewis family – and, by association, off her.

'And did you ever get over your broken heart?'

'You ask a lot of questions.' He drained his glass, just plain irritated now, and Jenny saw she'd overstepped the mark.

'People interest me. Most people I meet like talking about themselves, I find.'

'So you're a secret voyeur too.'

'It's hardly the same thing!'

'I disagree. Asking someone personal questions is just like asking them to take their clothes off and pose for a painting. It's peeling away conceits to show the naked truth. I'd rather strip off any day. That's a lot easier. Nothing feels more naked than revealing the truth about your past. Ask me anything else and you'll be talking to my skin.'

Her blush was like a furnace now. 'I was just making polite conversation.'

'Trust me, my love life is not a polite conversation,' he said quietly.

'We'd better get on.' She stood and gathered up the plates. 'Do you want more coffee?'

He stayed out and smoked a cigarette. Jenny snatched her electronic replacement to her lips for a few puffs, then washed up and made very strong coffee. Gunter had already been inside to polish off the cheese, ham, butter and bread she hadn't put back in the fridge, although he'd left the olives and the last of the salad.

Hearing a splash, she hurried to the door and saw a long streak of tanned muscle powering an underwater length of the pool.

Please don't let him be naked, she willed.

As he flipped direction at the far end and swam back towards her, she could definitely make out two taut pale buttocks amid the darker skin. 'He *is* naked!' Hurriedly she backed inside.

The stereo system was playing Gershwin now, which was far too sultry and suggestive for her overwrought state. She hurried to the touchpad and tapped on 'track' until it shuffled to some suitably funereal Mahler.

Gunter came sloping inside again to cool off, tongue lolling out of a guilt-free smile as he greeted her with a cheesy burp. He cocked his head at the Mahler and decided it was safe enough to heave himself up on the sofa. Jenny joined him.

Her coffee, too disgustingly strong to drink, went cold as she sat there wondering what to do about the naked artist in the pool. Waiting for him looked a bit sad, but she really wanted him to hurry up and finish his painting so he would go away.

The wine and the heat had made her incredibly sleepy. She closed her eyes and listened to a few bars of Mahler, now accompanied by Gunter snoring and the scratch of chalk against board.

She snapped her eyes open.

Euan was studying her intently, fully clothed and perfectly dry. Had she dreamed him swimming? Had she dreamed lunch? Lying on her ankles, Gunter smelt strongly of French cheese and chorizo.

'What time is it?' she asked, unable to believe she could have been sleeping.

'Afternoon,' he said vaguely. 'I prefer drawing you asleep. You don't ask questions and your face loses all the hate.'

'What hate?' She forced her face into a sleep-creased

approximation of benign. Vivaldi's *Four Seasons* was playing in place of Mahler. The sun was low over the shrubbery, so it must be close to six. She'd been asleep for at least two hours.

'You tell me.' He tapped the pencil against his chin. 'What do you hate so much?'

'I have no idea what you're talking about. I'm a very loving and forgiving person.'

'I think something or somebody hurt you very badly, made you turn in on yourself.'

'Not at all!' She sat up irritably, glaring at the striped sunlight and shadows on the wall that now reminded her of prison bars.

'Nothing feels more naked than revealing the truth about your past.' His focus returned to the board.

There was a fresh bottle of wine open beside him. Was that bottle three or four in payment so far? They had to be halfway through.

'You drink too much,' she told him.

'I prefer drawing you when you're asleep,' he repeated. 'Close your eyes.'

Jenny guessed it was better than 'Take your clothes off.' She scrunched her eyes closed, still sitting upright.

'Lie back.'

'I'm not going to sleep again,' she insisted, as Vivaldi's violins sang around her – the Adagio movement of 'Spring', so light and sweet, a fecund foreplay interrupted by the angry hornets' buzz of strings that echoed the Presto to come, music so impossibly sexy she'd never sit still.

'Of course not.' The chalk swept to and fro. She imagined he must be drawing her hair, still gratifyingly thick, if practical and neatly bobbed, any grey streaked out with low-lights once every six weeks, courtesy of Luca, her stylist. Her sister, who'd been battling menopause with soya milk and red clover for three months and eschewing her beloved Molton Brown for fear of going yet balder, now had a parting widening like the Red Sea, surfed with a white tide each side. Ageing was a hideous process, Jenny reflected.

'There's hate again.' Euan sighed.

She snapped her eyes open. 'It's justified.'

'Tell me.'

'I'm not going naked in mind or body.'

'So I'll paint both from my imagination.'

'You will not!'

'Which are you going to show me first?'

'Fully Clothed Woman Reclining On Sofa. With Dog. Saying nothing.' She closed her eyes, feigning sleep.

He laughed and drew on as Vivaldi's 'Summer' came over the speakers, predictably potent with breathless sex appeal. Jenny gritted her teeth throughout, grateful when 'Autumn' took over, its Allegro as safe and predictable as the opening credits of the antiques show it accompanied. But then the melancholy Adagio cut through her self-control, a harpsichord string at a time, the saddest of laments, calling a frosty, smoky halt to life in full bloom. She turned her face away. The next movement was back to antiques shows and she started to drift among the sun-soaked scatter cushions.

When Jenny woke up again, Euan was no longer perching on the table with his board. Two empty wine bottles stood sentry where he had been. Sitting up groggily, she registered that her lips and tongue were dry, her chin damp, and realized, to her shame, that she must have been asleep with her mouth open.

The blinds were shut, the sunlight streaming in from a low

angle, striping the upper walls and ceiling. At first she thought he was outside having another cigarette, but Gunter was missing too.

One of her legs had gone to sleep. Pins and needles raging, she extracted her feet from beneath her thighs and hopped across the room to open the french windows.

There was a note on the table. *Walking dog past cats. Back in ten. Prepare to strip off. E.*

When half an hour had passed with no sign of Euan or Gunter, Jenny tried not to worry. Instead she occupied her increasingly drumming fingers by Googling 'Intimism', the movement he'd talked about. She was relieved to find that it was an early twentieth-century artistic trend for painting subjects in rooms, or 'an intense exploration of the domestic interior'. Most of the examples were fully clothed ladies drinking tea or flower arranging, although a few were admittedly lolling nakedly on beds or in baths with dogs curled up nearby. She loved the brightness of Pierre Bonnard's work, which had echoes of Euan's paintings.

She then Googled Frida Kahlo and was depressed to see the mono-brow and moustache just as she'd remembered; Diego Rivera had been no more appealing. They were hardly Javier Bardem and Penélope Cruz. She was certain she and Roger made a more engaging pair.

She checked her gmail account (offers from Wendy at Lakeland and Johnnie Boden), Facebook (more home baking and selfies, plus 'shares' of starving dogs, abused children and romantic proposals that had gone viral on YouTube), and her horoscope (surprisingly good). When he still hadn't returned with Gunter as the church clock struck eight, she started to get seriously worried and annoyed.

How would she explain this to Richard Lewis? Should she

go in search? The dog was in her charge. Euan might be a friend of the family, but he struck her as decidedly unreliable.

Panic rising, she Googled 'Euan Henderson' (also spelled Ewan and Ewen). It threw up an enigmatic smattering of pictures and reviews for the original spelling, a lot of ceramic pots for alternatives. There were no obvious links to dog theft or kidnapping.

Euan finally burst through the garden gate as dusk fell, dragged towards the house by Gunter. Both were covered with burrs, mud and brambles.

'You can keep your clothes on.' He held up his hands as he let Gunter go. 'He is never going to walk past a cat. Nor, as I have just discovered, will he walk past a bitch on heat.'

'I thought he was . . . ?' She mimed scissors.

'Clearly not.' He flashed a weak smile, wiping away sweat.

'Did they . . . ?' She mimed something between an eighties Nescafé ad shake and an obscene gesture.

'There was a logistics problem that bought us some time, and the owner carried the Yorkshire terrier to safety. Middle cottage next to Myrtle. Best avoided.' His forehead was creased with apology.

'You know Myrtle?'

'Everybody knows Myrtle,' he said, looking up at the dark sky, eyes gleaming in the gloom. 'I'll start painting tomorrow. There's no light left now.'

'I'm quite busy tomorrow. Can't we finish now?'

He looked at his watch. 'Depends how naked you're prepared to go.'

'You just said—'

'Nothing feels more naked than revealing the truth about your past, remember?' He gave her a half-smile. 'I told you my story. Pour me a drink and tell me some truths, Jenny.'

'It's "I'll tell you some lies",' she corrected. Still intensely irritated that he'd abducted Gunter for some local canine sharking, she was in no mood to ruin her essential detoxing sleep in the build-up to Roger Roger Night by watching Euan Henderson wave a glass of red wine around being offensive.

'On second thoughts, I'd rather have a quiet night in alone. Thank you for walking the dog for me while I was having a nap.' She cleared her throat, trying not to think of the dribbling narcoleptic he'd left on the sofa. Her school-marm side took over. 'And I know you meant well, but on reflection, my letting anybody else exercise Gunter is an abuse of the trust Richard Lewis and his family invested in me. As is sharing my personal secrets.'

He stepped back, brows lowering. 'If that's how you feel.'

'I prefer to keep this professional.'

'Of course.' He held up a hand and backed towards the gate. 'You're sitting this house, not for me.'

She'd offended him. Jenny felt suddenly embarrassed. 'I might manage to sit for a short while tomorrow if you come early!'

'Sure.' The gate swung shut.

A niggling current across her skin told her she'd got that wrong, although her thick armour of self-preservation remained without a chink.

It was almost dark and stars were already piercing a purple sky. A huge full moon was rising in its midst. A bat flew across it, sending Jenny rapidly inside to where Gunter was waiting to goose her and demand supper, looking unrepentant and smelling strongly of ditch.

'Nothing feels more naked and revealing than telling the

208

truth about yourself,' she told him, beckoning him to follow her through to the wet room where she gave him another wash-down, picking yet more burrs and brambles from his fur. 'So what's with the Yorkshire terrier? Why the tiny bitch? You're such a cliché, Gunter.'

He gave her a mournful look.

'You're on the landing tonight,' she insisted. 'I have my own seduction to prepare for. Roger Roger Night is minus forty-eight hours and counting . . . '

VII

Wednesday

25

TO DO LIST

DO something EXTREMELY URGENT
about depilation
Eat super-food (NOT toast)
Swim 40 lengths
Do not drink
Quit electronic smoking
Treat your body as a temple for next
24 hours
Have SEX with Roger

If Jenny dreamed about her younger self swimming naked, she had no memory of it when she woke, the sun-strip still on the ceiling overhead. She was wide awake before six, having dozed so much the day before, and a curious sense of well-being encased her, beneath which stirred the faintest unfolding of butterfly wings; she put it down to Roger Roger Night minus thirty-six hours.

'Nothing feels more naked than telling the truth about your past,' she remembered, sitting up and stretching. She and Roger knew so little of one another's true history. They'd spent minutes at a time trying to pinpoint the year Laurence Olivier had died and whether Sharon Gless had played Cagney or Lacey, yet she had no idea what sort of child he'd been or how he'd met his ex-wife. Neither had he ever shown any interest in her past.

She wriggled her feet out from beneath Gunter, who had broken in from the landing in the night again, like an SAS commando, and crept onto the bed.

In the bathroom, she forced herself to look at her reflection, grateful at least that she wasn't wearing her glasses and the blind was lowered, casting her in blurred glow. Roger will see this tomorrow, she reminded herself. One naked truth, but not who you really are.

She knew that she wasn't the girl who swam naked any more, or the fat, unhappy wife who cried in the bath, but she had always found it impossible to see herself as others did, her criticism far harsher, her desire to hide herself acute.

Putting on a robe, she headed downstairs to make fruit tea – in line with her pre-Roger two-day detox – then took it to the french windows, which she opened to let Gunter stretch his legs across the dewy lawn. Early-morning mist hung cool and sweet in the air and a wood pigeon was cooing, its throaty repeat as familiar here as lawnmowers, bicycle bells and car alarms in North Oxford.

She turned back to the table and picked up Euan's board, the white marks over-layered and intensely detailed now, a ghost figure emerging. She could see an indistinct essence of herself, beautifully drawn yet without the depth and substance of colour and no sense of the person behind the form. There was no hate in her face: it was just a mess of white wool through which her features somehow appeared, brilliantly depicted, every angle uniquely hers, even though it was no more than dust on board, an ephemeral conceit of lines.

How incredible to have been born with such talent, yet so frustrating to have had no encouragement from home. She could imagine Euan's strict upbringing, the heat and heartbreak of his long summer rigging, the wanderlust that had kept him moving, the lovers who came and went, the family tragedy that had brought him home and now Richard's generous patronage, a blessing and an anchor. She'd thought him ungrateful, but he was just honest.

'Nothing feels more naked than telling the truth about your past,' she repeated, laying down the board and picking up his sketchbook, flipping through the sketches he'd done of her to the start of the book and on towards earlier work. The sight of Perry's girlfriend, naked and lustful in a houseboat berth, made her snap it shut and pick up her tea, wincing as she tasted its fragrant healthiness. She must be pure and glowing for Roger, she reminded herself.

She and Roger were entirely different beasts from Euan, their lives conducted in concentric circles – work, friends, marriage and family, each with its own life cycle. At one time she'd wanted desperately to travel: she had dreamed for a while of a road trip through Italy with Robin, but it had never happened, the sum total of her world exploration being family holidays and school trips. She'd even chosen interior-designed comforts here in Buckinghamshire over yomping in the Peaks.

A memory stirred and she caught its tail as it ran through her head. A circular, stone-walled room in the Lake District, a night intended for passion that had gone horribly wrong.

Jenny found herself looking out for Euan as soon as she got back from walking Gunter on Beacon Common. By late morning, when he still hadn't appeared, she was illogically furious. She told herself that she wanted to get this obligation out of the way, to pay her debt by posing, but she knew she was bored and fractious.

He hadn't actually said *when* he was coming, she reminded herself. He hadn't promised anything. He might even have gone off the idea. He was probably painting Perry's girlfriend, who was all too willing to strip off and have her beautiful body immortalized again.

A text from Roger showed that he was also on countdown and wanted to bank some flirting. *Looking forward to tomorrow :-)*

Hey! Me too. X, she replied, refusing to stoop to an emoticon, although the 'hey!' was happy text speak she'd picked up from Amalie and now found impossible to drop, along with the 'hahaha' of laughter, the 'yay' of delight, and the 'heh' of a sarcastic guffaw. Roger had picked up on it too.

Yay! Is there anything you are allergic to? Gluten? Lactose? Seafood? :-)

Jenny sighed. They'd been on over twenty dates during which she'd eaten cioppino, spaghetti alle vongole and tiramisu on a regular basis. Her phone beeped again.

Oysters, asparagus, figs, watermelon, melted chocolate . . . ;-)

She felt the butterflies stir. Roger was being witty. Or was he making serious menu suggestions?

She gave him the benefit of the doubt. *Hahaha! Will I be saying, 'Waiter, waiter there's a Spanish fly in my soup'?*

Chilled or hot soup? :-}

Now she really didn't know if this was a jokey flirtation about aphrodisiacs or a helpful exchange while he walked around Waitrose in Headington. Was :-} a cheeky smile or a chef's moustache thing? *Avocado and chilli is my favourite.*

You wild woman! ;@

That was ironic wit, wasn't it? And what was ;@? Lip implants?

Heh!

Et pour le dessert? Que voulez-vous manger, Madame? ;-x

Oh, God, it was all getting a bit sordid now. He was texting in bad French. They'd be at cross purposes over *crème brûlée* and *tarte Tatin* soon. *Text later. Just going for a swim. Happy shopping!* x

She put on her faithful bobble-bottomed Speedo, cap and nose clip and plunged in. This time she attempted a lot fewer than forty lengths and took her time. The cool embrace of the water was bliss. She dived down and spun onto her back, spreading her arms and legs to float back up. As she did so, a face appeared above the surface, indistinct through the ripples, though distinctly dark-haired and smiling, with a dog silhouette bouncing alongside.

The butterflies seemed to whoosh her up at double speed. She burst out, gulping air and pinching the clip from her nose. 'I thought you weren't coming!'

'Did Mr Lewis not explain we're always here Wednesdays?' said a strong local accent, laughing as he deflected Gunter's kisses.

It wasn't Euan. The face was unfamiliar, round and young. Jenny pulled off her cap, spotting a bright blue polo shirt with Home Counties Poolcare embroidered on the chest. 'Just need to check the levels and backwash, love. You can carry on swimming, if you like. I won't be more than half an hour.'

'No, no – you're fine!' Hurrying up the steps to cover up in her robe, she went inside to make him a cold drink, checking her phone as she passed. Roger had opted for *strawberries . . . whipped cream . . . Gü.*

She tried to work out what emoticon Gü could be, but it was beyond her. Replying *Hey!* x seemed to cover all bases.

Wine? he replied, before she could put the phone down again.

Wishing he'd show a bit more initiative, she wrote, *Surprise me!*

The pool man chatted amiably about the heat when she took him out iced elderflower pressé. It was almost unbearably close now – heat seemed to prickle off every surface, like an army of stinging ants. 'Might be a record-breaking July, they reckon.' He mopped a sweating forehead with his shirt sleeve. 'Days like this, I hate my job. Don't get me wrong, it's great work, but looking after pools without being allowed to jump in them is tough.'

'You can jump in this one if you like,' she offered, feeling sorry for him. She still felt guilty about denying Shelley the cleaner's family a swim, verruca sock and all.

He shook his head, smiling politely. 'I'd lose my job, love.'

Jenny recognized herself in him. Cautious, conservative, self-denying. They were life's J. Alfred Prufrocks. She longed to be the sort of person who took off around the world on a whim, who thought nothing of drinking wine before lunch and jumping naked into a pool to cool off.

'I won't tell.' She laughed. 'Go on. You know you want to. What's the harm?'

He took a step back, glancing over his shoulder, as though he might need a quick getaway. 'Really, I can't, love. I have a fiancée and young baby.'

Appalled to realize he might think she was hitting on him, she moved back too, so that they were soon reversing around the shallow end, like synchronized swimmers about to dive in from opposite sides. 'Never mind! Just got to text my boyfriend, Roger. He's coming here tomorrow.' We are going to make love all over the house. I am *not* a cougar. My MILF porn channel is very exclusive, very tasteful, and mostly stars Nice Married Matt or Benedict Cumberbatch. You're far too young and sweaty.

There's 20% off Prosecco, Roger had written, *or would you prefer the Pinot Grigio Blush which is 2 for £10? I've already got Colombian coffee and after dinner mints. ;-)*

'I have measured out my life with coffee spoons,' she breathed, typing *Why not get both – and cognac and crème de cacao? I'll do anything for an ice cold randy Alexander x* She pressed send, then groaned. *Brandy Alexander!* she corrected.

He didn't reply.

The pool man had gone when she wandered back outside. She thought about diving back in, but didn't want to overdo it. It was almost one o'clock and there was still no sign of Euan.

Her new bank card hadn't come in today's post, so she couldn't yet tackle her list of repairs, and it was far too hot to iron. She needed a cooler, calmer head to reread *Tour Divorce* and find the thread-line faults and inconsistencies still hiding in Carla's earthy, well-argued prose.

Jenny had never been good at having nothing to do. Even sitting for a portrait was something to do – in fact, she'd quite embraced the idea now that she knew she didn't have to bare all. She wanted the white chalky ghost of herself on the board filled in with those bright oils. She couldn't help worrying that she'd really antagonised him yesterday by packing him off so prissily.

She went upstairs and changed into shorts and a T-shirt, scraping her sweaty hair up into a band, then picking up *Bonjour Tristesse* and putting it down again, unable to face the overpowering philandering father, Raymond: 'Sin is the only note of vivid colour that persists in the modern world.'

Jenny longed for colour. The afternoon stretched ahead in a hazy heat-wave of parched, dusty nothingness.

Back downstairs, she gathered some blank sheets of A4

and set up under the shade of the pergola to have another go at copying the faded page of *The Storm Returns* from the Sapphic sex scene, carefully replicating the loops of the *y*s in *slithery* and *slippery*.

A shadow fell across the table as she laboriously forged *mouth greedily drinking her nectar like a honey bee from a snapdragon.* 'Marking homework?'

She quickly covered up what she was doing.

Euan looked half asleep, still wearing yesterday's T-shirt with the *Nude Reclining in Bluebell Wood* paint stains, green eyes pinched with tiredness.

'Long lie-in?' she said brightly.

'I haven't slept. Can you sit?'

'It's what I do here.' She smiled up at him, embarrassed by how delighted she was to have been forgiven and to have some company. 'I'm a house-sitter.'

26

'I'm not drinking today,' she told Euan, when he fetched wine and glasses. 'I'm detoxing for a date.'

'Sure.' He poured her some anyway and pulled boxes of paint tubes from his bag, lining them up alongside him, like rows of twisted silver slugs. He squeezed a few onto an old chopping board and thinned it with linseed oil. Then he propped the board on his knees and studied it.

'Why don't you use an easel?'

'You ran over it.' He glanced up. 'It was just cheap old tat. I always used to work without. I'm cool with sitting you on my lap. I'd rather you were naked, but that's your choice.' His tone was easy-going, his mood hard to read. He certainly didn't seem upset any more, but Jenny found his detachment almost more disconcerting.

She felt her cheeks heat up. 'Do you want me to put on the same clothes I was wearing yesterday?'

'I'm only interested in you from the neck up for now. The rest can do what it likes.'

It sounded as though she could lay her decapitated head on the sofa and jog around for a bit. 'Does the same apply to Gunter?'

'We both know he's largely empty space from the neck up. Let him stay cool.'

Gunter flopped out in what little shade he could find. In concession to the airless heat of the day, the doors stayed ajar as the blinds were lowered, striping the room in light and shade.

There was no music today. Instead, Euan told her to talk to him: 'You can tell me lies, truths, the plot of the best movie you ever saw, explain the life cycle of bees – I don't care as long as you care about what you're saying and you don't bore me. Unlike most artists, the last thing I want you to do is keep your face poker still. I need it animated and full of expression, and I'll tell you if I need you to shut up for a bit. You have very characterful features.'

Jenny supposed she should be grateful that she'd been promoted from 'bony' and 'unusual'. She might never be beautiful, but characterful was good.

'What do you want me to talk about?'

'You could start with your life story and work up to the movie plot and bees that way.'

'"Nothing feels more naked than telling the truth about your past,"' she quoted back at him.

He half smiled as he mixed another colour, looking at her cheek then his palette. 'I knew that would get you thinking. Talk about the future, if you prefer. Who's your date with?'

Jenny contemplated her plans for tomorrow evening and swallowed. *I'm* the conversational interviewer, she thought uncomfortably. I always ask questions and draw people out. 'First, tell me what's on your mind that's preventing you sleeping?'

He pretended not to hear, trying a new line. 'Are you house-sitting somewhere else after you leave here?'

'Is it the exhibition that's worrying you?'

'Will you be seeing your kids soon?'

'You said you still needed a lot of paintings?'

'Okay, I give in.' He started to paint in short, deft strokes. 'I can't sleep because I've fucked something up very, very badly. It's inevitable someone I care about – several people – will get hurt.' He looked at her, his eyes fierce with the effort

222

of saying it out loud. 'Now I've taken off one layer and I've got to work, so you talk.'

'I have no firm plans after I leave here,' she said.

'Liar. People like you always have plans.'

'What do you mean, "people like you"?'

'Organized people.'

She thought about her wall planner at home in the museum of marriage, neatly marked out with the coming weeks, the theatre trips and visits to friends and family, Jake's homecoming and exodus to university, then the preparation for her autumn term sabbatical to escape and write the novel she'd been planning for almost ten years.

'I'll come and see your exhibition,' she hedged. 'That's a plan.'

'Do you live nearby?'

'Oxford.'

'Beautiful city.' His brush dabbed from makeshift palette to board. 'Did you grow up there?'

Jenny smiled, aware that she was being manoeuvred into revealing those truths. Somehow she didn't mind as much as she'd imagined she might. Talking made her less self-conscious, and she certainly didn't feel naked describing her childhood.

'No, I grew up in Warwickshire – Shakespeare country, as my father was proud of boasting, although he preferred the golf cart to the Bard. Dad was a dentist: "For there was never yet philosopher that could endure the toothache patiently" – *Much Ado*,' she explained, as his eyebrows shot up questioningly. 'He took us all to the RSC with much the same long-suffering dignity he took us to theme parks and ice rinks. I think I was alone in loving it. My sports-mad sister used to do buttock and thigh lifts in her seat through five acts, and our geeky little brother always smuggled in a Walkman.

'My parents live in Hampshire now. They moved last year to be closer to my brother – who promptly took a job in Toronto, but that's another story. It's a country house converted into apartments for the over-fifty-fives – *definitely* not a retirement home, as Dad will explain at great length if you ask. There's a mini spa, café and nine-hole golf course, so it suits them perfectly. They're very conservative. As Dad's Iranian by birth, lots of people assume he's one step away from ayatollah extremism, but he has no truck with religion and just lives for longboats, am-dram and bird watching. Mum was always a home-maker, the full bread-kneading, biscuit-baking, dress-sewing, veg-growing, make-do-and-mend package. She struggles to do much now because of her arthritis – her fingers are like ginger roots, poor darling.'

'Which parent do you take after?'

She smiled. 'A bit of both. There's a lot of personality there to share out. My sister was always the confident, go-getting one. My brother was "difficult" and clever. I was the polite, bookish perfectionist. I found happiness in fiction, dreaming of becoming Tintin's co-reporter on adventurous assignments with Snowy. I lived in an imaginary world with an address book full of imaginary friends. By the age of twelve, I read a book a day, often more. Of course, there were no virtual online worlds then, apart from my little brother's Spectrum on which he played hours of Manic Miner. We had one television that was only ever on for the news or sport, so fiction was my escape.'

'You were a loner?'

'Not really. I was part of a group of close school friends who loved reading more than pop videos and *Neighbours* – we were the sort who posed around river-banks in long scarves and floppy hats, imagining ourselves Warwickshire's answer to the Bloomsbury Set. We had no interest in hanging out by the chip shop on the parade swigging cider, or painting our faces white and nails black and lurking in graveyards. We were top-set students, arty swots, and we all got into university. I was the golden girl who made it to Oxford.'

'And you stayed there.'

'I almost fled home after a term. I found that transition tough. There were so many riverside poseurs there that I lost my way. I made a few good friends who I still know well today, had a couple of flirtations that made me think I understood love, and developed a huge crush on a student who was way out of my league – all standard stuff – but I never really settled and enjoyed the ride. I was the small-town dentist's daughter who needed to justify her place with constant A-plus grades and a chippy attitude to keep pace with the oiled tracks of the privileged. By my second year, I practically lived in the library. I didn't mind because it meant I could be close to Robin Rees – my big crush – although he had no idea I existed then.'

'So Mrs Rees got her man?' He studied her over the board.

'Yes. "Reader, I married him." Robin was a PhD student, a Rhodes Scholar who was so bright he practically glowed in the dark. The entire English department at my college was in awe of him, and not just because he looked like a young Warren Beatty. He had a rock-star ego with an academic's dedication and was impossibly cool, tall, fiercely intelligent, by turns as funny as Woody Allen then intense and inter-nalized like Walken in *The Deer Hunter*.'

He was watching her intently, brush in hand, brows knit-ted together, as though something about her face wasn't right any more, although she wasn't aware of moving her head or the light changing.

'Robin was totally obsessed by his work,' she went on. 'His doctorate was obscure, highly political, impeccably indexed and handwritten in a scrawl nobody could read. When he put a postcard up on the notice-board advertising for somebody with typing skills, I deciphered it before anybody else could. I grabbed it and the chance to get closer to him. My second-year exams were fast approaching and I should have been studying non-stop, but studying Robin Rees at close quarters was all I could think about. I bought an electric typewriter with what was left of my living allowance – who needed food for the rest of term when they had Robin? – and I turned up at his rooms with it, along with my Tintin pencil case and a ream of cheap paper, announcing that I was the woman for the job.

'I'd done a secretarial course the summer before I went up to Oxford – my father insisted I needed a fall-back for the future – so I could at least type. I didn't hide the fact I fancied the pants off him, and I was precociously outspoken about the Americanisms and spelling in his dissertation. I simplified his ideas a little so they could be understood, clarified his arguments, picked holes in his wilder assumptions. I edited it as I typed, and he soon stopped griping and started telling me I was the cleverest girl he'd ever met. He fed me lots of toast and cups of sugary coffee, laughed at my tenacity and told me I was Simone to his Jean-Paul. I realized I'd never loved anybody as much in my life.'

Euan hadn't painted another stroke. He laid down his brush, its metal collar carefully propped on the edge of the palette, and reached for his cigarettes. 'You're still in love with him.'

'Of course I'm not!' she scoffed. 'We've been divorced almost three years.'

Saying nothing, he stepped outside.

She hurried to find her electronic cigarette. Then, breaking the pledge, had a big gulp of wine.

Why had she told him all that? She was like a ranting depressive in therapy, going on and on about herself. She must apologize.

She stepped outside onto the decking alongside him. 'I am *so* sorry. I didn't mean to bore—'

'We're two refugees, you and me,' he interrupted.

'I'm sorry?'

He looked at her and she knew straight away that he carried the same pain as she did. There was no hiding it from him. He'd seen right through her. 'You mean you . . . ?'

'The same.'

He handed her his cigarette and, without thinking, she puffed it.

'I want to hear your story if you'll share it,' he said, 'every naked truth.'

27

Jenny needed the whole glass of wine to talk about falling in love with Robin.

'We first slept together on May Morning after staying up all night talking. I remember the bells and cheers outside, and thinking it was just for us. I was pretty inexperienced sexually and he was ten years older than me, so I took his lead. I thought it was high passion, but looking back it was fumbling and awkward and drunken. I was so besotted with him, it hardly mattered. We'd sit up until dawn drinking bourbon and reading poetry to one another. He called me his muse. I was totally blown away, fearless and uninhibited. There wasn't anything I wouldn't do for him.

'When he went back to the States to take up a position as a junior lecturer at NYU that summer, I pined like mad, although he insisted I must stay on for my final year to bag the first he was convinced I'd get. After that, he promised we'd be together and travel, like Sartre and de Beauvoir. We exchanged long, handwritten love letters and saved up for transatlantic calls. He visited twice and they were little lifetimes of happiness I'd have died at the end of. He promised to take me to Paris after my finals. I scraped through them, but my degree wasn't nearly as good as predicted – I couldn't concentrate on anything but the thought of seeing him again, so much so that the day after my last exam, I cashed in the Post Office savings account my grandparents had set up in my name and used it to buy a flight to New York and surprise him.

'When I got there he was different, distant and cold. There was none of the intimacy that we'd shared in those visits or our letters. He said it was because he was stressed out, that he hated the department he worked in, his roommate was driving him mad and he missed Oxford. He put me up in this terrible motel out of the city. We still drank bourbon and made love, but he was bad-tempered and distracted. He kept making excuses not to take me into campus or to meet his family, who lived in Connecticut.

'On the third night, he broke down and admitted that he was married.'

Having been painting in concentrated silence, Euan looked up sharply. 'Go on.'

'He explained that he and his wife had been high-school sweethearts. Their families had known each other for decades – her father and his were best buddies. He said he loved me, but she was a part of his family and like a sister to him. His father was seriously ill – a spinal tumour that was slowly killing him – and he couldn't break his heart by leaving his wife, however much he loved me and wanted a future with me. His father's greatest wish was to see his son start a family with the girl who was like a daughter to him. Robin's an only child, so he felt his duty was to stand by his word.

'I left the next day. I was devastated. I thought my world had ended. I couldn't sleep or eat. I just wanted to forget he ever existed. Why aren't you painting?'

'Your face is too sad.'

They went outside again, wine in hand. This time he gave her a cigarette of her own to smoke.

The sun had dropped to its teatime glow spot over the churchyard yews.

'So Robin Rees broke your heart twice.' Euan squinted up

at two wood pigeons flapping furiously in the tallest yew's crown.

'You could say that.' She watched them too, wondering if it was courtship or battle.

'Did he follow you back to England?'

She shook her head. 'Not at first. We had no contact for almost a year. I moved in with some friends in a flat share in North London and temped with a trade-magazine publisher. My career ambitions were on hold – I just needed to pay the rent – but the job worked out better than I'd expected. It led to sub-editing, and I soon got a permanent job on a weekly title. It wasn't the glamorous end of the publishing process, but I got to write the headlines, which I liked, and I was quickly talent-spotted and bumped up to work across several titles. I started to enjoy it – I had over-inflated dreams of becoming editor of the *Times Literary Supplement*. I still read a ridiculous amount – in those days it was lots of dark social commentary and dystopian literary fiction.

'I had a few dates and a short-lived office romance, but nothing matched up to Robin. I was off men and into hedonism. I partied very hard during those months – my drunken rebound through London club-land. I turned into a reckless wreck who sometimes went into work in yesterday's party dress, still drunk. Believe it or not, I was always good at my job, no matter how little sleep I'd had or how much party fuel I'd put into my body, chemical and human. I had super-human stamina and resilience – I suppose one does when one's young. And I'm not proud of my behaviour, but it stopped me thinking about Robin most of the time.

'It was only when I stood still that I felt the floor give way beneath me. I missed him like a physical ache that never really goes away and throbs almost intolerably through every nerve ending when you lie still. I started a hundred letters to him, but I sent nothing. I'd forced myself not to contact him, or pass on my address. I tried to cauterize the pain, but it wouldn't go away.'

She saw Euan wince and knew he'd been there. That was why he'd kept moving so long, unable to settle. She'd clubbed her way around London, he'd kept on moving around the world. But she'd done it for a twentieth of the time he had and – for a while at least – she'd got love back.

'Then on my twenty-second birthday, Robin sent a card care of my parents,' she explained. 'It was postmarked Oxford. In it, he said his father had died a few months after I'd visited New York. He was now getting divorced because he had realized once and for all that he was totally in love with somebody else. He had taken up the offer of a research fellowship back at his old college, and said that, if I could ever face seeing him again, his greatest wish was to bow down and beg my forgiveness in person.

'The day after reading it, I handed in my notice and caught a train to Oxford. I believed he'd sacrificed everything to come back to me, and I was ready to give him all of myself in return.'

'I bet he didn't deserve a tenth of you.' He looked into his glass, saw it was empty and drifted inside. 'Come. Keep talking. We need more wine.'

'I really can't.' She followed him in. 'I must stay legal enough to drive so I can take Gunter out.'

'Then we'll go together now so you can talk as we walk.' He pulled the doors shut, glancing over his shoulder. 'Or is it an abuse of Richard's trust?'

She blushed. 'I'm sure it's fine. I'm really not boring you?'

'You mustn't stop talking. Gunter agrees.'

Gunter had cottoned on to the prospect of a walk and was bounding around, barking his head off.

It was pointless to protest, she decided, so she went to the utility room, reached up to the hidden cupboard for the car key, then set the alarm. Euan wandered in behind her to pick up Gunter's lead.

The drawer containing Geraldine's half-ironed manuscript was still open, she saw in panic as she tapped the keypad. She entered the wrong number and got a shrill warning beep.

'1887,' he reminded her.

'I know that.' She re-entered it and got the timed beeps counting her out of the house.

She tapped the manuscript's drawer shut with her hip as she passed it and shot through the door past Euan. In her haste, she didn't see that she'd inadvertently put her foot through a loop of the slip lead. Brought down like a lassoed steer, she thought for a terrifying moment that Euan was attacking her.

'Shit!' He dropped the lead and stooped beside her. 'I'm sorry. You were moving like Usain Bolt.'

'I'm honestly fine!' She scrabbled up, ignoring his offer of a hand. The beeps were ringing out more urgently. 'No harm done! My fault!'

'Did marriage make you this self-effacing?'

'No. It just made me face certain facts about myself.'

'I want to know.'

They both looked up as the last long beep sounded, then dashed for the door.

28

'I moved into Robin's rented flat in Jericho and he proposed within forty-eight hours,' she said breathlessly, as they walked into their own long shadows, taking the opposite direction to the houseboats, ducking clouds of midges and watching riverboats puttering by, full of pensioners in Panamas drinking sundowners. 'Six months later we had the big white winter wedding at the college – it had snowed and was utterly beautiful – and we spent our honeymoon in Venice, impossibly romantic out of season. It felt like we had it to ourselves. My parents found Robin tricky to get along with, but they loved how happy I was and how prestigious the match was; Robin was Oxford's young don pin-up, and he'd just come into a small fortune from his father, which Mum thought an auspicious start. We lived a charmed life amid high-flying academics. My friends were still clubbing and partying in London, single girls living in shared flats and climbing career ladders, but my life was suddenly totally different, revolving around college and the Oxford set. I was determined to belong amid the dreaming spires, to fit into the role of wife. I took it very seriously.

'Robin had inherited more than enough for us to buy somewhere to live befitting a glamorous American academic and his new wife. We both fell in love with a Seckham villa near the university gardens, barely touched in fifty years. It was far too big for just the two of us, but we filled it with friends and visiting family – at least, I did. Robin's antisocial tendencies were more deeply established, but he indulged my every whim in those days. I imagined myself as a heroine in a grand Victorian novel tasked with attaining moral perfection. He said he couldn't wait for me to get pregnant. As an only child, he'd craved siblings and always wanted a big family of his own. His mother had died when he was three, so he had this idealized notion of motherhood. He loved the way my mum had brought me and my siblings up – the home-baking, craft-making maternal devotion – but I was convinced I could top that, being thoroughly modern and emancipated. I mugged up on conception, quit the late-night bourbon drinking, switched drunken pleasure shags for scheduled ovulation missions and set about ripping out the warren of small rooms to create a child-friendly space in the eccentric old house – inadvertently taking away three of the things Robin loved most: getting drunk with me, fucking and being surrounded by dark, historic corners.

'The house became an obsession, and I can see now that he was jealous of my devotion to it, but at the time I thought I was creating our own Taj Mahal love palace in Park Town. I persuaded him to let me get the builders in and transform it into a layer cake of living and entertaining perfection. I devoted hours to the project, poring over catalogues and colour samples. Robin quickly lost interest, although he was always happy to write the cheques.

'But his mood became very black. His mind worked differently from anyone else's and deciphering it was my constant challenge. His critical essays and lecture notes were always genius, but utterly chaotic. I worked incredibly hard to iron them out and make them comprehensible to lesser mortals. I often ended up more or less rewriting them, which was when we connected best – me at the old IBM computer

234

with its glowing green words, him pacing around behind me talking through points into the early hours.

'And despite the big house renovation, my life in that first year of marriage revolved around Robin. I was devoted to him, to writing up his papers, discussing his work, assessing his students' essays with him, planning his terms. It was the ultimate job share, and life share, and I loved it, although I wanted to keep a sense of myself too and I got a sub-editing job on an upmarket local paper. I'm like a Border collie – I need to work all the time. I can't stand still. It was chewing-gum work and Robin made no secret of disapproving, but I loved the social side away from the college protocol, and I even got to write a column for their monthly magazine sup-plement. It was called 'Academic Goddess' and catalogued the life of an Oxford don's wife, recounting my trapeze swings between ivory tower and Acrow prop in the battle for domestic perfection.

'I got passionately into cooking – it was the era of the competitive dinner party, when you felt inadequate if you didn't have your own *sous vide* machine and a vacuum dewar of liquid nitrogen in the larder. I was Oxford's answer to Nigella, and the column got a big following. Not every-one liked me – I got quite a postbag of green-ink offence saying I was a disgrace to the sisterhood. But I was funny enough to be kept on, and the Headington yummy-mummies adored me, as did a surprising number of undergraduates who nicknamed me "Honorary Dig Rees". Robin seemed mildly amused, if disparaging about my prose – it was only much later I understood how mortified he was by the attention. The awful thing is, I wrote them to impress him in those early days. I think I already knew that I had to work hard to keep him, but I went about it the wrong way. I totally overdid it, trying to prove my worth. I

235

was just as nuts about going to the gym three or four times a week, playing tennis, attending art classes and learning to play the piano. I wanted to be superwoman and super-wife.

'Then, after eighteen months of marriage, I fell pregnant with the twins and was determined to add super-mum to the list.'

They sat on a bench dedicated to Alma and Bob Whitehead, watching swans drifting towards them as Gunter plunged in and out of the reeds further along the bank, furiously hunting dragonflies.

'I'm not going to talk any more.' She rubbed her face. 'I've bored the pants off you already.'

'You're going to keep talking until you end this story. I won't give you the car key back unless you do.'

'You have the car key?'

He held up the little black fob. 'You dropped it.'

'It's a keyless car. Technically speaking, that's not a key.'

'Technically speaking, it stays here with me until you talk.'

'Am I really not boring you?'

'Only when you say you're boring me. Do you feel naked yet?'

'I'm down to my bare bones here,' she admitted, looking sideways at him, amazed that the more she said, the more he seemed to want to hear.

He was surprisingly cheerful, as though her ancient-mariner act was feeding some sort of elixir into his veins. 'Then I'm not the one whose pants are coming off right now, am I?'

'I'm keeping my pants on, Euan. Think of me as bones in pants.'

'I need to see all of you to paint you. The pants will come off. Keep talking.'

An elderly jogger gave them an odd look as he panted

236

alongside their bench, then on past Gunter, who was too busy going in for the dragonfly kill to notice the gentle pounding of small white trainers behind him.

'Is this art therapy?' she asked, suddenly feeling vulnerable and silly. She wished she'd said nothing, hadn't let the wounds of the past gush out like blood from a severed artery. 'Did you ask Perry's girlfriend to tell the bare, naked truth?'

'Perry's girlfriend?'

'The girl on the houseboat,' she clarified.

'Femi? She took her clothes off so I saw the naked truth that way. And she's not Perry's girlfriend. What's she got to do with this anyway?'

She ran a hand around the back of her neck, which was silted with drying sweat. Now she just felt sillier and more vulnerable. 'Let's go back to the car.' She stood up.

'Wait.' He reached out to catch her arm but she snatched it away and called Gunter, who bounded up, body-slamming them both.

'Tell me how Robin reacted when you told him you were pregnant.' He fell into step.

She marched on, trying to tie off the artery, but it was pumping harder now. She was almost talking to herself. 'At first he was besotted with the concept of our unborn children, especially the idea of twins, our Artemis and Apollo, Viola and Sebastian, Princess Leia and Luke Skywalker. But then I developed pre-eclampsia in the second trimester and was so sick that I ended up in hospital. Robin was totally stressed out by it, and his reaction was to drink too much, throw himself into college work more and get depressed – backing away from me.

'In fairness, I must have been a nightmare to live with. I was so scared of losing the two tiny lives growing inside me

237

that I treated my body and the house like temples. The dinner-party *haute cuisine* was replaced by pregnancy superfood. I banned Robin from smoking anywhere near home, even in the garden – we'd both been dedicated puffers, although I'd been a Camel Light poser who found quitting easy in those days, whereas Robin was a forty-a-day Marlboro man. Nor could I bear the smell of alcohol – he could sink a bottle of Napa Valley's best every night in those days and he loved his bourbon. I slept badly and got too hot if he spooned me in bed, so he was banished to the spare room most nights. We still made love twice a week – I'd read it was good for the babies and that it might even help with the pre-eclampsia, but it was about as romantic as pumping up the tyres in the car. Robin would shower and go through the motions soberly while I dictated positions and diligently exercised my cervical muscles.

'In the final stages, I felt so ill and frightened that I withdrew even that privilege. I didn't want Robin to see me as anything less than perfect. It never occurred to me that his lack of interest in our unborn children challenged perfection too. My mum came to stay for a bit, looking after us both. I hated being forced to rest so much to keep my blood pressure down. I was in and out of hospital, and I had to give up the sub job early, although I kept the column, describing my nurturing and nesting overdrive.

'With so much enforced rest, I read more than ever. I devoured books about pregnancy and escaped into women's fiction, no longer interested in shaping Robin's theories on Shakespeare's sociopathic political subtext. I was an emotional sponge while pregnant – I needed to laugh and cry, and I found the self-indulgence of academia infuriating. I guess a part of me resented the fact that Robin was spending longer hours than ever in college, sometimes staying overnight if he had a paper to write or a faculty dinner. He came to a couple of antenatal classes, but I felt I got more support from the birthing ball and sag bag. He hated the repetitive, condescending inanities and complained that most of the expectant mothers were old enough to be grand-parents and should have started families earlier. But I saw them differently. I looked at these connected, loved-up cou-ples, so many of the women indeed much older than me, much wiser, more worldly and successful, and felt *I* was the one who had got it wrong by gazing up at our ceiling rose in the throes of passion before I'd got close to the glass ceiling, squatting in the birthing pool before I'd swum with sharks in life's ocean.

'When the twins were born, none of that mattered, of course. I had intravenous love pumping through my veins twenty-four hours a day. Robin was incredibly proud, but he wasn't a natural father. The pre-eclampsia had meant an elected Caesarean, which he hadn't been able to bring him-self to watch, and he seemed equally terrified when these two tiny pieces of us appeared swaddled in waffle blankets. I kept thinking he'd suddenly get it, but it never happened.

'I was advised not to have more children – the risks were too great. I knew how much Robin wanted a big family to fill our huge house, and I felt a failure, more so because our two beautiful, precious children seemed to bring him no joy. I sometimes wondered if it was because they were twins – there's a bond between them that's quite amazing and totally self-contained – but I think I was just looking for excuses. The noise and ever-demanding repetition of babies drove him mad, the need for a structured routine and the impos-sibility of leaving the house *en famille* without planning ahead and taking bags full of changing stuff. As toddlers, their furniture-coasting invasion into his quiet space alienated him just as much. He seemed permanently irritated by us all. I found myself keeping them all apart like an umpire. It was obvious that both children felt rejected by him at times when they were young, and their desperation to please him broke my heart. Amalie now jokes that her father only took an interest in her once she could write an essay of more than five hundred words. That and the time her best friends went from spotty brace-wearers to gorgeous young things and he could sidle up to them and say, "Are you thinking of trying for Oxford? I'll put in a good word." Thank God poor Am never knew what else he had plans to put in. Unfortunately, by then, I did.'

They had reached the car, which obediently flashed its strips of pretty lights like a party boat as Euan reached the keyless tag from his pocket, lighting up the scorched dusk.

'Can I drop you somewhere?' she offered, as they climbed in.

'You're not dropping me.'

29

Talking about the next stage of her married life was probably not the wisest move while driving. Even navigating the short run from river to Old Rectory with the aid of a sat-nav required some sense of vision, and hers was horribly tearful. But he prompted her gently and persistently until she started spilling while they were stuck behind a tractor pulling a towering Giant's Causeway of hay bales at fifteen miles an hour.

'Maybe our marriage might have ended a lot sooner if I'd spotted the signs earlier, before I lost so much sense of myself. I now know that Robin's affairs with his students dated right back to the first weeks of my pregnancy, but I was blissfully ignorant in those days. I blamed myself for his distraction, and did everything in my power to compensate for the fact he clearly felt excluded after the twins were born. I tried harder than ever to be *über*-wife and mother, to make the twins and Robin feel safe and loved. I made family time a big thing, but the more picnics and play days I organized, the more Robin absented himself. So I determinedly tried to make time for just the two of us. Looking back, I probably resented it all like mad, however hard I tried to convince myself we needed to recapture the spark. I threw myself back into the Oxford set, into old friendships, dinner parties and weekends away, dragging my mother down from Warwickshire to babysit.

'We had one particularly awful weekend staying at a romantic folly in the Lake District, which Coleridge was supposed to have used as a writing room. It was obvious Robin didn't want to come, but it was my birthday so he grudgingly acquiesced. I'd bought lots of luxury food and champagne, deciding I was allowed to let my hair down and get a bit drunk for once, but I just ended up making a fool of myself trying to seduce him. It had been over six months since we'd made love. He was far drunker than me and said he wasn't in the mood, then got angry because I was upset, shouting that life wasn't all about me and storming out. While he was gone, Mum called to say Amalie had a temperature of a hundred and four. Then Robin reappeared, white as a sheet, saying we had to talk and he burst into tears, but I had already packed everything up, beside myself with worry, insisting we could talk in the car. Shit!' She tried to overtake the tractor and had to swing back in as a car passed within inches, leaning on its horn. 'You can see why Robin decided that wasn't the greatest plan.' She laughed nervously. 'Being very upset while driving is one multi-task I've never mastered.'

'Does it still upset you that much?' He looked at her closely.

'No, but it might if this goes wrong.' She swung out again, and this time they powered past the tractor.

Exhilarated, Jenny told the rest of the story with a soft curl of cynicism lightening the harsh brutality of that night. 'Robin and I had a huge row that evening at the folly, with him refusing to leave until he'd said what he had to say and me demanding he say it *now* and him crying and shouting and drinking more and not saying it – it was like a terrible Pinter play where everything is insinuated and nothing happens.

'In the end, I insisted on driving home with or without him. He took the ride, smoking out of the window furiously and still not saying whatever it was. We didn't exchange a single word the whole way back. I was terrified I was over the limit. I remember crying so much at first I could hardly see the M6. I still have no idea what he was going to say. Perhaps he wanted a divorce. I would have fought that with every molecule – I loved him so completely.

'It turned out Amalie had meningitis. We almost lost her. I wish I could say it brought Robin and me closer together, but I think that was the point at which he realized he no longer loved me. I was totally lost to terror and an obsessive need to be practical, always at the hospital, or making lists and packed lunches and thanking everybody who saved her. I desperately needed him to tell me everything was okay, that I was doing okay, but he withdrew interest and affection totally.

'He became domineering and impervious, living by his own agenda. He was generous to a fault when it came to money, but in everything else he put his own needs first and there was a detachment I could no longer penetrate, a lack of time for and interest in us. He talked about the children as though they were two of his brighter undergraduates. An outsider would see him as a proud father, but from the inside it was torture. This wild, exciting man I adored had removed his love and energy from our relationship. He switched off from me totally, and I didn't know what I'd done wrong, apart from bearing his children and loving them as much as I loved him.'

'Why didn't you stand up to him?'

'I've often asked myself the same thing. When the children were little, I was too busy crouching over them trying to protect them. When they started standing up for themselves, I found I was too broken-backed to join them.'

They were back on the Old Rectory driveway. The garage door opened, like Moby-Dick's jaws, to swallow them.

*

When the alarm beeps rang out, Euan strode ahead to key in the code. Jenny leaned back against the front door. 'There's no light to paint.'

'I don't want to paint you yet. I want to see you naked,' he called, the alarm silenced. A moment later, wine was glugging into glasses.

Jenny knew what he meant, and she already knew she couldn't stop. She'd never talked like this in her life. Whatever was happening had gained momentum to become addictive. She'd started to suspect that her history was background music for him, but that almost made it easier: she wanted to say it and he wanted to hear it.

They went outside so he could smoke. The noodles were bobbing beneath the diving board – the neighbours had clearly popped in for an evening dip.

She jumped as the pool turned luminous turquoise, rippling like silk. Euan had flicked on the light. Black bugs bobbed on its surface like pepper grindings. There were midges everywhere. He lit the nearest citronella candles, then handed her a cigarette. She handed it back. 'I mustn't. My kids hate it.'

'They're not here.'

She smiled, tucking it behind her ear. 'I started smoking again after that night in the Lakes. I used to steal Robin's cigarettes and sneak to the end of the garden after the twins' bedtime. Isn't that awful? The irony is, he'd just got his first mobile phone and used to sneak out there to call his girl-friends. We'd bump into each other by the bins and both frantically pretend to be composting carrot peelings.'

'Did you confide in anyone?'

She shook her head. 'Of course not. I was far too proud. I pretended all was well to the outside world. My old school and university friends all thought I was an alien, but they hung on loyally when we met up as I passed around endless photos and talked about potty-training and first words. They were all at a different life stage, just starting to break up long-term flat shares and co-habit, and at that point there wasn't much more to my world than Annabel Karmel recipes, mother-and-baby groups and, of course, the "Academic Goddess" column. When those old friends of mine visited, Robin lit up and found them fascinating in a way he no longer found me. Eventually, I stopped inviting them, deciding my true friends were other new mums – or old mums, given that the average age of my circle was forty. I was only twenty-six but acted like a ring-leader. I started up a babysitting circle so that we could go out to concerts or the theatre and come back for baby-friendly kitchen suppers afterwards. I set up a baby music group, toy recycling, and a co-operative childcare network for mothers who wanted to return to work. To the outside world, I was the sort of multi-tasking high-achieving career mother who probably needs pushing off a cliff for making most young mums look idle, but in reality I lived on nervous energy and adrenalin, and I screwed lots of things up by taking on too much, always in a bad-tempered screaming hurry with no quality time. My idea of a me-treat was a Boost bar in the car.

'"Academic Goddess" was at its most popular by then, and I'd got a lot more opinionated, sparing no blushes. Even the local sisterhood had decided I was okay. Flaky fathers were my bugbear, and I had a lot of examples to draw from. Robin thought it was all about him, but I very rarely used our home life. Something about having the twins stopped me wanting to share personal secrets and I heard more than enough from my new-mother friends to fill a decade's worth of columns. In fact, Robin came out of it rather well, our marriage painted a far rosier colour in print, along with the house I kept redecorating. I changed the décor constantly, always looking for more child-friendly, family-oriented space to try to glue together the fractured Rees clan, unaware that Robin had already bagsied the naughty step pre-partum.'

They seemed to have migrated to the table under the pergola, storm lamps and citronella candles flickering, although Jenny had no idea how they'd got there. Her glass was empty, but there was a full bottle open. Euan lit a cigarette and offered it to her, although there was still one tucked behind her ear.

She took it, drawing in the bittersweet poison. 'Will you promise to forget I said all this tomorrow?'

'No.' He poured the wine.

She smiled, looking up at the stars, which were competing for attention overhead, like high-carat diamonds on a jeweller's velvet cloth.

'It's curious how you can share a house with someone who is gradually becoming a stranger simply by retaining those things that are familiar about the relationship – the routine, the social circle, the repetitive conversations and one's own need for nervous distraction.

'When the twins started full-time school, education became my new obsession. I joined the PTA, mugged up on child psychology and Key Stage One, and relayed tales from the school gate to eager local readers. I'd started looking around for more full-time work, although I had no great desire to return to a sub's desk where technology had already taken leaps beyond my knowledge-base, stealing much of the creativity. Nor did I work on Robin's papers any longer because he always accused me of dumbing down his ideas. As a result he was published and quoted less, the college no longer seeing him as quite such a jewel in their crown. His most recent work was parked straight in the back of the reference section.

'I desperately wanted a career to give me a new identity, one that I might feel proud about. The twins adored me as I did them, but they were now at school every weekday and went to bed at six, after which I struggled to feel good about myself. I shared long calls with friends, and read a lot of books, writing furious notes in the margins.

'Robin was rarely home before nine, often much later. He had a host of bright young things hanging on his every word, students he inspired who had adopted the handsome, scruffy, genius Yank who drank too much and avoided his controlling wife. By that point, I'd guessed he was having affairs – there were the furtive calls, the times he stayed all night to work in his college rooms, the mood swings from guilty hyperbole to malevolent depression. But I survived with denial, still thinking myself *über*-wife and mother, believing my own hype, running scared only in the deepest veins, unable to bear what it would do to the children to edge closer to the ledge of truth. My "Academic Goddess" columns became the ultimate bittersweet lie, filled with sugary little yummy-mummy tips and acid-sharp observations, hiding the taste of fear in my mouth. I started to lose readers' interest and my edge.

'Around that time, a friend I'd kept up with since NCT classes who was head of media studies at an Oxford girls' school invited me in to talk to her sixth-formers about writing a regular column – I'd love to say I was a local celebrity by then, but the London journalist they'd booked cancelled so they needed a last-minute replacement. Ironically my own editor sacked me by email that morning, thanking me for six years of fun but pointing out that times had changed and they needed more space for advertorials. It's weird because I found I could still talk about the process to the pupils, even telling them I'd just been fired, and it went down really well.

They laughed and listened. I seemed to connect with them without really thinking about it, inspired by how clever they were and how much I'd loved my own education at that age. My friend cornered me afterwards and told me that the school was looking for another member of the English department and that applicants could train on the job. Teaching suddenly became a vocation I couldn't deny.'

She heard the church clock chiming the hour and counted the strokes. Ten. It felt like early evening, not the point at which she normally yawned her way through the news wishing she'd gone to bed earlier. Talking non-stop – smoking, drinking, not eating – she suddenly felt like her student self again, Jennifer Asadi, the girl with a lightning-fast mind who could stay up all night. She didn't feel remotely drunk. It was warm as day outside.

She looked at Euan, his profile glowing blue in the reflected pool light. 'You must be tired. You didn't sleep.'

'I'm not tired.'

'Hungry?'

'No.'

'Neither am I.'

'I bet you're a bloody good teacher.'

'I'm better than I was. I was a bit overeager at first. I threw myself into it with such passion, I was the mutant child of Miss Brodie and Mr Chips. I spent all those lonely evenings planning lessons to inspire young minds, and I hardly cared what – or who – Robin was up to.'

'You were a good wife too.'

She laughed, shaking her head. 'Our home life was just shared space and resources. We'd barely made love since the twins' birth, and that was only when he was drunk, and any compliments were also long gone. The public face of the Rees double act was a joke, the cracks showing through the false smiles. I blamed my body, because otherwise I'd have lost my mind.

'I remember one night when there was a hugely important white-tie do. At the last minute I realized I couldn't fit into my best formal dress and had to borrow something that I wasn't sure suited me at all. I desperately needed cheering up, just a kind word to help me survive, but when I asked Robin how I looked – fatal mistake – he said, "Very full of yourself as always." I asked him what he meant, and he picked up a thesaurus and read out twenty-seven synonyms for "fat". He made out that it was a joke, but he knew it was a terminal wound to my self-confidence. At the party, he couldn't wait to dump me on the dean's wife and bolt. That night, I felt as though my real self was standing alongside Robin Rees's eager, overweight young wife in her hideously unflattering dress, watching as she spoke very fast, laughed too loudly, asked endless questions, shared forthright opinions on education, talked too much about her children and tried too hard to be liked.

'In coming months, I joined a gym and took up tennis again in a half-hearted attempt to get back into shape, but I was very self-conscious about it, and it was my brain I wanted to exercise, not my body. I no longer craved the burn as I once had. The twins and the house kept me happy enough to survive, along with teaching, which I loved. I had my holy trinity – motherhood, home and career. My husband no longer saw me as sexually desirable and neither did I. Nor did I ever look at other men that way, and if they looked at me, I wouldn't have known.'

'Men always looked at you in that way. It's what we do.'

He was gazing at her very intently. Was he looking at her in that way now? Jenny wondered. Surely he'd already seen far too much of her mind stripped naked in an unflattering light. Dismissing the idea, she took a gulp of wine, feeling uncomfortably hot as the muggy night grew closer. She stared into the dark garden which was under threat of becoming as dry and barren as her marriage in its darkest years, insects humming and thrumming in its borders, like the first crackling sparks of fire. She was gripped by the desire to give it life before it was too late.

'This needs watering!'

A moment later she was wrestling with the sprinklers,

'Stop!' Euan laughed incredulously, striding after her. 'It can wait.'

'Everything will die.' She turned on the taps.

'I'll do it.' He grabbed a sprinkler and towed it out onto the lawn. 'Tell me about teaching.'

'Don't be ridiculous. I'm irrigating.'

'And I'm interrogating.' He threatened her with a revolving perforated yellow egg. 'I'm a professional at this, remember?'

'Teaching was a revelation,' she said, as water jets puttered out, catching them both. Yet they stood still, eyes focused on one another as Jenny talked. 'It provided the mental stimulus I needed, and I loved it. The pupils gave me the sort of respect and approbation I'd never believed I was worthy of, showing me that I made a difference, that my enthusiasm and dedication were appreciated. By belonging somewhere, I got some self-esteem back.'

She leaped away as one of the hose ends blew out and started snaking around.

Euan didn't seem to notice. 'Go on.'

'My marriage became more bearable,' she said, grabbing it, 'although Robin still blanked me emotionally and sexually. But he relied on me practically and that lent life the rhythm of respectability.' She clicked connectors together in rapid succession to redirect the flow through the sprinklers. 'He isn't a practical man. He needed a family framework. By then, I knew about his serial love affairs with students, but I trusted he was far too cowardly to walk out on us and they never lasted longer than two academic terms. There!' She stood back and admired the moonlit mists of water, oblivious to the fact that she and Euan now looked like finalists in a Mr and Ms Wet T-shirt competition.

'You're amazing.' He laughed.

'And you're shit at irrigation, but I'm sure your weeding is better.' She looked at him sympathetically, wringing out her shirt front and going to reclaim her wine as they settled back by the pool.

'I prefer bedding beautiful things.' He pulled off his T-shirt to wring it out, and she hastily averted her eyes from cobbles of muscle gleaming in the half-light. When he pulled it back on, his eyes were on her from the moment they appeared through the neck hole. 'How many affairs did your husband have?'

'I stopped counting after double figures. He preferred the foreign students on a one-year exchange, which ensured a clean break at the end. Mature students were tricky – there was one particularly pushy redhead from Ottawa who called at the house begging me to let her have him. Thankfully, I was toughened enough by his extracurricular activities to think quickly, and I knew he wasn't about to leave me, so my first thought was to get her out of the way before the children got back from school.'

'How could you put up with it?' He poured more wine.

'I used to confront him in the early days – so upset I often couldn't speak for tears – but the contrition he showed and the promises he made became hollow eventually. He always promised it wouldn't happen again. He always said sorry a thousand times over. And he said, repeatedly, that it was "just sex", as though that was somehow more excusable. I once made the mistake of demanding to know why he wanted sex with his students – was it because I wasn't exciting enough in bed, or too old at twenty-eight or too overweight? Didn't he desire me at all any more? He said it wasn't because he didn't desire me, it was because he desired them more.

'I didn't want to know any details and a part of my survival relied upon a hefty measure of see-no-hear-no-speak-no, and on being too busy to stop and think. Of course, there was always an urge to lift the curtain, to flip through the texts on his discarded phone, scan the credit-card bills, pop into college when he was working late, but to do that was self-harm on a grand scale and I was good enough at beating myself up already not to need it. By day, our children and my career came first. By night, I already spent too much time crying in the bath. I mourned my lost sensuality, the pleasure my body had once given me. I blamed Robin for stealing it and not giving it back, but most of all I blamed myself. I'd started drinking more, misery-eating more. The fact that I'd lost my confidence physically and sexually became my unspoken secret, just like the affairs were my husband's.'

'Do you have a photo of him?'

She smiled into her glass. 'You may have accused me of still loving him – which I dispute, even though I've talked about him all evening without pause – but I don't carry his photograph around.'

'What does he look like?'

'To you? Ordinary. Six foot, average build, bearded, a bit scruffy, thinning on top. To me, nonpareil. He grew better-looking as he got older, young Warren Beatty ageing just as beautifully, with a dash of Gerard Butler and Nicolas Cage.

The hair thinned but not the charm, and nothing about him thickened, no matter how much he drank or how many home-made Stroganoffs I fed him. We shared a bed until the marriage ended, but it was more of a silent reading room than anything else. Ironic, given that the library was where I'd first watched him with such an overwhelming teenage crush. I think I might have found it easier if my desire for him had faded in line with his for me, but while I certainly didn't crave the all-night sexual marathons we'd once shared, I never wanted anybody else. It was his touch I pined for, his body I longed to feel inside mine. Sometimes, on a purely visceral level, I wanted him so badly it hurt.'

She drained her glass. Now she was starting to feel drunk – and naked, very naked. The church clock was striking eleven.

Euan was looking at her, green eyes unblinking – perhaps he'd fallen asleep with them open. Gunter was leaning against her, staring up at her adoringly, which was almost certainly because she still hadn't fed him.

'Did you ever make love?' asked Euan.

'Once or twice a year at most. He still went through brief bouts of desiring me – or at least appreciating the availability of unprotected sex with a warm, welcoming vagina he didn't have to prise open with gifts or lubricate with clever flirtation and cunnilingus. In hindsight, I think the sex with me was usually when one of his affairs ended badly, before he'd lined up the next, or when he was frenzied with desire for somebody new he hadn't got into bed yet. At the time I fooled myself that I was still desirable to my husband, that if I tried harder I might rediscover the man I'd once sat up with all night drinking bourbon, reading poetry and fucking for fun. He was happiest when I said nothing, avoided eye contact and tried nothing more ambitious than HBO – hand, blow, then the big O, his, not mine. It was technical pleasure rather than emotional. We both preferred the lights out. I wish I'd had enough self-respect to deny him, but I needed to feel wanted physically and it was all I had.

'As my husband turned me into an occasional trick that could be turned for free instead of fifty quid on the Cowley Road, I matched this private shame with a new outspoken sexual morality among friends, ranting against media distortion of women, internet porn, over-sexualization of youngsters. I was on a crusade, my sword aimed straight at my husband's chest before I turned it on myself and fell on it. Yet every time Robin and I shared a good moment, the laughter we could still trigger in one another, a debate on a controversial book, an animated discussion of a news event, or those rare touches in bed that meant he wanted me to open my legs, the feminist agenda melted away. I was a lousy feminist, the only equality I sought being my own husband's love and desire. I still so bloody loved him. Fuck, I'm drunk.' She buried her face in her hands. 'I don't swear. Mrs Rees does *not* swear.'

His fingers touched hers and scalded them, hot as brands enclosing her knuckles. She didn't immediately pull back, instead feeling the heat run through her.

Then she snatched them away and reached for her glass. 'Fuck it, I'm going to get legless.'

30

'Did you never think about having an affair yourself?' he asked, as the church clock struck midnight.

Under Euan's encouragement, Jenny's words were flowing as freely as the wine he kept pouring, just as full-bodied and robust. To her surprise, he seemed to find them just as intoxicating too, his eyes never leaving her face.

'I'd stopped seeking out that sort of male attention when I married. Then I became far too lost to know how to find it again, or feel I had a right to. There was an electrician who did a lot of work for us, always staying hours to talk. He said he liked me, but I dismissed it as a bit embarrassing and inappropriate, and I actually thought less of him for fancying me. I couldn't even look at myself naked in the mirror. If I masturbated – which was almost as rare as having sex with my husband – I did so by remembering Robin's unstoppable sexual appetite for me at twenty. By my early thirties, I felt I'd been buried alive in a stranger's body and life.

'My old school and college mates were all hitting career highs, getting married and making babies, all loved up and happy. My kids were pre-teens, my husband was a philanderer and the money had run out. As I've said, Robin's hopelessly generous. All his lovers had received gifts – first editions, antique jewellery, weekends away – his overseas lecture commitments had trebled with no appreciable income, and we'd already taken equity from the house to fund the Rees lifestyle. An Oxford don doesn't earn a big salary. The twins' school fees cost almost as much as he earned. Beyond that, we lived off my teaching salary, ate economy food and waited for the house to regain value in the property boom so we could borrow more, pretending all was well. There were no jolly parties with the Rees family in Park Town any more. I dreaded being on show at weddings and christenings and often made a feeble excuse not to attend. It's a big, hurtful thing to miss a close friend's wedding, and some of them understandably melted away afterwards. I'm deeply ashamed I was so selfish, but my act was starting to crack.'

'What about your family? Surely they knew what was going on?'

'They were going through a tough time themselves. Dad had suffered a series of heart attacks, the final one very serious, meaning he had to take early retirement with a reduced pension. My sister was going through a messy divorce at the time, and our younger brother had just come out as gay. I wasn't about to load them down with more, but I spent a lot of weekends in Warwickshire, which the twins loved because there was a hot tub and satellite television. I liked escaping there, chatting to Mum about novels, gossip and holidays, both of us pretending all was sunny and well.

'It was after one of those visits that I came home to find Robin having sex in our bed – the ultimate cliché – bum bouncing merrily with a Japanese student, too enthralled to have heard me coming through the front door. Thank God the kids were on a school skiing trip. I remember thinking they could have bloody used one of the spare beds because I'd only just changed our sheets. Then I threw a bedside light at them and sat in the garden smoking all his cigarettes and working out how to leave him. He was predictably contrite. The girl was duly dumped, the promises made, the marriage patched up with Elastoplast from which a red river seeped steadily beneath Mrs Rees's baggy, brightly coloured clothes. But that episode gave me a very deep body wound that never really stopped bleeding.'

'Why didn't you leave him?'

'I contemplated it many times – inevitable whenever the truth came too close to the surface for comfort – but I couldn't bear to put the twins through it. Neither could I bring myself to leave our beautiful house and the familiar heartbeat of co-dependent life. The only time I'd seriously tried to do it was on our tenth anniversary. Tintin-gate.' She winced into her wine glass, remembering it.

'Tintin the cartoon character?'

She nodded, setting her glass down. 'I'd been a huge fan as a child, Robin knew that. When I was sorting through some of his research notes, I found theatre tickets for *Hergé's Adventures of Tintin* at the Barbican. They were dated for the night of our tenth wedding anniversary.' She looked away, fighting back the first tears to betray her, refusing to let them take grip. 'I was impossibly touched. The tenth wedding anniversary is tin, you see. I'd always made such a big thing of each year's meaning and Robin was horribly cynical about it, but this time I thought he'd made a huge effort. I didn't want to ruin the surprise by letting him know I'd seen them, so I put them back and said nothing. But a couple of days later he told me he was attending a seminar in London that evening and would be staying overnight. He'd obviously totally forgotten it was our anniversary. The tickets weren't intended as a treat for me. They were part of a romantic night away with another Tintin fan, who was probably barely more than a child herself. That was when I decided to leave him. I booked an out-of-season holiday cottage for us to hide in, packed bags for us all while the children were at school and stashed them in the car boot, tidied the house and even

257

left notes for Robin explaining how everything worked. But then the school phoned to say Jake had fallen off the climbing frame and fractured his wrist.

'I promised myself I'd leave Robin once Jake was back to strength, but I never did. I thought about it too much after that, which is fatal. I should have just done it.'

'I wish you had,' he said, with feeling.

'I promised myself I'd take the twins to *Tintin* and I never did that either.' She smiled sadly.

'I'll take you to see *Tintin* one day.' He raised his glass, the glint of his green eyes revealing how drunk he was too. 'Brussels pretends to be all starchy and bureaucratic, but it's sexy as hell underneath. We'll be total tourists. We'll meet by the fountain in the place du Petit Sablon, admire the view from the Mont des Arts, drink ourselves silly at la Champagnothèque, pig out on Belgian chocolate and then you can get your fix at the Musée Hergé before we take a suite at the Royal Windsor.'

'Thank you.' She stole one of his cigarettes. 'The kids will appreciate that.'

He smiled, lighting it. 'We can't smoke in front of them.'

'Absolutely not.'

'How will you introduce me?'

'The man to whom I told my life story,' she said, then thought it sounded far too romantic and added, 'Who has an uncanny knowledge of Brussels, unlike his very limited knowledge of garden sprinklers. Kids, meet Euan Anderson. He's a sprouts, not spouts, man.' She found this ridiculously funny, realizing even as the laughter ripped the breath from her lungs just how sloshed she was. Wiping her eyes, she made to throw away the cigarette, then changed her mind, suddenly wondering if she could blow smoke rings. It had been over twenty years since she'd tried.

'You are absurdly lovely,' Euan said, watching her spluttering attempts. 'It's Henderson, not Anderson. And your husband was a bastard,' he added emphatically.

She smiled through the smoke. 'Robin just fell out of love with me. And you do learn to survive a toxic marriage. The betrayal still hurts, but we cushioned ourselves with routine and bad habits, work and friends, the sense that anything else out there could be infinitely worse. We were always friends, but long-distance friends trapped in close quarters. We were also pretty good at holidays, which helped. The kids saw another side of their dad on the annual Rees getaway, and they loved it, especially as they got older and their expensive education finally paid off. It gave them the code to decipher the incredible complicated genius who had fathered them. We went from "I hate Daddy" to "My old man's a dood!" in the space of two historic European city breaks. Robin was a walking encyclopaedia, Baedeker guide and street theatre all rolled into one.

'Then when the twins were in their first year of A levels, he left us. There was no warning, no sense that this love affair was different, but it certainly was. She is a fellow New Yorker, another Rhodes Scholar, as bright and shiny as he'd once been, and as madly in love with him as I had been that final year in Oxford. She was also expecting his child.'

He reached to take the cigarette from her and draw on it. 'That must have hurt.'

'I wasn't the first Mrs Rees he'd done it to. In almost eighteen years of marriage, it had never occurred to me to find out what had happened to Robin's first wife, the childhood sweetheart he'd left in the States, the girl he'd claimed was his best friend. But I think I worked it out the day he left me. I think she had read a note just like the one he wrote for me, beautifully phrased, minimalist yet moving, filled with regret but leaving no doubt that this was final. He wrote to the children as well, explaining that our marriage had been over in all but name for years, and that nobody was to blame. I wanted them to blame him, but they didn't. They blamed themselves. We all did. That's the crucifying thing about divorce.'

She looked up as the church clock struck one o'clock. Or was it two?

'Robin now lives in New York with his new family – third wife Lindsay, one-year-old daughter, Honey, and a bump that's going to be a boy. He's a senior lecturer at NYU and writes bloody good papers – I hear he has a terrific editor who takes no shit. He's had a lot of therapy at Lindsay's request, too. So very American. He wrote to me a while back as a part of his "healing circle". He now says he wasn't ready to have kids when we got together – he was rebounding from his father's death and we were both too immature to be parents.

'But that doesn't make our children any the less amazing. And they are amazing. They love him to bits. He's a lucky guy. Amalie's studying at NYU and sees him all the time. Jake's staying there on his world trip. We're very lucky parents.' Jenny had soared to an evangelical, wine-induced high, but now her wings started to smoulder as she dropped down to earth.

'I totally disagree with Robin that I was too immature to be a mother,' she picked up her glass angrily, 'but I'm not going to argue the point with him merely for my own gratification. I know what I am, and I'm not "full of myself" as he once accused me. I'm hollow. I wish I could afford to buy three thousand dollars' worth of therapy to forgive myself for my marriage failing, but that's not an option. I just pull up my hood and jog on. I don't drink as much and I don't comfort-eat. I started smoking again, which wasn't so good, but I'm down to electric stick things now.' She blinked at him, eyes skewered, remembering too late that she had a cigarette in one hand and a glass of wine in the other.

Euan was smiling at her, face moving around a lot. 'You've spent so long associating food with misery and drink with forgetting that you can't remember what it's like to sin for pleasure.'

'I'm not sinning for pleasure, Ian.'

'Euan.'

'I said Euan. Thing is, Ian, I'm plastered. And naked.'

'You have all your clothes on.'

'I'm talking metaphorica-li-lially. Can you stop moving?'

'I am sitting perfectly still. You need coffee and sugary food.' He stood up.

'I don't eat a lot, Juan. Punch me in the stomach and you'll feel the difference from two years ago. Then it would have wobbled a lot. Now I'll punch you straight back.'

He laughed, ruffling her hair as he passed, but she was too drunk to notice. 'My friends and colleagues have been shtrordinary through all this,' she went on, not realizing he was out of earshot. 'I had no idea how much support I had out there and how much it helps to admit you might need them. People *like* to help. I do. They've been wonderful, and Jake and Amalie's friends have been too. Losing the house hurt. I'd put so much of myself into it, and for all its sadder hours, I loved all those walls, which had the twins' childhood wrapped up in them. It was like selling a member of the family. I cried myself to sleep for weeks after I left it – longer than I cried over Robin. I still won't walk or drive past it. I'd pleaded to keep it until they'd finished their education, but Robin fought that one right into the divorce court, knowing I couldn't afford to buy him out. In our

261

marriage's lifetime, it had become a million-pound des-res, and he got his father's money back in triplicate despite the second charges. Not a bad return on eighteen years of marriage.'

'He lost you.'

A cup of coffee landed in front of her, so strong that she got a double espresso's wake-up hit simply from inhaling.

There was a large pile of *pain au chocolat* on a plate by the coffee cups. Where had it come from? Was he Mary Poppins or something?

'I'vegorralifeIlike, June,' she told him earnestly, munching on a pastry and struggling hard to enunciate. 'The twins are incredibly well adjusted and getting on with their lives.' That was better. She sounded like Angela Rippon now, so all good. 'I'm deputy head of department, and the school is top of its league.' Oops. Going a bit Joyce Grenfell. Get a grip. 'I see lots of my friends, including old ones I lost touch with when I was so unhappy, I have far too many hobbies and pastimes to keep on top of.' Stop! Widdecombe. Steer it back. 'But no obsessions that consume me. I've even started dating again,' Esther Rantzen – it would have to do, 'through the internet. Embarrassingly, my kids signed me up. It's called Ivory Towers.'

'Is the date you're detoxing for from Ivory Towers?'

'Yesh.' She nodded earnestly, reaching for his cigarette packet. 'Roger.'

'Roger?'

'I know.' She held up a hand. 'The name, which makes everyone think of a retired jobsworth police officer, isn't ideal. But there's a lot to like about him. He is admittedly a bit stuffy and OCD, but so am I, according to our online match criteria. He's three years older than me, a solicitor, divorced with no children. He is fit, well dressed, good-looking and he always smells of lovely aftershave. We've been seeing each other for six months.'

'Six months is a long time.' He looked surprised.

'In your terms, Yun, it probably is.' She nodded kindly. 'He's coming here tomorrow evening. We are going to have sex.'

Euan – who was still on the wine, swigging thoughtfully – spluttered a red mist.

Jenny didn't notice. She was listening pensively as the church clock chimed three, emotions bubbling without warning, 'The trouble is, Jan, I'm frightened that imagining having sex with Roger – which I've done rather a lot in the build-up to this – will be infinitely better than joining with Roger in having sex. I don't love Roger, which means I cannot make love to Roger, nor he to me. I can only roger Roger. Over and out.' Without warning, her head landed among the *pains au chocolat*.

Somewhere, in her half-conscious mind, Jenny could hear Euan swearing. With great effort, she sat up straight. 'I'm fine!'

His chair tipped back, then forward again as he peered at her. 'You're decimated.'

'No, honestly, I do this – seeming to be very pissed, but actually quite sober.' The effort of speaking as though she was brightly taking the register on a school morning was killing her. This was back to the clubbing-all-night London years, but her body was no longer capable of the rapid turn-around from wasted, sweaty ho to sitting pretty pro. Yet somehow it seemed vitally important not to fall asleep or dribble in front of him again.

'You called me "Jan".'

'Some of my closest friends are called Jan.' She reached for the cafetière and stood up. 'More coffee?'

Standing up had been a mistake. Moving in straight lines was impossible, and being by a swimming-pool in charge of a glass coffee jug marked high danger, but by following the plank lines of the decking very carefully, she made it into the house and reeled towards the kitchen. Thank goodness he hadn't followed her, she thought, as she cannoned off the island and against the surfaces like a pinball.

Once the kettle was on, tiredness and nausea over-whelmed her and she took advantage of Euan being out of sight to take a brief rest somewhere cool as she waited for it to boil.

31

'You're lying on the floor, Jenny.'

'Mmmmm?'

'You're lying on the kitchen floor.'

'Mghwooaway.'

'Let's go up to bed, shall we?'

'Don't think goingtobedtogether susha good idea.'

'I meant let's get *you* to *your* bed, Jenny.'

'Not ready for bed. Want coffee.'

'It's almost four in the morning. It's like communicating with a Neanderthal. I want to see you in bed right now.'

Jenny rallied the all-night clubber again, remembering how her head would jerk up from nodding off in the Tube, the bracing walk along Chancery Lane via the coffee shop, the deep breaths in the lift, the cool splash at the hand basin in the Ladies and two squirts of antiperspirant before she swiped her key card to the open-plan office and burst into action.

With great effort, she sat up. 'I'm flattered, Ian, but—'

'Euan.'

'I'd rather keep my clothes on.'

'I think they already came off tonight, don't you?'

Rubbing her eyes, she looked down at her body to check he wasn't talking literally and then up at him groggily, trying to remember if she'd done something drunkenly shameful. His face was really quite kind beneath its thick mop of black hair, the square features smiling, green eyes pinched with tiredness yet also dark with concern. Then she groaned in horror.

Even with the self-obsession of drunkenness, Jenny had a feeling she might have gone on a bit. She had talked for HOURS. She had told him everything shameful and painful about her marriage, with the possible exception of the in-growing toenail she'd developed not long after being promoted to deputy head of English. 'Oh, fuck, will you ever forgive me?'

'Mrs Rees never swears.'

'Mrs Rees will swear on her life right now that she will never, ever bore somebody with her life story again. Christ, why didn't you stop me?'

'Because I wanted to hear it,' he said simply. 'I'll make more coffee.'

Back outside, now on two of the wicker recliners in the little hidden garden beyond the library, which got the first of the morning light, they watched the sunrise as they drank strong coffee and listened to the dawn chorus. She was grateful for the silence as she felt the coffee take hold. Then he told her about the dawns he had watched break across five continents, and she was equally grateful for the rough, melodic scratch of his voice and the amazing pictures it painted, pictures his hands had also often captured along the way but traded for food, accommodation and lifts.

'Don't you ever sleep?' she asked him eventually.

'Not much at the moment,' he admitted. 'Are you tired?'

'No.' It was true.

'Then I'd like to paint. Now you're naked.'

She glanced down again to check. While no longer tired, she was feeling increasingly spaced and random. 'I need a shower first.'

*

As Jenny stepped into the shower, head spinning, she distinctly recalled a friend at Oxford who had sworn that the correct combination of coffee and wine, taken in tandem with flirtation, poetry and attraction, was better than any Class A drug.

'Ah, yes, that was Robin.' She snorted, pointing at herself, fingers gun-shaped, in the mirror.

This time she kept her eyes open as she turned beneath the water, watching herself disappear into the steam gathering on the antique-looking glass. Her body was suddenly far more than a collection of ever-more-sagging fault lines to obsess over. It was her protective shell, her armoured truck that drove on through life regardless of traffic, accelerating away from her car-crash marriage. While some people spent a fortune customizing and beautifying theirs, others tinkered with the engines and many coveted a chassis they could never have, she'd largely taken hers for granted. It was too late to trade it in for a new model. She just wanted to put her foot down and drive as fast as she could.

Euan Henderson was no smooth ride, but he was a great rally co-driver to have through a night stage en route to an epiphany moment. Roger Roger Night was fast approaching.

She dried herself quickly, aware that coffee on top of wine had made her hyper, yet still quite drunk, a *Through the Looking-Glass* state of mind she rather liked. Hearing a splash outside, she pulled back the blind and saw her younger self swimming. As she searched for clean clothes in the bedroom, she heard voices and went to the window, watching through the wisteria leaves as Euan stooped by the pool and talked to the girl. She was standing in water up to her shoulders, her back to the house, hair in wet snakes over her butterfly tattoo.

Jenny strained to hear, but apart from Euan's low chuckle, she couldn't make out anything that was said. Pulling on her dressing-gown, she hurried downstairs.

The blinds were closed. She edged closer to the door, but all she could hear were rhythmic strokes now.

'She's the neighbours' daughter.'

Jenny spun round. He was watching her from the kitchen. 'You know her?'

'She's sweet. Go out and say hello. You'll like her.'

She remembered Richard mentioning the brilliant scholar destined for Somerville. She'd probably always known that the young swimmer wasn't a dream, the *Through the Looking Glass* mirror impenetrable after all, only the truth looking back at her. 'She's naked.'

He carried a jug of juice to the table. 'So?'

'It bothers me, just like her parents' *outré* swimwear bothers me. This is Buckinghamshire, not Benidorm.'

'Drink some juice.' He poured her a glass. 'I can't do anything about you being reactionary, but we can fix the dehydrated sugar low.'

'At least you've stopped drinking wine.'

'Actually I still am.' He reached for his glass and lifted it. 'Now get into pose.'

She pulled her dressing-gown tighter and perched in position.

'Were you always this body-conscious?' he asked.

'Yes, especially when fat.'

'You're very thin now.'

'Am I?'

'You have no real idea, do you? You just don't like what you see.'

She pulled a cushion onto her lap without realizing what she was doing, thinking about her reflection disappearing in the shower, her new-found resolve to open the throttle on this body's life. 'It's fine.'

'Earlier you told me that loving someone, however ordinary others find them, made them nonpareil to you.'

'Without equal.' She tucked her feet beneath her to stop Gunter licking them winningly. 'I didn't put it exactly like that, but yes. I'm hardly alone in that outlook. It's a pretty common theme in literature and life.'

'You deserve to be nonpareil. Does Roger think you are?'

She closed her eyes. It was Roger Roger Night minus twelve hours and counting. She'd just stayed up until dawn talking about herself and was now posing for a portrait, still slightly pissed. If she was without equal, it was because she was beneath contempt. Roger would definitely have had his not-so-happy face on if he had witnessed her behaviour last night.

She knew something was happening to her. It was what was keeping her awake, pumping adrenalin through her, sharpening her senses and stealing her appetite, despite the hollow stomach and lack of rest. She knew she must stop it happening. Yet she couldn't move. Being with Euan made her reckless and daring.

'How does your wife fit into all this?' she asked, determined to take a reality check.

'I'm not married.' His gaze didn't leave hers and she felt her skin prickle, remembering how callous she'd thought him when he'd joked that he would buy Carla's book in case he ever divorced. She'd assumed that meant he already had a wife.

'I love it when you blush.' He tilted his head. 'It's like your skin whispering to me.'

'You're just painting my face right now?'

The green eyes watched her over the board. 'You want me to paint something else?'

269

She didn't move. 'How much more naked can I get?'

The eyes didn't blink.

For a moment she was going to do it, to slip off the robe in a dawn liberation, like a streaker at an all-night tournament. But Gunter let out a frustrated groan and stretched his full length on the sofa, almost propelling her off it with his back legs as he buried his head in the cushions.

The moment of madness passed. Jenny laughed. 'Poor Gunter. We've kept him up all night.'

'He's used to it.' Euan set down the board and went to the wall pad to select some music.

Gunter must have been genuinely exhausted because he barely stirred when a sweet, melancholy voice filled the room, singing of love and loss. As the beat tapped its way around them, the intimate Caribbean beach hut was back, only to Jenny it now felt like Dorothy's cabin in *The Wizard of Oz*, swirling through the sky on its private trajectory.

'Ayo.' Euan turned back to her with a half-smile.

'Hello,' she said quietly, heart thumping suddenly.

The half-smile curled a little more as he went back to the table to gather up his brush and board again. 'Ayo's the name of the singer. Nigerian father, Roma mother, voice of an angel.'

Jenny couldn't disagree. Trying to slow the freefall force still rushing though her, she stared fixedly at one of the paintings on the wall, an old one of Euan's featuring a joyful array of country characters. 'And you are Scottish father, Scottish mother, God-given talent. Where did you paint this?'

'The Borders. I need you to do the talking,' he reminded her. 'You are Persian father, English mother, kind soul.'

'I'm not talking about myself.'

'Tell me more about Roger, then.'

She snorted, glancing across at the clock. Roger Roger Night was now fifteen minutes closer. Was it too late to cancel? She could feel panic rising. 'I'll recite something,' she offered, self-consciously aware that it was what she'd done staying up all night as a student. Everything about last night felt like rediscovering that lost romantic insomniac. 'I learned great swathes off by heart once. I can still remember some.'

'As long as it's not Walter Scott – all that Scottish swash-buckling isn't my thing.'

'T. S. Eliot? Byron? Queen's *Greatest Hits* Volume One? I've been trying the lyrics out on Gunter to help him get over his pop-music phobia. He's a big fan now.'

He smiled slowly over the board. '"Rock me".'

It was time to say goodbye to Ayo. Smiling back, Jenny thumped her flat hands down on her thighs twice, then clapped them together once – thump thump, clap, thump thump, clap, thump thump, clap . . .

Euan painted in total concentration for an hour, by which time Queen's *Greatest Hits* had been loudly and tunefully remembered with buxom cyclists, champions, lonely hearts and fandangos. The sun was sneaking at an oblique angle through the slats of the blinds and Gunter was pacing from sofa to door, eager for his walk.

'I must take him out soon.' Jenny stifled a yawn, sleep finally catching up with her.

'He'll survive just this once. I can't stop now.'

She glanced at the clock.

Catching her, Euan smiled. 'I'll be long gone for your date with Roger.' He seemed to put little ironic brackets round the name, emphasized by the Scottish accent.

'I need to clean the house up and pamper myself.'

'You're perfect as you are.'

271

'Heh.' Jenny's hair had dried in a muzzy tangle, her face makeup-free. Her dressing-gown was falling open to reveal a bony chest and less than pert cleavage. Pulling it together, she stretched away the stiffness, then sagged back into position, amazed by how relaxed she felt. She tilted her head to look at him cynically and found her eyes glued there as Euan looked straight back, and this time he wasn't working out the angle of her brow or the precise skin-tone of her nose. He was looking her straight in the eye, and neither of them could look away.

'Take it off,' he said quietly.

She no longer felt so relaxed.

'Take it off,' he repeated.

She was back in her first Oxford digs, having smuggled in a fellow undergraduate for her first pre-Robin full-frontal, a terrifying, sensational rite of passage.

Jenny knew she wanted to do this. It was shedding her old skin, the cold-blooded, battle-scarred scales of a bad marriage.

Standing up, she slid the knot apart and let it fall. It was like casting off the heaviest, rustiest chain mail. It hadn't been so hard after all. For a long moment she felt proud of her liberation, her body and its history, and floated back onto the sofa, like a feather.

Eyes not leaving hers, Euan smiled. 'As Tintin would say, "Great snakes."' Still smiling, he returned to his board and carried on painting. 'Christ, this is going to be good.'

Shame mugged Jenny, one arm flying to her chest while the hand of the other covered her groin. It wasn't the imperfections of her body that embarrassed her, or the thought of having them immortalized: it was its honesty she couldn't control, her nipples instantly hardening to pips, a hollow beat hard and fast beneath her pubic bone. Flashing at Euan

Henderson, her erogenous zones were now practically giving blues and twos to let him know how turned on she was.

Apparently unaware, Euan painted on, his eyes on her face again.

Sitting it out, Jenny waited until her heartbeat slowed. The tightness that had spiralled her areolas eventually slackened, the beat between her legs calming from *presto* to *largo*. Then she let her arms drop to her sides, tucking her feet back beneath her and looking at the figures in the painting on the wall, aware that her cheeks were scarlet. With a rush of relief, she remembered Queen's *Greatest Hits* Volume Two. She needed a kind of magic, she decided.

An hour later, when she had half sung and half recited half-remembered hits with double-vision exhaustion, Euan finally laid down his brush. 'I'm beaten. I can't see straight for tiredness. Let's go outside.'

She put on her dressing-gown and joined him in the hidden library garden where the sun was cooler and the sprinklers, which were still spitting all over the main lawn, wouldn't catch them. It wasn't yet eight, yet it felt like the end of something, the shared student spliff in a punt at dawn after the May ball re-enacted in middle age on the creamy cushions of a wicker sofa with the last Marlboro in the packet.

Having lolled naked in front of Euan until just moments earlier, and having been talking all night before that – not to mention communicating in Queen lyrics since dawn – Jenny found herself utterly lost for words. He seemed equally taciturn, sitting forwards with his elbows on his knees, tapping the end of his cigarette repeatedly, his face hooded with tiredness. Eventually he said, 'I think you should put him off.'

She knew he meant Roger.

'You said you don't love him and he doesn't love you, so what's the point?'

Sex, she thought tiredly, eyes aching so much she had to close them.

'I think it's just sex,' he said out loud.

She cranked one eye open, offended. 'We both like the theatre.' It came out as one mangled word – webofflicktheatre – but he seemed to understand.

'Theatre is good.' He nodded. 'And he's going to cook for you, you said, which is good too. You *do* need to eat.'

Watching his profile, she had never felt less like eating a Waitrose ready meal in her life. 'You really think I should put him off?'

He rubbed his face with paint-stained hands. 'I just want to finish the painting.'

A snap of irritation pinched her along with cramps of tiredness. 'Well, I'm sorry if my sex life doesn't revolve around your exhibition preparation.'

He slumped back beside her, crossing his arms over his face.

'You need sleep.' She remembered groggily that he hadn't slept the night before, a marathon of insomnia coming to an end. 'Where do you live?'

'Come to bed with me.' He spoke from beneath his arms.

Despite her tiredness, the pulse started up through every vein like a cricket's thrum. She took a long time thinking up her reply. 'Ask me that again after eight hours' sleep,' she said carefully.

He didn't answer. After a while, she realized he'd already taken her up on her eight-hour challenge and fallen asleep, although whether he'd heard her say it was debatable.

She went to turn off the taps feeding the sprinklers, her feet and ankles wet as a beach paddler when she returned.

He'd stretched out on the big wicker sofa now, one arm still across his face while the other dangled down towards the grass. Her skin prickled as she studied the sinewy width and strength of it, the fingers relaxed, speckled with the paint he'd used to capture her light and shade. She wiped her sweaty forehead with her sleeve and dropped to her haunches to lift his arm and tuck it back alongside him. It was incredibly heavy. As her fingers slipped through his, she felt his grip tighten. Inside her, the beat started up faster than ever. Then his hand slipped away and he turned his back towards her, curling into the sofa.

Jenny was so spent she felt as arthritic as her mother when she straightened up, yet something deep inside her body had been rejuvenated: the part of her that believed in crazy, sexy infatuation was back in business. The pulse still thudding in her groin told her categorically that it was nothing to do with Roger.

She went back inside, yawns racking her. As she passed the table, she looked at the painting. Euan had made no changes to her chalky fully dressed body. He'd only painted her face, and it was mesmerizing, so full of life it seemed impossible that it was just layers of oil and pigment.

VIII

Thursday

32

TO DO LIST

Sober up

Jenny showered again, then lay on her bed, shaky and hollowed out from lack of sleep, yet her mind was running faster than ever. She needed the thought-numbing, cool submersion of the pool, but she couldn't go down, let alone swim, while Euan was sleeping so close by. The beat wouldn't stop thrumming between her legs now. She wanted to go downstairs and wake him, bring him up to her bed, but her head was too addled by tiredness to trust her judgement or co-ordination.

Her heartbeat spiked crazily when a heavy weight landed on the bed, but it was just Gunter, flopping down beside her and panting. It was too hot now for him to want a walk. Within seconds, he was snoring loudly.

She closed her gritty eyes, certain sleep was beyond her.

The beep of a text arriving woke her: *ETA 1900 hrs. Looking forward to you . . . .and Gü ;-)*

What was this Gü emoticon thing? Jenny thought groggily, as she read it with her one open eye an inch from the screen. The time-sent stamp said 11.57. Then she sat bolt upright. It was past midday. Roger Roger Night was minus less than seven hours and she had the hangover from Hell, a bikini line shaped like a Hebridean island and a heart that had set sail towards the Scottish mainland.

Just thinking about Euan made the beat start up between her legs. Was he still asleep in the library garden?

Dressing with headachy clumsiness, she groaned as she remembered talking about herself endlessly, then taking her clothes off and singing Queen hits.

She made the bed with a perfunctory drag of duvet across mattress, forfeiting her plans to strip and wash the bedding for Roger, to arrange scented candles and conceal the condoms in the bedside table. She knew she had to call a halt to Gü.

Grabbing her phone, she headed downstairs. Empty wine bottles, glasses and coffee cups littered the kitchen surfaces. The blinds were still lowered, casting it in its Caribbean stripes, but Euan's painting things and the portrait had gone from the table.

A loud electric buzzing started up from the garden.

She clutched her sore head, praying the neighbours hadn't brought some sort of mechanical plaything to indulge their pool pleasures.

A loud rap on one of the french windows made her jump. They were all still ajar.

A thin, wild-eyed man wearing nothing but dungarees and a back-to-front flat cap was glaring at her. 'Was it you set those bloody sprinklers up?' he demanded, in a strong Welsh accent.

'Yes.' She peered past him to another figure, also in dungarees and a flat cap, waving a strimmer around by the shrubbery. They looked like two long-lost members of Dexy's Midnight Runners. 'Who are you?'

'Roy the gardener. I take it you're the house-sitter. No offence, but you should have left well a-bloody-lone. This garden already has an integrated irrigation system. State-of-the-art it is. Now it's like a bloody bog out there.'

'You're the gardener?'

'That's right. But I'll be telling Richard any more nonsense like this and he'll have to find somebody else. Any chance of a cup of tea?'

He stepped back in surprise as she rushed past him, almost falling into the pool as she rocketed past it, jumping down the steps from the decking in one and hurtling into the library garden.

Euan wasn't there.

To the ongoing irritation of the dungaree-clad gardeners, Jenny didn't make them any tea. Instead, she paced backwards and forwards across the small library garden, arms tightly crossed, Gunter bounding behind her. An argument was raging in her head, the beat between her legs refusing to be stilled.

Why did Euan let me think he was gardening here to supplement his income?

He never actually said that he was. You made that assumption.

What else was he doing here with a pair of secateurs first thing on Sunday morning – trying to prune the cottage ghost?

You were the idiot who kept believing he had green fingers, even after he revealed his hand.

He's done nothing dishonest.

Where is he now then?

She sat on the sofa, its cushions still indented where he'd slept. Just as quickly, she sprang up again and dashed back into the house.

'Cup of tea would be nice!' called one of Dexy's Midnight Runners from the herbaceous border.

She marched restlessly from painting to painting. God, he was talented. How could she ever have thought he needed to hoe and weed to justify Richard's patronage?

Then she went into the snug and found the portrait of the Lewises taken down, the safe on the wall open.

She fell back as though punched. 'Oh, God, no.'

Call the police. Call them now.

But she hesitated, climbing onto the sofa to peer inside the metal recess. There was a tall column of bank notes divided up with paper belly straps, along with multiple velvet cases that probably held jewellery, leather files of paperwork pushed further back and several keys that looked like they belonged to safe-deposit boxes.

Call the police.

Heart hammering, she shut it and hung the picture back up.

What are you doing? *Call the police.*

She went to the utility room. The key cupboard was open. All the keys were hanging up exactly where she'd left them, except for the set with the *Ironman Cozumel 2009* key-ring that she'd found in the door of the garden cottage.

Euan had lived in Mexico, she remembered. He said he'd used the cottage as a painting studio for a while. If they were his, why hadn't he just asked for them?

Taking down the spare set of cottage keys, she hurried back out through the garden.

'Any chance of a cup of—'

The door was already open. The mess had been moved around, but it was impossible to tell if anything had been taken. For a premeditated burglar who had bided his time all week, Euan was useless at covering his tracks. Then again, she remembered painfully, he'd been as slewed on a sleepless high as she had. 'Come to bed with me,' he'd said before passing out. Then he'd ransacked the place.

282

Jenny sat down heavily on the sofa, then stood up again to remove two CDs and a pen lid from beneath her bottom. Familiar writing littered the floor around her. She sat back down, thinking hard. *The Storm Returns* manuscript! She stood up again, hurrying out. Gunter ran after her.

'Any chance of a—'

The manuscript was still in the drawer of the utility room, her attempts at forgery neatly placed on top. She lifted the top sheet, confused, certain her efforts hadn't been this good. It looked exactly like an original, copied verbatim. Jenny knew she hadn't finished one side of the page, but there was the Sapphic sex scene in all its slithery, slippery, ripe-papaya glory. Her brows creased as she read a line describing a tongue tracing the wings of a butterfly tattoo. Then she slammed the drawer shut.

She picked up her phone and Googled a number for the local police station. Just as quickly, she closed the app and pressed the handset against her forehead.

What sort of burglar apparently takes nothing, apart from the time to cover up one of somebody else's crimes?

33

Roger arrived at exactly seven o'clock, his black Mercedes freshly valeted, supermarket cool bags neatly stacked in the boot alongside a small overnight bag, which he left discreetly alongside the AA emergency breakdown kit as he turned to hail Jenny, who was emerging to greet him uncertainly from the shadows of the porch.

In the past few hours, she'd picked up her phone to cancel him as often as she'd picked it up to call the police, but she had done neither, mostly pacing the house and garden with Gunter. They'd walked miles that day without leaving the Old Rectory grounds.

Still wearing his suit trousers with his striped work shirt, Roger looked cool and crisp, the glacial hair barber neat, the aftershave as fresh as a lime grove when he stepped forward to kiss her. It was a firm, confident kiss, lips slightly parted, telling her that tonight he meant business. Jenny waited for a flutter of anticipation. None came, just the reassurance of seductive intent after Euan's betrayal. Roger would get her back on track. She could tell him a potted version of what had happened and he'd know what to do.

He handed her a watermelon as heavy as a bowling ball. 'For breakfast.' He looked at her sideways through his pale lashes, smiling widely. 'You look wonderful as always. What a marvellous place!' He turned to gaze up at the Old Rectory's austere face. 'Wouldn't mind somewhere like this myself, if I ever decide to settle down away from the city centre.'

'Who wouldn't?' She smiled in agreement, wishing she'd cancelled. But she really didn't want to be alone tonight. Her head still pounded, no matter how many painkillers she popped, her thoughts revolving like a zoetrope, yet she could see nothing but Euan. She was wearing a lot of makeup because her skin had dried to parchment after her night on the tiles and her eyes were shrunken red bugs, but she was already sweating it off. Her only decent dress that was cool enough for the muggy evening was an overtly flowery boot-strap concoction she'd bought for a holiday last year but never worn because she thought it was too see-through and so long she'd keep tripping over the hem.

She tripped over it now as she followed Roger's very upright striped back inside, listening to his admiring architectural lecture. 'Wonderful trefoil relief work on the mullions – undoubtedly nineteenth-century revival. This oak staircase is very grand, and the barrel-vaulted ceiling is most unusual. Must date back to a previous incarnation.'

He was less impressed by Gunter, who woke up from another deep heat-wave sleep on the patchwork sofa to throw barks and bear-hugs at him, then goosed him non-stop.

Dumping the watermelon on the side, Jenny took Roger's grocery bags before he dropped them.

'I insist you leave dinner to me,' he said manfully, trying to hold Gunter's nose away from his crotch. 'I'm chef tonight – and I must say I'm looking forward to playing with all this gadgetry. What a magnificent kitchen.'

'Yes, it's a high-tech house,' Jenny agreed. 'Remote-control kitchen, remote-control garden, remote-control dog.'

'Can you switch him off?' He laughed anxiously as Gunter caught him unawares opening the 20-percent-off Prosecco, and inhaled deeply.

'I melted the control collar,' she admitted, as the cork popped, sending Gunter scuttling into his cage, which made a terrible clanking noise. 'And he broke his bedroom.' Realizing she could no longer keep the awful truth of her custodianship of the Old Rectory a secret, she blurted, 'He also ate the car and I ripped a valuable portrait, but that's nothing on the artist who pretended to be a gardener, then asked me to pose for him before stealing back his keys and ransacking the place. This morning in fact.'

'What a character.' He handed her a brimming glass, touching it with his own. 'To us and our wonderful dinner venue.'

He hasn't taken in a word, Jenny thought in horror, setting her champagne flute down. The smell of wine made her stomach churn.

Roger's blue eyes were shining into hers. 'I'm ready for the guided tour.'

'Of course!' She felt an automaton click in, the one that had got her through dozens of college dinners and drinks parties a decade earlier. 'We'll have to put the food out of Gunter's reach. He's a terrible thief.' The word made her wince.

Roger gave Gunter a wary look as he carried the bags to the cavernous larder fridge, then whipped them straight out again as though they'd been contaminated. 'There's lots of out-of-date food in here, Jenny.'

'Is there?'

'We'll have to throw it away.' He set his bags down on the island again and went to start unloading the fridge. 'Does the kerbside collection take foodstuffs?'

Roger was immensely practical. It was one of the things that had attracted Jenny to him in the first place: his per-nicketiness had always seemed to match her own. Within

286

moments, he had a system in place as he scooped ageing guacamole and pâté from plastic tubs to a food-waste bag then handed the containers to her to rinse for the plastics and recycling bin. In, too, went cheeses, salads, cold meat, quiches and the olives Gunter had rejected.

'I'm sure lots of this stuff is still fine to eat,' said Jenny, who hated seeing things go to waste.

'Can't take any risks.' He slotted his cold bags onto the empty shelves. 'Let's have a top-up and you can show me round.' He helped himself to more Prosecco.

Jenny deliberately left her glass behind as she took him around the rooms, tripping over her hem, feeling very proprietorial. When she'd first arrived at the Old Rectory, she'd been eager to share it, excited by the idea of an evening here with Roger, fantasizing that it was their home. Now she was protective and reluctant to reveal its secrets, wishing even more that she'd cancelled.

'Some of these paintings are a bit way out.' He was peering at Euan's vibrant depiction of the Old Rectory's austere façade above the fireplace in the library.

'How do you mean?'

'I suppose some people like all this cartoony naïve stuff. I'm more of a Turner fan.'

'He was considered pretty way out in his day.'

Jenny hadn't intended to show Roger the bedrooms, but he was already bounding up the stairs two at a time. Seeing so many house details and surveyors' reports must have made him feel he had a professional right to roam, she supposed. She hadn't even considered looking at the Lewises' private rooms until Gunter had gone missing, yet Roger enjoyed a good snoop in each, stopping in Richard's dressing room to whistle admiringly. 'Now *this* is a room I'd like.'

'I didn't think it would be your taste.' Jenny hung back,

remembering the Ashmolean dash. Now in his favourite playpen, Gunter pogoed from chaise-longue to chaise-longue in the main bedroom, cushions flying.

'I believe public art should be epic. Private art is another matter. Some of these paintings are much more like it.' Roger was admiring the claret-red walls. 'The girl with the butterfly tattoo is particularly well executed.'

'The what?' She hurried to his side. The picture was so small and hung so high on the wall that she hadn't noticed it before. It was a deliberate reworking of Degas's *La Toilette*, its nude subject turned away, her thick hair swept up over her head, the butterfly tattoo clearly visible. Euan had painted the neighbours' daughter in the nude too. Jenny's neck suddenly ran with angry pulses.

'Very pretty,' Roger stroked her bottom as she studied it. 'Who's the artist? Signature looks like a sink plunger.'

'Or a lamp on its side,' she said hollowly. 'You need another drink,' she noticed gratefully, turning to leave, tripping over her skirt again.

'And you're a little tipsy already, if I'm not mistaken.' He chuckled, casting another lingering look at the little nude.

Having topped up Roger's glass, Jenny took him out into the garden, desperate for fresh air.

'Terrific pool.' He raised his glass at it. 'Might try that later if I'm allowed.'

Her mind was on overdrive again. *He's drinking so much he clearly doesn't think he's going to drive back to Oxford tonight. He thinks this is a done deal.*

It's time you had sex again. You trust him. Nothing has changed.

I can't roger Roger.

'Christ, whose fag butts are these?' He reeled back as he

stepped under the pergola and spotted an old sand-filled terracotta flower pot brimming with them.

'The gardeners'.' She had a sudden image of Euan handing her his cigarette, her lips taking the filter where his had
been, and the heartbeat started between her legs. 'They were
here today.'

'Revolting. Must light one from the other. Still, seem to do
a good job.' He stood on the prow of the decking and sur-
veyed the walled explosion of colourful herbaceous fireworks
and luscious Jackson Pollock annuals with a deep, appreciative sniff, like Gunter at a particularly fine crotch. 'Yes,
this would do very nicely. Lucky bastards.'

Jenny hadn't seen the aspirational side of Roger until now,
and she wasn't sure she liked it. Neither had she seen him
drunk before, but as he sauntered back inside, winking at her
in passing, she registered that she was about to. A moment
later, she heard the second Prosecco cork pop.

'I've just seen what's in the bottle recycling!' he called out,
a hint of disapproval in the jovial voice. 'Have you been
throwing parties?'

'Ha-ha!' She closed her eyes, thinking about Euan sketch-
ing and painting with wine and coffee always on the go,
plying her beyond her limits so that she told him all her
secrets. The heartbeat speeded up and she pressed her face
against the inside of her arm to cool it.

'Do you know what wattage the microwave is?' Roger
called.

Seeing Roger cooking was another first. Lining up the
luxury ready meals in a row, he drew his reading glasses
from his top pocket and studied the instructions carefully.
Then he read the microwave manual – which had to be
unearthed from a nearby drawer – and used a pad and paper

to plan his pinging schedule with military precision between swigs of Prosecco.

Jenny's first glass remained untouched. Desperate to get in the mood, she went to the magic touch pad and put on some music.

'What's this juvenile racket?' He laughed as a lilting voice burst out from speakers all around.

'Ayo.'

'Got any Gershwin?'

Remembering 'Rhapsody in Blue' playing when she'd first sat for Euan, Jenny felt the beat in her groin again. She needed it to stay there. Soon the clarinet was singing its familiar cheeky opening and Gunter took refuge under a chair.

'You seem different tonight, Jenny.' Roger lowered his reading glasses and peered at her over them.

'Really?' She could feel the clarinet run right through her.

'Have you lost weight?' He was synchronizing his watch alarm with his notes.

Even now, when friends kept telling her she'd lost too much, it was a comment guaranteed to cheer her.

Watching Roger microwaving to the chirpy, sensual music was a refreshingly comic distraction. Jenny felt comforted, a sense of normality returning, the rhythm of twenty dates forming a chain-link fence around her. He's a good man, she thought fondly, as he danced from trough to trough, stabbing the cellophane surfaces with the alacrity of Norman testing out Bates Motel's shower curtains.

Euan Henderson is a bastard, she told herself emphatically. Roger has far more backbone and credibility: he would never ask a stranger to sit naked in front of him.

Remembering the 'chaps' nights out' he occasionally slotted into his diary with work colleagues and kayaking cronies, she changed her mind and moved quickly on, certain at least that Roger wouldn't break his way into a safe and ransack the house while she was sleeping upstairs.

'Must be worth a mint, the Lewises.' He threw ready-tossed salad into a bowl. 'What's their security like?'

'Fort Knox.' She eyed him warily.

Roger would never get her drunk.

'Top-up?' He shimmied up with the Prosecco.

Or ask her about her sex life.

'I was thinking, it must be a while since you invited a man for the night . . . When was the last time?'

'I haven't actually invited you for the night, Roger.'

But he didn't hear, having hurried back to his pinging microwave and handwritten schedule.

'I couldn't get that chilled soup, so I opted for assorted dim sum and mini Yorkshire puds with beef and horse-radish.'

Jenny's stomach lurched. It's a man thing, she reminded herself, thinking of the parents' evenings and club nights when she'd asked Robin to pop into the late supermarket for supper and found herself eating pork pie and pasta on the same plate. 'Shall I lay the table outside?'

'Too much insect life out there. Let's do the laying inside tonight,' he growled, taking ten seconds out of his microwave schedule to stroke her bottom again as she raided the cutlery drawer. He dropped a kiss on her shoulder. She closed her eyes. Gershwin was hotting up, sweet and ironic. The sexual beat thrummed faster inside her. But the kiss disappeared as fast as the microwave pinged.

'I bloody well hope you like this.' He laughed, pulling one out and inserting another. 'Hard work!'

Jenny smiled at him over her shoulder, remembering her dinner-party days, the frantic multi-tasking between soufflé, *jus*, choux pastry and spun-sugar cage. 'Thank you. I love being cooked for.'

'Must be nice being a lady of leisure.'

She looked back in the cutlery drawer. 'A rare treat.'

'Pity we poor foot soldiers who've worked a full day. You were no doubt still sleeping soundly in bed when I got up at seven with only John Humphrys and an electric toothbrush for company.'

She slid the drawer shut with her fluttering belly, reliving the moment she'd stood up and slid the gown from her shoulders. The beat thrummed from pelvic bone to spine now.

'Rhapsody in Blue' had been replaced with 'Summertime', unbearably sensual. She wiped the hot skin of her upper lip and raked back her hair, now heavy with sweat.

Roger was laying dim sum and mini Yorkshire puddings on what appeared to be Emma Bridgewater cake plates. She took the cutlery to the table, imagining Euan sitting there, board in hand, intimately familiar with every contour of her face.

'Dining room, I thought,' Roger redirected, in a voice thick with seductive intent, making her think of Fielding's lusty Tom Jones supping with Mrs Waters.

He followed her through, carrying his plates aloft, like a *Masterchef* contestant, as she laid two places as far apart as she dared. Opposite ends would be too kinky and lonely.

'Opposite ends, I thought.' Roger's voice was increasingly adenoidal. Taking a setting to the far end, she was grateful that the music was piped through speakers in here too, keeping the beat going inside her. 'Summertime' had given way to 'The Man I Love', the Billie Holiday version, which always broke her heart.

'Ella Fitzgerald sings it better, although purists say Sarah

Vaughan nailed it,' Roger said, picking up a box of matches and looking at her above the spark as he struck one. 'Wine, Jenny.'

For a moment she thought he wanted her to make animal noises. Then she realized she should open the two-for-one blush Pinot Grigio. She tripped over her skirt on the way out.

'No sneaky tipples when I'm not looking!' He started lighting candles.

Grateful for the excuse to delay the moment when she had to eat Cantonese dumplings served alongside micro Sunday lunch, she ran back to the kitchen, past Gunter who had already got the microwave packaging from the surface to lick clean, and out to the poolside to breathe in chlorine and hot night, the last streaks of light fading from the sky, the moon rising.

'Remember Roger is a good man,' she told herself, stepping inside to change the music to some feisty Kirsty MacColl.

She grabbed the wine and returned to find the dining room almost in darkness, the shutters closed, a few candles sputtering in corners. She fumbled her way across it to locate Roger at the head of the table. He already had his mouth full of dim sum. 'This is very good. Try.'

Kirsty MacColl was singing about an Elvis impersonator in the local chippy.

'Is this a DAB channel?' asked Roger.

'Guess so.' She headed to the opposite end of the table, grateful that the darkness meant he couldn't see her feeding everything from her plate to Gunter, who wolfed it with grateful snaps of his jaws.

'I love a woman with a good appetite!' Roger growled from afar, wine glugging into his glass.

293

'It's lovely,' she called back.

'Always makes me think of oral sex,' Roger said.

At first Jenny thought she'd misheard him.

'Eating dim sum. Like oral sex!'

'Yes?' she said brightly, as though he'd commented on the weather, too shocked to say more. Roger never talked about sex.

'The soft, moist folds giving way to a sweet, succulent interior!'

'Absolutely.'

'Mmmmmm.' He made ecstatic, slurpy, gobbling noises as he ate.

Think sex, Jenny told herself. You and Roger Roger Night. A rite of passage. You may both explode in ecstasy. Give it a chance. But even as she thought it, she visualized Euan sitting in front of her at the garden table eating an *ad hoc* lunch, knees pressed inadvertently to hers, ripping bread with those paint-spattered fingers and feeding it into his mouth between talk and laughter, and she knew which was the greater turn-on.

'I have to say something,' Roger shouted over Kirsty McColl. 'You are so . . . fucking . . . sexy . . . tonight.'

'Thanks.' Jenny wondered if the polite thing was to say, 'You too.' In the end she left a sexy silence.

Gunter belched underfoot.

The wine glugged again at Roger's end. He can't have drunk a glass already, Jenny thought anxiously. She'd already snuffled every Alka Seltzer in the house.

'Chef could probably do with some help clearing away and carrying here!' He headed towards the kitchen, glass in hand.

Clearing the two love-hearts tea plates to the sideboard and deciding it would be sexier to stay away from the kitchen than listen to the microwave descant, Jenny went in search of the electronic cigarette she'd left in her bag in the main hall and puffed it furiously in the kids' television room. She felt anger mule-kick her back against the cushions, the confusion of the past twenty-four hours throwing her into a tight curl, like a yachtsman staying aboard in a storm. She knew she was just one of a long line of Euan's models, following hard on the heels of the girl from the houseboat who wasn't Perry's girlfriend and the Oxbridge entrant with the butter-fly tattoo. Had he cracked a safe and frisked a house while *they* slept? Had they told him their deepest, darkest truths? Had they sung 'I Want To Break Free', stark naked, in the early-morning light?

She tipped forwards, curling up again, telling herself this would look a lot better after a good night's sleep. And sex.

She made it back to the dining room just as Roger carried in the main course accompanied by Kirsty MacColl's 'They Don't Know'.

'Fusion Sino-Indian duck *français!*' he said proudly.

He'd arranged microwaved crispy Peking duck, potatoes dauphinoise, sag aloo and creamed spinach on two star-shaped serving plates decorated with Christmas crackers and icicles. She wanted to cry. He was making such an effort and her every urge was to run away screaming. Keep the heartbeat, she told herself, picking up her fork. Keep the anger. Keep the faith. This is Roger Roger Night.

'You like?' He watched her, hawk-like, through the gloom, Michelin-starred chef to diner.

She had no choice but to eat, indigestion raging, tears still prickling. 'Tasty.'

'It *is* rather good,' he agreed, as he devoured his between slurping the two-for-one blush. Was that the second bottle? she worried. Surely not.

You need to see him naked, Jenny told herself. Not literally – at least, not until he's finished his duck – but metaphorically, as naked as you have been in the past twenty-four hours. You both need to go naked.

'Tell me about your marriage,' she asked.

Roger neatly choked on a chickpea. 'Why d'you want to know about that?'

'It's part of you.'

'Right. Well. Not much to say. Met through friends. Together twelve years, married eight. Grew apart. You know all this.'

'Do you regret not having children?'

'Well, not after the divorce, no.' He downed the best part of a glass of wine in one and topped it up.

'And during the marriage?'

'We tried, but it – it didn't happen. Karen wanted to take the IVF route, but I wasn't ... well, that didn't happen either.' More wine was tossed back.

'I'm so sorry. That must have been hard.'

'Not at all. Karen was fine about it in the end. We got two Burmese cats. There was a bit of a wrangle over their custody after the split, but that all got sorted. Lovely creatures. You?'

'My kids didn't want to see their father at first. Jake was particularly adamant, but I insisted the calls and visits were in place from the start. I probably overcompensated, making them Skype twice a week and email too, sorting flights months in advance, and always insisting how much their father loved them and that they mustn't blame anyone for life happening because that's what life did. Now they seem to want to be with him all the time.' She sighed, smiling at him sadly. 'I pretend it doesn't hurt, but it does.'

There was a long, thoughtful silence. Then he said, 'Actually, I was asking whether you'd ever had any cats.'

When he reeled off to prepare pudding, she returned to the television room and puffed the electronic stick some more, heart burning and aching. I'm not sure I fancy him, she admitted to herself. I'm not sure I ever have. He hides his emotions, clipping them away, like unsightly nasal hair. He finds them embarrassing. When we go to the theatre and watch actors speaking through their souls on stage, I'm up there with them, but for Roger, it's just social sport.

'Jenny! Where are you? I think you're going to like this . . .'

In the dining room, Roger had dispensed with the Bridgewater plates. On the place setting in front of him he'd lined up a clear plastic carton of strawberries, a tub of cream and two little plastic pots of chocolate fondant in a box marked 'Gü'.

Of course, the luxurious little puddings. She cheered up a little, remembering that Amalie loved them, stacked up in the supermarket dessert section, like little double dream shots. Life always looked a lot better after a chocolate fix, she told herself. Roger was trying his hardest after all. If his biggest displays of emotion were text smileys, then that was fine. Gü might not be an emoticon, but it showed his sweet centre as surely as any confession of burning heartache and child-substitute kittens.

He'd clearly fiddled with the wall pad in the kitchen and changed the house music to Sade's 'Smooth Operator'. Its clichéd seductiveness, dating him as surely as rings in a tree trunk, made her feel choked and tearful again. She sat down.

At the opposite end of the table, Roger was holding up the little plastic pot. Through the candlelit gloom, Jenny could just about make out his big suggestive smile. 'I'm going to bring it to you.'

'You really don't have to.' She stood up, guiltily aware she'd been distinctly idle that night.

'Sit!' he insisted. 'I will walk across the table on my hands and knees.'

'I'm sorry?'

'I will come to you across the table on my hands and knees and spoon-feed you, mistress.'

'No!' Anger flared inside Jenny. She was nervous enough as it was without him free-running across the Lewises' furniture in the name of seduction. And why had he just called her 'mistress'?

There was a long silence. Eventually he said, 'That wasn't quite the reaction I was expecting.'

Jenny rubbed her lip with her thumb, wondering if she'd overreacted. Poor Roger was probably as nervous as she was under the drunken bravado. They'd spent twenty dates sharing wit, culture, good Italian food and farewell clinches that had made her stomach tighten in something close to a lover's knot. It wasn't his fault that her time here had retied that knot into a tight, confused tangle. An expensive Waitrose meal had been reduced to leftovers for the compost caddy and black packaging shredded in Gunter's cage; a giddy build-up of expectation was under threat of being similarly destroyed. Dessert was the only course she actually wanted to eat. She wanted Gü and she wanted it now. She was certain they could get this back on course. She needed the bass beat inside her again.

'How about you meet me in the middle?' she suggested.

He was on the table faster than a stag-party exhibitionist in Hofbräuhaus. 'Hey!'

'Don't say "hey".' She kicked off her shoes and clambered up.

Bad idea, she told herself, as she crawled towards him

around the candles, her knees catching on her skirt constantly, pulling her head and chest down towards the oak.

'Miaaaow.' Clearly Roger thought she was doing some sort of cat impersonation.

She tugged the skirt up and held it in one hand. He is handsome, he is fussy, he is the man to tame this hussy, she chanted in her head, still in tune with Kirsty MacColl, ignoring Sade breathily cooing her famous coronation anthem for lovers.

Already at the candelabra, king of love Roger was wrestling with the gold foil lid sealing the small pot of chocolate pudding. As Jenny drew close, he wrenched it off, dipped his finger into the Gü and held it towards her lips. 'I'll suck yours if you suck mine.'

She sat back on her haunches. 'Actually, Roger, could I have a spoon?'

'We can spoon in bed,' he said huskily. 'We'll take this as slowly as you want, Jenny. We have all night.' He kissed her gently on the lips. It was a sweet-tasting, familiar kiss. 'I think we should take this upstairs, don't you?'

Twenty dates, Jenny reminded herself. Roger was attractive and smelt good; he was never late, he had never lied, he had offered her an exclusive package. There was no reason to change her mind after one sleepless night with a predatory, unconventional thief. Euan might have turned up the tempo, but Roger was still playing the tune. She was certain things would get back on track upstairs. It was time, she told herself. Roger Roger was finally happening.

While Roger nipped outside to fetch his discreet overnight case and Gunter finished off the washing-up in his unique, anarchic way, Jenny sat on the loo in her mirrored bathroom upstairs with her head in her hands, adding 'fuck' and 'scaring me' to 'Your Love is King', which Roger appeared to have put on repeat.

She was having a huge wobble at the prospect of having sex again, most especially sex with Roger. She had two minutes max to get the pelvic heartbeat back, or escape out of the window, or alternatively to tell him that in the past two days their twenty dates had been eclipsed by a few hours with an artist who was a safe-breaking, house-breaking liar, but who made her feel eighteen again.

It was too late. She could hear him coming upstairs, ordering Gunter to stay back.

She washed her hands, splashed cold water on her throat and the back of her neck, then went into her sexy Provençal room.

'My name is Roger,' he swaggered in with a tray, 'but tonight you can call me – Randy Alexander!' He'd brought up two bottles of liqueur, cocktail glasses, the cream and a 1920s shaker.

'Wow.' She smiled over-brightly. 'You remembered.'

'I'd do anything for you,' he said in a Sean Connery drawl, setting the tray down and consulting a piece of paper on it before starting to measure out precise proportions.

Oh, shit, Jenny mouthed to herself, turning away to look out of the window, past the fronds of wisteria to the darkened garden. Then her pulse skipped as she saw something glow like a cigarette end.

'What are you looking at?' Roger was hip-jigging eagerly around the bedroom with the shaker, like Tom Cruise in *Cocktail.*

'Fireflies.' She stared out into the darkness, seeing nothing now.

'Did you know that fireflies can synchronize their flashing?' He poured the drinks.

The pinprick of orange light glowed again, making her heartbeat treble, the beat flying between her legs.

'Close the curtains.' Roger pressed himself up against her and kissed her shoulder, handing her a martini glass brimming with creamy *digestif*.

34

While Roger couldn't put together a dinner menu to save his life, he mixed a mean Brandy Alexander. Jenny managed to get through most of hers by alternating it with strawberries, spoonfuls of the chocolate pot and long kisses. It was surprisingly moreish. In fact, invigorated by a sugar rush, she felt more awake than she had all evening. She was ready to break her three-year barren patch and her twenty-two years of fidelity to Robin. Roger might have ambitiously planned a Tom Jones scene on the dining table, or maybe a Lady Chatterley moment in the shrubbery later, but she was happy with the comfort and safety of a standard-issue bedroom seduction, plus Gü.

Roger Roger night minus three . . . two . . . one . . .

Sade finally gave way to Bryan Ferry, and Roger fixed Jenny with a look that meant business, reaching up to unbutton his shirt. As each button started to come undone in time to the beat, she realized that he was doing a strip-tease. He appeared to have practised – there were disconcerting leg kicks and hip shakes – but once he was in the buff, she could see he *was* buff. Square shoulders, flat stomach, neat cock, professionally waxed man foliage, he sauntered towards her, growling, 'Your turn.'

It was too late to panic about her own personal grooming. This was her hot, sticky sexual comeback. She was too far from the switch to dim the auditorium lights as planned. Last night she'd stripped off in front of a near stranger she had never kissed, let alone shared six months of flirtatious build-up with. How hard could this be? Hooking her fingers under the bootlace straps of her dress, she remembered last night's liberation when she'd undressed, the feather lightness, the hot wash of arousal rushing in. The dress dropped six inches then stopped, its hanger ribbons caught in her bra clasp. She tugged it down with a loud ripping sound, inadvertently dragging her bra half off.

'Beautiful,' breathed Roger, as Bryan Ferry cooed around them.

The bra was shed, still attached to the dress, her breasts springing out, nipples still soft as marshmallows.

'Oh, Mama,' Roger growled, semi-erect now.

The knickers slid off and, just for a moment, Roger's eyes fixed on the Hebrides before returning to her breasts.

'Hallelujah!'

'Now turn the light out,' she squeaked.

In darkness, Roger and Jenny embarked upon polite, fumbling HBO sex, with a lot of 'hey baby' gusto from Roger (she wished it didn't make her think of Austin Powers) and occasional muttered apologies from Jenny when she accidentally elbowed him.

It started to go wrong when Gunter bed-bombed them somewhere between H and B, crashing his way in from the landing, banking the bed, then bounding off to raid the pudding tray for leftovers.

'Ignore him,' Jenny insisted, grasping the initiative once again. Roger's initiative was refreshingly smooth and sanitized. It tasted incredibly clean, as though he'd rinsed it in mineral water just beforehand.

After five minutes of groaning and 'hey', Roger muttered,

'That's enough now' – like a father telling a child to stop playing on the Wii – manoeuvred her back towards the pillows and angled himself above her.

'Have you got a condom?' Jenny tried not to feel resentful that he hadn't shown the slightest inclination to offer her any delights in the HBO mix, his fingers barely kite-surfing round the Hebridean coast, let alone paddling there, far more interested in motor-boating her boobs.

It transpired that Roger hadn't added condoms to his Waitrose loyalty-card buys, and he seemed as surprised to be asked to wear one as an A-lister required to put on a tie in a restaurant. 'Don't you have that end covered?'

'We're covering your end too,' she told him firmly, handing him the small foil packet, which he ripped into with slightly less enthusiasm than he had the Gü lid.

As he rolled it on, she wriggled back to get into a better position, propping herself up on pillows and dipping a discreet finger between her legs to check his welcome was guaranteed; the heartbeat that had revved in her groin on and off all day had left her constantly slippery. She felt her muscles tighten in anticipation again now as she turned her head and looked towards the closed curtains. Unable to stop herself, she thought about Euan, imagined his green eyes watching her window. The muscles drew in further, craving touch. Roger angled himself for entry again. Then, as he plunged in with a 'hey, baby' and a gasp of release from Jenny, Gunter reappeared on the mattress with a big, panting grin and chocolate Gü on his whiskers.

'Jesus!' Roger withdrew and covered his genitals as thirty kilos of panting hairy dog bounded around the bed, eager to join in.

Sitting up, Jenny fought terrible giggles, a nervous reflex. Having seen the funny side the first time – or pretended to – Roger was now extremely put out. 'It's frankly perverted having a dog in the bedroom,' he said, through gritted teeth, erection wilting in its Fetherlite wrapping as Gunter rolled over and flashed his white-eyed upside-down smile. 'We have to shut him away somewhere.'

'His cage is broken,' Jenny explained, still battling giggles. 'He trashes any room he's shut in. He can be distracted by tripe sticks, but I've run out.'

'Right.' He sprang off the bed determinedly. 'We'll see about this.'

He gathered up the pot of cream from his cocktail tray, which Gunter had yet to spot, and, whistling, led him through to the bathroom, returning a few moments later. 'That should keep him busy for ten minutes or so.'

Ten minutes, Jenny echoed silently, trying not to feel short-changed. No magic fingers, no tongue longing to taste her, ten minutes left on the clock. 'You just threw cream around my en-suite?'

'It'll wash off.'

'It'll smell terrible.'

'Let the cleaning ladies worry about that.' Roger resumed position with a perfunctory kiss to get things going again. 'Now, where were we?'

She swallowed a small fireball of indignation, pulling away. 'What happened to the dim sum course?'

'I'm sorry?'

'You said eating dim sum was like oral sex.'

'We're already at dessert.'

'I feel like dim sum, Roger.'

'Now?' He looked as if she'd just asked if she could relieve herself in his car glove box.

'Yes.'

He blew out through his lips in much the same way Robin

had whenever she reminded him that he hadn't cleaned his teeth.

After a lot of fuss rearranging the duvet behind him, he knelt above her. 'You have a beautiful body. Is that a Brazilian?' He seemed to be making conversation to delay the moment.

'A Jura,' she told him. 'It's all the rage.'

'Beautiful.' He dipped his head and kissed her pubic mound, much as a politician would kiss the thin fluff on a baby's head. Then, straightening up, he fixed her with a look that gleamed eagerly through the darkness. 'Will you order me to do it?'

'I'm sorry?' It was her turn to sound alarmed.

'Order me to lick you.'

Jenny found the idea faintly off-putting, but she was squirming with the need for physical release now, the beat in her groin, ears, pulses and nipple ends.

'Please make me come, Roger,' she entreated.

'A bit more demanding, maybe?'

'Go down on me, you bastard!'

'That's a bit harsh.'

'Roger, if you don't get on with this, the dog will be out of that bathroom bouncing around with us again.'

'Yes, mistress.' He cleared his throat and got to work.

It was the throat-clearing that truly killed the moment for Jenny. It reminded her of her dental hygienist, who always cleared his throat before scraping off tartar. Then Roger started dibbing away with his tongue as though he was moistening Christmas stamps.

'A bit higher would be great,' she suggested.

'It's fine. I know what I'm doing,' he muttered, like a driver irritated by a map-reading wife. 'Enjoy the ride.' He dibbed some more.

Jenny suddenly pitied poor Karen with her husband's air-freshener erection bringing hygienic pleasure but no babies or enjoyable oral sex. No amount of Burmese cats could make up for that. At least in the old days Robin had shown boundless enthusiasm and skill. A deep sigh of regret drew through her for what she'd lost.

Roger's face reappeared, looking very pleased with himself, ball of his thumb wiping his mouth carefully. 'Enjoy that?'

He thinks I've come, Jenny realized, her solar plexus still resounding with hollow need that no amount of dibbing would satisfy. Having him inside her would surely do something to meet the craving. She wriggled back up the pillows, but he fixed her with those gleaming eager eyes again, voice thickening. 'Now you can do something for me.' He glanced towards the bathroom, from which they could still hear faint sounds of a cream pot being rattled around and destroyed.

Jenny could have pointed out that she'd already stroked, gripped, licked and sucked at length while he'd merely bestowed a Tory PM kiss and dibbed for precisely twenty seconds, but she was hoping that whatever it was might get them back on track and finally sate her bubbling frustration.

Clambering off the bed, he hurried towards his small overnight bag, drawing something out with the reverence of a knight pulling Excalibur from a stone, then turned back to face her.

'What is that?' she asked, alarmed, as she saw something resembling a giant fancy dress nose dangling from his hand.

'A strap-on,' he breathed, as he loomed over her, his eyes huge with excitement. 'I always knew it would take a special someone and that someone is you, Jenny. I want you to wear it. Hang on, I brought lube.' He headed back to his bag.

With a bleat of horror, she scrambled upright, pulling the

sheets around her as she watched him fumbling around in the zipped sections. 'I won't wear it!'

There was a short, angry buzz of a holdall zip closing. 'I came all this way.'

'I'm so sorry, Roger, but it really isn't my thing. I absolutely can't do it.'

'I cooked you supper. I just went down on you.'

'This isn't a trade-off.'

More zips buzzed and growled back and forth. 'This is a big thing for me. I wasn't going to share it with you just yet, but you shared your needs. I thought we had a connection.'

'We did – we do. I think perhaps we're just trying to run before we can walk here, Roger.'

'Why walk when you can fly?' He laughed hollowly, another zip closing. 'Ouch! Fuck!'

'Have you caught yourself?' She peered through the gloom anxiously. He had his back to her, the pale moons of his buttocks clenched tightly together.

'I'll ... be ... fine.' He spoke in staccato bursts of pain. 'I'll ... sleep in another ... room. I should be gone by dawn. I have a breath-test kit with me.'

'Your breath smells fine, Roger, honestly,' she insisted before realizing he meant an alcohol breathalyser.

He was snatching his clothes up off the floor now, so joyfully discarded in his Slave to Love striptease. 'I can't drive for at least six more hours. As soon as I'm legal, I'll be out of your hair. I think it best we don't see each other again.'

'Roger, please let's not—'

'You need to lose some inhibitions, Jenny. And, speaking purely out of kindness, I think the jury's out on the Jura.' As insults went, that was about as hard core as Roger got.

IX

Friday

35

TO DO LIST

Eat lots of super-foods
No alcohol
Quit electronic smoking
Take a break from depilation
Never have sex with Roger again.

Roger was gone by dawn, leaving two Prosecco bottles and two blush alongside the forest of green Montrachet empties in the Lewises' recycling bin. He took the brandy and cacao with him, along with his cold bags and the watermelon, which Jenny was quietly relieved hadn't featured in his sexual overtures.

She made herself a cup of tea and tidied the debris left from Roger's military microwaving. There wasn't much – Gunter had appropriated most of the packaging, after all although Roger appeared to have used an inexplicable number of tea towels.

Hearing a splash, she looked up to see the girl with the butterfly tattoo swimming.

'Hi there.' She stepped outside, frantically averting her gaze.

Swimming under water, the girl didn't hear her, but when she bobbed up for air, she spotted Gunter bounding round the pool edge barking and turned. 'Hi! I'm Lonnie. We haven't met, but I know who you are. Isn't it glorious out here at this time?' She had a sweet, lisping voice.

'You're obviously an early bird.'

'Are you kidding?' She laughed. 'I haven't been to bed yet.'

Oh, to be young and party all night every night, Jenny thought. Euan probably got much more value from her than he did from me on his insomniac, wine-fuelled painting marathon.

'I'm stacking supermarket shelves as a holiday job,' she explained cheerily, dispelling Jenny's myths of nocturnal Buckinghamshire debauchery.

'I've seen the picture of you in the house. It's lovely.'

'Fabulous, isn't it? I was so flattered to be asked, although Mummy insisted I mustn't pose front-on. She's a terrible prude. Dad and Hilary were cool about it, though. They have one hanging on the mezzanine. There's three more going on display in Euan's exhibition in September.'

'I'm certainly looking forward to that.' Jenny tried for a carefree laugh, but it came out as a demented cackle. 'Do you know where I might find him, by the way?'

'I'm not sure where he lives. I sat for him at his studio – it's one of the converted barns on the Thame road.'

'Thanks! I have some stuff to return to him.' She headed inside, her heartbeat like a kettledrum in her ears.

Running upstairs, she pulled on the first clothes she could find, then hurried to the dog car.

Thrilled to be back on the early-morning-walk routine, Gunter leaped around behind the patched-up grille, even more excited when he realized that they were detouring to the Thame road on their way to Beacon Common.

She found the barn complex easily. All the units were secured and deserted at this time in the morning, although the main gates were unlocked. Parking behind an old half-timbered milking parlour that now housed Graffix Web Design, she let Gunter out of the boot to help her search. Eventually, she tracked down a sagging single-storey brick-and-flint barn in a far corner with a small hand-made plaque outside bearing the sideways-lamp signature. There was no sign of life. The dusty windows were too high to look through, the double doors padlocked.

Returning to the car, she scrabbled in the glove box, found a pen and an old vet's vaccination receipt, and wrote on the back, *I hope that if you found what you were looking for, it was worth deceiving me. I wish you'd just been honest; I think you owed me that. You know why.*

Was this aiding and abetting? She wanted to add something that might trigger him to make contact, but in the end she simply signed it *Jenny* and slipped it into the box beneath the sign on the barn. Then she pulled it out and added. *PS Did you copy a manuscript page for me?* She pulled it out a second time and added a *Why* at the start of the PS.

She had got into the car and started the engine when she decided to add a PPS. She ran back and fished it out again, adding, *Thank you for listening.* Then she crossed out the first PS.

'Enough', she told herself firmly, pushing it in again. She was going to take Gunter on an extra-long walk around the gravel pits to make up for her negligence yesterday.

It was even hotter than it had been the previous day and, despite the early hour, Gunter soon started to fade, flopping down in the shadows of tree-trunks and splashing in and out of the cloudy grey water to cool off. Jenny was pouring sweat by the time they got back to the car. She'd parked in the shade, but the seats were as hot as bubbling caramel. The bottles of water she'd left for herself and for Gunter's drinking bowl were warm as tea.

As soon as she was back at the Old Rectory and Gunter was wolfing breakfast she peeled off her sweat-soaked shorts and T-shirt. It was even too hot for her faithful Speedo. Leaving on her bra and knickers, she jumped into the pool. The cool water enveloping her was beyond bliss.

She floated up to the surface, starfishing there for as long as she could, enjoying the silence as she looked down at the blue pool floor, its perspective distorted, her shadow a strange crab.

She saw another shadow a split second before she was knocked sideways by a great bow-wave and a body plunged in beside her, surrounded by a halo of bubbles. For a moment, she thought Gunter had jumped in with her, but then a strong arm encircled her and started towing her towards the side.

Blinded by her hair swooshing across her face and now swallowing a lot of water, Jenny struggled to break away, but the arm tightened. By struggling, she swallowed more. Arms flailing, lungs filling, her fingers closed around soft cotton which she pushed and pulled to try to free herself.

When she burst up into the air, lifted by the unseen arm, she was by the steps at the shallow end. Towering over her, Euan scooped her up to carry her out.

'Let me go!' she spluttered. 'What in hell do you think you're doing?'

'I should ask you that, you bloody fool.'

'I was swimming!'

Caught off balance by one of Gunter's bear-hugs, he staggered a few steps before dropping down on his knees and depositing her on the grass.

She glared up at him, silhouetted by the sun and dripping water everywhere.

'I was swimming,' she repeated.

'In your bra and knickers? Floating there like a corpse?' He carried on dripping water on her, his face inches from hers.

'I was starfishing.' Realizing she was still gripping his T-shirt, which was why he was leaning so close, she let go.

He didn't move. She could feel the hard muscle of his chest against her ribs, breaths punching in and out of him. 'I got your note.'

She wanted to sit up, but he was still pinning her down. She turned her wet face to wipe against her shoulder and looked up at him curiously. 'You didn't think I was going to do something silly?'

'It sounded very final.'

'Why would I kill myself? You think I'm so guilt-ridden for trusting you and letting you loot the Lewises' house that I'd drown myself in their pool?' Sighing angrily, she lay back on the grass and looked up at the flawless blue sky. 'It was just a note. I want an explanation.'

'Why didn't you call the police?'

She slid her eyes towards him and the heartbeat started up in her solar plexus, furious and urgent. She knew exactly why. The shallowest of all reasons. The reason Bonnie hadn't dobbed on Clyde. 'You didn't actually take anything, did you?'

He shook his head. 'I was tired and pissed and clumsy. I meant to cover my tracks, but the gardeners turned up. I thought it best to clear off and find a way to apologize. By the time I got back, your date was here.' He was still unbearably close, his skin hot against hers.

Perhaps it hadn't been a firefly after all, Jenny thought, the beat increasing. Panting up behind her, Gunter flopped alongside, sandwiching her tightly. She could hardly breathe for being so close to Euan now. He dipped his head, a black and white cowlick of hair flopping over one eye, and she was suddenly so turned on words slipped away. She longed to reach up and touch it. Sweat was pouring off her again. She had to cool off. 'Please let me finish my swim.'

He moved his arm and sat up so that she could roll away. Grass cuttings were sticking all over her, like a fur coat. To her embarrassment one boob had popped out of her bra, nipple hard as a marble. She hurriedly put it back and stood up, adjusting her knickers where they'd rucked up around her bottom and hurrying back to the pool to dive in with an accidental belly flop.

Each time she bobbed up from swimming a length, she saw that he was still stretched out on the same patch of lawn with Gunter, drying off in the sun.

'You'll burn,' she told him, as she turned at the shallow end.

'I never burn.'

'So what was it you were searching the house and cottage for?' she asked, on her next turnaround.

'A painting.'

Realizing that this wasn't the speediest means of cross-examination, she stayed in the shallow end, letting the pressure filter in the pool wall massage her back with its jet of water. 'Is it for the exhibition?'

'No, it's personal. I need it back.'

She bit her lip, guessing it had to be the second Lewis family portrait that she had ripped.

'How was Roger?' he asked, his shadow falling across the pool.

She turned to him, letting the jet blast her collar bone. 'Roger's over and out.'

Even though his face was in shadow again, she could see a huge white smile burst out.

'But I'm not suicidal about it.'

'Good.' He squatted down to sit on the side of the pool in

front of her, dropping his feet in the water. He had a birth-mark on one ankle, she noticed, suddenly longing to kiss it.

'What went wrong?'

'We're not compatible.' She closed her eyes briefly, trying not to remember the dibber tongue and the prosthetic secret in his overnight bag. His advert was probably already live on the dating website again, his Thursday slots unexpectedly available.

She let the water jet run over her shoulders, pummelling away the aches of a restless night. When she opened her eyes, her face was parallel with his calf, the muscle as defined as an overhang on a rock face.

She grabbed the side of the pool, moving closer to the jet, which was trying to push her away. It caught her breast and a bolt of instinctive pleasure cut straight down through her.

'What changed your mind about him?'

'It was a bed thing.' She moved her breast against the jet again, the nipple glancing through the stream, and felt the bolt so intensely she shuddered.

Blushing, she moved quickly away, appalled at herself. His shadow dipped forward just as quickly and he reached his hand around the back of her neck. 'What bed thing?'

Pleasure bolts were flying in every direction now, even though she was nowhere near the filter. She ducked her head away and his hand dropped. 'Did I say bed? I meant food.'

'The food put you off?' His voice was half suspicious, half teasing.

'Seriously random menu.' She'd crept closer again, could feel the outer edges of the water pressure catching her. 'Plus he got very drunk.'

She squinted up at his dark outline and he leaned for-wards so that she was beneath his shadow, his eyes serious. 'Did he frighten you?'

317

'God, no. He's a bit of a wimp, really.' She was alongside the jet again. One step to the left and it would be nipple nirvana. 'Poor Roger.'

Euan's eyes didn't leave her face. She remembered the firefly glowing in the dark outside. Had he been there to watch out for her, or to ransack the cottage again? She couldn't trust him. He'd propositioned her once, then promptly gone to sleep, later plundering his way round the Lewises' house. Yet she looked at the tanned, muscular legs dangling to either side of her and knew that if he'd been in her bedroom last night she wouldn't have been left squirming in frustration, caught up like a fish in a net above a perfect ocean reef, gasping to be released.

She felt his fingers touch her now and the electric surges coursed through her as their tips traced her shoulders then around her back, very gently unhooking her bra and drawing it over her shoulders, his breath warm in her wet hair. 'Move to your left.'

She stepped left. The warm pounding pressure on her nipples shot her through with such bolts of sensation it knocked her off her feet. Still sitting on the pool ledge, Euan reached down, hands beneath her arms. He held her there, through almost unbelievable pleasure.

His hands tightened on her ribcage, taking her weight in the water now and pulling her up to his mouth, his lips hard against hers. The jet was pounding against her navel, meeting the instinctive beat thumping back. She gripped his shoulders for balance.

Kiss deepening, Euan pulled her higher, his thighs closing around her hips to support her as she was suspended out of the water, like a dancing dolphin, his hands through her hair, strong thumbs stroking the hollows behind her ears.

'Did you fuck him?' he demanded, as he kissed her.

'Yes – no – sort of.'

At this, he tipped off from the poolside so they both plunged in. Coming back to the surface amid a shoal of bubbles, Jenny felt his arms still around her. Before she could take in what was happening he'd scooped her up and was marching up the steps to carry her inside, dripping water across kitchen flags and hall boards, straight up into the room of a hundred mirrors where he deposited her in the bath and turned the big mixer tap on full blast, emptying half a bottle of her best Sanctuary pampering kit into it.

'That's oil!' She slithered precariously.

'I'm sure you don't need any more of that.' He rattled through the bottles, finding foam wash and emptying it in too. Soon she was slipping around amid great white popping peaks.

His green eyes bored down on her as he leaned over the bath. 'Wash.'

'What right have you to tell me to wash?' She reached for a bath mitt, but his hand was already against her skin, fingers sliding from her navel to her groin. She flipped back with a spasm of pleasure, spine bull-whipping.

He slipped a finger inside her and she came, embarrassingly instant and eager, with such force that she had no time even to blush, her forehead pressed to his arm.

Euan slid his fingers through her hair, cupping her head as he tilted it back so she was looking up at him. His eyes were hard with desire, green irises almost all black. 'I'm taking you to bed. How much longer are you here?'

'A week,' she said breathlessly, shock bolts still running through her.

'It's a start.'

'Cooeee!' a voice shouted from the landing. 'Ladies Who Launder Va Va Vacuum! Did you know the dog is in the pool again? He's got tangled up in a bra.'

319

36

Gunter had one lacy shoulder strap around his neck, wearing Jenny's bra like an apron as he swam around the shallow end. Coaxed up the steps, he charged around the garden with it swinging behind him, like a superhero's cloak, thoroughly overexcited by his rebellious dip.

Euan pulled Jenny behind a big scented shrub rose and kissed her as Gunter thundered around. 'I can't promise you anything.' His lips made their way up her throat. 'I'm unreliable and I never stick around. I'm a lost cause.'

'I had gathered that.'

'I have no prospects, no regular income. After this exhibition, I'm travelling again.'

'Where?'

'As far as I can get. Christ, I want you.' He buried his face in her shoulder, his body tight against hers. She could feel the swell of him against her stomach, remembered him standing on the houseboat. He must have slept with so many women, seducing them as nonchalantly as she took a new book to bed. Yet right now she didn't care. She'd never wanted anyone as much in her life.

Gunter panted past again, bra still swinging. The cleaning ladies were having a cigarette out on the balcony, talking loudly about the latest episode of *Broadchurch*.

'I can't wait.' His mouth found hers again, a heady tongue twist of lips and words. 'We'll go to my studio.'

'The ladies will be off soon.' She groaned, as his hand slid up beneath her shirt. 'I can't leave the house unlocked.' His lips on her neck made her dissolve against him. 'Someone might break in ...'

They leaned against one another in a brief, silent kiss of laughter. She felt seventeen again, her pre-Robin life of sexual awakening fuelled by *The Dust Storm*, INXS, *Dirty Dancing* and fierce crushes, with stolen kisses on doorsteps and illicit fumbles on sofas while babysitting.

Gunter was panting past in the opposite direction now. Seconds later, there was a loud clatter of pointer slamming against garden gate, then gate falling off its hinges.

On the balcony, the Ladies Who Launder let out caws of surprise. 'You see that? Straight through. Bonkers that dog.'

'My neighbour had an Italian Spinone just the same. Stallone, he was called, but we knew him as the Dogfather. All the local mutts looked like him after a while. I reckon Gunter must have a lady friend. You couldn't keep that dog in Alcatraz if there was a bitch on heat nearby.'

The silent laughter became almost painful as Euan and Jenny clung to one another, attraction and amusement fusing into the most exquisite arc. Then they stopped, catching their breath, both thinking the same thing.

By the time they tracked him down to a quiet corner of the churchyard, Gunter was past the ecstatic beast with two backs thrusts and at the post-coital Instagram selfie stage with a very satisfied-looking Yorkshire Terrier standing prettily on a church bench to enable entry, like a tiny cheerleader with a giant basketball star. Hurrying to separate them, Jenny saw they were still attached.

'Don't try to drag him away,' Euan warned. 'Dogs don't stare into each other's eyes after sex,' he explained, reaching in his back pocket for his cigarette pack. 'They go back to back, plug in and fertilize. They're tied. We can share the pillow talk while they work it off.' He offered her a cigarette.

'I quit.' She waved the pack away, horrified at Gunter's antics. 'How long does it take?'

'A few minutes.' He cast his eyes around the churchyard. 'I'm sure we'll find somewhere private to keep a discreet eye.' He wrapped an arm around her and drew her into the cool shadow of the porch where he pressed her up against the thick column supporting the arched stone door surround, his lips against her cheek, his soft breath in her ear making every tiny hair on her body do Mexican waves.

Impossibly turned on but deeply embarrassed to be snogging by the hymn books, like a hooligan, Jenny pulled away.

The church clock was striking midday. Hearing a bark, they realized Gunter and his tiny bride had already separated. She was trotting off without a backward glance while he sauntered in the opposite direction to relieve himself against a gravestone. He was still wearing Jenny's bra around his neck.

'You might be a lost cause, but I do expect you to behave better than that.' Jenny turned back to Euan. 'And definitely not wear my bra during sex.'

Laughing, he threaded his fingers through hers and kissed each of her pink fingertips. Jenny had never known that fingertips could be so sexually charged. They felt as though a lightning bolt was stored in each one.

'However short-lived this thing is,' he held her hand against his chest, his skin hot through his T-shirt, his heart a rhythmic hammer strike, 'let's never regret a moment of it.'

She kissed him again, fighting an urge to pull the T-shirt straight off and be a hooligan after all. Then, as they broke apart to breathe, she ran her lightning-bolt fingers up to his face. 'Naked truth?'

Nodding, Euan turned to kiss her fingertips again, charging them up once more.

'Tell me about the missing picture.'

His teeth snagged her ring finger. Saying nothing, he reached up to take her hand and led her back towards the house. Almost at the broken gate, he jinked right and towed her beneath the canopy of the biggest yew, its trunk thick as a factory chimney and cleft with deep arteries. Gunter followed, flopping ecstatically in the cool, shadowed dust.

'It could really hurt the family if I don't find it.' Hanging his head, he looked up apologetically.

She bit her lip, having already guessed which one it had to be. 'It's with the repairer. I damaged it.'

'You saw it?' His head lifted in amazement.

'I ripped it.'

His eyes moved between hers. 'You can't have. It's painted on board.' He shook his head, looking away. 'It's very small. I should have destroyed it when I had the chance, but I couldn't bring myself to.' He sucked in one cheek with a soft popping sound, staring at the dusty needles beneath them. 'We knew it was wrong when I painted it. Her mother disapproved of her posing for me, but that just made us more determined to do what we wanted. The pose was her idea – she was crazy sexy. There was nothing she wouldn't do.'

Jenny was finding breathing hard, what felt like an armoury of bayonet blades now in her chest. Euan Henderson, insomniac wine-drinking artist, was bad through and through, just as he had told her – an unreliable lost cause. He'd promised her no more than this. But her veins ran red hot nonetheless, blistering inside. Lonnie was barely out of school.

'What exactly is she doing?'

'I don't want you to see it.' He stepped closer, his head

dipped, breath warm on her throat. 'I'm not the man who painted it any more, believe me. I've given up on him.' His lips landed beneath her ear.

'For how long?' She laughed hollowly, jerking her head away.

'Let's start with this week.' His hands slid to either side of her face, pressing her up against the yew trunk, her spine uncurling and the beat starting up as he kissed her.

She tried to keep her mouth closed in a tight line of disapproval, but for a moment her lips yielded, letting his tongue slide against hers, his body fold into hers, his mind lead hers towards bed, however many Warning, Keep Out tapes he was pulling away.

'YOU FUCKING BASTARD!' screamed a voice across the churchyard. 'SHAGGING MY BABY GIRL! I'LL KILL YOU!'

Euan swung round. Gunter looked up with a worried grunt.

'YOU'VE BEEN SPOTTED, YOU PHILANDERING BASTARD! I HAVE IT ALL ON CCTV!'

Beyond the veils of yew branches that hid them from view, a determined figure was moving across the churchyard.

'Is he after you or the dog?' Jenny whispered, terrified.

'The dog, of course.' Euan turned to her, offended. 'It's the man from the middle cottage.'

Slinking towards them, Gunter hid behind Jenny's legs.

'I WILL *KILL* YOU WITH MY *BARE* HANDS!' The voice came closer.

'We have to get Gunter away,' Jenny breathed urgently, reaching down to grab his collar and muzzle his mouth with her hand as he growled. They heard the broken gate to the Old Rectory creak open and crash shut. 'Take him to your studio,' she told Euan. 'Stay with him. I'll come in the dog car later.'

He dropped onto his haunches, taking her face in his hands, nose and forehead against hers, their eyelashes forming criss-crossed sabre arches. 'I don't want to leave you with that angry bastard.'

'I'm good at playing tough battleaxe,' she promised. After which, Mrs Rees is going to haul you over the coals too, Euan Henderson, she added silently, then felt ashamed to find herself making a mental note to put her condoms into her handbag.

37

'Right, Mrs Rees. The gentleman in question has been formally cautioned for trespass and animal cruelty threats, and is aware that any repeat of this incident could lead to a criminal prosecution. There will be no further action taken against the dog.' The policeman checked his notepad. 'Gunner, is it?'

'Gunter. And thank you.'

'Where is Gunter?'

'Still out walking with a friend. Likes plenty of fresh air . . . especially after . . . '

'Yes.'

'Maybe there'll be a happy event in a few weeks.'

'The gentleman is taking his little dog for a canine morning-after-pill as I speak.'

Jenny closed the door gratefully on a silent house, which smelt of disinfectant and clean sheets. The Ladies Who Launder had long gone, leaving stripes on the carpets and points folded on the loo rolls again. It was still way below her standard, but at least the Old Rectory felt purged of late nights, too much wine and self-doubt, leaving a crisp new leaf instead.

The cleaners had taken in the post, among which was Jenny's new debit card. She could finally buy her own food and make repairs, although she doubted whether anybody sold heart-mending kits locally. She thrust it into her pocket and went to grab the dog-car key, then stopped, wondering where she would secretly conceal a painting in the Old Rectory. It hadn't occurred to her to ask what such a compromising painting of Lonnie Clifton was doing there. Had Richard Lewis discreetly bought the picture of his neighbour's daughter in a risqué pose? She could see no other explanation, however much it saddened her. Men were all as bad as each other, Euan for painting it, Richard for coveting it. She closed her eyes and breathed in the comforting cleanliness of beeswax and Cif.

She was now absolutely certain Euan would hurt her beyond her pain threshold, and she had to try to stop herself falling. She would not lower herself to the level of a dog in a graveyard.

Her phone was ringing. She chewed her lip as she picked up the regular call from her mother, distractedly eyeing the walls around her for hidey-holes in which one might conceal a highly compromising painting of the girl with the butterfly tattoo.

'What a week, Jenny! I so envy you lounging around in that lovely house. You cannot imagine the stress here. Just *wait* until you hear the latest ...' Her mother's warm, waspish voice launched into an attack on the Carmichaels' guests' parking.

'... *all* three guest spaces and the emergency vehicle slot, which is frankly selfish, given poor Frank Jamieson is in such a precarious state ...'

Now that she had several minutes during which she was required to contribute nothing more than encouraging monosyllables, Jenny went upstairs to the claret-walled dressing room to search, knowing it was the obvious starting point, but she couldn't bring herself to sift through drawers, and there was no other logical place.

'The kipper culprit is still at work ... they're sniping random bins now ... '

She looked around the vanilla-sex bedroom, then glanced into Geraldine's dressing room.

'Mrs Montgomery thinks it's the travellers from Lime Woods coming to dump them there ... '

RUN AWAY WITH ME was still on the mirror. A spider had festooned it with a gossamer web. She tutted. The Va Va Vacuumers were sloppy.

'"Out flew the web and floated wide ... "' She remembered the Tennyson quote that formed part of the dedication to 'RL' at the start of *The Storm Returns*. She'd thought Geraldine's dedication to her husband so romantic at first, but now she wasn't so sure. From what little she'd read, the book was very dark and bitter: Jack and Victoria were in turmoil, the latter slithering around like a ripe papaya when Jenny had left her seducing the young teacher with the butterfly tattoo. The Lewises' marriage, which had clearly been in crisis, seemed to have been immortalized in the pages of Geraldine's new book. She was certain that the couple were playing a complicated game of marital one-upmanship in which Lonnie was an important chess piece.

'Is that "The Lady of Shalott"?' a voice demanded in her ear.

'Well recognized. "Out flew the web and floated wide, the mirror crack'd from side to side".' She finished the quote with the famous line that followed.

'It's so romantic when she looks out to see Lancelot riding by and knows that the curse will claim her.' Her mother sighed. 'I always thought that brief deep love infinitely preferable to a lifetime trapped in that room weaving away.'

Jenny walked to the mirror, her face staring back, huge-eyed and hollow-cheeked. She had the beginnings of a tan, cheeks sun-touched and hair sun-streaked, the sleeping dead awakening. She stepped forward and peered behind the mirror. There was nothing there but an old Q-tip and a lot of spiders.

'Bloody Suzanne Goodenough is determined the next am-dram will be a Beckett.' Her mother had moved on. 'We all tell her the Haven can't take people buried in pots. We need farce or crime – lots of banging doors or guns to keep the oldies awake . . . '

Jenny hurried downstairs and out through the french windows, raced across the walled garden to the cottage, fumbled to find the right key to unlock the door, then tripped through the mess to the cracked mirror above the little fireplace.

RUN AWAY WITH ME.

Tucked behind it was an unframed picture, painted on board. It was much smaller than she'd imagined, hardly bigger than A5, yet it was exquisitely detailed. The model's joyful expression was as rapturous as any woman might dream to feel. Painted from the side, she had her shoulders turned away but she was looking towards the artist, long neck thrown back, one arm scooping up a great weight of hair while the other disappeared between her thighs, its purpose implicit. There was no butterfly tattoo on the smooth, creamy nape of her neck, and pure, shame-free abandon in the face. She was stunning, tendrils of fire blonde hair escaping over her shoulders, wide mouth open in a spontaneous laugh, body curled in a taut S of sheer physical ecstasy. It was an intoxicatingly sensual, intimate, beautifully painted picture.

Jenny looked at it for a long time. There was no sideways lamp signature. But she knew without doubt Euan had painted it. And she knew it was Geraldine Lewis.

329

She turned it over, *En ta paume, mon verbe et ma pensée*.

In the palm of your hand, my word and my thoughts. Euan had quoted it. Bonnard had painted lovely colourful tableaux of naked ladies bathing and dogs curled up on bathmats. Euan, meanwhile, had painted his rich patron's wife self-pleasuring, and from the expression on her beautiful features as she shared the moment with the artist, that wasn't all they'd shared together.

'The Kermodes are having a ruby anniversary party next weekend.' Her mother was still talking. 'Betty wants to dye all the food with beetroot juice to go with the theme and you know what your father's allergy's like – beets bring him out in terrible hives . . . '

Jenny turned the picture over again. He'd told her it could cause untold pain if it got into the wrong hands. No wonder he wanted it back. The painting was startlingly intimate, a picture that could only have come out of a love affair. It was now obvious that Euan Henderson couldn't help seducing every woman who sat for him. This one was high-grade and dangerous, a married woman with a young family. He'd told her that he was no longer that man, but she didn't believe him. Like Robin, he would never change. His cause was far too lost.

'Mum, I have to hang up.'

'Is there an emergency? I haven't even asked you about your man.'

'Low battery. Sorry. We'll speak Sunday. And my man is . . . ' she took a deep breath, looking up at the writing in the mirror '. . . lost.'

'Oh, Jenny dear, I'm so sorry. Hasn't he got a sat-nav?'

Jenny dared herself to go up the cottage stairs, feeling the same self-punishing heart tremors as she had when going through Robin's text messages, knowing that what she'd find there would hurt her yet unable to stop herself. There were two pale-walled bedrooms with polished oak floors, one of which had been set up as a painting studio, now deserted apart from a long, scuffed bench covered with empty bottles, old jam jars and the carcasses of spent pigment tubes, scabs of masking tape hanging from the walls where pictures had been ripped down in a hurry. A splattered red stain by the door hinted at a glass of wine being thrown at it. The other room was much smaller, dominated by a huge king-size mattress on the floor, with crumpled cream sheets, suggesting little sleep and a lot of sex. There were clothes abandoned everywhere – soft, faded jeans and old T-shirts, all covered with paint. More empty wine bottles were lined up by the skirting board. Framed on the big mattress in a square of bright sunlight spilling through the low dormer was a pair of frilly white knickers, barely more than lacy elastic. Lying beside them, like a tragic Othello alongside his Desdemona, was an abandoned pair of black jockey shorts.

She backed hurriedly out, the taste in her mouth all bile and betrayal, uncomfortably aware of her intrusion into a love affair. She was just a one-week fix, taking up where Geraldine and the girl on the boat had left off, a passing distraction in Euan Henderson's priapic, bohemian life.

She picked up the painting as she left the cottage, trying not to look at it. She knew it was shallow, but the thing that kept stabbing her was how beautiful Euan had made Geraldine look compared to her own haunted, hollow face in his half-finished painting of her.

Jenny drove to the studio in the converted-barn complex, like a zombie playing Gran Turismo, oblivious to fellow road-users waving their fists and flashing lights at her. She could hear Gunter barking before she even cut the engine.

The boys from Graffix Web Design were having a barbecue, burned-sausage fumes pluming across the courtyard. They beckoned her to join them as she passed. She held up a hand with an apologetic smile and marched to the barn with the saggy roof.

Euan wrenched open the door, hair on end, black mop veering one way, white streak the other, tanned chin gravelled with stubble. He looked so delighted to see her and so absurdly sexy that she wanted to crash her head against his chest, her body into his arms, imprinting everything about him there before it was too late.

She was grateful to Gunter, who slammed her back a few steps with welcoming devotion as she held up the little painting with the writing side towards Euan like an idiot board. 'Does this mean I have you in the palm of my hand?'

'Oh, Christ, Jenny, I didn't want you to be the one who—'

'The police came,' she interrupted, which shut him up. 'It's okay, they didn't want you.' She handed the picture across. 'Now we're partners in crime. We'll have to put Gunter in a witness-protection scheme.'

Gunter was still body-slamming her, whimpering and bear-hugging as though she'd disappeared on a three-hundred-mile Incredible Journey with a bull terrier and a Siamese cat. She hugged him back, wiping away her tears on his coat before Euan could see them.

'Thanks for looking after him.' She straightened up. 'I'll take him home.'

'Come inside.' His voice was roughest sandpaper, his eyes black jade. He put his arm around her back, thumb and middle finger sliding up into the hollow behind her ears, pulling her closer.

Jenny looked at his lips, purveyors of such pleasure, knowing a kiss was about to hit her like an express train that would flatten her resolve, dragging her along the tracks to a place she'd never gone in her life, a place that would take her breath away. But now the hurt it would inevitably bring frightened her far too much to lie down on the parallel lines.

She held up her hand between his face and hers.

'*En ma paume, mon verbe et ma pensée,*' she told him, trying to stop her voice shaking. 'Read my palm, Euan.' She struck him hard across the cheek, grabbed Gunter and hurried back to the car, cheered all the way by the barbecuing web designers, beer bottles aloft.

'Wait!' Euan ran after her, catching up as she fumbled for the keyless fob. He wrapped his arms around her, trying to make her turn back. 'Jenny, it's not what you think.'

For a moment the urge to turn almost overpowered her, but she forced herself to wrench free, opening the boot to let Gunter in. 'I don't want to know, Euan. It's best we just forget any of this ever happened.'

'You can't say that!' he protested. 'Come back and talk.'

The web designers were watching the car-park confrontation open-mouthed. Agitated by the high emotion, Gunter was barking and circling now. Jenny tried to slam the boot, forgetting it closed automatically, and it continued gliding down at its own pace while she slapped at it ineffectually.

'Jenny, just come inside.'

'No! I don't want to see you again.' She was terrified she was going to cry.

One of the web-design boys sidled up, full of beer and bravado. 'Is he bothering you?'

'Fuck off!' Euan snapped over his shoulder.

The geek stepped back, tripping over a reserved parking sign and pitching into a flowerbed, much to his mates' raucous delight.

'I'm fine.' Jenny got into the car, still not looking at Euan, her voice low as she said to him, 'It's your decision to live your life as you do, Euan. It's my decision to have nothing more to do with you. Please respect that.'

'You're different,' he said.

She looked up briefly and wished she hadn't. No brush-strokes could have captured the despair in his face right now.

'You're different,' he repeated, almost whispering.

'Why do I think it's not the first time you've said that?'

'Because I just said it twice.'

He almost had her then, the sad-amused expression, the dark-filled centres to the tired green eyes that promised con-fessions, wine, insomnia, ever-lower inhibitions and almost certain seduction. But she could already smell the pain and regret that would come with it.

'I won't say this again. Goodbye, Euan, and good luck.'

She started the engine, reversing back with such blind speed that she almost ran over the web designer stepping out of the flowerbed.

X

Saturday

38

TO DO LIST

~~Finish ironing GS's manuscript.~~
Eat super-food (NOT toast)
Swim 40 lengths
Do not drink
Read a novel a day
Quit electronic smoking

Jenny had spent most of the night ironing the remainder of *The Storm Returns* like an automaton, determinedly not glancing at its contents, the repetitive monotony of her task calming her as she removed every water crease and put each page neatly back in line with its companions. She walked Gunter just after six, marching around the Beacon Common gravel pit so fast that she left him far behind, sniffing tree trunks and making his regular pee stops.

When she got back, she set about cleaning the Old Rectory with fervid attention to detail, making up for the Va Va Vacuumers' slapdash lack of precision by getting lime-scale from around taps, dust from picture tops, messages from mirrors. It was another searingly hot day, so close and airless it was like working in a steam oven, but she didn't care, her sweaty hair scraped back in a makeshift Alice band and her vest top sticking to her, like wet tissue, as she scrubbed and polished and rinsed.

The neighbours came to swim mid-morning, chuckling and canoodling as they shared a Lilo and floated around like two fat seals, loved up and adrift on a piece of flotsam.

Irritated, Jenny retreated upstairs with an Ecover bottle in each hand to clean all the mirrors in her en-suite, trying not to look at her pinched, angry face reflected everywhere, so different from the round, laughing ones outside. At least I have cheekbones, she thought savagely, as she attacked the dirt ingrained in a carved frame with a cotton-wool bud.

Gunter was standing on her bed, barking at them through the window now. Unable to bear the noise, she marched across to close the curtains, then stopped in appalled amazement as she saw them standing on the diving board, like Jack and Rose on the prow of *Titanic*, the board dipping down almost to the pool's surface under their combined weight. The husband had his arms wrapped around his wife's bulk, his chin on her shoulder, cheek resting alongside hers. They both had their eyes closed and were singing.

Shushing Gunter, she strained to hear a crooning comedy rendition of a Céline Dion hit, but what she heard was far sweeter: 'It Had To Be You', sung in perfect harmony, accompanied by the coo of wood-pigeons and the percussive buzzing of bees raiding nectar cups.

Watching them through the wisteria leaves, Jenny realized, with a painful tightening of her throat, that she envied them. She envied the fact they adored one another without self-consciousness or self-criticism, that they didn't seem to care or notice the physical imperfections in one another or themselves. They were growing old together disgracefully.

338

She turned back to the room and looked at the bed, scene of the disastrous Roger Roger attempt, now neatly made up with the freshly laundered counterpane. Roger wouldn't have been a fun companion through life; he would never have sung a duet with her on a diving board or challenged her to play-fights with pool noodles, although he had admittedly challenged her to join in his own fetish. Jenny had always believed herself far too self-controlled to entrust her sexual fantasies to another like that. Her MILFy porn moments had always been top secret, the shame of enacting them far too great to risk sharing with a new lover. They were also bashfully slow-burning. If she'd been told at the start of this week that a man would help her find nirvana almost instantly, she'd have bet any amount it wasn't possible. If she had been told that that man would not be regular-date Roger but a philandering artist – also a burglar, a forger and possibly homeless – she'd have packed mace spray and a personal alarm.

She went back into the bathroom and started cleaning again, unable to shake the memory of Euan carrying her in and depositing her in the bath, his simple touch enough to make her melt. Reliving that hot, heady weightlessness, she dropped onto her haunches, folding her arms across her forehead, body leaning against the end of the bath. What she wouldn't give for that touch again now.

'He'll hurt you, he'd hurt you, he's hurt you,' she breathed. 'Keep cleaning.' Opening her eyes and spotting a dark line of dirt under the lip of the bath, she reached for the Ecover spray.

Gunter was barking again, further away in the house. She could hear a bell ringing.

*

A small, stooped figure in a flowered sunhat eyed Jenny over a Dr Barnardo's collection tin.

'This is a ruse,' Myrtle said matter-of-factly. 'I hear there's been some bother.'

As if aware that his accuser was on the doorstep armed with a charity sabre, Gunter stayed behind the big artisan umbrella stand, barking through the handles, like Chewbacca goading droids in a *Star Wars* battle.

'There really wasn't anything I could do.' Jenny was immediately defensive, voice raised above the barking, trying to keep calm and smile. 'Gunter didn't break in and commit rape. The Yorkie got out and they met in the churchyard. It was too late by the time I got there.'

'How charmingly *Romeo and Juliet*.' Myrtle rattled her tin at Gunter, who whined, fell silent and sat uncertainly. 'However, the situation I'm talking about isn't to do with the dog. May I come in?'

Hot, flustered and wishing she'd thought of a quick excuse, Jenny led her through the hallway.

'I do like this house.' Myrtle admired the tapestries. 'Gosh, it's rather stuffy in here.'

'The neighbours are using the pool,' Jenny explained, as they arrived in the kitchen, which was stifling and striped in shadows because she'd lowered the blinds. Silhouettes moved behind them, pool noodles aloft.

'Lovely couple, the Cliftons.' Myrtle moved away from the Aga, already turning very pink. 'Terribly close to Dicky. I think they're good for him. God knows he needs a positive influence. Have you met the daughter?'

'Briefly.'

'She posed for Euan Henderson, you know.' She took off her hat, fanning herself with it.

'Drink?' Jenny pulled open the fridge, realizing with a

sinking heart what the bother Myrtle had referred to might be. She took a deep breath of cool air.

'Elderflower, thank you. Lots of ice. They've all posed for him, even Geraldine.'

'So I gather.'

'You did too,' Myrtle said, with *j'accuse* relish. 'You've been spotted.'

Jenny held the cool pressé bottle to her collar bone, heart jumping. 'I had no idea Neighbourhood Watch was so vigilant these days,' she said tightly, adding, 'He really only did a few quick sketches.' She hoped nobody had seen her fling off her dressing-gown and flash amid the scatter cushions while Euan painted no more than her face.

'I thought he started a painting?'

'Unfortunately I'm now too busy for him to finish it.' She poured the cordial over ice with a shaking hand, increasingly unsettled by the small, elderly Gestapo invasion. She hated to imagine what parish-council meetings were like round here. 'I've brought lots of work with me, plus I don't want to neglect Gunter.'

Gunter had retreated beneath the dining table and was grumbling through his whiskers.

'As I keep telling Dicky, that dog is thoroughly spoiled.' Myrtle was trying to scale a tall, slippery bar stool by the island.

Watching her struggle valiantly, Jenny carried the drink to the table. 'Let's sit here, shall we?'

As Myrtle followed with relief, Gunter relocated behind the patchwork sofa with a low whine, chin resting on its back, eyebrows moving anxiously.

'I've always been a cat person,' Myrtle said, settling in the shadowed streaks of sunlight. 'The Cairn was my late husband's. Serial shagger and terribly undomesticated, but mellowed by age.' She smiled fondly. 'Thank goodness, his son couldn't be more different.'

Jenny didn't like to ask whether she was talking about her husband or the dog.

Now striped like a small, ferocious tiger, Myrtle fixed her with an unblinking stare. 'I take it you know that Euan Henderson is packing up his studio? He's leaving tonight.'

Feeling as though she had been plunged under water, her boat capsized, Jenny experienced a strange, submerged calm combined with almost suffocating panic so deep it had no vent. 'Where's he going?'

'Quite far, I should imagine.' The tiger pounced on Jenny's upturned boat, like Mr Parker on Pi. 'You *must* stop him, Mrs Rees.'

'I hardly know him.' She was trying not to think about the hours she'd spent on the patchwork sofa pouring her heart out to him, or the brief moment of intense intimacy she'd shared upstairs.

'This really is most inconvenient,' Myrtle went on huffily, lobbing an ice cube at Gunter, who caught it with surprise. 'Setting aside the fact he is quite the most entertaining company that this village has seen since that pop star rented the manor, Euan owes Dicky some loyalty. He *can't* just bugger off without a by-your-leave. Please reconsider, Mrs Rees.'

'Why would he stay if I asked him?' She couldn't resist saying it, her heart in her throat.

'It's you or Papillon Clifton, and I sense you're much more discreet.'

'Lonnie is short for Papillon?' She let out a sarcastic snort, the lump turning into an angry fist.

'Thank goodness she wasn't christened Limace or she'd have a tattoo of a slug.' Myrtle nodded, bright berry eyes narrowing. 'She's hopelessly in love with Euan Henderson and terribly pretty, and I know he wanted to paint more pictures of her, so she might talk him into staying awhile, but it's a long shot. He owes her nothing. You are different.'

'How?' She felt the fist in her throat open its hand in welcome now as she heard the same words Euan had said to her. *You are different.*

'Because you found the painting of Geraldine and gave it to him.'

Her heart now felt as though it had stopped beating, still trapped in her windpipe, clenched in the fist again. Jenny eyed Myrtle's determined little face, the cheeks two deep pink rosebuds, the eyes fierce.

'You know about that?' She tried to sound casual but her voice was a strangled soprano.

'I've never seen it, but I gather it could finish off the marriage if Dicky finds out about it.'

Jenny said nothing, reluctant to give away any more. For all she knew, Myrtle could be fishing for scurrilous gossip to share at the Hadden End over-sixties' lunch club.

'What Euan doesn't appreciate,' Myrtle fumed, 'is that by leaving now he will throw suspicion on himself just as much. Dicky worked very hard to get him this career break. Leaving before the exhibition makes it obvious he's got a guilty conscience.'

Jenny pictured Geraldine Lewis's head thrown back and the ecstatic smile, sharing the sweet, unrivalled sensation that had driven so many to betray husbands and lovers. Euan's brush had captured it, but his magnetism had sanctioned it. She thought about the girl from the houseboat writhing on a narrow berth, the young neighbour with the butterfly tattoo mimicking Degas, and herself on the patchwork sofa just behind her, nipples like spark plugs, libido roaring into life after being garaged for years.

With effort, she lowered her voice to a Margaret Thatcher alto. 'I think he *should* go.'

'You're wrong.' Myrtle took on Thatcher with a bass Denis Healey. 'Better by far to stay and brave it out. After all, Euan swears nothing improper happened between himself and Geraldine.'

Jenny snorted, thinking about the Othello and Desdemona underwear lying together on the bed in the cottage.

'You've heard a different story?'

'I know absolutely nothing about any of it,' she insisted, angrily aware that she had shared every intimate secret about herself with Euan, yet knew nothing of his recent chequered past.

Myrtle lifted her collecting tin. 'Cross my palm with silver and I will tell you more.'

'I literally have no cash.' Or any desire to know.

'I'll take an IOU.' She placed the tin in front of Jenny. 'Shall we start with the portrait Euan Henderson has been painting of you for his exhibition? If you ask him to finish it, he will stay.'

'Absolutely not.' She shook her head, starting to feel angry, questioning what right this cat-loving old biddy had to march in and play marriage-saving matchmaker. 'All this is none of my business, Myrtle.' She stood up. 'I'm just here to look after the house, and I don't see that it's my place – or yours, quite frankly – to interfere in the Lewises' marriage, or stop Euan Henderson leaving.'

'He wants to see you again. He told me today.'

'You saw him?'

'He dropped something off for safekeeping with me. He was very agitated.'

She felt her knees jellify, making her lurch slightly as she took her glass to the sink to gulp more cold water. Her heart felt as though it was pounding against each rib in turn, like a child's stick along metal railings.

The house phone was ringing. She grabbed it without thinking, hoping Myrtle would take the cue to go.

'Mrs Rees! How fares all?' It was Richard Lewis, in Mauritius and imbibed. 'Is my house still standing?'

'Yes. All fine here.'

'Dog behaving?'

'Is that Dicky?' demanded Myrtle in the background.

Jenny frantically signalled her to stay quiet.

'Is that my mother?' Richard laughed. 'I knew she'd never stay away.'

'No, it's ...' Her voice faded and she looked over her shoulder.

Myrtle's eyebrows shot up. Suddenly Jenny saw the family resemblance.

39

'Geraldine and I fell out,' Myrtle explained, topping up her elderflower with a slug of gin from the drinks cupboard. 'In fact, it would be more accurate to say we declared war, but the peacekeeping force has us at bay now. Are you sure I can't tempt you to an elderflower spritzer?'

Jenny shook her head, throwing open the doors while Myrtle topped up with tonic, cucumber and ice. The Cliftons had gone, the sun directly overhead now, the heat of the day at its most skin-searingly intense.

'My late husband adored Geraldine,' Myrtle told her, stepping outside and squinting in the bright sunlight. 'They flirted terribly. Before he died, we lived in Amersham and Dicky's lot were in Highgate, which was a good Sunday-lunch hop. After I was widowed, I downsized to my cottage here – I've always loved the village. The Old Rectory came up for sale not long afterwards, and Richard got this romantic notion that it would be marvellous to be out of London, and he persuaded Geraldine to move the family here. She had terrible writer's block at the time and he hoped it might break the cycle, but if anything it got worse.

'I admit I was against it.' She turned to Jenny, her light-sensitive glasses now rap-star dark. 'The marriage had always been volatile. A mother should never get between her son and his wife, but it was hard to stand by and watch Geraldine combust daily. She has great charm, but she's totally self-destructive. If she can't work, it's like a tsunami ripping through the house from one end to the other without let-up. Dicky and the children suffer terribly.'

'Why does he put up with it?'

'He loves her – worships her, in fact.' She settled on the large, shaded swing chair and patted the cushion beside her for Jenny to join her. 'And it's an open secret that she's the breadwinner – earns five times his income, almost all of it still on the back of *The Dust Storm*. It's sold over twenty million copies. That's one copy for every man, woman and child in Australia. She bought her parents and sister a house here in England. And she paid cash for this place.' She cast her eyes from pool to house. 'She bought it for Dicky. He loves working here, the sermonizing biographer. It's a great fit.'

'And Geraldine's less happy?'

'Hard to tell. She's terribly contrary. When they moved in, she announced that she was switching genres – which I have to confess worried me because I misunderstood and thought she was getting gender reassignment – and she wrote a historical crime thriller filled with vengeful parlour maids in Gothic vicarages. I looked after the children while she worked on it, collecting them from school, giving them supper and helping them with homework. That was when we first declared war. The children were doing their nativity play and I'd made their outfits and practised lines *ad infinitum et ultra*, then Geraldine swanned in at the last minute to take all the credit and bagsy the seats with some London yummy-mummy friends, which meant I couldn't even go to watch it. It was a petty show of jealousy, but lethal in mother-/daughter-in-law politics. After that, we engaged in furious battle. She announced that she wanted to give up writing and be a full-time mother. It didn't last, of course, but she baked and sewed and planted seeds, wafting about in gingham for six months, deliberately getting up my nose.

347

She became the village darling, joining every fund-raiser and evening class. She took me on at the fête, her jams sweeter and flower arrangements more sculptural. She gave Dicky a puppy, which meant he couldn't pop across the churchyard to see me without a long ritual of bribery and imprisonment.' Myrtle nodded at the figure now watching them from the shadows beneath the pergola table, eyebrows still moving like hairy caterpillars.

'I'm ashamed to admit I retaliated with very low blows, squirting glyphosate on her vegetable garden and going online to leave rude reviews of her books, but it was jolly good fun to plan evil deeds and I think we were both rather enjoying the warfare in the end.

'Then her book came out and the murderer was an ancient frustrated lesbian housekeeper called Mabel Louis with a Cairn terrier and a ginger cat. I probably could have sued, but it was such a good book, and she's so entertaining that I wouldn't have dreamed of it. That's the thing about Geraldine. Everybody adores her. She's so clever and such fun, you forgive her anything, even coveting Euan Henderson. After all, who can really blame her for that? The man should come with a health warning. I'm eighty-five and having him in my house makes even me feel skittish.'

Jenny rubbed her teeth with her tongue. 'You know him well, then?'

'He's lodged with me on and off. He was in the garden cottage here for a while, but that became far too close for comfort. They needed the big wall between them.'

'So they *were* having an affair?'

Myrtle gave a minimal shake of her head, almost a shudder. 'I think they're in love with one another, which might be rather worse.'

Jenny felt a hard weight land on her chest, like a huge

book thrown with force. She tried to breathe round it so that she could speak without giving herself away. 'What makes you say that?'

'Goodness, it's hot. I need another drink.' Myrtle stood up with effort, leaving Jenny swinging back and forth on the chair. When she finally struggled off to follow her inside, she found her barring her entrance with the collection tin. 'Do I get my IOU?'

'Not just yet.'

Myrtle turned huffily back in. 'I'm being horribly indiscreet, but you have a trustworthy face, and I do desperately need you to persuade Euan to stay. He simply won't listen to me when I tell him it will all blow over. It always does.

'Geraldine is prone to infatuations.' She helped herself to another elderflower spritzer. 'Nothing as serious as this, admittedly, but it's not new. In Highgate, she was always smitten with a writing protégé, a flirty restaurateur or a neighbour's pretty undergraduate son. Ironically that was part of Dicky's reasoning for getting her out of London, but here the lack of new blood meant the infatuations have lasted longer and are less satisfying. Then Euan arrived.

'It was as though she was lit up from inside. She was just exhilarated. She started writing so fast it was frankly unhealthy. I don't think she slept much at all. There were notes and pages everywhere. She danced around with the children, threw parties and cooked extraordinary meals. This book she's just written, this *Storm Cloud* thing, burst out of her like a parasitic worm. Poor Dicky was deeply agitated, but he knew how much she needed to write so he tried to ignore it.

'It wasn't as if the two of them were cooing lovingly. Euan was here to paint a family portrait, and you've never seen a more reluctant artist. I picked him up from the station when

349

he first arrived and he looked like a man at the gallows. They seemed to loathe each other at first. Geraldine took totally against the first painting he did – she was livid, saying it looked nothing like her, and she demanded that he start again. He wasn't allowed to over-paint.

'That was May. He'd been based in the garden cottage then – the idea was that he'd use it as a studio to build work for the exhibition this September, but then Geraldine announced she was commandeering it to finish her book in total isolation. Euan came to me for a while and I found out how kind and funny he is, as well as being extraordinarily talented. That goes a long way when one's a bit arthritic and forgetful. Not that he was around much. Dicky rented him the studio and he more or less lived there, with different life models trooping in and out day and night. Geraldine got even more frenetic. I'm quite sure Dicky's behind the decision to make Euan's exhibition just nudes – that's very much his *modus operandi*.'

'So he knew what was going on?'

'He knew Geraldine had an infatuation but, frankly, the enmity between her and Euan was such that he could be forgiven for believing it was somebody else. And, for now at least, Dicky *does* think it's somebody else. She flew very close to the wind with Lonnie.'

'The neighbour's daughter?' Jenny remembered the Sapphic sex scene only too well, having copied the slippery papaya sentence more often than a naughty schoolgirl writing *I will not talk in class*.

'I think Geraldine was very jealous that Euan had persuaded Lonnie to be a model, so she decided to annex her for herself, persuading her to become a research assistant on the new book instead. Lonnie was totally awestruck by Geraldine, as so many young women are, and they were

350

holed up in the cottage together a lot, giggling their way through YouTube videos of Australian sheep shearers at work and swimming naked in the pool late at night. I don't think poor Dicky knew whether to be excited or jealous. Geraldine also has this terribly flirty long-distance thing going on with her American publisher – lots of late-night texting and tweeting – and that's where his current suspicions lie. It's been obvious the marriage is under tremendous strain. They argue a lot, and Geraldine has become increasingly vocal about how unhappy she is and that things can't carry on as they are. Dicky knows that whoever she's infatuated with it's about as bad as it gets. He booked this Mauritius holiday in a desperate attempt to patch things up.

'I wouldn't have suspected Euan either, had I not found out about the existence of the painting. Geraldine took it from my cottage, you see. Just before they set off on holiday, she came to see me in a terrible state, saying that she and Dicky had just had an awful fight, and that she had never been so unhappy in her life. I had no idea things had got that bad. You know they lost a baby last year?'

Jenny shook her head, eyes instinctively pricking with tears.

'It was ectopic. They were both devastated – Geraldine's forty-six. They think it was their last chance. They bought this glorious old house intending to fill it with more family, but it never happened – it was too late for more babies. I think that's why Dicky commissioned the portrait – trying to make her see the beautiful family they already had together. Instead, she saw her lost bloom of youth.

'That day, she begged me to go and talk to Dicky on her behalf, to explain that she just needed time alone to calm down and think. She must have gone in search of the painting as soon as I left the cottage. Euan kept a bag in my

351

spare room for the odd occasions that he actually wanted to sleep, hardly more than a backpack's worth, but he travels light by nature. The painting was among those things apparently. I suppose he daren't keep it at the studio in case Dicky saw it. The night Geraldine and Dicky flew off on holiday, Euan practically pulled my cottage apart looking for it. He only stopped when I told him I thought Geraldine might have taken whatever it was he was trying to find.'

'Did he tell you that she was the subject of a very private portrait?'

'One look at his face and I just knew. And I knew that if Dicky found it, those children would no longer have a mother and father living under the same roof, and I couldn't bear that for them.' Her eyes filled with tears. 'He's put up with so much, but this would break him.'

Jenny rubbed her throat with crossed hands as though she could push away the huge lump still amassed there, remembering her own desperation for her children to have Robin in their lives daily, not a pick-up-Friday-drop-off-Sunday father or, worse still, the transatlantic dad he'd become.

'That's why you wanted the keys to the garden cottage,' she said, 'to look for it. I'd disturbed Euan trying to get in there when I first arrived, and taken the keys he left in the door, thinking they were Geraldine's. Then when I caught him trying to break in I mistook him for the gardener. He only offered to paint me in the first place to have access to the house so he could keep trying to find where she'd hidden it.'

'She hid it well, I take it?'

'Very. I don't think Richard would have stumbled across it. I wish I'd never found it.'

'Thank goodness you did. It's a weapon that she would have used against Dicky one day, don't you see? That's how

352

she operates. In the heat of an argument, she can't help herself. Tell me, is it terribly, terribly risqué?'

'It's in that zone.'

'No wonder Euan is running away like a thief now. Dicky's no fool; he'll smell a love rat if he comes back to find him gone, not to mention the money and face he'll lose if the solo show is cancelled. That's why I need your help.'

'I'd rather keep out of it.'

'But now Euan *must* finish that painting of you, don't you see? When Geraldine sees it, she'll know he's already moved on.' Myrtle pressed her palms together in front of her button nose as if in prayer. 'Dicky will see it too and assume his dissolute artist was straight in there with the house-sitter, which takes any suspicion away from his wife.'

'I'm sure there are other Henderson originals which will better serve your purpose,' she muttered. 'You need to talk to a girl called Femi.'

'Yours has the freshest paint,' Myrtle said determinedly. 'It's the perfect distraction. This will all blow over, and Richard need never know about his wife's private portrait. The exhibition *will* go ahead. If there's one thing I learned from the unhappier years with my husband, it's that the quickest route back to contented family life is to act as if nothing has happened and move on. And I'm determined my grandchildren will have that happy family life.'

'By me making an exhibition of myself?'

Myrtle held up the collecting tin. 'Call it a charitable gesture. Save my son's marriage.'

Jenny remembered afresh the devastation of her divorce, the loss of her own family home, the bone-scraping pain of betrayal. 'I'm not sure he'll stay even if I ask him.'

Myrtle consulted her watch. 'He'll be gone if you wait any longer. Will you talk to him at least?'

Jenny picked up her phone. 'What's his number?'

She looked delighted. 'He doesn't have a mobile phone. You'll have to drive there. The painting of you is at my house. He dropped it off when he came to collect his things. He asked me to give it to you after he'd gone. It's all wrapped up and I haven't peeked, so you don't need to blush. I confess I *did* read the label, but I don't understand it.'

'Is it French?' She felt flame licks of anger.

'No, it's some sort of nonsense poem about fandangos.'

Jenny didn't need to read the label to remember sitting naked on the patchwork sofa singing 'Bohemian Rhapsody'.

When she drove to the studio barn, stopping off at Myrtle's cottage to pick up the painting en route, she selected something far more self-protectively hardcore than Queen for the car stereo. Accompanying Pink's 'So What' at the top of her voice, she flipped down the sun visor and floored it.

40

With Gunter barking and spinning excitedly in the back of the dog car, thoroughly overexcited by her angry 'na na na na na na na' singing, Jenny turned into the gateway to the barn units. The car park was deserted, apart from Euan's battered pick-up truck that was reversed up to the doors of his studio.

She parked out of sight behind the furthest barn and put her face into her hands, summoning strength. 'Na na na na na na na, na na na na na na!'

A tap on the window made her jump so high that she banged her head on the roof of the car. It was Euan, his face amazed, the black bin bag he was carrying dropping to the ground with a crunch of breaking glass.

Jenny wanted to shout, *I'm not ready!*

Instead, she wrestled the door open, flustered and almost faint with the instinctive body jolt reaction to seeing him.

'How did you know I was here?'

'You're parked in front of the bins.'

Glancing out of the passenger window, she saw she'd blocked access to an enclosure housing a row of galvanized refuse bins.

He picked up the bag and hurled it over the car roof into an open flip lid with more crashing of glass.

She pressed the boot release for Gunter and stepped out. 'You should recycle.'

'I was in a hurry.'

He watched her guardedly as she straightened up and folded her arms, leaning back against the car, like a defensive motorist discussing a prang. 'I've come here to ask you to complete your painting of me. I hate seeing things left unfinished.'

'Has Myrtle put you up to this? Don't answer that.' He dropped his chin, smiling. 'She's a wily old trout. I'll miss her.'

'Please don't go. This exhibition is so important.'

His gaze found hers again. 'Not to you.'

'Your portrait of me is.' She swallowed, uncomfortably aware that her eyes were having an entirely different conversation with his, the attraction between them painfully close to enmity. 'I have the rest of the wine to pay you.'

'Share it with friends.'

'Please finish the painting.'

He grimaced, turning away, then swinging back, brows curled sceptically. 'Is that what you really want?'

Jenny found she suddenly wanted it very badly indeed, along with all sorts of decadent things that his gaze and hers were already conspiring about, from which she was determined to protect herself. She looked away, hating herself for blushing. 'I'd like to keep this strictly professional. We should have done that from the start.'

'Sure.'

'I would prefer to stick to daylight hours only, and not drink alcohol, smoke, or talk about myself.' She glanced at him. 'You may do all three, of course.'

He smiled, his eyes mugging hers, silently agreeing that she didn't stand a chance. Then he turned back towards his studio. 'Follow me.'

Gunter bounded ahead, his excited barks echoing in the building.

There was almost nothing left in the barn, apart from neat stacks of paintings leaning up against the walls, some three or four deep.

'That's a lot of nudes,' she muttered.

'It's up to Richard what he does with them.' He was flicking off lights. 'They're his, in lieu of rent and good manners.'

'Staying for the exhibition would be the more noble gesture.'

'I don't do noble gestures.'

'You're finishing the painting of me,' she pointed out.

'Only because I want to sleep with you,' he said matter-of-factly, as he flicked off the last row of lights.

Jenny had been about to ask what he was planning to do with the painting of Geraldine, but she was far too wound up to trust herself to speak.

He picked up his canvas bag and the big bunch of keys. 'I'll follow you back.'

Grateful to be able to 'na na na na na na na,' again in private, she drove deliberately slowly to delay the moment they arrived. Euan's big snarling radiator grille was all over her back windscreen. The thought of sitting alone with him in such intimacy was winding her up like a coil.

Even if he left the area straight afterwards, the painting of her should be enough proof to stop the Lewises' marriage disintegrating. But did she really want to risk losing her heart and her dignity like this for them, a family whose house she loved, but whom she didn't know, whose psychotic dog had cost her a small fortune and whose resident portrait artist had ridden roughshod over her fragile self-esteem once already? It would be one thing if she could keep the picture at home to remind her of her moment of empowerment, and perhaps by the age of seventy or so, she might even envy herself the slightly sagging middle-aged body she had now. But she didn't want her naked form to be Exhibit A in a marital dispute.

By the time she signalled to turn into the Old Rectory's drive, she had na-na-naed her way to a definite 'no no no' and talked herself out of it.

Then she looked at her rear-view mirror and saw she'd lost Euan's snarling truck grille. He must have changed his mind too, she realized, illogically furious. He was probably heading at speed for the M40 and freedom right now.

'Bastard!' She careered up the drive, snapped back the wing mirrors of the car by driving it into the garage before the doors had fully opened, and stomped into the house with the painting. Throwing it down, she pulled out her mobile and selected a trusted speed-dial. She badly needed advice, and Rachel was her wisest friend, who had always been her closest confidante. But before Jenny could begin to rant about her predicament, she was cut short by Rachel apologetically dealing with a small child vomiting into a bucket. 'We all have norovirus,' she explained weakly, when she came back on the line. 'I was going to call you. We'll have to rain-check our lunch.' She sounded absolutely terrible. 'Is everything okay, Jenny?'

'It doesn't matter. You concentrate on getting well, you poor loves. Call me when you're feeling better.' She rang off and tried Carla, whose phone was on voicemail as usual, and who, she could already predict with total certainty, would think her current dilemma a liberating tango on her post-divorce sex-life dance-floor. She then tried a couple more close friends without success, before giving up and pulling open the french windows to let in some air, already so hot that sweat was sliding from her temples around her ears. As she did so, Euan appeared through the newly mended gate in the churchyard, his forearms covered with engine oil. 'My truck just died on the side of the road.'

'I didn't see.'

'So I gathered.' He was even sweatier than she was, having walked a mile in forty-degree heat. 'Do you never look behind?'

'Do you need the AA?'

'No. I need a drink.' He carried his canvas bag inside, dumping it on the table and turning back to face her. There were tired black smudges under his eyes and he hadn't shaved. He studied her face closely. 'You've changed your mind.'

Looking at him, the na-nas faded in Jenny's head, her eyes already having a private conversation with his that she couldn't control. She wanted the painting finished. She couldn't face the thought of him leaving just yet. 'No talking, no boozing.'

'If that's what you want.' He pulled his T-shirt up to wipe his face, revealing a rock face of muscular stomach.

'It is.' She walked inside past him, a sensation not unlike passing a chocolatier during a fast and forcing oneself not to look or step inside. 'How long will it take?'

'A couple of days at most.'

'Good. Let's get started, shall we?' She pulled her T-shirt over her head, but she was so hot and sweaty it stuck to her skin. Now unable to see, her arms in the air, she struggled to get it off.

'Here.' His shadow appeared and she could feel his body near hers as he tugged it over her head, freeing her arms.

Her heart was roaring in her chest, its beat echoing around her body, no more so than between her legs. *Don't look into his eyes,* she told herself firmly. Don't let him hurt you.

'Thanks,' she muttered, turning quickly away and kicking off her flip-flops, then lowering her shorts. As she fiddled with her bra, she could hear him unscrewing the top from a bottle of wine.

One bra hook was stuck fast. She wrenched at it furiously. Then she sensed the hot body close up again, and this time the beat in her belly trebled, turbo-charged.

'Let me.' He took over and the speedometer broke as his fingers accidentally brushed against her back. A split second later, the bra was unclipped and her boobs were released, like statically charged helium balloons, attached to her revving, rolling insides with tight ribbons.

Increasingly undignified and angry with her body for being so rebelliously carnal, she hurried to the patchwork sofa, whipping off her knickers in a stealth move practised over a long and increasingly inhibited marriage and sliding them under a cushion as she resumed her portrait position. 'Is this where I was?'

He'd disappeared again, a full glass of wine left on the side.

'Bastard!' she muttered, pulling two cushions across to cover herself, now very hot and feeling increasingly silly.

Just when she was starting to suspect he'd done a runner, he reappeared with the blue and white throw from her bed, which had been on the sofa when he'd sketched out the composition, and her dressing-gown, which he threw over the back of a chair.

Saying nothing, he handed her the counterpane and she hurriedly crammed it beneath her as he took up his board, slurped some wine and studied her minutely.

'Tuck your hair behind your ears and look slightly to your right. Chin higher. Your left leg was further over. More than that. A bit more.'

She edged it out, embarrassingly aware that she was going

to be flashing at him in a minute and might reveal something already slick with excitement. She needed a cold shower. She found Euan ordering her around disturbingly erotic and equally infuriating. Her giveaway nipples were like two bullets now – she half expected to hear the click of a safety catch releasing. Anger and longing bubbled in equal measure inside her.

'Arms back. A little further. Further.'

The sweat was pouring off her. Gunter clambered up alongside, adding his bristly, panting heat to the mix.

'That's it,' Euan said, looking from her to his board. 'Hold that.'

Hopping down from the table, he closed the blinds and pulled the doors ajar, then went to the music control pad, which bleeped as his fingers scrolled.

'Is there any Alanis Morissette?' Jenny called out tetchily. 'Or rap maybe?'

'Rap?'

'Yes. Something edgy and hardcore.'

'Eminem?' he suggested sarcastically.

'Perfect.' She had no idea what it sounded like, but she hoped it was suitably mind-numbing.

As the beat thumped into the room, she focused on a point in the mid-distance, trying to empty her mind, but it just made her body all the more finely tuned. The angry music seemed to make her pulses pound faster, the words hot in her bloodstream, crude and urgent. Having never really listened to rap before – apart from the noise that reverberated through her children's bedroom doors and the earphones of iPods she confiscated at school – Jenny found it all-consuming. She gritted her teeth and wondered how much longer she could endure before she suggested some Bavarian accordion music.

'I haven't been having an affair with Geraldine Scott,' Euan said, wiping sweat from his forehead with his wrist.

'Fine. Your business.' The music ground on, Eminem growling about mistakes and regrets, his pain impossible to ignore.

Euan was talking quietly. 'I loved her a long time ago.'

She only half heard as the rapper's angry voice talked to his children, fast and loud, explaining his reasons for leaving them. 'She has a lot of fans.'

'In Australia.'

'Worldwide indeed.' Her nose was itching. She wrinkled it and lifted her chin.

'I was eighteen.'

'I was about that age when I discovered her.' She twitched her nose some more.

'It's a drip of sweat,' he muttered.

'A what?'

'On your nose. A drip of sweat.'

She wiped it away irritably. Eminem had moved on a track and was telling her he wasn't scared of anything. She liked his spirit.

'When Richard started collecting my work, I knew she was his wife,' said Euan. 'It's why I didn't want to come here to paint the portrait.' He tilted his head, staring at her leg, then made a mark with his brush before laying it down. 'But twenty-five years is a long time, a lifetime. I thought we'd be fine.' He picked up his cigarette packet. 'Turns out we weren't.' He went outside, taking his glass of wine.

Jenny sat very still, feeling stupid and startled as she finally took in what he had said. Euan had known Geraldine in Australia. They'd met at eighteen. He had loved her.

She stood up shakily, grabbing her robe to pull on, hurrying to Geraldine's office to search out a copy of *The Dust*

Storm. After a few false starts with German and Dutch editions, she located one with a familiar sepia jacket, her coming-of-age motif. She turned to the dedication page.

For EH. *En ta paume, mon coeur.*

'In your palm, my heart.' She pressed the book angrily to her forehead.

'If her heart had been in my palm the year that was published, I'd have crushed it.'

He was in the doorway, cigarette dangling between his lips, wineglass at his fingertips, Gunter panting at his feet with her knickers in his mouth.

She hurried forwards to grab the pants and wave cigarette smoke out of the room. 'You can't bring that in here. Lose it now!'

'Yes, Mrs Rees.' He stepped forward and handed it to her with a half-smile. 'No smoking, no drinking, no telling the truth.'

She held it like an unexploded bomb, looking round for somewhere to put it out. Then she gave into temptation and drew on it, almost groaning with pleasure at the head-rush of relief. She could feel Euan's body doing its thing of being hot nearby, and she stepped back. He stepped forward in time, like a waltz partner, handing her the glass.

'You're like the devil on my shoulder.' She sipped, tongue waking up to the rich Burgundy blackberries and pepper.

'And you're the angel on mine.' He took back the cigarette and glass. 'Let's go outside.'

She followed him out into a setting sun, leaving Eminem still unafraid. The pool was lapping coolly at its filters, midges hovering, shadows in the garden lengthening. She could feel his arm close to hers as they stood side by side.

363

'Geraldine was the girl you fell in love with when you were rigging at the sheep station in Australia.'

He nodded, handing the cigarette across. 'We spent six months turning into one person, then she ripped herself out of me, went to university in Sydney, moved on. At the time, I thought my world had ended. I felt like I'd been turned to stone.'

'So you became the rolling stone that gathered no moss.'

He gave a gruff, sardonic laugh. 'After a while, you long for moss.'

'You're Jack from *The Dust Storm*,' she said, in sudden amazement, remembering the descriptions from the book that had become so real in her teenage imagination, the black hair and green eyes, the intense stare and Atlas wide shoulders. Euan wasn't *her* Jack: her Jack had existed entirely in her head, like the Jack every reader had conjured, but standing in front of her now was unmistakably Geraldine Scott's Jack.

'Nothing like me.' He sucked his teeth, gaze sliding along a jet's white tail streak in the darkening sky. 'I heard he gets the girl. I never finished it – I read so slowly I had time to get too angry so I stopped. Then I caught the film on television. I was in South America at the time; it was dubbed into Spanish. Jack said, "*¡Por Dios!*" a lot in a voice as deep as a blue whale.'

'That actor with the melting brown eyes who was always in rehab wasn't the Jack I knew.' She had hated the film. 'We were all in love with our own Jack.'

'Apart from Geraldine.'

She turned to look at him in profile, too caught up in literary interpretation to check herself. 'Victoria falls in love with Jack in the book. Nobody writes that intensely without loving in real life.'

'But does she stay in love with him?'

Jenny thought uncomfortably about the handwritten sequel she'd sneaked looks at, depicting Jack's descent into drunken debauchery. Her fingertips jumped against his as she took his glass and drained it. 'The light's going.' Turning back inside, she silenced Eminem as she passed, his angry, honest pain no longer helping.

Slipping off the robe again was a blessed relief in the relentless heat. She slid gratefully onto the sofa as Euan went to refill his glass and pour her one of her own, her professionalism slipping.

'What was it like seeing her again?' she asked, as he resumed painting.

'Emotional. Move your left leg out again.'

She moved it slightly.

'More.'

'Emotional how?' she repeated, keeping her leg where it was.

'It's like wine. You bottle a vintage love like that and it tastes bitter and dusty when you open it, but then it rests awhile in the open air and the flavours start to come out – dark, rich and incredibly complicated.'

'Was Geraldine the one who said that?'

'Yes.' A pained smile dimpled his cheeks as he ran his brush slowly through the mix on his palette. 'She's the one who's good with words.'

'How did it make you feel?'

'Fucked up. Twisted apart. Angry. Sick.'

'Vintage Liebfraumilch, then.'

'It's not a Liebfraumilch,' he said angrily, reaching for his glass. 'It's something I've waited half a lifetime to taste again. It takes a bit of getting used to.' He drank, eyeing her thoughtfully. 'You've caught the sun. I'll need burnt sienna.'

Setting down the glass, he rooted through the tubes beside him.

She had a sudden image of the nude he'd painted of Geraldine, so raw with white-hot sensuality and love. Wiping another patina of sweat from her sunburned skin, she held in her stomach, edging her left knee in prudishly.

'How did she break your heart?' Even to her own ears, her voice sounded harsh, Mrs Rees demanding that a GCSE student define Charlotte Brontë's concept of eternal love in twenty words or fewer.

'Usual way.'

'You followed her to Sydney, didn't you?'

'Her father made her go. He was a bastard, but a clever one. He hated me. He guessed that as soon as we were apart she'd find other distractions. Isolated on the west coast with the nearest town an hour's drive away along a dust track, all she lived for was me. In Sydney she had a twenty-four-hour social life and her studies. She begged me to follow her, but by the time I got there, she had new friends and I was just a stranger with a funny accent who couldn't read a book.'

'She must have had serious regrets. She created Jack while she was at university. That's you.'

He shook his head. 'She'd already written *The Dust Storm* by then. That was what we did. I painted and she wrote. And we fucked. We thought we were the Rossettis.' He cast the board aside and stood up to refill the glass he'd already drained.

That's why it was so incredibly real, Jenny thought. Geraldine Scott had always maintained that she'd written the book at university, somehow cramming it in between wild parties and working hard for her double first. Young fans like Jenny thought she was Superwoman. But she'd written it at sixteen or seventeen, reporting live from the front while experiencing the first love she described so well.

Euan turned more music on as he returned to paint again, a familiar, lilting classical rhythm.

'Fauré's Pavane to soothe you.' He picked up his board and tutted as he looked at her over it. 'Move your left leg.'

'Tell me about meeting her again.'

'Move your leg and I'll tell you.'

Irritably, she moved her leg and felt cool air between her thighs. She turned her face away, already feeling it reddening, the beat deepening in her pulses

'Move your head back where it was,' he ordered. 'Look at me.'

She did as she was told, now able to see the brush working hard, dancing from palette to board, eyes on and off her in a constant slow, rhythmic sweep.

'I've told you everything,' he said, gaze alternating from body to brushstroke. 'I came here at Richard's invitation.'

'Where did you paint her?'

'In the library.'

'Christ – that was a bit close to home, wasn't it?'

'Richard chose it. The light is incredible. The family sat individually, but everyone was in there most of the time.'

'I'm talking about the nude.'

He selected a tube of paint and squeezed out a pip of cadmium red to mix with the skin-tones spread out on his palette, her naked body on a board. 'That was in a bathroom.'

She edged her knees closer together. 'She looks very happy.' It sounded ridiculously prudish.

'She was.'

'But you were both angry when you met again, right?'

'We didn't hit it off straight away.' His brush was a rhythmic conductor's baton between board and paint. She could tell from his eye-line that he was painting her arms. 'She seemed to think I was rubbing her nose in it, swanning in from my world travels while she was suffocating in middle-aged middle England. She's self-conscious about her body. She beats herself up about ageing. You and she have a lot in common.'

'Great,' she said tightly. 'I'm sure we'll enjoy bonding over that some time.'

'She accused me of trying to be a modern-day Picasso, drinking too much and sleeping with my life models.'

'You do.'

'Not the one who's got so deep under my skin I can't sleep at all.' He looked at her levelly, his eyes burning into hers.

'You should try Nytol.' She felt hot brands searing into her cheeks. 'I heard she was jealous of Lonnie.'

'Myrtle's been stirring.' He sighed, glancing at her then back to his mixing brush, pulling in more of the red pip. 'There's nothing disingenuous about Lonnie Clifton. She's a great kid, but she's barely kissed a boy. I'm not interested.'

'Geraldine was, I gather.'

'Stop bitching.' His eyes were on hers, but she refused to meet them, far too frightened of losing control, particularly as his unblinking gaze was now lighting fireworks inside her and holding sparklers against her skin.

She reached for her robe. 'The light's gone. We should stop.'

A hand clamped on her arm. 'Sit back. I haven't finished.'

She sprang into position again, arm now buzzing as though it was wrapped in a TENS massager.

He worked on in silence.

Fauré's Pavane gave way to his Requiem, so unutterably tragic and beautiful. It was impossible to listen to it without tears nudging. It was one of the first pieces of music Robin had taken her to hear, performed by the New College choir, his hand in hers throughout, his square-topped thumb running back and forth over her heart line. *En ma paume, mon coeur.* Blinking hard, she tried hard to think about something else. Your body is naked, she reminded herself. Don't show more.

'What's making you so sad?' Euan asked.

'Let's just get on with this painting.' Despite the heat, goose-bumps were popping all over her skin as self-consciousness crept back, her inhibitions returning in full flood. She squeezed her thighs together, no longer protected by the gauze of detachment. Her bullet nipples shrugged on full metal jackets.

Gunter's eyebrows were starting to twitch between her and the door, small impatient groans starting in his throat.

'I must take him out,' she said, as the light finally slid away.

When she headed to the door to take Gunter to the river, alarm beeps sounding, she found Euan waiting for her in the cool shade of the porch, a grand Gothic replica of the church's ancient little one in which they'd kissed just the day before. 'I could use a lift. Can you drop me at my truck?'

'Where is it?'

'I'll show you on the way back.' He watched her pull the door closed. 'I think it's my turn to walk and talk, don't you?'

41

Gunter charged ahead as they walked along the riverbank into the last pink glow of the sunset, past Perry's houseboat, which was deserted.

'Femi's Perry's niece by marriage,' Euan explained, without prompting, answering the question that had been burning her tongue, 'his brother's step-daughter, I think. She was looking after the boat while Perry was away for part of June and July, and she offered to model for me. I liked painting her. Her skin-tones are breath-taking. Plus she also has the cheekiest arse and face, and she flirted as default. Then when Geraldine went to Mauritius, I went on the rebound so . . . ' He raked back his hair and shrugged.

'Femi floated your boat.'

'Neither of us was very buoyant, but we were interrupted halfway through by a woman with a badly behaved dog.'

'Sorry about that.' Jenny put on a burst of speed.

'Forgiven.' He caught up and kept pace, his loose-limbed stride easily matching her half-jog, hands plunged into his pockets.

'Do you love her?' she asked, already breathless.

'Femi?' He laughed. 'C'mon, Jenny. We're not all star-crossed. Sometimes sex just ticks the box.'

'I was talking about Geraldine.'

The white streak in his hair had turned salmon pink in the sunset again, she noticed, just as it had the first time she'd seen him.

'That crazy little thing called love was once very big between us.' He glanced across at her, eyes turbulent. 'It's hard to lose the madness.'

She was embarrassed how much it hurt to hear it. 'Star-crossed *and* ticked, then.'

'Something like that.'

'It must have been hell seeing her so unhappy.' She stopped, and he loped on a few paces, then turned back, the low sun directly behind him.

'She's so defined by her creativity. She was such a huge critical success so young – it's the scale upon which she judges herself and she's never matched it again. She was the bright young thing, but there are much younger, brighter things now. She feels her life is passing her by and taking all the wrong directions. Richard adores her, but he's stuffy and needy and pedantic, and she struggles to feel the energy and passion she needs to write freely.'

'But she has it with you?'

'She wrote night and day after I finished the portrait.'

'It must have been like Brontë Parsonage.' She pictured the bottles lined up by the mattress in the garden-cottage bedroom along with the Othello and Desdemona knickers on the bed, the painting of Geraldine pleasuring herself in the bathroom. 'Maybe not quite so close to God.'

'She was exactly the same at eighteen. Once she starts writing, she can't stop.'

'I'm surprised she found the time for adultery.'

'She didn't. We agreed not to take it any further while she was still with Richard.'

'I've been in the garden cottage, remember, Euan.'

'And what did DCI Rees find there?' Anger snapped in his voice.

She bit her lip, unable to say it out loud. It sounded

371

sleazier than ever, faintly ridiculous and acutely embarrassing to confess to snooping so thoroughly that she'd unearthed the evidence. In the end, she said vaguely, 'It's a mess.'

'A mess?' His eyebrows lifted.

'I hate mess,' she muttered. Then she looked at him levelly, eyes challenging. '*Run away with me.*'

His eyebrows shot up, and she realized he thought she was making a suggestion. 'It was written on the mirror above the fireplace in the cottage. She hid the painting of herself behind it. *The mirror crack'd from side to side.*'

'I threw a bronze at it when she told me she was going to Mauritius with Richard.' He ducked his head. Across the river a proud mother mallard was taking her ducklings for a swim past two swans. 'She'd seen the pictures of Femi and was jealous. She wanted me to destroy them, but I refused. Then she told me they were going away.'

'She chose to try to save her marriage.'

He turned back to her. 'She deserves the happy ending she creates for other people. She works crazy hours creating the most vivid, imaginative, exciting escapism, yet she admits to having been suicidally unhappy before I turned up. Richard's a good man, and he loves her. I just want her to be happy again.'

She watched Gunter plunging into the river to cool off, sending the duck quacking away with her charges and the swans hissing to the opposite bank. 'No *Schadenfreude*, then?'

'Is that like Liebfraumilch?' He half smiled.

'Vintage *Schadenfreude* tastes just as bad.' She picked a lacy parasol of hogweed from the hedgerow. 'It's good you want the marriage to work.'

'I didn't say that.' He dipped his head and looked up through his thick forelock. 'I said I want her to be happy.'

372

They started to walk again, Gunter diving in and out of the long grass to either side of the path to dry off.

'To be honest, I've spent most of the past four months wishing I'd never bloody come here,' Euan said. 'The odd thing is, I changed my mind this week.'

Jenny nodded, understanding that Geraldine's decision must have led to some sort of closure, however painful.

'If I hadn't come here,' he said softly, 'I wouldn't have met you.'

She felt his hand brush against hers as they walked, then his fingers curled between hers. Her thumb crossed with his, like a bird's wings folding together. Every neuron in her body seemed to be feeding currents to her hand now.

They jumped, handhold breaking, at a shrieking squawk nearby and Gunter sent up a barrel of brown feathers that hurtled out of a nearby thicket and took off into the woods behind them. With a delighted, baying bark, he shot past the 'Trespassers Will Be Prosecuted' sign into the darkness after it.

'Shit!'

It was his favourite pheasant-slaying wood.

'GUUUUUNTEEEEEEER!' She sprinted towards the nearby gate, clambered over it and landed at the other side almost on top of a quivering heap that had come to sit there.

'Gunter!' She dropped to her haunches in amazed delight, hugging and kissing him. 'You came back! This time you came back!' He licked her face.

She heard twigs breaking and the sound of a quad-bike engine coming towards her from deeper in the woods, a voice shouting, 'If that's the bloody dog that's been killing my pheasants, I'll shoot the bugger right NOW!'

'Oh, Christ.' Jenny grabbed Gunter in an ungainly struggle of long legs, turning back towards the gate. Euan was already there, leaning across to take him before helping Jenny back over, her T-shirt ripping as it caught on the barbed wire holding the 'Keep Out' sign to the gate.

The quad bike was getting closer, tyres crackling through the undergrowth.

'We'll hide in the houseboat,' Euan said, in an urgent undertone, grabbing Gunter's collar. 'I know where the key's kept.'

Together, they ran back along the bank, lungs burning. They could hear the quad engine cut out then the clatter of someone climbing over the gate, but they didn't look back, hurtling around the weeping willow on the river bend, which afforded them enough cover to get to the boat. There, Euan grabbed the keys from beneath a tub of lavender and unlocked the low doors, just in time to push Gunter through the hatch and tumble in after him as their pursuer came into sight.

'I'm sure he's seen us,' Jenny whispered in terror, running to the dusty window and ducking as she peered out. 'Shit! He really has got a gun!'

Euan wrapped his paint-stained fingers around Gunter's muzzle to stop him barking as the footsteps pounded closer, then carried on past. The dog writhed and whined, breaking free to let out a loud bark.

The footsteps slowed and pounded back.

'There's dog food and chews in one of the galley cupboards,' Euan hissed.

Pulling open cupboards in the kitchen and clattering through them, Jenny located the Rottweilers' stash and pulled out a roasted hock bone to thrust at him. Conker eyes bulging with greed, he took it reverently and retreated beneath a bench table.

Jenny and Euan crouched by the window, trying not to make a sound as the shadow moved back past.

'*Was* he the dog that killed the pheasants?'

'Twice.' She nodded.

'The guy came here and accused Perry's dogs of doing it. He wanted to put a bullet in them.'

'Oh, hell.' She lifted her head again, saw the glint of red sunlight on a gun barrel and dropped down, wiping her hot face on her shoulder and realizing it was covered with blood.

'You've cut yourself.' He leaned over her in concern, pulling back the T-shirt where it was ripped and seeing a gash from the barbed wire on the gate.

'It's nothing.'

'It's not nothing.' Still on his hands and knees, he pulled open cupboards and drawers searching for a first-aid kit.

'Ssh – he'll hear.'

He located a pile of clean, folded tea towels and held one to her collar bone to staunch the bleeding. 'It might need stitches.'

'It won't.' She lifted the towel to check. 'It's just a nick.'

Back on the hunt for a first-aid kit, he opened a tall cupboard and a pile of drawings slid out. He tried to gather them up before she could see, but there was no mistaking the pouting perfection of Femi posing naked.

'She wanted to keep the rough sketches,' he explained.

She picked up one that had landed beside her, immediately understanding why Geraldine had been upset, jealousy nipping at her throat and pulse points. 'That's pretty close-up and personal.'

Drips of blood landed on the drawing. She cast it aside and held the tea-towel tighter.

'Femi is beautiful, but as dull as a still-life compared to drawing you.' He shoved them back into the cupboard and lifted a green tin down from another shelf, peering out of the window as he passed. 'I think he's gone.' He settled down beside her and doused some cotton wool in TCP.

She winced as it touched the wound.

'Perhaps it's not as bad as it looks,' he said, with relief, dabbing at the cut. 'You just bleed a lot. Comes from having such a big heart.'

'Thanks.'

He stopped dabbing, but didn't move away, his head close enough for her to smell his hair and feel the warmth of his breath on her shoulder, the heat rising off his body. Then, very slowly, he bent his head and kissed the skin beside the wound.

It shouldn't have been as sexy as it was – they both reeked of TCP and there was something kinkily vampirish about it – but it was one of the most singularly erotic moments Jenny had ever experienced. Her body seemed to drop lower, weighed down with lust. As his lips found hers, she knew without doubt that she had to sleep with this man, even if it meant playing Russian roulette with a fully loaded gun.

They jumped as they heard footsteps on the gangplank, and he wrapped a protective arm around her, cursing under his breath.

'Did you lock the door?' she whispered, instinctively turning to check Gunter, but he was working on the bone obsessively, temporarily zoned out.

'It's latched.'

A fist pounded on the hatch. 'I know someone's in there!' Gunter snarled.

'Fuck.' Euan stood up. 'You hold the dog. I'll deal with it.' He pulled off his T-shirt.

'What are you going to do?' she squeaked, in alarm, as he moved to the sink and doused water over his hair and chest. 'Greek wrestling?'

'Pretend we're screwing. It worked before.'

'You weren't pretending last time.'

He dropped to his haunches, green eyes level with hers. 'I'm not this time, either.'

The kiss that followed was wet-skinned, urgent, breathless, and almost turned her inside out with lust, the blood pumping so loudly in her ears she could no longer hear the banging on the door because she wanted Euan inside her right now. When he pulled away, he ran his thumb across the plump wet softness of her lower lip, his gaze locked with hers. 'Hold that thought.'

Pulses pinging crazily, she hurried to stop Gunter breaking out from beneath the table. But far from launching an attack on the stranger, his only interest was in guarding his bone and, right now, he thought she was the biggest threat. He slunk back further into the shadows with it, hackles and neck scruff raised, snarling a warning.

She could hear Euan outside complaining that he didn't appreciate being interrupted on a Saturday evening, the pheasant man arguing that he had every right and he knew the dog was on board.

Gunter crunched loudly on the bone, a low growl reverberating in his throat.

Realizing he wasn't going anywhere, Jenny crept closer to the voices shouting beyond the hatch.

Euan's accent was at its gruffest, a fierce clansman warrior protecting his quine: 'I'm in the middle of something seriously fucking epic here, and I want you to get tae fuck!'

'I don't believe you,' the man shouted. 'All you have in there is a murdering dog.'

Jenny steeled herself. Anything Femi could do, she could do with bells on. She pulled off her ripped T-shirt and sweaty bra, kicked off her shorts and knickers and grabbed a towel.

'Who are you calling a murdering dog?' She stepped outside, discovering too late that she'd grabbed a pair of towelling oven mitts.

The man's jaw dropped, his eyes on stalks. 'I apologize, madam. I had no idea ...' He saw the blood, which had started to drip again, spattering the white mitt.

Jenny hadn't bargained for several cyclists pausing on the bank to drink from their carry bottles and witness the confrontation, but she brazened it out. Keeping her back to the river, one mitt high and one low, she smiled. 'Would you mind leaving us to it?'

'Of course!' The man cast a final uncertain look through the open hatch, but Gunter was well out of sight, chomping with silent and feverish concentration.

High-powered air rifle beneath his arm, he retreated to the bank and set off back to his woods, cyclists wobbling in his wake.

'You are amazing,' Euan breathed.

Behind them, a whoop went up from the river and two canoeists slid silently by, admiring Jenny's naked backside.

She and Euan fell back into the boat, leaning against one another in silent laughter, wiping tears away.

'Amazing.' He kicked the hatch closed and started kissing her again as she backed into the room and they slammed against the fitted cupboards, then the fridge, then the table, from beneath which came a furious snarl.

'I don't think we'll get him out of here for a few hours,' Jenny breathed between kisses.

'Suits me fine.' He dropped his mouth to her nipple, sending the statically charged helium balloons high in the air. Then, tipping her back on the cushioned bench seat, he kissed lower.

Where Roger had dibbed and dabbed, Euan feasted,

fingers threaded through hers, eyes on her face. It was a sensation like no other Jenny had ever experienced, and almost too much to bear, by turns ecstatic, then deeply shaming.

'Relax.' He lifted his head. 'I love doing it. I love watching you as I do it.' His tongue dived in again and she felt an electric heat scorch through her, holding his gaze now, laughing and gasping in wonder.

Fingers sinking through his thick hair, she drew him up to her mouth again, wanting to give him pleasure, to admire that part of him she'd first seen bulging for another, but that was now bulging all for her. She didn't care if that made him a cocksman and her a hussy. She was on the dance-floor right now and she didn't want to come off.

When he pulled open his belt and unbuttoned his flies, she bit her lip in delight at the long, smooth harbinger of pleasure that sprang out. 'That's so beautiful,' she breathed, reaching up.

He laughed. 'It's been called many things in its time – and I've been named after it in less than flattering terms once or twice – but never that.'

'It's my kind of beautiful.' She ran her fingers around it and guided it towards her lips, kissing the end like a giant Chupa Chups and deciding it tasted just as good, the silky, salted caramel skin stretching beneath her lips and tongue.

He groaned, his fingers in her hair, holding her there. 'God, we're going to be good together.'

As Jenny licked and sucked every inch, a mill race of anticipation was bubbling between her legs now.

There were footsteps on the gangplank again. This time Gunter started barking beneath his table.

'Please, Christ, no,' muttered Euan.

A shaft of evening light fell across them.

'Fuck me.' Perry's short, squat silhouette was framed in the door, gripping a Rottweiler collar with each hand. Seeing Gunter, the dogs plunged against his grip, snarling and straining to attack.

'I wish you'd drop me a bloody text if you're planning to use my gaff, Euan,' he shouted, over the din. The boat now sounded like an illegal dog-fighting pit.

'Can you give us five minutes, Perry?' Euan threw his T-shirt at Jenny and pulled up his shorts.

'I'd love to, mate, but Femi will be here in two. And I know she's not exactly broken-hearted, but this is rubbing it in. So hop it.'

Gunter made a savage hullaballoo as he and his precious bone were extracted from beneath the table, picked up and transported at speed past his baying enemies.

Dressed in Euan's damp T-shirt and her creased shorts, scuttling past the boat-owner, like a babysitter caught sexting, Jenny no longer felt liberated, but dirty and smutty and one in a long line of Euan Henderson's conquests. She was sticky with sweat, ashamed of the swollen excitement still wet and welcoming between her legs. The T-shirt was clinging painfully to her cut, which was bleeding again.

'I'll drive,' he insisted, when they got to the car. 'You need to hold something against that cut.' He fished around in the glove box as they set off down the road that ran alongside the river, pulling out a packet of tissues.

Jenny pressed one tightly to her collar bone and stared fixedly out of the passenger window, the sight of him with no shirt on too disturbing a reminder of what they'd just been doing together.

'This is the long way round,' she protested, as they turned into the woods.

'I need you to understand that I'm not normally some sort

of shitty Don Juan who struts around seducing women,' he said. 'I know that's how it must seem.'

'I went into this with my eyes open, Euan. We both did.' Gazing unseeingly out of the window at the tree-trunks sliding by, unable to calm her raging blush, Jenny could still vividly picture his eyes looking up the length of her body and straight into hers, the memory doing nothing to still the frustrated excitement still buzzing shamefully against the hot car seat.

'You are different.'

'So you say.' Twice Femi's age. Old enough to know better.

'This is more than just sex.'

'What just happened on the boat was largely sex-based, Euan.' She felt another body-wash of embarrassment at being discovered *in flagrante*, and in the same place he'd seduced another woman little more than a week earlier. Had he pulled the same moves on Femi? Had he looked her in the eyes as he kissed her before, behind, between, above, below too?

'I want you like crazy,' he said urgently. 'I'd park the car in a clearing now and pull you into the back seat if you weren't bleeding all over the front one already.'

Jenny wondered if it would be terribly slutty to suggest that parking now was fine as she had the tissue.

'You have to believe me when I say that you're different and I care about you and I'm not just some debauched libertine who thinks with his dick,' he went on.

'You're the one who told me you're an unreliable lost cause who never sticks around,' she reminded him.

'I am sticking around,' he promised quietly. 'I'm not going anywhere.'

She chewed on an emerging smile as they drove out of the woods. Gunter was panting loudly in the boot, realizing they were almost home.

Jenny's phone beeped in the central cubby where she'd abandoned it. She picked it up, seeing the voicemail notification on the screen. Unplugging the charger, she dialled 1 and held it to her ear, anxious to ensure it wasn't an urgent message from one of the children.

'Welcome to your voicemail.' A recorded voice announced loudly over all sixteen surround-sound car speakers. 'You have *two* new messages . . .'

The high-tech Bluetooth connector was playing hands-free. She stabbed at the phone screen trying to grab it back to the handset, but nothing happened.

'Hi, Jen, just Carla. Sorry I missed your message. You sounded a bit strained. Did Roger Roger Night not go well? Call me.'

Clearing her throat, she tried frantically to end the call, but her screen had frozen now.

'Jenny, it's Roger. About the other night. I must apologize. I was very drunk and very nervous. I've been thinking about it a lot – all the time, in fact – and I feel we should try to put it behind us and give this another go. Forget the – um – strap thing. It really isn't that important to me. You are much more important, and you're quite simply gorgeous, Jenny Rees. What you did – that thing with your tongue – it was sensational. I can't stop thinking about that either. I had no idea you were such a wild cat in bed.' He let out a little growl. 'You are different, Jenny. Call me when you get this. I was thinking *Merry Wives* on the fifth?'

'Guess we both went into this with our eyes open,' Euan said quietly.

They were driving past his abandoned pick-up truck now. There was striped blue police tape on it. Noticing the driver's window had been smashed, he slammed on the brakes, cursing under his breath as he pulled the Evoque up onto the verge and jumped out.

Jenny hurled her phone onto the dashboard and pressed her palms to her brow, appalled at the Bluetooth gaffe. Then, remembering that all of Euan's studio equipment had been in his truck, she tried to get out too and found a hedge right up against the door so she couldn't open it.

He appeared at the driver's window, wild-haired and bare-chested. 'They haven't got into the back, thank God – just trashed the cab. There's a police number to call. I'll have to get it towed tonight. Will you be okay to take the car the rest of the way?'

'Of course.' She tried to sound calm, but she was panicking that he'd just heard Roger's call and knew she was just as guilty of repeating the same sexual tricks – even though his harbinger of pleasure had been a million times lovelier than Roger's sanitized one.

'Can I borrow your phone?' His voice was terse and practical. 'Do I need to get in the car to use it?' He caught her eye and she found herself looking guiltily away.

'I think it's fine now the engine's off.'

She moved across to the driver's seat while he stood on the grass verge making the call. The hot car reeked of TCP and Gunter's roast bone, making her feel nauseous.

'Thanks.' He handed it back through the window, less tetchy now. 'A tow truck's on its way. Then the local bobbies want me to pop into the station and go through some details.'

'You have no shirt on,' she reminded him.

'It's a heat-wave. They'll forgive me.'

'Have this back.' She pulled his T-shirt over her head and handed it out through the window. 'Call me if you need a lift.'

'You're amazing,' he leaned in to kiss her, then breathed into her ear, 'and so sexy. I'll see you later tonight. Roger's right. That thing you do with your tongue is something else.'

She pulled back, mortified by her week of blow-jobs, canal-boat dogging and topless driving. 'I'm never normally like this, you do know that?'

'The first – correction, second time I saw you, you pulled your dress off.' He smiled easily, dropping a finger to trace her bare shoulder.

'You know that's not true. I refused to pose nude.'

'You were about to dive into the pool to rescue Gunter.'

'You saw that?'

'I'd come to get my stuff from the cottage, hoping Geraldine had hidden the painting somewhere obvious. When I heard the splash, I saw what was going on and charged out ready to blow my cover to dive in too. But you were already pulling him up to the surface.'

'I didn't see you.'

'You had a lot of paperwork to worry about.' He offered the ghost of a smile.

'Christ, I've been so guilty about that.' She ducked her head. 'You forged that page, didn't you?'

'I might not be a prolific reader like you, but I liked that scene.' The smile widened. 'We'll try it out later.'

'It's a lesbian love scene,' she said awkwardly, blush rising as she had uncomfortable images of him inviting Femi to join them, of Roger and his urges, of Geraldine's teasing Sapphic flirtation that titillated and frustrated both husband and lover. She wasn't at all sure she was ready for this.

'I think we can adapt it.' His fingers had traced down from her shoulder and along her forearm to her hand, slotting through hers and guiding them downwards, sliding them beneath the fabric folds and buttons of her shorts to the place where her libido was still wired to the mains. It felt intoxicatingly wicked and brought her seconds away from meltdown.

Then, hearing a car horn beep as it passed, Jenny jolted back into reality. 'We can't do this. It's obscene.' She pulled her hand away. 'I'm not doing filthy things in parked cars or re-enacting any scenes written by your ex. This isn't me. I'm not an artist's model or a bohemian voluptuary,' she rushed on, sounding starchier by the minute as Mrs Rees took over to cover her embarrassment. 'I really don't like talking about myself or taking my clothes off or listening to Eminem. I'm just a full-time teacher and occasional house-sitter, who loves reading and hates mess.' She punched at the ignition button. 'You know that's the real me, don't you?'

'Sure,' Euan laughed as the engine roared into life, 'and I'm looking forward to kissing every sweet, reactionary inch of her later.'

'Fine.' Face absolutely flaming, she put the car into drive and lurched forwards, forcing Euan to jump back. 'I'll see you later, then.' Even more embarrassed by her bad driving, she tried to look as though the manoeuvre was intentional, signalling and waving before driving off at speed. In the back, she could hear Gunter throwing up pieces of his bone.

As Jenny braked to turn into the Old Rectory drive, she spotted Myrtle bearing down on her along the pavement, tugging the elderly Cairn and waving frantically. Gunter went into a flurry of barking in the back, churning up the dog sick.

Myrtle tapped on the window, mouthing, 'How's it going?'

Jenny tried to open it just a fraction, but it whizzed right down. 'Fine! All in hand.'

Taking in the strong pong of regurgitated bone and

noticing that Jenny was driving in her bra, Myrtle adopted a fixed smile. 'Jolly good.' Then her smile turned into one of bulging-eyed horror as a liver-spotted hand landed a greeting on her shoulder, and she was forced to introduce Jenny to the chairman of the parish council through the open window.

Jenny cleaned the car of regurgitated bone and blood as best she could, then had a long bath, writhing in soapy frustration, reliving the way her body had exploded right here, and wishing the warm welcome between her legs would dissipate instead of staying there, taut and uncomfortable, like an inflated wet water-slide after the holidaymakers had left.

'He will be here later,' she told herself, soaping every inch and slipping back beneath the water to rinse her hair.

But he didn't come later. She stayed downstairs until long after midnight, pacing from the clock to his painting gear to the window and back to the clock, then went to bed to lie awake, body slick with worry and anticipation.

When the house phone rang at close to two in the morning, she fell out of bed in her hurry to get to it, sending Gunter into a frenzy of barking, but it had already taken a message and the caller had rung off by the time she reached a handset. Playing it back, she heard Richard's patrician voice, slurred with extreme drunkenness: 'Know I'm calling at silly o'clock UK time, and there's really nothingwassoever-worry 'bout, Mrs Rees, but could you give me a call in the morning when you get this?'

She checked the clock, calculating that it was six a.m. in Mauritius. She couldn't face calling straight back, and he clearly didn't expect her to. Let him have a few breakfast coffees first.

Yawning, she checked out of the windows again, seeing only blackness. She trailed up to bed.

XI

Sunday

42

TO DO LIST

HaVE SEX

'Wake up, beautiful.' A cup of tea was set down on the bed-side table, along with a plate of buttered toast. 'We have a painting to finish and the light's amazing. I want to catch it before the storm breaks.'

She rolled onto her back and looked up at Euan. She could smell the toast and the warmth of his skin. She surely couldn't be dreaming.

'How did you get in?'

'There's a spare key to the house in the garden cottage.' He ducked away, laughing as Gunter gave him a bear-hug.

Jenny was reluctant to reveal how pleased she was to see him, blinking up at him suspiciously, the awkwardness of their car journey and her departure still stinging. 'I waited up for you last night.'

'It took hours for the truck to be towed, then with the police.' He was still wrestling Gunter, the mattress bouncing beneath her. 'It was late and I didn't want to wake you, and I had something I wanted to do first, although seeing you like this now, I need certifying for wanting to be anywhere else.' He wrestled Gunter off the bed and gazed down at her.

'But I want to prove that I know exactly who you are, Jenny Rees, and you're not a bohemian volunteer.'

'Voluptuary,' she corrected automatically, her heart pounding so hard she half expected the sheet to flap up and down. 'A person devoted to sensual pleasure.'

'I know what it means.'

She rubbed sleep from her eyes, sitting up, acutely aware as she did so that she was wearing nothing but a crumpled cotton sheet beneath which every sensual part of her was currently getting tighter and wetter and ever more eager for pleasure.

But he was loping back across the room, Gunter bounding at his heels. 'I'll take the dog out to Beacon Common. You enjoy your breakfast in bed. We have a lot of painting to do.'

Completely forgetting about Richard Lewis's late-night call, which had to be returned, she listened to the car retreating along the drive, Gunter barking in the back, and banged her hands twice on the mattress, then clapped them once, banged twice, clapped again and started singing 'We Will Rock You' at the top of her voice.

'Move your left leg out . . . further . . . further.' A slow smile spread over Euan's face, casting the dimples into deep grooves beneath his cheekbones. 'Oh, Christ, I'm not going to be able to resist you much longer, but we need this light.' The brush moved on the board.

It was a magical, eerie light, the horizon black as night, the brightest blue halo of sky overhead, from which the sun blazed, casting the landscape in luminous multicolour against dark monochrome. At the far end of the open kitchen, the patchwork sofa was seamed with golden rays and Jenny's body seemed spun from light.

As the storm rumbled in the distance, Gunter hid beneath the table, guarding the remnants of his bone from which he could still not be separated, eyebrows flicking nervously towards the ever-darker horizon.

The first heavy drops landed on the surface of the pool as Euan scratched his sideways lamp signature into the wet oil in the bottom right-hand corner of the painting. 'I have nothing more to add, except that I intend to take you to bed right now and keep you prisoner there for the rest of this week.'

She stood beside him, still naked, staring at the extraordinary energy bursting from it. The model in the painting wasn't as beautiful as Femi, as sexy as Geraldine or as young as Lonnie, but she was extraordinarily vibrant and charismatic. It was impossible not to stare.

'Wow,' she breathed.

'Wow,' he agreed, but he wasn't looking at the painting, his fingers already tracing her throat and gliding down to her nipples, his head tilting to watch them harden.

There was a great rolling clap of thunder overhead, followed almost instantly by a flash of lightning. Gunter and his bone retreated behind the sofa.

'Come to bed and hide under the covers with me.' His fingers trailed lower, bumping over her ribs, dipping into her navel and off-roading into the Hebrides.

'Don't be such a scaredy-cat.' She reached down for his belt buckle, releasing his beautiful pleasure harbinger and taking it in her hand, drawing it to its full length while he leaned against her with a groan of delight. 'Are you frightened this might be struck by lightning?'

'With you doing that to it, there may be a running risk.'

'Come outside and dice with death, Zeus.' She kissed him hard on the mouth before running out, leaping into the pool, water pounding down around her. Another great thunder-clap almost deafened them as Euan plunged in alongside her. They laughed and kissed as they trod water in the torrent, forked lightning shredding the sky overhead.

Euan towed her to shelter under the diving board, one hand gripping it above their heads while she rested her arms on the side of the pool. They kissed on as the storm raged and turned day into night, his free hand pulling her closer. Eyes not leaving hers, he angled her hips up towards his.

He's going to be inside me any second, she realized, with dizzying excitement, her nerve endings jangling crazily.

'How can we do this when you're not touching the bottom?' she asked, to cover her hyperventilating embarrassment.

'Good idea.' He slid his hand under her bottom and lifted her up onto him, sliding inside her. As he did so, she felt every nerve ending stop jangling and start humming in harmony.

Above the drumming rain, they could hear Gunter barking. Then they heard a woman's deep, agitated voice with a distinctive Australian accent: 'Mrs Rees. Mrs Rees. I'm back early! Where the fuck is the woman?'

Euan closed his eyes, his hand dropping silently from the diving board.

Jenny gripped tighter into the edge. She could feel him sliding out from inside her.

Geraldine was outside now, her feet moving around on the wet boards just behind the diving board. 'Mrs Rees? Are you there?' There was an audible sob, heartbreakingly lost.

Another crack of thunder split the air, then another sob. The sky lit up, Euan's face white in front of Jenny's. They could hear Geraldine crying, followed by a strange scraping noise on the decking as Gunter – so terrified of storms – conquered his fear to come to comfort her.

392

Euan's eyes snapped open. He pressed a finger to Jenny's mouth, his face tortured, the green gaze locked on hers, spilling words he couldn't say.

The sobbing continued for an agonizing minute. Then the footsteps retreated. The finger released.

Jenny gasped for breath, feeling as though she'd been punched hard and repeatedly.

Euan pressed his forehead to her breastbone, huge shoulders rearing out of the water, arms wrapping tightly around her. The rain pounded harder than ever, thunder rolling like a roulette ball around a wheel.

'You have to go to her.' Why am I saying this? she thought, the instant she said it. Why? Stay with me. *Stay*. But even as her conscience fought itself, she heard her pragmatic head say in horror, 'She'll see the painting.'

He flipped his head back as though his chest had been harpooned.

Jenny dropped lower in the water, arms scraped raw against the decking ledge, her heart sinking on down, dripping stone-like to the pool bottom. He still loves her, she thought wretchedly.

'Wait in the cottage,' he whispered, his hands cupping her face now. She could feel how much they were shaking. 'I'll meet you there.'

Euan's lips landed hard against hers, speaking more from his heart than he had time to say, which was no more than 'Forgive me.' He then kicked out from beneath the board and swam to the pool ladder. A moment later, he was gone.

Jenny turned to the pool wall, pressing her face against it, fighting not to cry out in anguish.

She stayed like that for a long time, freezing cold now, teeth chattering as she hid from the storm beneath the board, which drummed with rain. Above its rattling percussion, she could just about make out raised voices, sobs, more barking from Gunter, a door banging.

She waited, mind churning, skin wrinkling. Amid the storm's cacophony, the church bells started to ring for evensong.

Eventually, she took a deep breath, slid underwater and swam to the steps at the shallow end, stepping out into the rain to run across the garden, lightning showing her the way in strobe-like bursts as she dashed behind the high hedging and let herself into the cottage, its tiny windows letting in the meanest grey gleam from the blackened sky outside.

Shaking uncontrollably, she stumbled through the darkness in search of something warm to wrap herself in. As she did so, it struck her that there was nothing but smooth floorboards beneath her, the path underfoot clear. The papers, pen lids, ashtrays and empty bottles had all gone, tidied away to the sides of the room.

Running upstairs, teeth like castanets in a frantic flamenco dance, she found the bedroom empty of all but a mattress and a folded blanket, no clothes scattered, the Othello knickers scene gone. Lit by intermittent white flashes through the little window, it had been stripped bare.

This was what Euan had been doing since the early hours: removing the evidence. Or was he taking away the mess she'd told him she hated? Either way, he had been cleaning his way through a crisis. Just as she had. She sobbed and laughed, her emotions all muddled up.

Curling up on the mattress, she pulled the blanket over her. She could still feel the length of him sliding inside her, the ecstasy of taking him there, the agony of being denied it. But nothing was as excruciating as the relentless pain in her chest telling her that he was still in love with Geraldine.

The storm was moving away at last, the thunder retreating, the walls around her brightening, reminding her that the sun was still above the horizon, that this extraordinary day still had hours to give, was still filled with other people's Sunday routines – her mother calling after lunch to bitch about everyone at the Haven, Amalie the transatlantic family peace-maker Skyping 'Mom', a friend or two texting with news or an invitation, Jake sending a message if she was lucky. None of her loved ones was aware that her life no longer dovetailed routinely with theirs. She was broken-winged suddenly, drowned by the floods, olive branch dropped.

Eventually she got up, wrapping the blanket around her and heading through to the second bedroom, which had a window overlooking the house. It still smelt of turps, but the old paint tubes and mixing bottles had gone, the table had been scrubbed clean, and the stain on the wall washed away so only its shadow remained.

There was no sign of life in the house, the french windows all now closed. Were they still talking? Had they run away together already?

She wanted to feel angry, but she was too hollow with shock. She thought about marching across there to demand to know what was happening – she was the house-sitter with a professional duty of care, after all – but she was too cowardly, especially without clothes. She went in search of something to wear, looking through empty fitted wardrobes and finding nothing but more blankets and bedding.

Downstairs among the tidied papers and books in the sitting room there was a folded pile of Geraldine's things. The frilly Desdemona knickers weren't among them, Jenny noted, but there was a long red jumper that she pulled on. Because Geraldine was so tall, it reached almost to her knees and was impossibly hot, smelling strongly of the expensive perfume she'd noticed when she'd met her. It felt strange and uncomfortable to be wearing the Other Woman's clothes, but at least she could venture outside.

The wet garden glistened as though freshly varnished, the greens acid bright, the colourful beds like splashes straight from Euan's paintbrush. She smelt cigarette smoke and realized Euan and Geraldine had just stepped out together on the balcony above the pool that led out from the master bedroom, both staring into the garden, speaking with stiff-jawed restraint. It was like a scene from *Private Lives*.

She ducked into the shrubbery, heart pounding in her ears, already imagining the scenario – rapturous reunited love-making in the Lewises' marital bed followed by a post-coital Marlboro. Her fingers and lips twitched for her electronic fag. Peering out through an azalea, she was grateful to notice that they were fully clothed. Flicking away his half-smoked cigarette Euan went back inside. Geraldine stayed out, raking her Pre-Raphaelite mane from one shoulder to the other before resting her forearms on the balcony rail. She seemed to be staring straight at Jenny's azalea bush. Jenny stayed frozen on the spot until Geraldine turned her head, then she bolted back into the cottage.

For the first time she noticed that the broken mirror above the fireplace was gone, a painting propped there in its place. It was of the garden of the Old Rectory, painted from the room above her, bursting with riotous colour, a glorious Euan Henderson one-off, filled with character and characters – the Va Va Vacuum ladies flapping towels from windows, the Come On Eileen gardeners wrestling with hoses, the roly-poly neighbours frolicking with pool noodles on Lilos, Myrtle on a ladder wagging a finger over the garden wall at Gunter, who was barking at the ginger cat perched superciliously beside her. Apparently oblivious to them all, a small figure was lying on a sun-lounger reading a book, wearing dark glasses and a floppy hat, painted toe-nails like rows of coloured beads at the end of balletic, flexed feet. She stepped closer, looking for a tell-tale mane of fire-blonde hair. But it was short and dark.

'It's for you,' said a voice behind her. 'Because you're not a voluptuary, and you didn't volunteer for any part in my messy, shitty life.'

She turned to face him. He looked terrible, his face ashen and hollow, the smudges beneath his eyes dark as the storm clouds that had just passed.

'She hasn't stopped crying since Mahébourg. She and Richard had a drunken row and she told him that she was leaving him, that she was in love with somebody else. Then she flew home. I managed to hide the picture before she got a look at it. She's in no mental state to take that on. She thinks you're at church.'

'At *church*?'

'It was the only thing I could come up with off the top of my head. I heard the bells. I told her I'd offered to stay in the house to look after Gunter.'

'And what does she think you're doing now? Taking Holy Communion?'

'Getting my stuff. She wants to get out of here.'

Jenny gripped the mantelpiece to stop herself swaying, blood rushing from her head. 'You're running away together after all?'

He looked away, a muscle slamming in his hollow cheek. 'That's the plan.'

'Where will you go?'

'A hotel.'

She wanted to hit him hard. Instead, she felt Mrs Rees step in front of her, standing up to silence thirty rowdy new classmates, cool as cucumber in Hendrick's gin. 'Have a nice time.'

'I'm so sorry, Jenny.' He moved towards her.

She darted away. If he touched her, she'd be lost. She had to be practical and organized. It was her coping mechanism. 'Am I supposed to return from "church" before you set off?'

'I'll put Gunter in his cage.'

'It's broken.' Like my heart, which is equally useless at confining a free spirit.

'It'll hold together long enough.'

She lifted her chin, swallowing blades of pain. 'You'd better go, then.'

He shut his eyes tight. 'Jenny, please—'

'No,' she interrupted. 'I won't forgive you.'

'I never meant to hurt you.'

She felt her brittle ice armour start to crack. 'It's not me that matters. It's the family, the children. Have you any idea how selfish you're both being? I saw what mine went through, the constant scar of betrayal that never heals. And what about Richard? How's he supposed to cope?'

He couldn't look at her. 'He's flying back now.'

The ice re-formed. 'I'll make sure the kettle's on.'

'I never meant this to happen.'

'You asked her to run away with you. She's doing that. You meant this to happen.'

'I'm talking about you and me.'

Don't show him how much this is hurting, she told herself frantically. Be cool, be angry, hear those screw-you songs in your head.

'I will survive, you know,' she said tightly. 'You learn, as they say,' she went on. 'Trust me, I'm not afraid.' She lifted her chin, feeling feverish pink hot spots flare in each cheek. 'There you go . . . so what?'

'Believe me, I'm torn in two.'

'I don't want to hear!' She covered her ears and found her own heartbeat thundering there. Not Natalie Imbruglia, please, God, not that. The ice melted around her as though blasted by a flame-thrower. 'I *won't* go through this "I'm torn" shit again. Robin did it. I was the one it ripped apart in the end. Because that's the most humiliating bit. He was *always* going to choose her. I got the torn speech as compensation, keeping that faint, pathetic flicker of hope alive that one day soon he'd see the torn half he'd rejected, the family he'd abandoned, and realize it was a mistake.'

'Maybe he *was* torn,' he said quietly.

But she still had her hands over her ears, shouting now: 'You really don't need to bother with it, Euan. Robin owed me it. We were together twenty years – we raised kids together. You and I have just been filling in time.'

'You don't mean that.' He prised her hands from her ears. 'It's much more than that.'

She wrenched her wrists from his grip. 'Please just go.'

He looked away, the sun-filled angles and hollow shadows of his face a sad, beautiful chiaroscuro. 'I have to do this, Jenny. I loved her until it broke me. I carried her around in my heart for over twenty years. Now she's given everything up for me. I'm the torn half that's been picked up again.'

'Good for Geraldine. Keep Britain Tidy.'

He let out a despairing breath. 'What if Robin had changed his mind, had chosen to keep your torn half too? Wouldn't you try?'

'I'd throw it back in his face,' she said angrily. 'I wouldn't let him hurt me any more.' Perhaps I'd have tried a year ago, she added silently, when the self-blame was still so raw. Perhaps even a month ago when Roger had got so amorous in the car that buttons and zips were undone, and I knew he'd never be able to make my body respond as Robin could. Perhaps even a week ago when Amalie told me she'd be in New York for Christmas and I was so angry I wanted his new wife to understand the pain I've felt every Christmas since he's been gone. Not now.

'I wouldn't want his new family to be hurt as his old one was,' she told Euan, with dignified certainty, then ruined it by closing her eyes and, in that brief second, seeing a tableau of betrayal. 'I certainly wouldn't shag him in a cottage across the garden from them.'

'What are you talking about? I haven't slept with Geraldine here.'

'I saw the knickers, her knickers, here upstairs, abandoned on the bed.' Oh, God, she sounded like Othello ranting on about the handkerchief.

'They weren't hers.'

'Well, that makes me feel a whole lot better.' Red mist blinded her now.

'I told you we didn't sleep together while she was still trying to make a go of it with Richard.'

'And now that she's left him, it's straight to the Travelodge. Lucky she's still packed from Mauritius. She'll barely notice the difference, apart from the mind-blowing sex, of course. What are you hanging round here with me for?'

'Oh, fuck, I've really screwed up.' He looked up at the ceiling.

'Unfortunate choice of words,' she hissed. She knew she was going to cry if he prolonged the agony any longer. 'Please just go.'

He rubbed his face in his hands. 'I can't leave you like this.'

'I'll make it easier for you.' She headed towards the door, holding the tears back with the balls of her palms, desperate for the agonizing final farewell to end. 'I'll come back from church.'

'You can't!' he pleaded.

She held up her arm for silence, Mrs Rees marching from the classroom. 'I know I'm barefoot and wearing her clothes. Her marriage has just ended. Trust me, she's not going to notice.'

43

'At last! Oh, my darling, I'm still crying, but it's honestly, honestly with happiness. Oh, Mrs Rees is with you! I'm so sorry about this. I'm sure this happens all the time when you're house-sitting. Please just ignore us. Actually, could you possibly help me carry these things?'

Geraldine didn't notice what Jenny was wearing. She barely seemed to notice she was there at all as they all heaved suitcases downstairs and into the boot of the sleek black Mercedes that had been parked beside the dog car in the garages all week. She'd packed an awful lot of stuff. They had to flip down the back seats, and even then the bags were crammed up to the car roof, like those of a student heading off for autumn term. Saying nothing, Euan looked wretched with guilt, pack-ponying from bedroom to boot, head bowed, cheeks quilted with taut muscles.

Looking equally miserable, Gunter sat whimpering in the hall as the bags went past, then glued himself to Jenny's side in the kitchen where she had retreated, hiding out to play the good house-sitter while Geraldine trailed around the house one last time, wailing noisily, collecting as many family photographs and *objets d'art* as she could carry, like a demented *Crackerjack* contestant.

Jenny looked away guiltily as she spotted *The Storm Returns* manuscript crammed beneath Geraldine's beautifully cleft chin, picked up from the chair in the study where it had been carefully replaced to hide the fact that it had been subjected to a week of creasing, soaking, drying and ironing. Geraldine now tipped it onto the kitchen table in a loose white spill of neatly ironed pages. 'Could you possibly take this and burn it in the garden incinerator, Mrs Rees?'

She stared at it in horror. 'Surely you're not destroying something you've written.'

'This is just my tatty longhand copy. It's already been transposed onto disk. I meant to shred it before we went away. Can't risk the bin men fishing it out of the recycling, or Richard reading it and accusing me of defamation of character before it's published.' Her voice darkened. 'The incinerator's just behind the garages.'

'Of course,' Jenny said shakily.

'I'll get this place in the divorce,' Geraldine vowed angrily, as she stalked back through the kitchen, picking up a hand-painted plate and fruit bowl to add to her collection. 'I paid for every brick and tile. He can keep his bloody books and paintings. Euan! Grab the Costa Book Award from the downstairs loo!' She hurried out.

Jenny didn't wave them off. She and Gunter retreated to hide in Richard's study. The Absolut bottle lamp had been knocked over and smashed, she noticed. She heard Euan calling her from the kitchen, but she stayed rabbit still. For once, Gunter did too, as though sensing she was in danger and the best protection came from steely pointer silence. When she finally heard the car engine retreating, Jenny pressed her face to his head and let the tears run out at last, hot as artery blood.

She let herself cry for five minutes, then forced herself to stop, thinking about her children, refusing to let self-indulgence take over. That way lay chaos. She had been there once, and that had been after sharing more than half her

403

lifetime with a man. She'd shared just a few days with Euan. She had to get perspective.

She broke down in tears again halfway out of the room, clutching the slate-topped desk and pressing her forehead against it, tears running along the hard, narrow threads of black stone.

'Stop this,' she said, out loud, with the kind but tough detachment of Mrs Rees soothing a hysterical twelve-year-old.

In the morning room, she caught sight of the patchwork sofa through the double doors and started to sob, cast adrift on a wide sisal carpet, remembering her naked epiphany, the feeling of being comfortable with her body again because it was admired for its lights and darks, its hues and tones, its lines and shapes, and the conversational frame set around it, not purely assessed for sex appeal.

'Stop crying.' Mrs Rees was getting impatient now, berating her pupil in the corridor outside the classroom. 'Buck up.' She headed into the kitchen and gathered up the manuscript that was spread across the table and, not thinking what she was doing, doubled back and carried it into Geraldine's study to put on the chair as though it hadn't been disturbed.

Having bounded eagerly ahead to the kitchen, Gunter trotted back, bushy eyebrows following Jenny with concern.

Noticing most of the family photographs were missing from the walls, she broke down silently again in the doorway, imagining the Lewis children still at their grandparents' house, blissfully unaware that their parents' marriage was ending, the pain in her chest so harsh that she felt as though she'd been shot. The thought of poor, wretched Richard Lewis, whose house-proud perfectionism she so admired, pulled the trigger that emptied the second barrel of heartache between her ribs. The reality of never seeing Euan again reloaded the shotgun and punctured one lung followed by the other.

'This stops now!' Mrs Rees issued her third strike, marching her misery to the headmaster's office.

Jenny blew her nose on Geraldine's red jumper sleeve and sank into the nearest chair. Gunter leaned against her supportively, resting his chin on her knee.

On the chair beside her *The Storm Returns* manuscript was positioned exactly as she'd found it the day she'd arrived.

Picking it up, she started to read on from where she'd left off.

XII

Monday

44

TO DO LIST

~~Read a novel~~ ✓
~~No alcohol~~ ✓
~~Quit Electronic Smoking~~ ✓
~~Swim 40 lengths~~ ✓
Incinerate GS manuscript

Richard Lewis's mobile phone was on voicemail. 'Hello, Richard, this is Jenny Rees returning your call. Apologies it's taken me so long to get back to you. I'm going to be out for some of the morning, but I'll be back at the Old Rectory by midday and on my mobile in the meantime. Speak later.'

Dear Myrtle, she wrote neatly, on the back of a postcard of Hadden End duck pond, *I'm afraid all didn't go according to plan. Best Richard explains. My apologies, Jenny R*

Pushing it through the letterbox, she drove to Beacon Common, veering onto the verge twice as she passed country-house hotel entrances she'd not noticed before, now convinced Euan and Geraldine were at the end of their long, tree-lined drives enfolded in one another's arms after a sleepless night recapturing their lost love on a four-poster.

She had a stitch the entire way round the gravel pit with Gunter, but she forced all thoughts of Euan from her mind by reciting 'The Lady of Shalott' loudly in a Cornish accent.

She emailed Henry from her phone as she sat in a High Wycombe car park, waiting for the shops to open. *Hi there. Hope all well. Can you advise what to do in the case of marital break-up while house-sitting? Do I stay put? Any news on Ibiza/the Riviera? Jenny. PS YKW forged and all other probs in hand.*

She sent Rachel a text straight afterwards. *Really hope Nobu better. Call me. Xx*

She then dropped Amalie a line apologizing for missing their regular Skype slot and lying that she had a terrible cold, the same lie that had appeased her mother. She cried just once and very briefly, stemmed with fierce self-control, carefully checking nobody was nearby in the car park to witness it. Jenny was an old hand at heartbreak, certain that if she kept busy and cleared her conscience, all would be well and the tears would stop.

The picture restorer had, as promised, made the Lewis family portrait look as though it had never been ripped. Jenny paid his bill with her new debit card, knowing she now couldn't buy food or clothes for a month, let alone the new Macbook Air that Jake coveted for university. She couldn't bear to look at the children's beautiful yellow-eyed faces smiling from it and asked the restorer to wrap it.

'I have a bouncy dog with me,' she explained apologetically, as she demanded more and more layers of bubble wrap and cardboard until it resembled a coffin.

Back at the car, Gunter had broken through the dog guard again and was sitting on the passenger seat chewing the trim from an air vent. She stashed the coffin in the boot and let him ride pillion to the out-of-town retail park.

The pet superstore didn't sell cages or training collars, the girl behind the till informed Jenny, glancing worriedly through the window to the Range Rover Evoque, which was shaking on its axles, horn blasting occasionally. But the whiskery-chinned woman loading discount rabbit food onto the belt behind Jenny informed her in an undertone that she needed Doggone Inc. at Far Furlong Farm. She paid for the large roasted knuckle bone in her basket, then hurried back to the car to Google them, feeding their postcode into the sat-nav and the bone into Gunter.

Then, holding together the shredded gear shift, which Gunter had just chewed, she drove to a remote smallholding on the Chiltern escarpment where a man in a string vest stepped grumpily out of a mobile home, cigarette in mouth, and disappeared into an adjacent lorry container to emerge with a black box like a handgun case and a rattling flat-pack dog cage. He would only take cash, so she drove back to High Wycombe to press her stretched debit card into the nearest cashpoint. Driving back up onto the escarpment, she veered wildly on the carriageway as she noticed more country-house hotels, along with boutique village hotels and spa hotels, in all of which she imagined Euan and Geraldine trying out increasingly challenging *Kama Sutra* positions. Chomping his bone beside her, Gunter was starting to look car sick.

The cage wouldn't fit into the Evoque, so Jenny and the man in the string vest strapped it onto the roof bars with rope that he charged her an extra thirty pounds for. She was too stressed to argue, although she bummed a cigarette off him, which she smoked out of the window as she drove back to the M40. It was maximum tar, its sickly sweet kick combining toxically with roasted-bone fumes. She stopped in a lay-by and jumped out, Gunter at her side. They both threw up into a ditch.

411

As they sagged on the verge drinking water, her phone began ringing through the Bluetooth speakers in the car. Jenny managed to lean through the open window to press the green icon in time to hear Rachel's voice: 'Noro is a virus.' She sounded weak. 'Nobu, meanwhile, is a shleb-tastic restaurant and I *know* you wouldn't make a typo like that unless it's serious. What's up?'

Jenny and Gunter crawled nauseously back into the car. 'You're still ill. It can wait.'

'No, it can't. I felt terrible I couldn't talk to you on Saturday. You never call unless it can't wait. You always text. The last time you called, Robin had left you. Even then, you waited until you had shingles, you'd found a spliff in Jake's sock drawer and the washing-machine had broken before you cracked enough to need to talk to me in person, and for me to say how amazing you are. *Ergo*, I'm going to start this call by saying that *you are amazing*, Jenny Rees. Now, what's up?'

Glancing at the car window beside her, Jenny remembered Euan leaning through it and telling her that she was amazing. She was suddenly so choked she couldn't speak.

Rachel was a patient soul, and she knew her friend well, the sound of cars swooshing past reassuring her that Jenny was still there. In the twenty-six years they had known one another, the situation had most often been reversed, the long sobbing calls coming from Rachel through her complicated, love-struck twenties and early thirties, tearful early-hours conversations that Jenny had crept groggily to the spare room to take, offering sympathy and comfort. Rachel had always been guiltily apologetic afterwards, embarrassed for intruding upon Jenny's already limited, sleep-starved hours between career and young children. But just as she'd relished the opportunity to help – glimpsing a world of party nights,

412

dates, flirtation and lust that seemed a lifetime away – now it worked in reverse: Rachel had the school run and nappy changes, and she had the single life and heartbreak.

'I could do with some advice,' she croaked eventually. 'About someone I've met.'

'Who is he? What's he like?'

'He's . . . incredible, life-changing.' Feeling the tears well, she stared determinedly out of the window at a Keep Your Distance road sign.

'For a woman who doesn't use words lightly, that's heavy,' Rachel said carefully. 'Do I take it Roger's a brown slice?' It was an old Trivial Pursuit joke they'd shared since college meaning 'history'.

'So is this one. He's in love with Geraldine Scott.'

'Oh, Christ, Jenny, not Richard Lewis? I know you prefer brains over beauty, but he's practically Melvyn Bragg. And he's married.'

'It's someone else who's in love with Geraldine Scott,' she said tightly.

'That sounds messy. I know you hate messy.'

By the time she'd told Rachel the full story – and they'd both paused several times for discreet nausea breaks – it was almost lunchtime. The sun was blazing overhead, the car's air-conditioning battling to beat back the heat and road fumes.

'I think you should walk away.' Rachel's kind voice was cautious as she tried to sweeten the bitter pill. 'You can't take on forever love. It's like trying to hit on widowed Heathcliff. We all know Cathy's dead, but he'll never pin any other woman against a craggy outcrop for more than instant gratification while her ghost's still singing Kate Bush songs at his window. If Euan lays her ghost, perhaps he'll follow. If not, don't look back. They're Jack and Victoria, remember?'

'I read the sequel to *The Dust Storm*,' she confessed.

'What happens?'

'They get back together.' She stared at the Keep Your Distance sign again, the words blurring and disappearing. 'They all live happily ever after.'

'You'll get all the slices and make it to the centre of the board,' said Rachel. 'Throw the dice again, Jen.'

Feeling more hollowed out than ever, Jenny drove back to the Old Rectory, unstrapping the ropes from the car roof and manhandling the new cage inside to replace the broken one, which she stashed at the back of the garage. Gunter eyed it in horror. But when she put his replacement collar on charge, he recognized the beep and hurried inside his new cage to test it for size, looking utterly betrayed.

'I'm sorry.' She crawled in with him to offer an apologetic hug. 'I don't make up the rules round here. I just break them. We both broke them.'

He rested his chin on her shoulder, shaking anxiously. She hugged him for a long time. She'd lost her heart to two very difficult males in a week.

The house phone called her out of her lair and she snatched it up nervously, summoning Mrs Rees in full Ofsted inspection mode. 'The Old Rectory, how may I help?' She seemed to have channelled Sybil Fawlty, now talking to a *Good Housekeeping* researcher who was ringing to brief Geraldine about her interview and cover shoot the following week.

'We're so looking forward to meeting her beautiful family,' the researcher gushed. 'The house sounds *amaze*.'

'The Lewises are away,' Sybil told her primly. 'Can you call back?'

I didn't keep a good house for them, she thought unhappily, as she hung up, looking around at the amazing kitchen she'd so envied when she arrived, so full of family and fun, still echoing with raucous footsteps, mealtimes, sibling scraps and laughter. Their lives will never be the same again.

She went into the snug and listlessly released the restored family portrait from its bubble wrap coffin and hung it back on the wall in front of the safe – averting her gaze from those happy yellow-eyed faces – before carrying the rejected first portrait back through to Geraldine's study. Setting it down, she caught sight of Geraldine's face in it. She could now see the marked difference between the two paintings, the sadness in this face, its wisdom and cleverness. It was a far more compelling face than its happier, younger-looking doppelgänger. This had been painted with love, she realized, the pain of loss cutting through her again.

It was only as she turned Geraldine's wiser face to the wall where she'd first found it that it occurred to her to look for the nude of herself that Euan had hurriedly hidden when Geraldine had returned. But despite throwing up every sofa cushion and rug, increasingly frustrated, she couldn't locate it. Desperate for clues, she went to the cottage and picked up the painting of the house, flipping it over, but all that was on the back was a scrawled marker pen sideways lamp signature along with the title, *The House-sitter*, and the date.

Was this painted with love? She examined the little figure on the sun-lounger. It was brilliant, observant, funny and charming, but it was a performance painting, a caricature to amuse and heart-warm. It was the house-sitter, who loved reading and hated mess, that she believed herself to be. Euan's nudes were the eye to his soul. His ability to make his female models come alive was extraordinary. This little figure had been painted from memory. Watching him paint her for hours on end on the patchwork sofa, she had seen herself come alive.

Steaming hot now, she carried the painting back to the house and laid it on the table, then headed upstairs to drag on her Speedo, rubber hat and nose clip. She swam forty lengths in the pool until every muscle was straining, like shredded elastic. Dropping beneath the water for a few strokes on every turn, she let her mind go blank. Bursting up again to grab air and life, she remembered Euan painting, listening, laughing, talking, raking back his hair, mixing paint, smoking with his shoulders hunched, looking at her. Looking at her for such a long time, gazing over the painting board, over the side of this pool, overhead as she lay in bed, under water, through glass and up from between her legs. Those amazing green eyes. Lucky, lucky Geraldine.

Heaving herself out, she flopped like a dead fish on the side of the pool, reaching up to reassure Gunter who had run the last few lengths alongside her on the decking and was now panting hotly between her and the sun. She was temporarily deafened and blinded as he threw up his head and howled, the sound ear-splitting, the bright sunlight straight in her face. He turned and sprinted away towards the house, still baying and howling.

Jenny's heart thudded crazily, hardly daring to hope. Ripping off her rubber hat, she hurried inside.

45

Richard Lewis was paying a taxi driver at the door, Gunter throwing himself at him in a hysterical, ecstatic welcome, one moment upside-down, the next bear-hugging, then goosing, then running around in puppyish bounds.

'Mrs Rees!' Richard greeted her over his shoulder, as he waited for a receipt, deeper-tanned and whiter-haired, but no less charming. 'Slight change of plan. The car's still at Gee's parents' house, as are the kids. Apologies for coming home early.'

'That's not a problem,' she said calmly, trying to look as professional as she could in a towel and flip-flops, expunging all pity and compassion from her face because that wasn't wanted. You did this too, Jenny told herself, as she hovered awkwardly. You acted as though everything was normal, talking in abbreviated sentences.

'Been enjoying the pool?' He marched inside and closed the door, Gunter now swinging lovingly from his linen jacket by the smiling jaws, conker eyes rolling. Richard didn't seem to notice. He turned to pick up the huge pile of post she'd carefully ordered on a hall side-table. 'Jolly good! Gather the weather here's been scorching.'

'Yes, it's been quite hot.'

'Marvellous.' He flipped through the envelopes. 'Geraldine had to fly ahead, as you no doubt know. Work thing. You saw her, I take it?'

'She collected some things yesterday.' She kept her voice as upbeat as his.

'Super. Good, good. I'll just take a shower and make some calls.'

She nodded, stepping aside so he could go upstairs ahead of her, well aware that after the ritual-of-normality came the ransack-of-hysterical-loss. 'Would you like me to do anything?'

'Yes, Mrs Rees. I apologize if this is somewhat short notice, but I think it might be best to curtail your house-sitting duties. You will be paid for the full duration, naturally. However, right now I'd be very grateful if you could quietly pack up and leave. Thank you.'

And that was it. Jenny threw her clothes into her suitcase, the neatly folded packing rituals abandoned, her heart roaring again. The broody mother hen could no longer sit on her temporary family nest imagining it her own, the love affair hers. What happened to Euan Henderson was no longer her concern. She would drive home to the museum of marriage, destined to veer off the road every time she passed a hotel, and try to pick up her life where she'd left off.

The Lewises and the Old Rectory were no longer her business either. She had no right to feel as though she knew them at all. She'd never met the children, just seen the three blond heads lined up in the car, the photographs keeping her company all week, their presence all around her. She had tidied the Barbies and Lego, followed their little footsteps up and down the stairs, smelt sugar-rushing children in the TV room and clean children in the bathroom. Neither did she know their parents, although the house had told her secrets she would always keep to herself: that Geraldine was earthier than she came across, rooted in reality for all her brilliantly spun fictional landscapes, privately hamstrung by self-doubt. That Richard was the tidiness freak, but also the idealist, the dreamer who liked the world – and his wife – painted brighter than it was.

She must return to her usual organized life, the fitness classes and book clubs, theatre trips and exhibitions, the holidays with friends and trips to her parents, the day-counting calendar watch until Jake came home to get ready to go to St Andrew's. Empty weeks stretched out beyond that, her sabbatical no longer holding any appeal. She needed the routine of school, the precise, monotonous rhythm to match her heartbeat to as she tried to get it started again. One day, maybe in a month or a year, she might read about the Lewises' marriage falling apart. She wanted to be busy when that happened. She wanted Euan Henderson to be a memory she'd sealed in a box and stored on a high shelf.

She came out of the en-suite with her wash things to find Gunter had bounded into the room, thoroughly over-excited that his master was home and eager to plunder her laundry basket in search of a gift for him. Disappointed grunts came from its empty wicker depths. When he burst back out and saw the packed suitcase, his ears inverted and his tail tucked anxiously between his legs; Gunter knew exactly what suitcases meant.

Shaking, he sat beside it, looking up at Jenny with forlorn, speckled eyes. She hugged him, battling not to break down and weep on his wiry shoulder. He pressed himself so tight into her that she could feel the hard bone of his domed head like a fist against her chest.

'You have been quite the most infuriating, stubborn and disobedient dog I have ever known, and I will miss you desperately.' She breathed in the nutty sweetness of his neck as he quivered in her arms and rested his chin on her shoulder.

Hearing his master's voice drifting up from a distant room, Gunter let out his bass bark and tore out of the door without a backward glance, the rug rucking up beneath him in his haste. Jenny was grateful; she had never been good at farewells either, least of all with those she cared for most. She carried her bags quietly downstairs. She could hear Richard talking in the kitchen, anger crackling through the quietly spoken words. At first she thought he was on the phone, but then she heard another voice, deep and forthright, and she realized Myrtle was with him.

They were sitting at the table. Euan's painting of the house-sitter in the garden lay between them.

'I'm going now.' She hovered behind the island.

Richard stood politely, coming to shake her hand. He looked as if he'd been crying. Gunter was glued lovingly to his side. 'Thank you for everything you've done, Mrs Rees. Do I owe you any money? I'll pay you for the full fortnight, of course.'

'I appreciate that, but Henry at the agency will sort it out.'

'Do you want a hand out with your things?'

'I'm fine, thank you.' She caught Myrtle's eye.

'I was saying to Richard, this painting is quite lovely,' she said loudly.

'Euan is very talented,' Richard agreed distractedly. 'It's charming that he painted this to welcome us home. Did you get on well?'

He still has no idea who Geraldine is with, Jenny realized. Her eyes were fixed on the painting. Richard thought it was for him. It was the only piece of Euan she had. She couldn't leave without it.

'He's—' She found she couldn't speak.

'Quite a character!' Myrtle finished for her. 'You know

he's having an exhibition in September? Fetch Mrs Rees a flyer to take with her, Richard.'

'Of course.' He headed towards his study, Gunter trailing him.

Watching him go, Myrtle sighed deeply, glancing across to the breakfast room to check her son was out of earshot, then speaking to Jenny in a deep, urgent undertone. 'He's not ready to hear it yet.'

'The painting's mine,' she managed to croak.

'Best not tell Dicky that now.' She looked down at the brightly coloured depiction of the house. 'I must apologize that I made a terrible error of judgement. I thought Euan was painting you in the nude. I should have guessed you would never be so unprofessional as to allow that to happen. This really is very sweet. I'll make sure you get it, if you give me your address. Easier to explain it to Dicky when all this nonsense has died down. Do you know where they've gone?'

'A hotel.' She started writing her Oxford address with a shaking hand, but dropped the pen as her mobile phone rang in her bag across the room. Euan didn't have her number, she reminded herself. He didn't do mobile phones or emails or instant messages, just painting and talking all night. Her eyes were drawn to the little central figure in the garden picture, noticing for the first time the laptop and smartphone stacked neatly on the table beside her, along with a cool drink. So cosily, prettily her. She didn't know that woman any more.

In her handbag, the call went to voicemail, but immediately rang again. It rang for the third time, and a great roar went up from Richard's study as he spotted the smashed Absolut bottle. 'She gave me that lamp for our fifteenth wedding anniversary!' he shouted. 'The base was engraved with our names.'

'Crystal.' Jenny sighed sympathetically, thinking of the hand-engraved champagne flutes she still had at home.

'Even for Geraldine, that's vindictive.' Myrtle looked terribly sad.

'I think it was an accident,' she said quickly, remembering Geraldine's *Crackerjack* pile.

'I'll check he's okay.' Myrtle stood up, tutting as Jenny's phone rang for a fourth time. 'Answer that. And don't go just yet. I want that address.'

She stared at the painting again for a moment, longing more than anything to be the happy, oblivious figure lounging by the pool.

When the phone rang for a fifth time, she went to answer the call, then gripped the handset white-knuckle tight as she heard a familiar voice say, 'Thank God you're there.'

His voice in her ear always floored her with heart-rush, a Pavlovian response she could never shake, never more so than when it was choked with emotion. Right now, racking sobs running hoarsely through him.

'Robin?'

'Oh, Jenny. Oh, Christ, Jenny. Help me.'

'Is it one of the kids?' She felt her face drain, her legs giving way. 'What's happened?'

'I didn't know who else to call.' He was weeping so forcefully he could hardly speak. 'She's left me. Lindsay's left me.'

XIII

September

46

TO DO LIST

~~Do washing (don't forget flight socks)~~
~~Go through post~~
~~Thank neighbours (bottle wine? Pot plant?)~~
~~Get Jake's things ready for uni~~
Stop writing To Do lists and just DO!*
*(unpack first)

Jenny flew from JFK to Heathrow with Jake and his girlfriend, trying not to intrude on their togetherness as they
came to the end of their year-long adventure. Having travelled side by side across three continents – their love
deepening as they wore the soles of their shoes thin – they
were now symbiotic, and parting to go to universities at
opposite ends of the country would be like splitting the
atom. Jenny feared a nuclear explosion of unhappiness
ahead. They held hands the entire way.

She tried to bury herself in her book, but it was a new
novelist Robin had recommended and she couldn't penetrate the plot's cold heart at all. He'd always had very dry
taste in reading, more than ever now. Since Lindsay's departure, he had moved through drunken denial and obsessive

hyperactivity and was now infused with a hurt, cynical anger towards the world in general and his estranged young wife in particular. Jenny knew it would pass. Experience had taught her an overwhelming sadness came next, long nights crying alone. Then, very slowly, the sadness lifted. It might take months or years, but Robin Rees would be fine. He wouldn't be alone for long: it wasn't his style, but neither was being a family man. Jenny – who had run the gamut of clichés from 'You've only brought this on yourself' to 'Time's a great healer' in recent weeks – knew he would never change, but he'd learned a very painful lesson that she wished she'd had the guts to teach him when she had been his Mrs Rees. Unlike Robin's second wife, his third hadn't turned a blind eye when, at five months pregnant with their second child, she'd discovered he was having an affair with one of his students, and had then uncovered a trail of previous infidelities leading back to her first pregnancy. Instead, she had flown into a blind rage and walked out. That Robin had reacted by picking up the phone to seek comfort from Jenny shouldn't have come as a surprise after she'd spent so many years absorbing his rebounds – in much the same way that her sense of triumphant pity was predictably familiar – but she'd been shocked by how little their ingrained patterns had changed since divorce.

As soon as she got home, Jenny was going to dismantle the museum of marriage. She'd sell the furniture that was too big and dinner services she never used, give away the tens of crystal glasses, the multiple coffee-makers and decanters. Her sabbatical would now be spent cataloguing and selling off the collection. She was ready to let it go: the family was all that mattered, not its history preserved in aspic.

Though a sweltering Manhattan August, she'd felt like a curator with no exhibits left to look after. She'd flown out because Jake and Amalie had begged for her help with their father's crisis, alarmed by his increasingly random behaviour: the hours of insomniac driving, the pages of indecipherable writing, and the repeated drunken viewings of Kenneth Branagh movies. All this was also achingly familiar to Jenny, yet she'd been grateful for her escape to New York, her overwhelming urge to be with her children undercut with the instinctive need to put as much distance between herself and Euan Henderson as possible. Perhaps – fool that she was – she'd also needed to see if her torn half still fitted anywhere in Robin's life. She now knew that it didn't: their torn halves no longer matched. Far from making her sad, she felt liberated.

For one heat-wave week in July, she had fallen back in love with the idea of love. It had slipped her grip, spared her no pain, left no mementoes for her museum, but it had a greater legacy for which she was grateful. She believed in it again, and she believed she deserved it. She now understood that, when Robin had fallen out of love with her, she'd fallen out of love with herself. That was the hardest love of all to recapture, and she'd only seen herself through somebody else's eyes. Euan had loved painting her. He had loved touching her. He had loved listening to her and talking to her. He'd loved being with her enough to make her see herself quite differently, even if he'd loved somebody else more all along. Perhaps they both had. Her children would always come first, after all.

She cast a look sideways at the young couple beside her, envying them such mutual devotion and trust, for all the sweet sorrow of parting that was in store for them. She hoped they might just survive long-distance love. They'd taken it twenty-five thousand miles together, after all; keeping it alive while they were four hundred miles apart could be done. She couldn't bear for Jake to suffer heartbreak just yet.

His girlfriend had fallen asleep on his shoulder, her long hair hanging down on his chest, like a strange Amish beard. He turned his head to Jenny. 'You okay, Mum?'

'Fine. Really good, in fact. You?'

'I'll be okay.' He rested his chin on the blonde head sleeping there and lifted two amber eyes to study the overhead panel, eyebrows shifting left and right, needing an ever-changing focus to stop himself going stir-crazy dwelling on the scary stuff ahead. So like Robin.

Like Gunter, she found herself thinking.

Don't, she told herself, glaring down at the clouds. But she was already wondering how they were, picturing the pool glimmering in its walled garden and the huge kitchen with striped sunlight spilling into it. And everywhere her mind looked, she saw Euan.

She'd hoped being so far from him would stop her thinking about him, but that wasn't quite the case. It just stopped her thinking she was about to see him in person – apart from one afternoon upon first arriving when she'd followed a good-looking dark-haired man with a witch's streak three blocks, her heart punching above its weight in her throat. She knew that the fantasy was going to grip her again the moment they touched down.

Her imagination had already played out and stored a hundred different daydream scenarios to wile away the hours, none of them remotely realistic – from getting home to find the outside of the mews painted with hearts and flowers and ILY (which would be frowned upon in a conservation area) to finding a pile of love letters filled with frantically sexy poetry quotes (unlikely given his dyslexia and the cost of stamps) to him abseiling over the

Oxford canal and into her little courtyard garden like James Bond (she rather liked that one), or strutting into the fresh groceries aisle in Waitrose, *Officer and a Gentleman* style, and sweeping her off her feet. In reality, she knew he was now fixing Geraldine Scott with that intense green gaze, but she couldn't stop herself making up romantic homecomings.

The mews house had no romantic Banksy-meets-Monet graffiti on its gold stone walls, and no one abseiled across the canal towards Jenny as she climbed out of the cab with her Odysseus son clinging to the hand of his Penelope. Inside, the house was dusty and neglected, the pile of post that the neighbour had been bringing in now towering higher than the well-watered pot plants that had turned into a jungle on the window-sills; the message counter on the landline phone was at max.

With an excited gasp, Jenny spotted a huge bouquet of flowers, which the neighbour had put in the utility room sink in an attempt to keep them alive, but which had long since dropped their petals and turned brown. Heart hammering, she ripped off the card and read it.

Thinking of you. Rog. x

Shot through with disappointment, she threw them into the composter outside the back door, returning to rifle through the post in search of anything resembling contact from Euan, but there was nothing very hopeful. A handwritten envelope raised her heartbeat but revealed a wedding invitation from a distant cousin. An airmail letter from Australia caused brief consternation – had Geraldine and Euan gone there? – but it turned out to be from her elderly uncle who had emigrated twenty years earlier and still preferred old-fashioned communication.

Yawns dislocating her jaw now, she sorted the rest of her post into piles before opening it – circulars, statements, bills, personal, brochures and parcels, which she raided greedily, hoping for a painting with a declaration of love on the back or, at least, Myrtle returning *The House-sitter* as promised – but there was nothing, apart from the vacuum bags she'd ordered before leaving and two complimentary copies of *Tour Divorce*, Carla's self-published book.

She flipped it open, tired eyes automatically running through for any missed errors.

To Jen, with love and thanks for a lifetime correcting my foul language. Now dance, bitch!

She snorted with laughter.

Looks great . . . and thank you. Wow! she texted, exhaustion sweeping over her in a tide of heavy-limbed shakes as she abandoned the pile, had a long bath and went to bed, leaving the star-crossed lovers to stay up on the sofa, still holding hands, giggling through their travel pictures together on their phones.

The next day, Jake travelled with his girlfriend to Bath to take her things to her new halls and then enact the tearful farewell at the railway station. Having called her mother in Hampshire, and endured a month's worth of low-down on the Haven residents' wheelie-bin and parking wars, Jenny resumed sorting through her post and checking her phone messages. Most were hang-ups or pre-recorded messages offering free financial advice. Her closest friends and family had kept in touch by text and email while she was away.

'Hey, Jenny. Rog! Not heard from you in a while . . . Have

you changed your mobile number?' *No, I barred you.* 'And my emails keep bouncing back.' *Straight to the junk folder.* 'Call me, huh? It would be great to hook up.'

She deleted the message, annoyed that she'd given him her home address and phone number. She'd been so keen at first, she remembered, heart skipping every time his number came up on caller display; now those displays of affection had numbered his days in her address book.

She opened another envelope, promisingly thick with an address label on it.

Private View – Euan Henderson

She had to sit down. Just seeing his name made her hands shake, her heart ricochet around her chest, an anvil of attraction dropping into her groin where hammers beat sparks from it. Even her taste buds felt as though they'd been doused in sorbet.

The Tythe Gallery, 9 September, 6 p.m. – 9 p.m.

That was three days' time.

The answer-phone was still in full flow. 'Rog again! Where are you? Return my ca—' *Message deleted.*

The painting featured on the invitation was a nude of Lonnie, the girl with the butterfly tattoo, looking coyly over her shoulder. Jenny flipped it over. No personal message. She looked at the envelope again, studying the label. Jenny Rees was just a name and address on a database. So why could she hardly breathe right now?

'Jenny, it's Henry from Home Guardian.' The machine beside her clicked into a new message. 'I've tried your mobile twice, but I think your mailbox is full. It's about that job you wanted this autumn. How do you feel about an Aegean island? It's a fantastic place, owned by a married couple, a Mr and Mr, so very stylish, very tidy, *just* your speciality. They have two dogs and a parrot to look after – rather lively characters, but all house-trained. Only trouble is, it's really short notice – you'd have to fly out early September. Call me as soon as you get this if you're interested.'

She checked the date stamp. It was last week. There would be no point calling back now: Henry always hammered the phone and filled a position in forty-eight hours. She deleted it. That was the last message the machine had taken before its memory had been full.

Carla rang her mobile as she made coffee. 'Welcome back!' She was having a cigarette break on the fire escape. 'You like the dedication, then?'

'I love it. I'm dancing as I speak.'

'The print run's tiny, but it's selling lots as a digital download. The divorcee dance-floor is trending. Talking of which, how's Robin hashtag bastard?'

'Increasingly misanthropic and very sorry for himself, which is ripe given it was his inability to keep his dick in his trousers and out of his female students that caused this in the first place.'

'I'm glad she left him. Takes a good ballsy American girl to walk out the moment she finds out what an unfaithful shit he is. You should have done the same fifteen years ago.'

'Water, bridges, under, old.' She picked up the private-view invitation, staring at Lonnie's beautiful smooth back, remembering that hers had been like that once.

'Less of the old. I want to know where you're going on this sabbatical. They're getting twitchy here about using up holiday allowance and I have a week in late October with your name on it.'

'I'm not going.' She looked around at the museum of marriage. 'I'm staying to de-clutter.'

'Like fuck you are. Where's your spirit of adventure? The bestseller you're going to write? You are going loco, even if I have to drag you there myself. You will be staring out to sea over a typewriter, Pavlos the hunky waiter topping up your glass, Cal the widowed millionaire neighbour waving as he runs on the beach with his still-hard, oh-so lonely body.'

'You should be writing this novel. Besides, I think you have an aggrandized view of house-sitting. The foreign jobs always get snapped up. There was something in the Aegean on offer, but that will have gone by now. I'll be lucky to get a fortnight in Croydon.'

'I want your arse back on the dance-floor wherever it is. You heard from that artist again?'

'Not directly.' She picked up the invitation, an electric current shooting up her arm just from touching it.

'But you've Googled him, right? I know you too well, Miss Marple.'

'Actually, I haven't.' It hurt too much. She'd tried once or twice, but it was like trying to put her fingers in a blender. She kept snatching them away from the keyboard.

'Then I will.' Having heard the whole story, Carla remained convinced that Euan's 'torn' speech had been a cry for help and Jenny's insistence that he leave as misjudged as Bogey pushing Ingrid onto the plane in *Casablanca*, but Jenny didn't buy it.

'Please don't,' she begged. 'I don't want to know.'

'Okay, but I heard a rumour about the Lewises' marriage through the girls who write the diary page here that I'm going to share whether you like it or not.'

Closing her eyes, she braced herself for the news that it was over.

'They're adopting.'

'Run that past me again?'

'Adopting. It's all very hush-hush and the story came from an outside source, so I can't confirm it, but somehow I don't think they're adopting a forty-something portrait artist. It's just a rumour but there's no smoke without fire.'

'It's all smoke and mirrors at the Old Rectory,' she said dismissively, but deep inside her headstrong eighteen-year-old self was stubbing out a cigarette and checking her reflection.

47

Jake and his girlfriend had said their tearful adieus and were now exchanging instant messages every five minutes. On the eve of his departure for St Andrew's, he and Jenny embarked upon a frenzied trip around Oxford buying new clothes, books, stationery and the coveted Mac Air. He was a terrible label snob, and the trip was a painful reminder that the days of bulk-buying combat trousers at outlet villages and raiding the covered market for bargains had long gone.

'Vintage is just jumble-sale stuff on coat-hangers,' he was fond of saying.

Having already paid for her New York trip with a credit card, Jenny knew she was the wrong side of the red this month, but at least selling off the museum of marriage would cover it

'I wish you'd let me drive you up,' she grumbled, as they tried to cram all the new purchases into Jake's rucksack and a trolley-case for him to take on the train.

'Mum, I've just travelled round the world. I can make it to Scotland.' He took a picture of his baggage on his mobile and sent it off. 'It's your turn to cross a few seas now. Jet off and enjoy your sabbatical.'

'I think I'll stay and sort out the house. You might need me around this term.' If young love fades, she added anxiously.

'Trust me, I won't need,' he said crushingly. 'And we can always Skype and Snapchat.' He took a selfie of his face blowing a kiss.

It's so different now, Jenny thought wistfully. When Robin had gone back to the States from Oxford, all they'd had was airmail and transatlantic calls that cost a pound a minute. Now you could see your loved one's face anywhere in the world. Unless you're Euan Henderson and don't possess a mobile or a computer, she reflected. Perhaps if he and Geraldine had been able to instant message when she went to university in Sydney, she would never have fallen in with new friends and forsaken him. And if Jenny and Robin had Skyped when she was in her final year at Oxford, she might have worked out he was married.

Jake opened his shirt and took a snap of his nipple.

'There are some things a mother would rather not see.' She turned away, then looked back over her shoulder in shock. 'Have you had that pierced?'

'We had his and hers done in New York.' He opened a new message and smiled fondly, adding distractedly, 'Dad said you'd hate it.'

'Your dad says I hate everything.'

'He thinks you're cool now. In New York, when Am and me asked if he'd ever thought about you guys getting back together, he said he had, but you'd never have him.'

'He's right,' she said archly, then grimaced in apology, a small furnace burning inside her at the idea that the twins still dreamed of a reconciliation, however hopeless their cause. 'We've both moved on.'

'That's it, though. You haven't moved a lot. Dad said you'd never really travelled because you married him so young, that you needed to spread your wings a bit. He reckons you two'll remarry each other at eighty.'

'He'll be—' she stopped herself saying 'a long time in Hell by then', staggered at the notion that he still saw them as

436

OAP dating potential '. . . very happily settled with another Mrs Rees.'

Jake was typing furiously into his phone. 'I hope she's a bit more upbeat than Lindsay. Honey's cool, though. Dad says he'll be getting her every other weekend and holidays soon. He's going to bring her to the UK to see us all, and Columbus Junior when he's born. The name's from Lindsay's family,' he explained, seeing his mother's eyes widen.

'Great.' She tried to look enthusiastic.

He photographed her face. 'That expression is *so* ballsed.'

'Is "ballsed" a good thing?' she asked uncertainly.

'Yeah.' He closed one eye and peered up at her from a low angle, smiling awkwardly. 'By the way, Am and me were talking in New York, and we both want to say that it's okay for you to have a boyfriend.' Cheeks streaking red, he read another incoming message and grinned, kissing the screen.

'A boyfriend?'

'We know you've been seeing someone called Roger,' he winced almost imperceptibly at the name, 'so if you want to, like, bring him out in the open – or anyone else *not* called Roger – that's cool with us.'

'Thank you.' She cupped his cheek and he ducked away with a wink, photographing his watch. 'Better get going, yeah. I know we've got to allow you ten minutes' crying time at the station.'

When they got Jenny's car out of the garage for the first time in over a month, it was wearing a mob cap of guano from the late-nesting sparrows that had been living in the eaves above throughout August.

'We *have* to go to a car wash on the way to the station,' Jake insisted. 'I'm meeting mates there.'

437

'It'll eat into my crying time.'

'Cry in the car wash, Mum.'

The train was delayed, meaning Jenny could indulge in an embarrassing amount of crying on the platform, then go in search of a *Guardian* and coffee – she even had time to do the quick crossword before she was called upon to cry again, hugging Jake tightly and secretly wishing she had a magic spell to shrink him back to six years old and smuggle him home. 'Call me as soon as you get there.' She reached up to cup his cheeks again. 'I'm glad we had our month in New York.'

'Me too.' This time he held her hands there, smiling his father's smile from lips as full as her own. 'Dad's right. You are pretty damn cool.'

Back in the car park, Jenny allowed herself three minutes' crying before she blew her nose noisily and texted Amalie and Robin to let them know Jake was safely en route. She then called Henry at the house-sitting agency. 'I know it's a long shot, but do the couple on the Greek island still need someone?'

'Jenny Rees, my secret weapon!' He laughed delightedly. 'Am I glad to hear your voice. The answer is almost certainly yes, although there is a slight problem. I've already had one of my best guys go there and come straight back. The dogs are certifiable, by all accounts. But you're one of the few I'd trust to be up to it. After all, you took on Gunter Lewis.' She could hear him shuddering.

'Are these dogs worse than Gunter?'

'No, but there's two of them.'

'Are they small?'

'Great Danes. I think the parrot's pretty neurotic too. But there is an infinity pool and a bedroom with three-hundred-and-sixty-degree views across the sea. You'll need to travel tomorrow if we can get you on a flight.'

'That's not a problem. Can you give me the address?'

She reached into the glove box where she had stashed the private-view invitation, now her constant companion, like a lucky rabbit's foot. Flipping it over, she wrote the details on the back.

She propped the invitation on the steering wheel and stared at it, thinking about Carla's diary-page gossip and romantic encouragement, and Rachel's insistence by contrast that forever love couldn't be hijacked.

She'd always known there would be no 'As Time Goes By' reunion in Rick's Café Americain, no 'Way to go, Jenny!' cheers in the Waitrose veg aisle. Her fantasies had kept her company and served her well across the Atlantic, but now it was time to face facts. A few weeks ago she'd told Euan she had no fixed plans, but she had promised that she would come to his exhibition. She would stand by her word. The thought already made her feel as light-headed and sweaty-palmed as the day she'd carried a newly bought typewriter and her Tintin pencil case up to Robin Rees's rooms.

48

The Tythe Gallery was far grander than Jenny had anticipated, a sumptuously thatched half-timbered barn
converted into commercial space in the centre of
Commuterland's most desirable and picturesque market
town, a straw's blow from London. Its car park was already
filling with high-class marques when she pulled into the furthest, most shadowy space and pressed her forehead against
the steering wheel, forcing herself to stay put and not drive
straight out again.

'Okay, so it's not warm Chardonnay in a little picture
framer's in Beaconsfield, but it's still fine. You'll go in, look at
paintings, say hello, and come out again. Five minutes max.'

She could hear the clicks of high heels and laughter drifting from Jags to entrance.

Jenny flipped down her sun-visor and studied the huge-
eyed, huge-lipped face of terror staring back. She repainted
her lips in a cherry red Amalie had talked her into buying at
Macy's that she'd complained was too bright for her. A
Japanese flag stared back. She wiped it off again.

'Great cheekbones,' she reminded herself, flipping the
visor away and reaching for her electronic cigarette to draw
deeply.

The dress she was wearing was another of her daughter's
New York coercion buys, but this was one she loved, a blue
and white sheath that reminded her of the Toile de Jouy walls
in the bedroom at the Old Rectory, and in which Amalie had

said she looked like a shapely Spode vase. Reaching into the back seat, she grabbed the heels she'd thrown there because she couldn't drive in them. She then pulled the invitation from the glove box, crammed it into her clutch bag, and headed inside.

One of Euan's paintings of Femi, the houseboat model, was propped on an easel in the entrance foyer, legs akimbo, a talented visual punch of sheer sex appeal to bowl guests over from the start. It already had an orange sold sticker on it.

Nobody asked to see Jenny's invitation. A girl in a cocktail dress was overseeing a big table covered with name badges, like an office sweepstake, yakking excitedly on her mobile phone that she'd just seen Alan Yentob. 'Yah, yah – trainers and no tie. Way cool. I have a Saatchi badge here and if it's claimed I'm so getting my camera phone out. No,' her eyes raked the table, 'can't see Trinny here.'

She didn't look up as Jenny pointed to her own name and was handed the laminated rectangle, the girl still talking, but in an undertone now: 'Not bad, usual stuff, tasteful porn, and there's a few dogs, too, which is cute. But there's this one painting here, yah, that is, like, *so* amazing it will blow your mind. The broadsheets all want pictures of it. It's this nude that totes jumps out at you. I *swear* you can smell the skin. The artist says it's not for sale at any price, which of course means the big buyers are writing blank cheques.'

Jenny felt panic rise, almost turning to walk straight out again as her ego twitched in its low lair, daring to imagine – to dread – that it might be a painting of a reluctant subject on a patchwork sofa, someone who had fallen into life modelling and fallen in love with life again. She hung her name badge's thick, corded lanyard around her neck and headed into the noisy throng.

441

There had to be over sixty people in the room already. A string quartet was playing on a raised rostrum in one corner. She took a flute of champagne from a circling waiter and smiled gratefully, downing it in one and handing it straight back to take another. *Thump thump clap, thump thump clap.*

Her heart was now channelling Queen. She looked everywhere for Euan, but his face wasn't among the crowd. *Thump thump clap, thump thump clap.*

The walls of the room glowed like a giant Chinese lantern with no obvious source of light; it seemed to be illuminated from its skirting boards, the eaves and the tree-trunk-fat upright beams that sprouted up and branched out to support its vaulted ceiling. The paintings on exhibition were mesmerizing, an orgy of ravishing nudes gathering orange sold and green reserved stickers, like roses with greenfly.

As Jenny waded hurriedly across a wooden floor as glossy as liquid caramel, she was knocked sideways by an ecstatic, loving rugby tackle and almost brought down.

'Gunter!' She dropped to her knees to embrace him as he wrapped her in a bear-hug, then goosed her and howled for joy, rolling over to offer her his belly with an upside-down smile, wriggling so ecstatically he polished the floor for several metres in a fast slide before flipping upright and bounding back. He had no remote-control collar on, Jenny saw in delight and amazement.

'COME BACK HERE!' boomed a familiar patrician bawl, as Richard Lewis strode across from a power clutch of suited men by the bar, champagne flute in hand. 'I'm so sorry, he's been much better recent— Mrs Rees! How wonderful. I had no idea you'd be here.'

'I invited her,' insisted a determined Denis Healey bass, as Myrtle burrowed through the crowd from the opposite direction looking startlingly like Grayson Perry in a full-skirted cocktail dress, her white beret of hair drawn back by an Alice band, her customary pink-rimmed glasses replaced by diamanté ones. 'You came!'

Jenny straightened up, emerging from Gunter's wet kisses. *Thump thump clap, thump thump clap.* 'It was very kind of you to invite me.'

'Nonsense. Richard still won't return your painting. It's most embarrassing.' She hooked her arm through Jenny's and towed her through the crowd, like a child pulling a kite. 'Euan's been cornered over here somewhere to give an interview to local television. He'll be so pleased to see you.'

As she tripped across the room in the grip of her small tugboat, Jenny recognized the Cliftons by the bar: Lonnie and her roly-poly pool-noodling parents laughing liberally. Houseboat owner Perry was there too, looking like a gangster in a white suit and black shirt, flanked by ravishing Femi and another tall beauty who could have been her mother. She thought she saw Euan everywhere, dark-haired and green-eyed, her head turning left and right each time she caught a tantalizing glimpse of dimples and witches' streaks, longing to swivel right round as her throat caught, her Queen heartbeat deafening her. *Thump thump clap, thump thump clap.*

'Euan's brothers are all here,' Myrtle explained, marching her on. 'And his mother. God spare the daughter-in-law who has to take on that woman. I'm a pussy-cat by comparison. Ignore the gawkers gathered around my son's wife. She's a dreadful exhibitionist.'

Jenny saw Geraldine, a head taller than almost everybody else, so magnificently crowned with her flicking fire-blonde mane that she was like a brazier lighting the way to the feature picture of the exhibition, small as a book, displayed alone in a panelled alcove, in front of which by far the

443

biggest crowd had gathered to look at and admire the *Mona Lisa* of the Home Counties Louvre, guarded by two huge monolith bouncers. Slipping Myrtle's grip, Jenny slid to a halt, recognizing the head thrown back, thighs lolling, the fingers at work, the face sharing that all-too-secret, all-too-universal pleasure.

Her *sangfroid* wobbled. She'd psyched herself up non-stop to see Euan and to encounter the Lewises in whichever way they were now divided up, she'd hoped to see Myrtle, and had had no doubt that she would see Lonnie and Femi many times in their painted naked glory; she'd even braced herself to see her own image on a patchwork sofa. But she hadn't prepared herself to see this picture again, the visual evidence that Euan Henderson had remained deeply in love with Geraldine Scott. This very personal, very overt declaration of shared sexual reawakening and obsession was a throat kick she still found hard to take. Perhaps she wasn't as ready for this evening as she'd imagined.

'I thought that was from a strictly private collection,' she said shakily as Myrtle returned to gather her again, hand held up like a blinker, refusing to look at it.

'It should be.' She shuddered. 'But Geraldine insists the publicity will be amazing for her new book, once word spreads that Jack is a real, live artist who painted this when he was eighteen.'

Jenny ran this back and forth through her head, uncertain if she'd heard it right. 'Did you say eighteen?'

'Euan kept it with him on his travels apparently.'

'It wasn't painted at the Old Rectory?'

'God, no! Look at it. That picture's over twenty years old. Geraldine has a waist. Apparently it was painted in secret at her father's farm when they were falling in love. I had no idea they'd met so young, did you?'

Jenny's head moved the pieces around faster than a street trader playing the shell game. The intimate portrait that she'd found hidden behind the mirror in the garden cottage, now displayed in glorious isolation, had been painted in Australia in the eighties. That's why Geraldine looks so youthful in it. She's barely a grown woman, and yet she is unmistakably, ravishingly, bright-eyed and sensual Geraldine Scott. It's why she stole it back, the eternal part of herself coming of age.

'Euan carried it with him the whole time he travelled?' There seemed no greater declaration of love than that. She wanted to duck her head down and blaze her way back out of the exhibition to her car, then drive home as fast as she could.

'Bloody fool should have taken a Polaroid.' Myrtle sniffed. 'He's livid it's on show this evening, but it's not his now, so he has no say. He sold it.'

'Who to?'

'Geraldine. She might say she bought it to protect her family, but she's a canny self-publicist and she knows that the story behind this painting will sell an awful lot of books. After all, it was painted when she wrote *The Dust Storm*. The real-life Jack's painting of the real-life Victoria? Imagine the furore when its sequel is released!'

'What does Richard make of it?'

'He absolutely loves it. Always had rather lewd taste.' She glanced at Geraldine again wearily. 'He knows everything. Hard to keep it from him when Geraldine came back and confessed all, swearing it was over and begging to be given a second chance. Dicky was remarkably sanguine about it, but I think it probably helped that Euan turned up and corroborated her story word for word, then let Dicky punch him around a bit, which always makes chaps feel better. By the time the children came back from Geraldine's mother, you'd never have suspected anything had been wrong. They *definitely* aren't allowed to see the portrait.

'It's on show here for one night only. Geraldine is very insistent that it can't be photographed or filmed. Those big security guards have been hired to snatch cameras and phones faster than pickpockets in Piccadilly Circus. The TV people aren't allowed to film it, of course.' She stood on tiptoe to look around, still only at armpit height. 'Where did they go? Euan must know you're here.'

Thump thump clap, thump thump clap. Jenny looked around too, but there was no sign of a television crew or Euan.

'We'll try outside.' Myrtle grabbed her arm again and tugged her onwards. 'He owes me twenty quid now. He swore you wouldn't come. I said you would.' Her eyes crinkled beneath the Grayson Perry makeup. 'How was New York?'

'You know I've been away?'

'Your neighbours told Euan that's where you'd gone. Your husband's based out there, isn't he?'

'Ex. Euan came to my house?' She suddenly saw hearts and flowers on her stone walls again, James Bond abseiling over the Oxford canal. 'Why didn't he leave a note?'

'You'll have to ask him, but I think he was a bit cheesed off. He'd just used some of the money Geraldine paid him for the painting to buy you some sort of present. Not sure what, but he said it was because he'd broken something precious of yours. Rather ruined the gesture to find you weren't at home. He came back in a frightful mood, banging on about Tintin being buggered by Robin, which confused me even more because I thought it was *Batman* and Robin.'

'He must have thought I'd gone running back to him after all.'

446

'I said he should paint you something to make up for Dicky stealing that lovely one of you in the garden. He's done a charming little canvas of me with my pets in front of the cottage that makes me look a fabulously feisty old bag.' She chuckled fondly as they reached an oak-framed glass wall overlooking the gardens. 'Ah, there he is!'

49

In a small courtyard bordered by Italianate potted bays and bronze sculptures with five-figure price tags, a local news round-up reporter, with a helmet of rigidly sprayed blonde hair like a Lego figure's, was doing her piece to camera. 'I'm here at Buckinghamshire's famous Tythe Gallery where a lot of local art lovers are getting *very* hot under the collar tonight, thanks to the exhibition that's running here from now to the end of the month, featuring the work of talented Scottish artist Euan Henderson. Tonight is the private view and we've come outside to film this because, frankly, the paintings in there are far too *risqué* to show you before the watershed, and one in particular is causing a *big* stir. More on that later when I interview bestselling novelist Geraldine Lewis, but first I'm going to talk to the man himself.'

Lurking with Myrtle behind two bronze boxing hares, Jenny grabbed the statue's marble plinth for support as the reporter stepped back to reveal Euan in a crumpled suit, his dark hair and distinctive witch's streak slicked back.

If she'd thought she'd prepared herself for seeing him, she'd clearly missed years of therapy and a tranquillizer prescription. Her entire body seemed to have been invaded by butterflies fighting for space; her Spode dress was now being held up by nothing but goose-bumps of excitement.

'We're both quite fond of him, aren't we?' Myrtle whispered indulgently.

The reporter had thrust a furry microphone at him. 'Euan Henderson, why nudes?'

'Naked women are beautiful,' he said simply, his accent at its most romantically gruff because he was nervous. 'I enjoy painting them.'

'You've been described by some of the less flattering critics as "Vettriano on Viagra" – how does that make you feel?'

As though drawn by fire, he saw Jenny, his face going very still. She tried to hide behind Myrtle so she didn't distract him from the interview – which she had a worrying feeling was live – but it was like a greyhound hiding behind a Chihuahua. And she was staring back now, incapable of blinking, let alone looking away, his green eyes having that conversation with hers that she'd never been able to interrupt.

'The Tythe Gallery is reporting almost half the paintings were sold before the doors opened, which is unprecedented for an unknown artist here,' the television audience was being told by their roving arts correspondent, as she struggled to fill her interviewee's distracted silence. 'I gather tonight is actually your first solo exhibition, am I right, Euan?'

He said nothing, still staring at Jenny.

The furry microphone was practically thrust up his nose. 'Tell me, is there a favourite painting of yours?'

'Yes.'

The reporter almost wept with relief. 'Tell viewers about it.'

'It's not on display.' With the cameras still filming, he walked out of frame towards Jenny.

'Back to the studio!' the reporter trilled.

'Thirty seconds to Sport Report – keep filming,' came an audible hiss from an earpiece as Euan walked up to the boxing hares and gripped their plinth too, his paint-splattered knuckles white.

Jenny opened her mouth in greeting, but he cut straight past it. 'Can we go somewhere quiet?'

She nodded, following as he turned and slipped between a potted bay and a bronze heron before striding away.

As they vanished from sight, Myrtle was already stepping forwards to the fluffy microphone. 'I know the artist very well,' she volunteered cheerfully. 'He was my lodger. He's terribly naughty and always sleeping with different women, but he's amazingly talented.'

Jenny followed Euan past the bonfire clutches of smokers huddled outside the Tythe Gallery's back doors and on to the car park.

His pick-up truck was parked even more antisocially than her car, sheltering behind some overgrown trees. When he beckoned her behind it, she thought for a ridiculous, knee-giving moment that he was going to press her up against it and kiss her, her insides spinning at the thought, but he just sprang the door and reached inside for his cigarette packet.

'You should quit,' she told him, as he lit it, realizing with a punch of regret that this wasn't going to be the life-saving mouth-to-mouth resuscitation of their short-lived passion, just a tetchy post-mortem.

'Have you?' He squinted at her through a curling plume, flicking his lighter closed. The witch's streak had defied slicking back and fallen across his forehead.

She shook her head, taking the cigarette gratefully when he offered, although her lips hadn't touched a real filter since she'd shared one with him by the Old Rectory pool. 'I *am* going to.'

450

Plucking the cigarette from her mouth, he flicked it away over her shoulder. 'Let's do it.'

His eyes were so close to hers now that she was again convinced he was going to kiss her, but then he turned away, raking his hair back and feigning fascination with a sign threatening illegally parked cars with clamping. 'How are you?'

'Good, thanks. You?'

'Yeah.' The answer hung there inconclusively as he turned back, and this time their eyes met and had a conversation that definitely said, 'Kiss.' But Euan wasn't listening. 'You look great.'

'Thanks.'

Gripped by the need to stop her knees collapsing every time she mistakenly thought he was going to kiss her, Jenny decided to perch on the truck bonnet. Unfortunately the Spode dress wasn't built for sitting on the snarling hood of a gas guzzler. After a few false starts – which an onlooker would have been forgiven for thinking was her attacking his car – she had to throw herself on, like a road-safety officer demonstrating RTA collisions.

Euan watched her curiously for a moment, then joined her.

As he slid alongside on the sun-warmed metal, her intake of breath seemed to suck him closer. The heat of his body drew her in further, like a magnet. They were far too close now, she thought, their sides connecting like two dodgems. An arm flew out and held her there before she could crash away.

They both turned their faces at once, an uncomfortable clash of cheekbones, noses and foreheads.

He ducked his head away first. 'I came to Oxford to find you, to say sorry.'

'I was in New York.'

'So I heard.'

'Robin's marriage broke up. Our children, the twins, wanted me there.'

'You're back together?'

'Never.'

He nodded. 'Good.'

The dodgems were parallel-parked now, his body still sending sparks up into the overhead cabling, ready to accelerate at the touch of a throttle, hers already pedal to the metal, nudging him out again.

Thump thump clap, thump thump clap. She closed her eyes.

'Did you sleep with him?' he asked.

Her burst of nervous laughter made a nearby pigeon take off. She glanced across at him, disconcerted to find the conversation going from polite, awkward catch-up to a main artery. Then again, Euan knew more about her marriage than her closest friends. He was looking at the clamping sign again.

'Once,' she admitted. *Thump thump clap, thump thump clap.*

'Like old times?'

'Only the worst ones. You?'

He knew exactly what she was talking about. It wasn't just their eyes that had shorthand conversations. 'We lasted two nights. We drove each other mad. She talked about her kids non-stop and cried a lot. I just talked about you.'

Thump thump clap, thump thump clap.

'I heard Richard beat you up.'

'It was more of a light hand-bagging, but he obviously felt like Rocky Marciano and his ego needed it. I think Geraldine enjoyed it too. They suit each other. They'll go the distance.'

She looked across at him and their eyes talked in private again. This time they wouldn't shut up. Forget the polite catch-up, they said. This sort of mutual attraction doesn't wear off. You might want to talk with stiff-jawed restraint, like a couple of toffs on a car bonnet at a polo match, but we're taking over where we left off.

The kiss burst out of them, like irrepressible laughter, meeting far too urgently for seductive angling, their teeth clashing first, tongues fighting, bodies slamming together. His thumbs were already in the hollows of her jaw, possessive and practised, drawing her into a longer, slower, exquisite kiss that left her limp with longing. She felt her body cling to his, threatening to slide right out of her Spode dress, like a sweet from its wrapper.

'Let's have that week.' He was pulling her into his lap now, his lips on her shoulder drawing her skin into eddies of pleasure. Any minute now they'd be copulating on the car bonnet, which was undoubtedly a clamping offence.

Jenny pulled away, desperately trying to salvage some self-control, certain she would melt again, embarrassingly quickly, if he carried on. 'I'm not really a one-week-stand woman.'

'We can try for longer.' His mouth chased hers, kissing her with incredible tenderness now, lips on her cheek then her ear, breathing, 'A month, a year, a lifetime.'

'A lifetime's a long time to stay in bed.'

'We'll get up every now and then.'

She pulled away again, refusing to let her eyes talk to his, staring down at her hands, rubbing her thumbs anxiously along her palms. 'I'm not a bohemian voluptuary, remember? I'd drive you just as mad as Geraldine – madder. I often talk about my kids non-stop, and about me.' She pressed her hands to her face, feeling the heat burn there as she remembered watching dawn break together. 'I sometimes cry too.'

'I'll beat anybody up if they make you cry, including myself.' He kissed her eyelids very gently. 'And I love you talking. I can listen to you talking all day. You're not allowed to stop talking.'

Eyelids feather light from being kissed, she looked up at him and was knocked backwards by the intensity of his gaze.

'I'm the one who'll drive you mad,' he insisted. 'I don't sleep a lot, I drink too much wine, I go stir-crazy if I can't paint every day, I like to keep moving. On the plus side, I'm completely in love with you and I just quit smoking.' His mouth landed on hers again.

She closed her eyes for a moment, succumbing to the intoxicating body rush. Then her eyes snapped open and she broke away. *Thump thump clap, thump thump clap.*

'Did you just say . . . ?'

He nodded. 'I might need patches and gum and those ridiculous electric things you use.'

'I meant the other thing.'

'You have no idea the cravings I've been through this past month. If you don't stick around after tonight, I'll be paved in ten-milligram Jenny Rees patches.'

Seized by her own all-consuming love and lust, she kissed him back with free-falling abandon and it all started to get decidedly MILF-fantasy-porn-channel before she was forced to remind herself that they were in a public car park.

Wriggling up the bonnet, she retrieved her bag and pulled that evening's private-view invitation from it, thrusting it at him. 'I'll be staying at this address for the next three months.'

He read it through the gathering gloom. 'When do you go?'

'Tomorrow. Apparently the light's beautiful there,' she said, talking too fast. 'Come and visit. Come stay. Come with me. Just come.' There were far too many 'come's in there, she realized breathlessly.

'How soon do you want me?'

'How soon can you come?' She winced as another slipped out.

'My bag's in the car.'

Thump thump clap, thump thump clap.

He looked up, eyes black coals. 'Richard made me agree to stay for this opening. After that, I always planned on getting as far away from this place as I could, starting tonight.'

'Can you divert via the Aegean?'

His eyes told her the answer long before he nodded, leaning forwards, lips against hers, smile spreading so wide that it tickled her cheekbones. 'Just try to stop me.'

They kissed for so long that night had turned the dimmer down on the last traces of daylight by the time they broke apart. 'Where were you planning to go?' she asked.

Euan ran his tongue over his teeth, smiling awkwardly. 'I thought I'd start in Belgium, then head on across Europe to the Dalmatian coast. I have some tickets that are still valid. I was going to take this woman I know who talks about herself a lot to see Tintin – and if she let me get a word in edgeways, I was going to tell her that I love her and ask if she could find some way to forgive me, travel with me, be my lover – but she was out.'

She held her breath as their eyes had a rapid-fire conversation that confirmed all these were still open offers. Then she laughed, raking her hair back, overwhelmed. 'God, I can't believe I missed that. I'd never have gone away if I'd known. It beats an officer's uniform in Waitrose any day.'

His eyebrows angled up questioningly, eyes dancing.

'I crossed the Atlantic like a raft with no compass,' she admitted. 'I knew I'd found love again, but I'd lost my heart to you.'

The kiss hit hard and fast again, shocking them both into silence. She landed against a windscreen wiper and the car alarm went off. It was a long time before either of them noticed. He rolled off the bonnet, pulling her with him, and reached in to silence it, still kissing her.

'Let's go now,' he breathed.

'We can't! It's your private view.'

'I prefer this view.' He tilted her chin up to look at her face. 'We'll go back in there and tell anyone who wants to know that this artist is going to enjoy this view every day from now on. I can't wait to paint you again. In fact, there's something of yours I should return.'

He pulled his bag from the back seat of the truck, a battered rucksack that had already seen a lot of miles. Clicking it open, pulling out randomly packed socks, art brushes, T-shirts and sketchbooks, he reached in far enough to draw out a rectangular board. Jenny covered her mouth with her hands, letting out a sharp breath of recognition as he held up the painting of her on the patchwork sofa.

'You bought this for nine bottles of Burgundy and the naked truth. I was going to steal it so I could take you with me.'

She took the board and tipped it into the light spilling from the truck's interior to study it, recognizing the vibrant, sensual woman gazing from the patchwork sofa, overwhelmed with joy at rediscovering her after so many years. Then she looked up at Euan, a cocktail of happiness, mirth and all-out lust in her tear ducts. 'You know, I think it's missing something . . .'

'What?' He looked offended. 'It's beautiful. You're beautiful. Even Gunter looks bloody beautiful.'

She reached up to kiss him, knowing she couldn't wait to get naked with Euan Henderson again. 'Have you ever thought of painting *Nude with Two Great Danes and a Parrot*?'

456

LANDMA...

**SHORTLISTED FOR THE SAMUEL JOHNSON PRIZE
FOR NON-FICTION 2015**

'Eye-opening, tongue-loosening, celebrates the microscopic verbal detail that
clarifies a farmer's, fisherman's or climber's view of earth, sea and sky'
Independent on Sunday

'There are not many books I would call life-changing, but this is one . . . This is
a book for all – it gives a glossary for the natural world to talk back, and for us
to listen' *Psychologist*

'Written with grace and suppleness, *Landmarks* is a classic in the making'
Tom Adair, *Scotsman*

'Wonderfully thought-provoking, an immensely original work. Beautifully written,
warm in tone and bold in content, Macfarlane makes a fresh adventure out of our
landscapes and our languages' *Mail on Sunday*

'Macfarlane's masterpiece, an exploration of the links between language
and landscape. Few books give such a sense of enchantment'
Amanda Craig, *Independent on Sunday*

'*Landmarks* is a "must read" for anyone who is interested in the literature of
the British countryside. Robert Macfarlane has long been one of our most
eloquent and knowledgeable writers about the way we interact with the natural
world, and anyone who loves great nature writing will find things in this book to
learn from and to cherish (I have been back to read the passages on J. A. Baker
several times, the mark of an important book). The theme of this book, that we
can lose our ancient knowledge and language of the land and become ever more
disconnected, and closed off from it, is a theme close to my heart'
James Rebanks, author of *The Shepherd's Life*

'For a dozen years Macfarlane has worked at the vanguard of a cross-cultural
movement that has tried to reanimate our wonder in and respect for the natural
world. Anyone who has read one of his works will know the feeling of heightened
awareness they engender. Go outside after closing one of them and bland
reality resolves itself into a series of small miracles. You perceive what medieval
theologians called haecceity, this-ness, all around you – whether "this" is a tree,
a rock, a bird' Geordie Williamson, *Australian*

'*Landmarks* is not so much concerned with reprising any decorative or "what-ho" tradition of intrepid literary adventurers, but rather with the urgent – as opposed to nostalgic – need to re-engage Britain's largely metropolitan population with the marvellously specific and intricate habitats that continue to be smashed by industrialization, population growth and sprawl . . . He forces us to confront what is a crucial underlying concept in the new self-reflexive resurgence of nature writing in the UK: "species shame". Ultimately, what Macfarlane leads us towards in *Landmarks* is a honing of our ability to see and understand what is still there, but always vanishing' Gregory Day, *Sydney Review of Books*

'The admirer of precision prose in others, Macfarlane's own writing has true "ammil" – the sparkle of sunlight in frost. If a more profound book on nature appears this year, I will eat dottle. (Don't ask)' John Lewis-Stempel, *Countryfile*

'There is a density in Macfarlane's prose, never flash and immensely precise, that is beautifully aligned with his material and . . . recalls the sparse style of Cormac McCarthy' *New Zealand Metro*

'His writing is addictive, but also functions as a gateway drug to other writers . . . While *Landmarks* is a celebration and defence of language, it is also a shield and lance raised by a champion of the land. Its moral thrust is explicit in a way that had hitherto only been implied in Macfarlane's previous books, but it is part of a strong tendency in his work' Peter Ross, *Scottish Review of Books*

'Impressive, fascinating. Macfarlane performs a miracle of resurrection' *Daily Mail*

'Joyous treasure troves of curiosity . . . Macfarlane remains without equal. An elegant, insightful and deeply humane book' *The Lady*

'Beautifully crafted reflections on the experience of establishing and enjoying contact with the earth, with another human being, and with one's own language . . . Mind-expanding glossaries accompanying each chapter. Together they comprise a wondrous word-hoard' Laurence Coupe, *Times Higher Educational Supplement*

'A concentrated trove of precious expressions, drawn together by a master narrator . . . Readers of landscape will love it. Writers of landscape will treasure it' *Trail*